Praise for *Say Hello, Kiss Goodbye*

FINALIST
2021 Contemporary Romance Writers 'Stiletto Awards'

"This sultry, yet sweetly heartfelt romance is a winner. Leia and Tarquin's chemistry sizzles...the playful and racy banter is delightful. Great for fans of Candace Bushnell and Alexa Martin."
— *Publishers Weekly Booklife (Editor's Pick)*

"As steamy as it is heartwarming...the two main characters are undeniably endearing. Romance fans will be grateful they picked up this novel."
— *The BlueInk Review (Starred Review)*

"*Say Hello, Kiss Goodbye* offers well-drawn, multilayered characters and stand-out sex positive romance.
— *Kirkus Reviews*

"Sweet, sexy, and overflowing with hope, *Say Hello, Kiss Goodbye* is the perfect romance for the modern romantic...it's groundbreaking in the way it approaches mental health...and is the gold standard all romance should aspire to."
— *Hypable*

Praise for *Until the Last Star Fades*

WINNER for ROMANCE
2019 The Independent Author Network

WINNER – BEST CANADIAN AUTHOR
2019 Northern Hearts Awards,
Toronto chapter of the Romance Writers of America

3x FINALIST
2019 Contemporary Romance Writers,
Toronto Romance Writers, and Las Vegas Writers
(all chapters of the Romance Writers of America)

The Certainty of Chance

Jacquelyn Middleton lives in Toronto with her British husband and her Japanese Spitz. She's an award-winning author who started out in television broadcasting back in the day when directors drank in the control room and indoor snowball fights with VJs were a thing. It's no secret that London owns her heart.

The Certainty of Chance is her fifth novel.

Follow Jacquelyn:
Instagram @JaxMiddleton_Author
Facebook @JacquelynMiddletonAuthor
Twitter @JaxMiddleton,
or visit her webpage at www.JacquelynMiddleton.com

Also by Jacquelyn Middleton

London Belongs to Me
London, Can You Wait?
Until the Last Star Fades
Say Hello, Kiss Goodbye

The Certainty of Chance

A NOVEL

JACQUELYN MIDDLETON

KIRKWALL BOOKS

Hi Abby!
Enjoy this holiday in London!
~~Best~~ wishes,
Jacquelyn xo

KIRKWALL BOOKS

USA – CANADA - UK

The Certainty of Chance

ISBN: 978-1-9992753-2-7
Copyright © 2021 Jacquelyn Middleton
First Paperback Edition, October 2021

Cover design by ThinkTank

Editing by C. Marie

This book is dedicated

to hopeful romantics

who believe in serendipitous salutations

and miraculous meet cutes,

fateful friendships,

and finding love where you least expect it.

And to Zoey.

My best friend.

Forever loved, forever missed. x

DEAR READERS,

The Certainty of Chance is a contemporary romance. Madeleine and Julian's story is a standalone that takes place in the same 'world' as my four previous books. There are laugh-out-loud moments along with the swoony, sexy stuff, but this book is not a rom-com.

I realize some readers stress if they don't know how to pronounce a character's name and it pulls them out of the story, so for reference Madeleine sounds like 'Mad-elle-lyn' while Micah is pronounced 'Mee-kuh'. Hope that helps!

Content/trigger warnings: coarse language, closed-door sex scenes, disenfranchised grief, unexpected death of a loved one (backstory), cheating partner (backstory), therapy, loved-up mentions of *Love Actually* and *The Holiday*, zero mentions of any pandemics...and lots and lots of London at Christmas.

P.S. I've included a glossary at the back of the book to explain a few terms that might not be familiar to all readers.

Love music? You can find *The Certainty of Chance* playlist under 'Extras' at www.JacquelynMiddleton.com.

ONE

"There's nowhere you can be
that isn't where you're meant to be."
John Lennon

MADELEINE

London, England – Six days until Christmas

"Pardon me! Sorry, sorry! If I could—oh, *come on!*" An irritated male voice stabbed the damp morning air. "This is an emergency! Would you *please* MOVE!"

Suitcases awkwardly scraped the pavement and British accents scoffed as a man draped in a long coat of obnoxious red and purple plaid lurched into Madeleine Joy's path, stealing the idling black cab hugging the airport's curb.

"What the hell?!" Her eyes popped beneath her umbrella as the tall blond launched himself across the back seat. "*Excuse* me!" she hollered, ripping off her headphones, their plump ear cushions curling below her clenched jaw. "*I* was next—"

"Sorry!" He reeled in his suitcase. "It's an emergency!" The cab door slammed, flinging dirty rainwater on her dark jeans and pristine suede boots, an early Christmas gift from her younger sister, Shantelle.

"So much for British manners!" Madeleine scowled, but her glare didn't penetrate the steamed-up window or sting its intended target. The oblivious silhouette barked at the driver then whipped out his phone as his boxy chariot chugged away, its rain-dappled exterior wrapped in a colorful advertisement celebrating Christmas chocolates.

"I knew it. I should've called an Uber..." she muttered, staring

1

at the dark splotches on her boots.

"Those high-flyin' City boys." Shaking his head inside his hood, the craggy airport attendant tugged his yellow reflective vest and tsked. "Selfish wankers." He gestured toward an empty cab creeping into the space vacated by her stolen ride. "Take this one, love. Happy Christmas."

Is it? A lump knotted Madeleine's throat as she adjusted the small backpack looped over her left shoulder. "Thanks. You too." She shivered into a half-smile and inched ahead, the thump of the driver's door a most welcome distraction.

The cabbie, wearing a navy sweater, black jeans, and a friendly smile—no coat—swung counter-clockwise around the nose of his car. He dipped his chin, hiding his tortoiseshell glasses from the downpour as he yanked open the passenger door. "Hop in, get comfy." His blue eyes urged. "I'll take care of your case."

Surrendering her carry-on, relief flooded Madeleine's chest. "Thank you so much." She collapsed her umbrella and climbed inside where a disco beat and an addictive '*la la la*' pulsed through the car's speakers. Her sleepy brain immediately clicked into work mode.

Kylie Minogue's "Can't Get You Out of My Head". Mid-yawn, she sat down with her backpack and pulled her cross-body purse onto her lap. *Great song. Always popular, always fun—for a Saturday night. Bit much for 6:30 Sunday morning, though.*

Her heavy-lidded gaze slid left. The cabbie parked her luggage on the floor, angling it away from her drenched boots and umbrella.

Could be worse. She gave his wavy, dark brown hair and wet sweater, clinging to the muscles flexing in his back, an appreciative perusal. *He could be blaring Christmas carols.*

He caught her stare and, with an amused nod, closed the door on the damp chill then darted around to the driver's side.

I lucked out on the cabbie lottery. This one's hot. Fat raindrops raced down the windows, blurring his movements. She unbuttoned her coat and glanced up to where menacing clouds swollen with rain hung overhead. Her eyes bulged.

2

The front door snapped shut and the one-man Kylie dance party died a quick death, replaced by watery plinks and plonks on the roof. The driver flashed a grin over his shoulder, peering through the cab's plastic partition. "Sorry about the music." His East End accent charmed its way through the intercom. "Just coming off night shift." He followed Madeleine's upward gaze. "Oh! Do you like it?"

She pulled her eyes away from Mother Nature's car wash sluicing above her head.

"The glass roof? It's new. Makes for a better sightseeing experience." He raked his wet hair off his forehead. "So, where we headed this glorious Sunday morning?"

Glorious? She winced. "My hotel. The Saint, uh"—her mouth twisted—"*something*. Just a sec…" Madeleine dove into her purse. "My sister only booked it like, five minutes ago." She dug past crumpled chocolate chip cookie wrappers, her wallet, and a pair of balled-up mittens as an impatient horn blared behind them. Glancing up, she offered an apologetic grimace. "Sorry…"

"Pay no notice," said the driver, removing his glasses. "Take your time." He wiped the lenses with a small, soft cloth.

Handsome AND helpful. Makes a change from the cabbies back home. Madeleine unearthed her phone and found Shantelle's rambling text. "Okay, it's the St. Pancras Renaissance Hotel on Euston Road."

"Got it." He slipped his glasses on then yanked his seatbelt over his soggy sweater. "Your sister sure picked a stunner." His attention shifted beyond the windshield and its hyperactive wiper blades waving back and forth. "The St. Pancras is a London landmark."

"Oh?" She clicked her seatbelt.

Checking his mirrors, he joined the parade of taxis fleeing the airport. "It's all soaring Gothic spires and Victorian opulence. If you've seen the Harry Potter films, you might recognize it from *The Chamber of Secrets*. Ron and Harry flew a car over it."

Madeleine's jaw dropped. "It's *that* building?" The buzz of an incoming text pulled her away.

Shantelle: Stop worrying, Maddie! I'll pay for it.

"Where you from?" he asked, drifting into cabbie small talk.

"Wisconsin, originally. I live in Boston now."

"Oh yeah? I have a cousin in Philadelphia." His eyes peered back from the rear view mirror. "First time in London?"

"Yes." She squinted back. A small wool dog twirled from a string tied to his mirror. The canine's long, sturdy body, stubby legs, and triangle ears were unmistakable. *Cute corgi.*

"Well, you're in for a treat. London at Christmas is pure magic. You here for business or pleasure?"

"Neither. I'm supposed to be on a plane to Paris with my sister."

He raised a dark eyebrow. "She left without you?"

"No, she's stuck in Thailand. And now I'm stuck here." Madeleine squeezed her phone and frowned, looking away from the back of his head. "The customs guy said the airports here and in France were closing soon. Something about a huge ash cloud..."

He winced. "The Icelandic volcano strikes again."

"*Again?*" Madeleine leaned forward. "It's happened before?" Her phone awoke with another sisterly text.

Shantelle: Airline says flights should resume in 2 days. See, told ya! I'll be in Paris soon-ish.

The taxi rolled to a stop behind a double-decker bus. "Yeah, several times," said the cabbie. "The bugger erupted for over a week, back in...2010, I think? Closed European airspace, disrupted things for about a month! Flights were grounded, people were stranded. No one flew in or out. Mad, eh?"

Over a week? Christmas is in six days! Unease thrashed in Madeleine's belly. "Shit." *I can't be stuck here on my own.* She sighed under her breath, dashing off a quick message.

4

Madeleine: Sorry, Shan. This is all my fault. I'm the one who picked Paris. I'm a travel jinx.

The cab accelerated again, overtaking the bus. "The volcanic ash has an abrasive quality that damages sensors and clogs machinery. If it gets into a plane's engines…"

Madeleine gulped. "They could fail?"

"Yeah. And who wants to take that risk, right?"

"Right." She wilted into the seat as another message appeared beneath her thumb.

Shantelle: You are NOT a jinx! Stop blaming yourself. None of this is your fault.

Her chest tightened. *But it is. This year, last year…* Thumbs flying, she sent her response.

Madeleine: Then why am I being punished? Of all places to get stuck, it's London. Fucking London, Shan! And rubbing salt in the wound, I'm alone and it's Christmas.

A prickling ache teased the back of her nose. Instinctively, she clasped the sterling silver musical note—an elegant quaver— hanging from a dainty chain around her neck. Her fingers fiddled with the charm until the three dancing dots on the screen gave way to a new text.

Shantelle: You're right, it's not fair. But hang in there, okay? We WILL be spending Xmas Day together in Paris. My psychic sees it.

Oh, well, if she sees it, it must be true… Madeleine huffed. Shantelle didn't get out of bed without consulting her psychic and astrologist. Before she could reply, a flurry of messages from Thailand arose on her screen.

> **Shantelle:** I have SO MUCH planned 'cause I know how much you luv Xmas!

I did...for thirty-two years. Madeleine swallowed, fighting the lump in her throat. *And then, all the color trickled away, out of my life.*

> **Shantelle:** Please don't be sad, k? Kellie wouldn't want you to be sad.

Is that supposed to help? Telling me how to feel? And you don't know what Kellie would want. She typed her answer, the letters blurring upon hitting Send.

> **Madeleine:** Don't make me cry. I'm in a taxi.

Wiping away the teary evidence, she hid behind her long hair and stared outside, but the gray cast of the bare trees flying by and the watery whoosh of passing tires plunged her further into a melancholy funk. Madeleine usually embraced change and the unexpected, a resilient trait her sister pinned on her being an Aries, "the astrological poster girl for making the most of life's precipitous twists". However, being stranded solo in London with the anniversary of her best friend's death looming was one shocking upheaval too many.

The cabbie glanced into the rear view mirror again, concern narrowing his eyes. "You know, Paris is still doable. You could take the Eurostar. The train station is connected to your hotel."

Madeleine sniffed and abandoned her phone in her lap. "I don't know." She shook her head. "The whole point was to spend Christmas week with my sister."

"In Paris? The entire time?"

"Yeah. I've never been, but my sister lived there for a while."

6

"Oh, that's cool." The driver checked his mirrors and changed lanes, passing a white van. "She'll have the inside scoop, then."

"I suppose, yeah." Madeleine blew out a big breath and toyed with the headphones hugging her neck. "So, *you* know London. If I'm here for a day or two, what should I see?"

"Easy." His answer arrived without pause. "The Christmas lights."

Oh no. No holiday stuff.

"London is spectacular during the holidays, it really comes alive. If you're short on time, I'd suggest Bond Street's peacock lights and Regent Street's angels. Oh, and Kew Gardens. They have a two-kilometre trail of starry installations and twinkly lights through their trees. It's a bit farther afield from where you're staying but worth the trip."

Madeleine smiled tightly and played along with a stilted "Sounds festive," too tired to change the subject and too kind to burst his tinsel-wrapped bubble.

"But if you'd prefer to stay central, I'd recommend Seven Dials and Covent Garden. Every year, they put up a tree in the piazza and hang massive mistletoe chandeliers in the market." He smiled over the steering wheel. "Time it right and you might catch carolers strolling along the cobblestones. Just add snow and it's straight out of a Dickens novel!"

God help me. I'm trapped in a cab with the British version of Buddy the Elf. She bit back her holiday malaise and plastered on a grin. "I bet! Maybe my sister's friends will join me." *For drinks, not sightseeing.*

Her phone launched into Pulp's "Disco 2000". The cabbie glanced over his shoulder, but Madeleine's quick "Hello" ended any ebullient mentions of mulled wine or candy canes from the front seat.

"Yay, you're not hiding in your headphones! I hope you don't mind me calling. It's easier than texting." Shantelle barely paused for breath. "How you doing? You okay?"

Madeleine shrugged. "Define okay." She slouched against the

window, lowering her voice. "It's cold and dreary and bucketing down."

Her sister giggled. "Welcome to London."

Madeleine scrunched her nose. "So, the Eurostar is still running. Is there any way you could meet me in Paris? You could fly to Zurich or Milan then take a train."

"And what?" Shantelle snipped back. "Barf the whole way to France?"

"Take your motion sickness pills. They've worked before—"

"Mads, have you *seen* my horoscope?"

She rolled her eyes. "I never read mine, why would I read yours?"

"OMG, it gave me goose bumps. No joke, it said Geminis should avoid travel today because *untold misery and misfortune will plague their journey!*"

Madeleine snickered. "You sure that wasn't meant for me?"

"Oh, yours wasn't much better"—Shantelle raised her voice over some raucous laughter and a loud, crunchy splash—"trust me."

"Where are you? I thought you were returning from the airport."

"No, I'm in the hotel's pool, floating on an inflatable avocado! Hate them in a salad, love 'em for lounging." She let out a satisfied sigh. "It's eighty-six degrees, not a cloud in the sky. Ahhh, bliss! I've had a grueling yoga sesh and a hot stone massage. Later I'm treating myself to some khao soi. It's my new fave!"

"Living the Hollywood life there, Shan."

"Well, what else am I gonna do? Everyone flew home to the States last night, and there's no point practicing lines for that animated Moomin thing. I might as well soak up some sun while I'm here." Her tone softened. "I know this sucks, but we *will* get to Paris. My psychic sees it. I see it. That stupid ash cloud has gotta clear, right? Santa's got places to go, people to see." Shantelle's laugh was drowned out by another apocalyptic splash.

"While we're on the subject, are your friends in town?"

Her sister slurped her drink. "Yeah, I'll text you numbers."

8

"That'd be great." Madeleine's voice faded as she stole a glance through her rain-splattered window. "Being alone here at this time of year is just—I don't know if..." Her breath hitched. *I knew the first anniversary would be tough but this—this makes it so much worse.*

"Aw, sweetie. I wish I could reach through the phone and hug you and make you fe—" Shantelle stopped short with a sigh. "I know it must feel like you're traveling through nothing but darkness right now, but Maddie, things *will* get brighter. Time always heals, right?"

Not this it doesn't. Madeleine bit her bottom lip.

"Call me when you've checked in?" asked Shantelle.

"Yeah."

"And spoil yourself, okay? The hotel has my credit card on file. Nothing's off limits. Order room service, raid the mini bar, relax in their spa," Shantelle urged. "Then explore, see London! It'll make you feel better. Promise me you won't turtle and stay in your room reading?"

Madeleine looked up from her lap with a frown. "I don't *turtle—*"

"You do lately! You go to work then come home every single night. It's not normal. It's not *you.*"

"Well, maybe it is now—"

A sharp slurp cut her off. "OH! Receipts! Get receipts for everything, including that cab."

"I can pay my own way, you know."

"Mads, for the millionth time! This trip is your present."

"But it's too much. I feel bad I can't reciprocate."

"I don't expect you to. Can't I spoil the best sister in the world?" Shantelle expelled an exasperated huff. "Please don't fight me on this, okay?"

"Fine! But I'm treating you to an expensive dinner in Paris."

"And I have the perfect bistro in mind! I can't wait to share it with you."

Madeleine played with the zipper pull on her purse. "I'll call when I get to my hotel."

"You better! Love and hugs."

"Love and hugs. Bye." Madeleine pressed her lips together and tucked her phone into her purse. Leaning back, she put on her silent headphones, cocooned in her coat, and closed her eyes. The hum of the cab with its gentle rocking and stuffy warmth lulled her into a restful slumber.

Thirty minutes later, she awoke with a jolt, her heart catapulting into her throat. "Where are we?!" Her stare ricocheted from the cab's partition to her purse then skated across the fogged-up windows.

"At your hotel. Just pulled up." The cabbie glanced over his shoulder as Madeleine peeled off her headphones. "Isn't she grand?"

As she swept her sleeve across the window, the opaque veil of condensation gave way to imposing red brick, Victorian arches, and soaring Gothic spires reminiscent of a historical cathedral. Madeleine gasped. "Holy sh…" Not even the rain could dampen the St. Pancras Hotel's majestic curb appeal. "It takes up an entire block!" She slowly prised herself away and squinted at the taxi's fare meter. "So, I owe you"—her brows peaked—"*eighty* pounds?"

"Erm, yeah. I take cash or credit, when you're ready."

She swore her wallet flinched. "I'll pay by card. Could I get a receipt, please?"

"Sure thing." He pulled a pen from the console beside his seat.

Thank god Shantelle's reimbursing me for this. Madeleine inserted her card in the reader and blinked into space, calculating her tip. By the time she'd punched in her passcode and rolled up her umbrella, the cabbie had opened her door and was hauling out her suitcase. The rain had slowed to a barely there sprinkle and sunlight flirted with the puddles, creating rainbow-hued splotches on the cobbled driveway.

She reunited with her luggage and raised her arms in a satisfying stretch.

"And this is for you." He handed over the receipt.

"Thank you." Madeleine's glance bounced from his elegant handwriting to the green oval, a taxi ID badge, hanging from a lanyard around his neck.

"By the way, if you're interested in sightseeing, I'm an accredited guide for Westminster and the City of London. I can do private tours by taxi, day or night." He smiled sheepishly as she looked up, meeting his eyes. "You can choose one of my pre-set itineraries or go bespoke, pick what you'd like, and I'll take you. It's the best way to see London, especially when you're short on time and the weather is…you know, British."

Madeleine curled her fingers around the receipt. "Sounds great, but I, uh, don't know what my sister's friends have planned yet." She extended the handle of her suitcase.

"Hey, no worries. If you change your mind"—the cabbie gestured at the paper in her hand—"my number is there. My taxi seats six, so plenty of room for friends, too." He stepped back, his blue Adidas Gazelles breaching the edge of a puddle. "Well, all the best to you and your sister, eh? I hope things work out."

What if they don't? A quiver rippled through her stomach as he rounded the front of his car. She raised a confident grin. "I'm sure they will. Thanks again."

Sizing up the twin Christmas trees guarding the grandiose hotel's entrance, Madeleine pulled on the handle of her luggage, but its broken wheel stubbornly skittered on the slick stones, dragging her in the wrong direction. She threw a curt glance over her shoulder, cursing her case, the volcanic ash, and the insensitive way the world carried on when her heart weighed so heavy with grief.

She gave the handle another yank, and the clatter of her suitcase's wheels was accompanied by a bouncy, electro beat, this time playing at a respectable Sunday morning volume. Madeleine's eyes vaulted toward the cab. Window down, the driver sat comfy behind the wheel, sipping from a thermos and bobbing his head to "Come Into My World" by Kylie Minogue. Above his windshield, the yellow TAXI sign glowed like a beacon, proclaiming *I'm available*.

He looked beyond his thermos in her direction, his friendly, familiar grin softening Madeleine's nagging loneliness. They'd only spent fifty minutes together, but who else did she know in London?

"Say bonjour to Paris for me. Oh, and *Happy Christmas*!" He waved and drove away in search of new passengers and adventures.

"Merry Christmas," Madeleine whispered, tracing the soft curves of his handwriting on the receipt. "Julian."

TWO

JULIAN

Five days until Christmas

"What's up with your phone, mate? Someone's eager!" Micah Cooper tossed his dark brown locks out of his eyes and scooped up an armful of plump velvet pillows. "Go on, spill! Who's the lucky lady?" His Mancunian accent teased playfully as he rounded his stockroom's doorjamb.

Not the pretty American. Dammit. Julian Halliwell furrowed his brow and followed his best friend onto the bustling floor of his homewares shop, Maison Micah. "It's Caroline."

"Again? Just tell her to piss right off and be done with it."

Julian weaved around a cluster of customers browsing a delightful display of ceramic crockery, oversized mugs, and small jars of orange artisan marmalade. "It's about Winnie." His eyes coasted over Micah's black shirt and slim tartan trousers. "She says I still owe her £1,650 for his surgery and rehab."

"Ouch. Is that like, half or the whole thing?"

"Half. I've paid some, but I don't have the rest—not yet."

Micah curled his lip. "There are vindictive exes, and then there's Caroline." He arranged the pillows in a nest of fuzzy throws on a sky blue love seat. "It's not like she's short of a few bob. She could spot you."

"She won't," said Julian.

"Talk about sticking the knife in, tight cow."

Julian stuffed his phone in his coat's pocket. "Yeah, but I'd do anything for Winnie, including falling into debt. I love the bones of that dog."

Admiring his cozy display, Micah stepped back and fiddled ab-

13

sentmindedly with his rolled-up sleeves and the tangle of beaded bracelets knotted around his wrists. "Caroline's such a pretentious snob. Your flat, your jobs, your friends—nothing was ever good enough for her. You're better off rid, Jules." He bent over and fussed with the pillows again.

"And I will be—once I get Winnie back."

"He's always been *your* dog." Micah raked his hand through his unruly, shoulder-length hair, nudging it from his eyes again. "Everyone knows that."

Julian's heart ached. "Caroline doesn't care. She'd rather get her jollies, dragging me through court."

"God, there's another expense you don't need. When's the hearing?"

"After the holidays." Julian pressed his lips together and tugged on the strap of his messenger bag. "So, you ready?"

"Yep." Micah motioned to his purple-haired sales assistant, clad in an indigo Victorian-style cinched waist dress, sorting through two boxes of needle felted animals. "Tash, we're grabbing lunch. Can I bring you back a salad or soup? One of those gooey gourmet donuts?" His eyes twinkled. "Go on, sis! You know you want one. All that orangey chocolatey goodness!" He crossed his arms over his slim frame and turned to Julian. "She's in there all the time. I reckon she fancies the trainee pastry chef."

"Ew." Natasha winced. "Brush away the powdered sugar and she's a toxic Twitter troll." Her gaze flitted from her older brother to Julian and back again. "Get me a butty from that place on Lower Stable Street? Anything but tuna. Oh, but—"

"No pickles." Micah nodded, tossing an empty energy drink into the recycling bin below his sales desk. "Got it."

A glint of braces snuck through her smile as she pulled a small fox and a rabbit from the bigger box. "Micah, these are super cute! You're getting so good at this."

Julian knotted his scarf and leaned in. "They look bloody real!"

"Cheers, mate. Yeah, they're selling well, too. Perfect stocking stuffers."

"You *have* to make me a koala and an otter," said Natasha. "Ooh, a flamingo!"

"Flamingo? Some goth you are!" Micah laughed, grabbing his coat.

Several customers peered over Natasha's shoulder. One woman reached around, snatching an adorable hedgehog.

Micah's big brown eyes narrowed. "Actually, Tash, can you put the fox and the rabbit aside? They're a special order. The buyer is picking them up later."

"No worries, I'll take good care of them." She bundled up the animals in blue tissue paper as the shop's phone rang. "Go! I'll get it." She waved them away, the sparkles in her blood red manicure glittering under the shop's soft lights.

"Won't be long." Julian held open the door, following Micah into the midday crush of Coal Drops Yard, a well-heeled, hip and happening shopping destination housed in two Victorian-era coal warehouses overlooking Regent's Canal. In a previous life, the re-vamped corner of King's Cross with its brick arches, cobblestone courtyard, and viaducts was a haven for drug dealers and midnight ravers. However, gentrification had swept away its gritty past, leaving all traces of discarded syringes and glowsticks a distant memory.

"Ah, it finally feels like the holidays now," said Micah, remov-ing a woolly hat from his coat's pocket. The joyful exuberance of the Salvation Army brass band's "Ding Dong! Merrily on High" added a bounce to his step as he tugged the black Manchester City beanie over his brown waves. "The shop's buzzin', customers keep ringing. I can't restock fast enough."

"Remember two years ago? Worrying it wouldn't fly? Now look at you. Run off your feet, you barely have time for a pint with your bezzie mate."

"Yeah!" Micah laughed, a puff of warm breath escaping his lips. "Just in time for my thirtieth trip around the sun, too. I've pissed about for so long, it's nice to finally be able to support my-self, you know?"

"And help Tash get back on her feet," said Julian. "I'm proud of you, man. A thriving business, a gorgeous flat—"

"No girlfriend, though."

"Ah, two out of three ain't bad! You're doing better than I am." Julian bobbed his head to the brass-heavy carols. "I thought I'd have everything sorted by the time I turned thirty. Three years past that and I still don't have much to show for my efforts."

"I hear ya." Micah squeezed Julian's shoulder and let go. "You know, the older we get, the more I believe that saying: '*What's for you won't pass you by.*'"

"Where'd you get that? A fortune cookie?"

"Nah, it fell out of a Christmas cracker few years back. It came with a pair of mini nail clippers. Just what one needs to navigate life: a paper party crown, an inspirational saying, and tidy finger-nails."

Julian laughed and nudged up his glasses, the sweet, smoky aroma of roasting chestnuts filling the air. "I usually end up with a crap joke, maybe a daft puzzle."

"I could've used a joke at the time. I was totally rat-arsed—I'd just split with Teagan."

"Oh, right." Julian cringed. "*That* Christmas…"

"Yep. I didn't need a load of new age wank making me feel worse, so I crumpled it up." Micah scratched his brow. "Next morn-ing though, the bugger found me again, stuck to the bottom of one of Mum's wine glasses. I peeled it off, read it again—then all hell broke loose."

"Let me guess—that drum kit you bought for your nephew?" asked Julian. Micah was *that* uncle, the one who bought gifts his older sister, Sadie, refused to buy her kids.

"No, wasn't that. Sadie was an absolute star. She bribed the kids with a cheeky Nandos and got them, Tash, and Mum and Dad out of the house so my head could pound in peace. For all the good it did. My mind starting racing, wouldn't frickin' stop! All these memories flooding back…"

"Like what?" asked Julian.

"Embarrassing hookups, wretched breakups—they ALL got a look in! It was like being stuck in an episode of *EastEnders*." Micah licked his lips. "Annnyway! There I was, double-fisting Coco Pops straight from the box, staring at that soggy saying when the penny fucking dropped. It was like my frontal cortex lit up or exploded or something."

"Messy git!" Julian raised his voice over the Christmas carols, growing louder with each step.

"Suddenly, everything made sense." Micah exhaled heavily. "Me and Teagan didn't end because I was a waste of space. We broke up because we weren't meant for each other. I wasn't her 'one' and she wasn't mine. If we were, we wouldn't have mutually agreed to split. We would've stuck it out. We'd probably be engaged or married by now."

"And your point is what?" asked Julian. "Successful relationships are predestined?"

"I think meeting certain people might be, but beyond that, each person has to proactively shape their own destiny. Any time you're gifted with a promising opportunity, you've gotta make the most of it. Kinda like volleyball."

Julian did a double take. "A sports analogy? Really? From the least athletic bloke I—"

"Hey! I *get* sports."

"Supporting Man City and playing a 2012 Olympics drinking game doesn't make you sporty, Meeks."

Micah huffed and stared ahead. "Just go with it, okay?"

"Carry on, Gary Lineker." Julian chuckled, name-checking the former football legend and current sports broadcaster.

"So, Player A sets up the volleyball for Player B to spike it over the net, right? But if Player B doesn't jump and seize the opportunity, they'll lose the point. The spiker's inaction could even cost his team the game."

Julian dug in his coat pocket as they slowed to a halt on the periphery of the Salvation Army band, the rumbly bass of the tuba vibrating through his chest. "But if Player B *does* spike the ball, they still might lose. There's no guarantee."

"Agreed, but at least spiker dude gave it a go. At least he was in the game." Micah removed his wallet from his trousers. "In other words, you gotta be in it to win it..."

Shaking his head, Julian pulled out several one- and two-pound coins and dropped the lot into the Sally Ann's donation kettle. The pink-cheeked flugelhorn player thanked him with an approving wink.

"Is this another thinly veiled attempt to persuade me to put myself out there and join a dating app?"

"Maybe..." Micah smirked, adding a crisp fiver to the kettle before moving on. "Listen, I know life's been pretty rubbish the last while and I'd be narked too if I had to deal with Caroline on the regular, but you're the kindest, most awesome person I know."

"Who drives a cab. Not the most sexy of professions, so I've been told."

"Caroline is a jerk, okay?! What does she know? You *will* meet someone, Jules. In fact, we both might! Sadie's bringing friends to my party..."

Oh, fucking hell! Micah's older sister had been trying to set up Julian for months. It wasn't that he didn't want to meet someone. She just had to be the *right* someone, and for a serial monogamist like Julian, hookups and flings weren't the way to find her. It also didn't help that Sadie's 'picks' were usually much younger, disliked dogs, and couldn't name a David Bowie song if their lives depended on it. He flashed a convincing smile. "Roll on, Wednesday."

Micah beamed. "Jules, it's gonna be off the charts."

They veered around a traffic jam of stalled tourists feeding a plague of cobble-pecking pigeons.

Julian glanced over his shoulder. "Is it just me or does London get busier each Christmas..."

"It's totally chock-a-block. Tash and I went out last night and tried five different pubs in Camden," said Micah. "Every single one—rammed solid. We couldn't get a look in."

"I had non-stop fares until midnight, then it dropped right off.

Bloody ride-sharing apps. They eat into my takings like nobody's business." Julian gazed quizzically through the metal-framed triangle stood in their path. Scraping the sky at thirty feet, the untraditional Christmas tree boasted a cornucopia of mirrored baubles and glass orbs, each one home to a mini terrarium of rubbery succulents. "I wish people realized modern doesn't necessarily mean better. No ride-sharing git with GPS knows London like we cabbies do."

"Preach, grandpa!" Micah laughed, side-eyeing the tree. "If you had your way, there'd be no apps, no ebooks, no music streaming."

"God, I *hate* streaming."

"Here we go!" Micah snickered.

"But seriously, does it add *anything* to the listening experience? No! At least with vinyl, you own the music, you get cover art and intriguing liner notes, not to mention that exquisite moment when the needle kisses the record. There's nothing like that warm, rich sound. Dynamics! None of this high compression crap—"

"Jules, I swear you love old records more than people!"

"Not all. Some." Julian bit back a smile, skating his fingers down the strap of his messenger bag. "What can I say? Music has been the one constant in my life. It has *never* let me down."

With a wistful grin, Micah glanced up at his friend. "I know I kid you about being a dinosaur, but I get it. If I was working my arse off at all hours and my profession was taking a beating from some newfangled appy nonsense, I'd be spitting nails, too."

"Yeah, well, I reckon my luck is about to change..." He fished out a set of keys from his coat pocket and proudly jingled them.

Micah gaped. "Are those what I think they are?"

"Yep!" Julian stowed the keyring safely back in his pocket. "Signed the lease and took possession two days ago—"

"Wahey! The taxi with the window—"

"—in the ceiling," they spoke at the same time.

Julian unzipped his bag and dipped inside. "Oh mate, she's a beauty. Electric-powered, wi-fi in the passenger area. It's quieter, too."

"How long does it take to fully charge it?" asked Micah.

"Thirty minutes at a rapid charging point, several hours at a slow one. Luckily, I know where most of the fast ones are." Julian pulled out a square plastic container as they turned the corner, leaving Coal Drops Yard behind. "I'm so chuffed about the glass roof. It'll be brilliant for tours."

Micah nodded. "I guess apart from airport runs, tours are the best way to guarantee a big pay packet nowadays?"

"Pretty much." Julian opened the container and removed half a sandwich. "The tour agency is hooking me up with some customers this week. Truth be told, I'd rather find them myself and keep all the profits, but I can't be choosy these days."

"It's great you have them as a backup, though." Micah's eyes zeroed in. "What's on the menu today?"

"Lovely cheese sarnie." Julian took a bite.

"Just cheese? Nothing else?"

He nodded, mid-chew.

"Jesus, you are skint!"

"Not skint, frugal. Things are a bit tight, but they'll pick up."

Micah stopped outside Sons + Daughters, a popular sandwich shop with a white delivery van parked on its roof. "I'm peckish, but I don't know what I want." He rubbed his chin and glanced left down Lower Stable Street. "Maybe a spinach salad from that place Tash likes…"

Julian's head jerked back. "You've got to be kidding me."

"What?" Micah's voice rose. "I eat healthy! Sometimes."

"No, it's"—he lowered his sandwich—"the woman I picked up at Heathrow yesterday. She's in the shop."

Micah laughed. "Random but okay."

"She was lovely. I tried to sell her a tour. She wasn't having it…"

"Oh?" Micah craned his neck. "Which one is she?"

"Wearing the purple coat and headphones," said Julian. "The brunette."

"With the long hair?" A slow grin tugged the corner of Micah's mouth. "Pretty. Obviously likes music." His eyes leapt back to Julian. "Eats sarnies for lunch. Oh, mate, she's *so* your type. Fuck the tour. Ask her out!"

"Micah!" Julian scoffed under his breath. "I don't proposition customers."

"Maybe you should make an exception. This one's *gorgeous*."

"She doesn't live here. She's American." Julian placed his barely touched sandwich in its container and twisted the other way. "So, made your mind up? Tash is probably starving."

Micah ignored him. "Look, she's coming. Ask her!"

"Would you stop banging on about it? That's so un"—Julian glanced over his shoulder as the shop's door swung open—"professional..."

Madeleine's gaze coasted over Julian and Micah, then boomeranged back. "Oh!" The single syllable bubbled with surprise. "Hey, I was in your cab yesterday!" She tugged off her headphones and they curved around her neck. "You drove me to my hotel?"

"I did." Julian smoothly slipped his lunch container into his messenger bag. "How are you?"

Her eyes fluttered down to his hand tugging the zipper closed. "Good." She met his smile. "I fell asleep reading yesterday, so I only started exploring this morning. I ended up here, somehow. It's pretty cool. Expensive shops, though."

"Not *all* of them..." Micah jumped in enthusiastically.

"This is my friend, Micah," said Julian. "He has a homewares shop around the corner."

"Which desperately needs me back! The holidays, eh? No rest for the wicked." He rolled his eyes and chuckled, avoiding Julian's narrowing stare. "But it's nice to meet you"—Micah leaned in—"sorry, I didn't catch your name?"

Cheeky git! I know what you're doing. Julian bit his tongue.

"It's Madeleine."

"Ah, such a pretty name! Isn't it, Julian?"

Micah, you bastard. He nodded. "Very."

"Right! Well, I'm off!" Micah smacked Julian on the back. "See ya later, spiker." With a wink and a turn, he flew down Lower

Stable Street in the opposite direction of his store.

He's bleedin' shameless. Julian's gaze flitted upward as he suppressed a laugh.

Madeleine gripped her takeout bag, its crunchy crinkle filling their pause. "I'm glad I bumped into you…"

Julian grinned. *She's changed her mind about a tour?*

"…you see, I lost the receipt you gave me, and my sister asked me to keep track of spending. She's expensing our trip and is a bit…persnickety."

His stomach sank with disappointment. "Oh. Well, no worries. I'll write you another one." He smiled kindly. "But my receipts are in my cab. It's about a five-minute walk from here. I can be back in like, ten minutes?"

"That's okay. I'll come with you. I could use the exercise." She bit her cheek. "Sorry I pulled you away from your friend"—her glance brushed across his messenger bag—"and your lunch."

"Oh, it's fine, really. I only stopped in to say hi." Julian gestured ahead. "Shall we?"

Madeleine nodded and they set off across Granary Square, a popular public space beloved for its dancing fountains and alfresco dining. "I'm a big fan of these pedestrianized areas." Her eyes strayed to their right and the wide cement steps that swept down to the canal's towpath. Bundled up in parkas, tourists and chatty locals sat interspersed, enjoying their coffees and takeout lunches, hoping for sun. "I'll have to come back and look around some more when I'm not so hungry."

"Oh, by all means, please tuck in—*eat!*" said Julian, ignoring the futuristic forest of green pyramid-shaped Christmas trees elevated on a platform above the square.

Madeleine winced. "But it might be kinda stinky…"

"Why? What'd you get?"

"Egg salad with miso mayo on a white bloomer."

"The one with truffle crisps inside?" he asked.

"It is! Potato chips in sandwiches—who thought of that? It's pure genius! I couldn't resist."

Julian chuckled. "Go on then. Enjoy."

Madeleine's shoulders relaxed. "Thanks. I get headaches if I don't eat regularly." She dove into the bag, lifting out her lunch wrapped in wax paper.

"That sandwich place is amazing. You're in for a treat."

"Yeah? Sandwiches are my favorite thing ever. Love 'em." She peeled away the paper. "So, a girl in line said putting chips inside is a British thing?" Pulling a crisp free from the egg, salad cress, and mayo, she popped it in her mouth and chewed slowly, muting its crunch. "Oh god!" she maffled. "So good."

Julian nodded as they strolled across the square's footbridge. "Crisp butties have come a long way. The ones we ate as kids were much simpler: soft white bread, a lick of butter, and a handful of crisps from the corner shop."

"That's it?" she asked. "No other filling?"

"Nope. Cheap and cheerful with precisely *zero* nutritional value! I still have them once in a blue moon."

"Well, have some now. Have my other half..." Madeleine hid her smile behind another bite of sandwich and offered its still-wrapped twin.

"Oh no, I'm good. Thanks, though." He glanced at the headphones resting around her neck. "What were you listening to?"

"Blur 'For Tomorrow'." She mumbled through her mouthful. "When in London, right?"

"Good taste. So where do you stand on the '90s Blur vs. Oasis debate?" asked Julian.

Madeleine swallowed. "You know, I never understood that, the idea that you could like one but not the other. If the music is good, who cares?"

"My thoughts exactly."

"That said, all Oasis albums sound the same to me," she said. "I'm not a big fan. What about you?"

"Uh, they're all right, you know, nothing special." He swept his hand down the strap of his bag and glanced away. "So, my cab's down this road here. If you want, I can take you somewhere after or bring you back to Coal Drops Yard?" Reuniting with her eyes, his gaze dropped, fixating on a small blob of mayo riding the edge of her bottom lip. "Um, you, uh"—he motioned with his finger—"have a bit of your lunch…"

Madeleine froze mid-chew then swallowed. "Jeez, you can't take me anywhere!" Halting on the spot, a small laugh escaped her wince as she pulled a napkin from beneath the sandwich's wrapping. "Thanks for telling me." She blotted her mouth, a blush blooming across her cheeks.

Julian looked across the street, gifting her some privacy. "One time, I worked an entire shift with broccoli in my teeth. Not a single passenger said a peep! I was smiling, laughing—it was really obvious! Felt like a right knob when I realized I had a bloody tree wedged in there."

Madeleine's tongue flicked her lip. "What's wrong with people? I get that it's awkward speaking up, but…" She blinked up at him. "Okay, how's it now?"

His eyes hovered over her soft, pouty lips. *Blimey, she's cute.* He swallowed hard. *And a customer. Tame that inner flirt, mate.* He nodded away all thoughts of fancying her. "It's gone. You look great, ready to meet the Queen."

"Or…at least the Queen's jewels? If I'm here, I might as well go see them, right?" Madeleine bit her lip. "And Tower Bridge and Buckingham Palace." She curled her fingers around her sandwich. "I guess I need a tour guide, huh? Any chance you're free for the rest of the afternoon?"

Julian broke into a huge smile. "Not anymore I'm not."

THREE

MADELEINE

Driving through Bloomsbury, Julian slowed to a stop on Guilford Street where it met leafy Russell Square. He flicked his left turn signal and glanced over his shoulder, waiting for the red light to change. "Madeleine, see the grand hotel on your right?"

"I can't take my eyes off it." Leaving her sandwich in its wrapper on her lap, she leaned on the arm rest and craned her neck for a better look. "London is killing it with gorgeous, old hotels." She gazed up at the landmark's thé-au-lait terracotta, arcaded balconies, and whimsical turquoise turrets.

"It's the Kimpton Fitzroy," said Julian. "The main entrance around the corner features four life-sized statues of British queens: Elizabeth I, Mary I, Mary II, and Anne."

"Beautiful. How old is it?"

"It was built in 1898. Charles Fitzroy Doll, the architect, made such a huge splash with its opulent style that he was commissioned to design the first-class dining room aboard the Titanic."

Her eyes widened. "Now there's a trivia question."

"Basically, he copied the hotel's restaurant and replicated it on the ship."

Madeleine pored over the façade's French-Renaissance style. "Well, if it ain't broke…"

"He also had a pair of bronze dragon sculptures moulded." Julian adjusted his eyeglasses. "One sailed with the Titanic and now lies on the ocean floor, the other graces the hotel's main staircase. Care to guess his name?"

"The hotel dragon? No clue."

"Lucky George."

25

"Oh man! That's just…" She sat back, picking up her sandwich again. "So I guess his twin is *unlucky* George?"

Julian laughed. "If you have time, you should look inside. It's incredibly glam, all soaring marble columns, gilded capitals. There's a mosaic marble floor featuring the signs of the zodiac…"

Shantelle would love that. Madeleine pasted on a smile as the red light changed to green and the cab eased left onto Southampton Row. *I'm trying, I really am. But being here, making small talk with a stranger, acting like the unthinkable never happened feels weird.* She fought back a yawn and picked at the crust of her sandwich. Grief had taken away many things—sleep, relationships, her concentration—but her appetite wasn't one of them. The ten extra pounds she carried didn't lie. Her attention hopped to the corgi swinging below Julian's rear view mirror.

'Happiness is a warm puppy.'

Letting out a shallow sigh, she tucked a tendril of hair behind her ear and revived her grin. "I love your corgi. So adorable." She popped the last piece of sandwich in her mouth.

"Oh, cheers. Micah made it. Needle felted animals are his latest side hustle."

"That's cool." Her eyes snagged on a pair of red telephone boxes on the eastern corner of Russell Square. Doors propped open, their windows were covered with signage, and office workers lined up out front. *What's going on there?* Swallowing her mouthful, she shifted around, peering through the cab's rear window as a guy in a parka handed a rectangular box to a well-dressed woman. *They're shops?!* Madeleine turned back. "Julian, what are they selling from those phone boxes?"

"Coffee and homemade tiramisu."

"Oh wow, what a lovely idea!" She smiled.

"You'll see others set up as corner shops, libraries, some even have defibrillators. It's great. Saves them from the scrap heap."

"I didn't think of that," said Madeleine. "I guess everyone uses cellphones these days."

He nodded. "Modern technology, eh? So what do you do back

in the States?"

"I work for Sensoria, the music streaming service."

Julian did a double take in his mirror. "Oh?!" His lips pressed together slightly as he broke eye contact and returned to the road.

"I'm a senior editor and content programmer," said Madeleine. "I make digital playlists for a living."

He paused for a beat. "How do you like it?"

"I love it! I'm a music geek, so it's a dream come true. It's such a cool place to work." Nodding, she balled up the sandwich wrapper. "I'm extremely lucky."

"Do you have a playlist specialty?"

"Definitely decades and moods, but my most recent playlists were pub-themed and for Christmas, funnily enough." Madeleine studied a pack of hunched office workers scurrying from the cold, steaming takeout coffees in hand.

"What about genres—got a favorite?" he asked.

"Ooh, tough question. I'm into everything, but I play indie music the most. And '90s stuff, especially Britpop bands."

"Hence you listening to Blur earlier—and your ringtone."

Her brow furrowed as the taxi met a red light. "My ringtone? How do you...?"

"Your phone went off when I picked you up from the airport."

"Oh right! Pulp—'Disco 2000'. Yeah, I love that song. I got the cassette single when I was seven, played it so much I wore it out." She stuffed the sandwich wrapper in its takeout bag and held it on her lap. "My dad was relieved. He hated it, said the lyrics weren't appropriate for a girl my age. He heard 'breasts' and went ballistic."

Julian smiled. "How does a seven-year-old American girl get into Pulp, anyway?"

"Dad's sister—my auntie—was a massive Anglophile and would fly over here for concerts. She'd come back with cassettes, CDs, t-shirts. Because of her, I was the only kid in my Wisconsin school with an Elastica tee."

"Dialing up the cool factor to eleven, eh? So, how'd you get the Sensoria gig?"

27

"Honestly, by pure fluke. I have a creative writing degree but couldn't find a job. A friend of a friend knew someone at Sensoria and got me in. My plan was to stay until I joined a magazine or wrote my bestseller. That was ten years ago." Uncoiling her headphones from her neck, Madeleine plopped them in her lap alongside the deflated lunch bag. "What about you? How long have you been driving a cab?"

"Two years behind the wheel, but before that I was studying The Knowledge."

"The Knowledge?! Sounds like something Yoda teaches in *Star Wars.*"

Julian laughed. "Well, it *is* old—dates back to the late 1800s." His taxi forged ahead, rejoining the flow of traffic. "It's a mandatory course all prospective black cab drivers take. It's intense and time-consuming, really challenging. The dropout rate is around seventy percent."

"That's brutal. What's it involve?"

"A lot of memory work. I had to learn 320 set routes within a six-mile radius of Charing Cross and more than 25,000 streets, plus 20,000 landmarks and points of interest. Everything from pubs, shops, and hotels to historic buildings, embassies, and hospitals."

Her eyes bulged. "Seriously? You know *all* of them? How long did that take?"

"Four years. Most of that was spent traveling around London, learning all the shortcuts and places of interest. Studying from maps only helps so much. You have to actually get out there on a moped to understand how London's road network is laid out." The cab eased to a stop behind a Tesco grocery store truck. "I was out and about at all hours. I pretty much existed on your new fave there, crisp butties."

"And that's bad?" Madeleine smiled as Julian changed lanes and they were rolling again. "Carbs are life!"

"They are...until you develop scurvy."

Madeleine laughed, her eyes hopping from storefront to storefront. Pizza Express, Holland & Barrett, Greggs: unfamiliar shop names whizzed by. "So much to remember. No wonder The Knowledge takes years to learn. Basically, you've earned a master's degree in everything London!"

"Pretty much, yeah."

They paused at another light, a bustling intersection where Southampton Row turned into Kingsway. A busload of suitcase-dragging tourists trundled past, rubbing shoulders with well-dressed Londoners chatting on their phones, their warm breaths rising mid-conversation.

Julian glanced over his shoulder. "It sounds mad, but I reckon my cab license was harder to earn than my journalism degree."

"Oh! You have a writing degree, too?"

"Yep. For six years, I wrote record reviews and special features for a UK magazine called *Words and Music*."

Madeleine's jaw dropped. "No! I LOVED that magazine! It was like, my music industry bible." Her mind raced. *Hang on! His name's Julian...* Leaning forward, she clutched her headphones and eased into a squint. "Wait a minute—you're not Julian Halliwell, are you?"

His forehead furrowed. "Uh, yeah. Why?"

"Holy shit!" She bounced back, sweeping her hair off her forehead. "I used to read your stuff all the time! You were my favorite! Oh my god, I can't believe this!"

"Bloody hell! I can't believe you've read my stuff." He grinned as traffic began flowing again and they crossed High Holborn.

How is this happening? He's the freakin' writer I idolized for six years! Madeleine stared in his rear view mirror. "Why wouldn't I? Julian, they were spectacular! Always cheeky and fun but fair and informative, too. And your artist profiles—the ones you wrote on Bruno Mars and Paloma Faith were so fucking good. I felt like I was there, riding the tour bus, hanging out backstage. I felt like I *knew* them." The prickly heat of a blush rose on her cheeks. *You're getting carried away, you big nerd!* Leaning back against the seat, her eyes drifted upward through the window in the ceiling where the leaf-free trees arched over the street, their branches mingling in a horticultural handshake. "Sorry, I'm fangirling wayyy too much." Her gaze dropped. "I'll stop."

"No, don't. It's great!" He laughed. "It's pretty much a first, let me tell ya."

"I was furious when the magazine went under," she said.

Julian sighed wistfully. "Yeah. Broke my heart."

"It must've been so hard."

"It was at first. My entire existence was connected to that job: my friends, my social life. I didn't know what to do with myself."

Madeleine's face scrunched.

"I contacted other magazines, but"—Julian shrugged as he stopped at another light, waiting to turn left onto Aldwych— "budgets were being slashed, friends were losing jobs, and the handful of new hires were recent grads who'd write for next to nothing. My industry experience and salary expectations were suddenly a detriment."

"That's terrible. Your experience should be valued, not held against you."

"You'd hope, right? I ended up freelancing for a few men's magazines but didn't make enough to live on. So I thought, enough of this bollocks, time to be my own boss, although I had no clue how I'd accomplish that. Then one night, Micah and I were sharing a taxi home and I had a drunken epiphany: I enjoy driving, love London and meeting new people. It was a no-brainer. Our poor cabbie, though. I drilled him with questions the entire journey. The next day, I leased a moped and signed on to learn The Knowledge. I spent hours traveling all over London, loving every minute—and still do! I wake up every morning wondering, *Who's gonna need a lift today?*"

"I bet you've met some real characters."

The traffic light switched to green. "Oh, you have no idea!"

"Any favorites?" she asked.

"A few, but if I could only choose one, it would be John, the World War II veteran I picked up on Remembrance Sunday a year back. He was in his mid-nineties and alone, wanted to visit the Animals in War memorial outside Hyde Park. On the drive over, he shared some incredible stories of working with Rocky, his search and rescue dog, during the Blitz. They located countless survivors in bombed-out buildings all over London. One time, Rocky refused to budge for ten hours until a little girl was recovered from the rubble."

Madeleine smiled. "If I didn't love dogs already. Wow."

Julian nodded. "John paid his respects to Rocky there every year since 2004. I think about him a lot..." He cleared his throat. "Anyway, London is full of stories like John's. One day, I'll turn my cabbie encounters into a book of short stories. It would be a shame to keep them to myself."

"That's a great idea. How far in are you?"

"Oh, haven't started yet. It's all in my head." He grinned. "But life is funny, eh? Turns out, being laid off was the best thing to happen to me. I found my true calling, driving around London."

"Have you lived here all your life?" she asked.

"Yeah, born and bred in the East End. Whitechapel."

"Isn't that where Jack the Ripper murdered people?"

Julian grimaced. "It is. You might've guessed it's not the poshest of postcodes."

"Maybe not, but if you don't mind me saying, your name is quite posh, though!"

"My parents had illusions of grandeur. They gave me and my brother Alistair aristocratic-sounding names hoping we'd grow into them, I think."

"Well, they should be really proud of you, for taking control of your life. Starting a new chapter..."

He gave her a tight-lipped smile in the rear view mirror and stared ahead again, falling into silence. Madeleine took the opportunity to stuff her headphones in her bag and text Shantelle.

Madeleine: Where are you? Did you get my message earlier?

Waiting for her sister's response, Madeleine scrolled through

31

the texts she had received from Shantelle's London friends that morning. Two of them were already visiting family in Scotland, while several others were on the train up to Manchester. She had left a message for one other girl but didn't hold out much hope of hearing back.

I'm so alone here... Her stomach ached. *It wasn't supposed to be like this.*

"Madeleine?" Julian beckoned through the intercom.

She looked up. "Yes?"

"We'll be at the Tower of London in seven minutes, give or take."

"Oh, perfect." Sitting up straight, she peered out the window, catching the red, white, and blue Underground roundel for Temple station sailing past.

"Don't let the name fool you, though," said Julian. "It's not just one tower. There are actually *twenty*-one."

"Really? Not only is that a major misnomer, it's also a major miscalculation."

Julian laughed. "True. The White Tower—the first tower—was built over nine hundred years ago. As time passed, they added defensive walls and more towers, and a moat around the castle keep."

I don't think Shan saw any of this when she was here. Madeleine checked her phone one more time, but her text remained unanswered. *Where the hell is she?*

The cab rounded Temple Place, joining another taxi waiting for a green light on the Victoria Embankment. Julian clicked on his left turn signal. "If you want the full experience, I'd recommend a tour with the Beefeaters. It's included with the price of admission."

"Are they the guys in the red coats and tall furry hats?" she asked. "They never smile, right?"

"That's the Queen's Guard. You'll see them, too. They usually keep watch outside the Waterloo Block where the Crown Jewels are displayed. Although at this time of year, the Guard pack away their red tunics and don gray coats instead." Julian looked briefly in the rear view mirror before turning left onto the Embankment. "You'll

love the Beefeaters, though. Their official name is Yeoman War-
ders, and they're former military personnel. Their duties are mostly
ceremonial, dealing with tourists, locking up the gates each evening,
but they're proper characters, always game for a laugh. Their tours
are peppered with bloodthirsty stories and bawdy humor."

"Bawdy? Where do I sign up?" Madeleine laughed, her eyes
glued to a six-foot-high stone plinth on her left, home to a snarling
cast-iron dragon painted silver and red. Below his fiery tongue, his
fierce claws held the heraldic coat of arms for the City of London,
marking the boundary of the ancient city.

"And unlike the Queen's Guard, you can talk to them," said Julian. "You should ask what it's like to live there."

"What?" She turned around, leaving the dragon behind. "*In* the
Tower?"

"Yeah, they live there with their families. The Tower walls con-
tain apartments. There's a pub, too, but only Beefeaters are allowed
inside."

"I'd have to be drunk 24/7 to live there." Madeleine squirmed
on the back seat, the River Thames flying by on their right. "All that
history of torture and beheadings, ghosts haunting the place..."

Julian snickered. "Word has it that Anne Boleyn, Henry VIII's
second wife, regularly roams the Tower Green without her head."

Oh god. A chill creeped up Madeleine's spine.

"And the two young princes believed to have been murdered
there in the late 1400s wander about, too. Some people have seen
them vanish through walls."

"Well, that seals it."

"What does?" asked Julian.

"You're coming in with me."

"Sorry?"

"I can't deal with ghosts," she said, her fingers digging into her
crunched up sandwich bag.

Julian smiled. "Madeleine, I doubt you'll see any."

"Doesn't matter! Look, I'll pay your admission. I'll pay your
parking and for your time. Just come with me...please?"

FOUR

MADELEINE

Leaving behind the Crown Jewels and the Tower's Waterloo Block, a puff of warm breath floated from Madeleine's lips. "That was incredible!" She beamed and hugged her Tower of London souvenir guidebook against her coat, ignoring the damp afternoon chill. "The crowns, the sceptres, Handel's coronation anthems—so perfect! I swear, I still have goosebumps."

Julian buttoned his coat and sidestepped around a slow-moving band of tourists. "What was your favorite?"

"No competition, the St. Edward's Crown. Five pounds of solid gold and gemstones, baby."

"Yeah, they sure didn't skimp on jewels back in the day," said Julian.

"How on earth did the Queen wear it during her coronation? My neck aches just thinking about it. That said, I'd still try it on in a heartbeat!" Madeleine let out a laugh. "What was your fave?"

"The Sovereign's Sceptre, the one with the cross?"

"And the world's largest cut white diamond," raved Madeleine. "Excellent choice!"

Walking in the long shadows of the White Tower, they passed a noisy gang of selfie-stick-wielding tourists and a Beefeater's tour of rapt Canadians. Madeleine looked up, studying the old keep's north side and two of its four turrets. Nearly 1,000 years old, the rectangular, medieval castle hadn't lost any of its ominous presence. "If stone walls could talk. It looks even more sinister in the dwindling daylight." She dipped her chin into her cozy scarf. "I knew about the gory executions but had no idea this place was a treasury or had a zoo. Imagine monkeys and lions roaming around here…"

"With the polar bear and elephan—" An old-school telephone ring erupted from Julian's coat. He slowed to a stop and retrieved his phone from a pocket. "Sorry, I have to..."

She pointed toward the far end of Waterloo Block and the gray-cloaked member of the Queen's Guard stood silently in front of his sentry hut. "Oh, no problem. I'll be over there taking photos." Strolling a few paces away, she stole a peek back over her shoulder, catching Julian's wince as he answered.

"Hey Caroline..."

Julian's been so accommodating—and fun. Granting him privacy, Madeleine continued on, admiring the sky in all its pink and orange glory as she rummaged through her purse. She pulled out her phone, its display earning a double take. *You're kidding? Quarter to four? Jeez, the sun sets early here.*

Wedging her Tower booklet under her arm, she stepped back and fit the guard and his tall, bearskin hat into frame. Even without the red tunic, he looked majestic, like a handsome soldier in a historical romance. She took a burst of photos then moved out of the way, allowing two women about her age to have their turn. Their laughter, easy banter, and Liverpudlian accents drew Madeleine in. *Best friends?* A heaviness knotted in her chest.

The curvy redhead hugged the short, earmuff-wearing blonde and extended her free arm, selfie-ready. "And no duck face, Jess! That was *so* Spain 2016!"

Jess exchanged a knowing look with her friend. "Yeah, like your thing for *chokers!*" She howled in mirth, glancing at the phone held aloft. "That trip! Flip-floppery, much?!"

The redhead's face creased as she squealed, "Oh gawd!" joining her bestie in shrieks of hilarity.

Inside jokes... An ache grew in the back of Madeleine's throat. *We had so many.*

Best friends come and go, but Madeleine and Kellie had been for keeps. At first, they bonded over music, a love of London, and writing fan fiction about their favorite movies, but fandom camaraderie blossomed into 'You really get me!' besties. Their hopes, dreams, secrets—nothing was off limits, everything was shared. Madeleine always joked Kellie would be her one phone call from jail while Kellie promised Madeleine if she ever needed a kidney, she was her girl.

Kellie wasn't *just* a friend. Kellie was family, a sister by choice.

They spoke daily, texted constantly, and supported one another 24/7 until last December. Until a panicked phone call split Madeleine's life into a stark 'before and after'. Her beloved bestie with the sparkling brown eyes and wit to spare, who adored her dog, Roo, and Taylor Swift and never met a taco she didn't like, died unexpectedly, age thirty-five.

Eight years of in-jokes, heart-to-hearts, late-night dance parties *just because* were all ripped away, leaving Madeleine's beautiful memories tangled with regret and guilt.

Australian Kellie and American Madeleine were online besties.

But they had never met.

If *only* they had met.

"Ohh, I look rubbish!" moaned Jess, pulling off her earmuffs as she flicked through her friend's photos.

"No worries, babe. I got ya," said her redheaded BFF. "We'll take more." Arms around each other, the pair smiled brightly in front of the stony-faced Queen's Guard and snapped away.

Madeleine sighed. *What I'd do for a single, crappy photo of me and Kel.*

When Madeleine told loved ones about Kellie's death, some dismissed their long-distance connection as superficial and insignificant, not a *true* friendship and definitely not one worthy of her breath-stealing sobs or debilitating despair. They had never worked together, never shared a hug or enjoyed a meal in person. "Yeah, but you didn't really *know* her. Not properly," said her brother, Antoine, one snowy afternoon, weeks after Kellie's death. Her Sensoria clique, who was always up for post-work drinks, wasn't much kinder, whispering behind her back, "How can she be *this* upset? This Kellie person, wasn't she, like, a *virtual* pen pal?"

Their insensitive comments stung, and when Madeleine didn't

immediately snap back into old-Maddie mode—going to gigs, meeting for brunch—most stopped listening and checking in, leaving her suffocating alone in the quicksand of unfathomable sorrow, desperately missing the one person who always lifted her up.

Weeks dragged in a blur of snotty, balled-up tissues and brain-numbing insomnia. With only one sick day from work remaining, Madeleine straggled out of bed, pulled on her sweats, and met with a grief counselor. Through exhausted tears, she spoke of how lonely grieving made her feel, of the peer pressure to "get over it already", and how, whenever she brought up her sadness, her so-called nearest and dearest and work acquaintances tried to cheer her up or insisted she be strong, which felt a lot like being shushed.

Yoshiko, her counselor, agreed, saying, "People are uncomfortable talking about grief, especially when it involves a loss or relationship they don't understand. And when they don't acknowledge a death like Kellie's or give it the usual empathy or support other losses receive, it encourages you to suppress the emotions you're feeling, and that hinders your ability to grieve openly and fully. Madeleine, what you're grappling with is disenfranchised grief."

Madeleine was surprised there was a name for it, but her counselor didn't stop there.

"Society has a terrible habit of dictating which deaths are worthy of grief and which ones aren't," said Yoshiko. "But grieving is a deeply personal thing. It's impossible for anyone to know the extent of someone else's pain. Losses should never be dismissed, judged, or compared. All grief is worthy—Madeleine, *yours* is worthy. It's real and life-changing and no one has the right to tell you otherwise or insist you 'move on'. Grief is a natural reaction to loss, and it doesn't come with an on/off switch or an expiration date."

For once, Madeleine felt seen and heard. However, her counselor was just one person. Madeleine still had the rest of the world to contend with. Who to tell? Who to trust?

Sometimes it was easier to stay silent, even if it left her feeling isolated and alone.

A brisk gust of wind scuttled crunchy leaves across the shiny boots of the Queen's Guard. *Oh Kel.* Madeleine sniffed as she glanced away from the giggly best friends, tears threatening, clouding her eyes. *So many everyday things remind me of you. Your absence is everywhere.* Dipping her chin, she sucked in a stuttering breath and hid in her phone, fussing with her email. *In three days, it'll be a year since you died. How is that even possible...* Her thumb hovered over an unopened message in the 'starred' file on the screen.

Subject: IN LONDON? OPEN ME!

Pictures snapped, the best friends swanned off, their laughter replaced by the gaspy shrieks of a crying toddler jarred by the cobblestone onslaught beneath the wheels of his stroller. Madeleine swiveled out of its path and blinked with purpose, quelling her own tears as she abandoned the email, unread.

"*Aaand* I'm back," said Julian. "Sorry for taking so long."

Sniffing one last time, she looked up, all signs of grief concealed. Or so she thought.

His smile faded. "Hey, are you all right?"

Shit. Red eyes? She rubbed her nose. "Yeah! Just had a sneezing fit."

"Oh, hate those. I get hay fever. So..." He motioned to her phone. "Want me to take some pictures? Prove you were here?" His eyes bore into the pastel-colored case and its assortment of smiling ice cream cones.

"That would be awesome." A grateful grin curved her mouth. "Thank you."

After several poses and one selfie with Julian, Madeleine reclaimed her phone and aimed it at the lantern bell-cote of the Chapel Royal of St. Peter ad Vincula, then took more photos of the half-timbered Queen's House overlooking the Tower Green where seven members of England's nobility had met their untimely deaths. Julian held her guidebook and waited patiently by her side until her photoshoot was finished.

"I got some good ones." She flicked through, sharing a few highlights. "Look at the ravens."

"Ah bollocks, you're missing the Christmas tree." Julian offered his hand. "Let me take one of you standing in front—"

"Oh no, it's okay." Madeleine suppressed her wince, avoiding any acknowledgment of the tall tree entwined with dazzling blue lights that twinkled and bobbed in the slight breeze. *How do I put this? I don't want to hurt his festive feelings.* She tucked a wisp of hair behind her ear. "Thanks, but...to be honest, I'm feeling more meh than merry..."

Julian opened his mouth to say something but stopped, settling into an empathetic nod before trying again. "That's understandable. Everyone's celebrating, seeing friends while you're stuck here on your own in suspended animation."

In more ways than one. She cleared her throat as they left the Tower Green behind. "Hopefully I'll get an update tomorrow morning. The airline seemed optimistic, anyway."

They traipsed down the stone steps leading toward the exit. Madeleine's stomach growled while Julian seemed lost in thought, taking in the fiery oranges and yellows streaking across the darkening sky. "They said on the news the ash might create some spectacular sunsets. At least it's good for something!"

"So pretty. This whole afternoon exceeded my expectations." Madeleine smiled softly, her compliment genuine. "I loved the Beefeater tour. His stories were worth the price of admission alone. And seeing the ravens, the crowns...all of it. Thanks for coming with me, Julian."

"My pleasure. I'm glad we ended on a high note with the jewels. You looked a little green in the torture exhibit."

Madeleine's lips twisted. "Oh god—the rack! I know it's a replica, but still! Gave me the creeps. I'm not good with scary things: movies, books, headless ghosts..."

Chuckling quietly, Julian flipped through her souvenir booklet. "Is there anything else you'd like to see before we leave?"

"Oh. Sorry!" Madeleine grimaced and held out her hand. "You

don't have to carry that."

"I don't mind. Makes it easier for you to take photos."

"Ah, thanks," she flashed a grin. *He's so nice. I still can't believe he's THE Julian Halliwell! I wish I could tell Kellie.* She snapped a picture of the imposing Bloody Tower up ahead. *Kel never teased, never laughed at me for fangirling over some stranger in a magazine. She understood. No one else did. No one else does...*

Halfway through the Bloody Tower's archway, Julian's phone rang again, its trill echoing against the aged stones spanning overhead. He wrestled it from his pocket as they swung left, passing Traitor's Gate, the entrance off the River Thames where many a prisoner passed during the reign of the Tudors. He gave Madeleine a quick smile before responding to the caller. "Hey..."

Walking ahead, she crossed the drawbridge spanning the fortress's grass-covered moat and gasped.

"Look at you!" Madeleine rushed across the cobblestones, swooning over the neo-Gothic grandeur of Tower Bridge stretching across the river. She leaned against the iron barrier and raised her phone for a quick capture of a red double-decker bus zooming along but instead received an eyeful of texts.

Shantelle: Just got in. Phone died on Koh Phi Phi. Such a beautiful island! You'd LOVE the beaches.

Shantelle: Got swarmed there by *Lost for Breath* fans, I'm all selfie'd out! So much sun and fresh air, I'm zonked! It's not even 11, but I can't keep my eyes open. My boo keeps texting. Ya think he misses me? Lol

Her sister's boyfriend was an Aquarius, a good match according to Shantelle's astrologist. Madeleine began typing her response, but another message landed before she finished.

Shantelle: Re: my friends—apologies! Everyone's scattering for the holidays. I'm sorry you've been on your own. How's it been? You didn't read all day, did you? Gimme goss, send pics.

Madeleine completed her reply, attached the selfie with Julian, and hit Send.

Madeleine: That island sounds beautiful. At Tower Bridge right now. I booked a tour with this nice cabbie. This is Julian.

Her sister's replies arrived fast and furious, bumping the conversation up the screen.

Shantelle: Nice?

Shantelle: Julian not nice

Shantelle: JULIAN SCORCHING!

Well, she's not wrong. Madeleine pursed her lips. *He's courteous and kind, too, which is even hotter. Must admit, my old crush is flaring again.*

Who knew? The good-on-glossy-magazine-paper guy was even better in person.

"So, Madeleine"—Julian's accent tangled in her hair—"you smitten yet?"

Her stomach dropped along with her phone. "Uh, sorry?" She squeezed its case, her 'Nothing to see here' grin contrasting with the wisp of pink blooming across her cold cheeks.

"Tower Bridge." Julian gestured toward the iconic landmark. "Isn't it grand, all lit up?"

Crisis averted. Crush undetected. She let out a breath. "Yes! Yes it is."

Julian's eyes searched the bridge's Victorian towers and its blue and white-painted suspension chains. "I was completely besotted the first time I saw it."

"I can see why." Madeleine took a few photos, including one

with her much-hoped-for red double-decker bus. "How often does it open up for boats to pass through?"

"About 800 times each year. The schedule is posted online. Did you know it opened for Michael Jackson once?"

"No way! He sailed the Thames?" she asked.

"Erm, in a matter of speaking." Julian grinned. "In June '95, Jacko had an album coming out. His record company hired a tug-boat and barge to float a giant statue of him down the river."

Madeleine rolled her eyes. "Oh jeez!"

"There was one problem, though. His doppelgänger was too tall to pass under the bridge."

"So they lifted it." She giggled. "That's bizarre!"

"It was! I saw it, you know. I was seven, pestered Mum until she agreed to bring me and my brother down. We got here just in time, saw the entire spectacle: Tower Bridge's bascules lifting and the King of Pop, immortalized in 32 feet of fibreglass and steel, sailing through." Julian pointed at the river. "They moored him here by the Tower for about a week."

"I wonder what the ravens thought of that!" Madeleine left his smile and admired the picturesque panorama again. "Ah, but what a view." Her gaze climbed the Shard on the far side of the Thames, the pointy skyscraper's spire alive with a shimmering display of dancing red and green lights. *This has been fun. Shame it has to end, like all good things…*

Julian held her guidebook against his chest. "So, where to next?"

Madeleine wanted a Tower of London magnet. Not that the cute cabbie needed to know about her nerdy collection. "The gift shop?" She shivered.

"Sure." His eyes jagged down to her balled-up hands hidden inside her pockets as they strolled along Tower Wharf, the jolly sound of passing carolers warming the crisp air. "If you'd like something hot to drink before we head to Buckingham Palace, they serve tea and coffee at the kiosk up ahead."

"Hmm, I might get a Coke and some salt and vinegar crisps or something. I'm hungry—again. I'm always hungry." She gave in to an eye-watering yawn and hid her open mouth behind her hand. "I'll probably order the entire room service menu when I get back to my hotel."

"You're not seeing your sister's friends?" he asked.

I can't let on that I'm alone. He's great, but still. Stranger danger and all that. She dropped her hand. "Oh. No, not yet. Maybe tomorrow."

"Well, here's an idea: instead of dining on your own, come to the pub quiz with us!"

I wasn't expecting that. She blinked, her countenance brightening.

"It's at the Castle pub on Pentonville Road, not far from your hotel. We go every Monday—me, Micah, his sister Natasha. It's great fun! Topics range from sports and hobbies to film and music, plus some general knowledge thrown in for good measure."

It's been a year since I've been out. I'd love a pub meal and a chance to talk more about music with him... She fought back another yawn as squeals of laughter arose from the seasonal ice rink filling the moat near the Tower's entrance. Projections of large white snowflakes swirled along the outer stone walls, their dance choreographed to a playlist of current chart hits. *But what if I suck at the questions?*

"They have prizes, too," added Julian.

Forehead wrinkling, Madeleine's gaze lingered over a group of wobbly teenagers clutching each other while rosy-cheeked couples held hands and glided gracefully around the ice. "Prizes, huh? It sounds amazing, but I don't want to hurt your chances of winning. I'm not really up to speed on British pop culture or history."

"Oh? You'll fit right in, then!" Julian nodded. "Don't worry, we're not hardcore trivia masters or anything. Honestly, it's just a bit of a giggle, really. And hey, you never know—they might ask a question about Lucky George!"

"Or pop music trivia...or American history?"

"Exactly! And I'll give you a lift back to your hotel after, no charge, of course. I'm our designated driver." He grinned. "Our crappy team could really use your help. Join us—please?"

A slow smile lifted the corners of her mouth. "Okay, yes. My final answer is yes."

FIVE

MADELEINE

The aroma of juicy burgers peppered the air and Bowie crooned with Bing as Madeleine and Julian joined Natasha around a reserved table in one of the Castle pub's cozy nooks. Steps away, Micah queued for drinks, shoulder to shoulder with slack-jawed tourists and Santa-hat-wearing Londoners let loose from nearby offices. The mood was jolly, the laughter warm, and a high-spirited competitiveness crackled through the Islington hotspot.

Even Madeleine wasn't immune. Sharing her day's adventures with Natasha, a buzzy anticipation raced through her veins. She sat back in the banquette's nest of plump pillows, unsure if it was the rare night out, her attraction to Julian, or her raging appetite responsible for the somersaults in her belly.

Or all of the above? Maybe.

Her shoulders rose in a gentle shrug. "I know it's such a cliché, American tourist visiting Buckingham Palace, but I'm glad I—" A passing server stole her focus, his prowess for balancing an armful of plates—*ooh, is that the beer-battered cod and chunky chips?!*—rousing an appreciative grin. He artfully dodged selfie-snapping influencers and seventy-year-old regulars, their shaky, weathered hands wrapped lovingly around precious pints of amber ale. Madeleine's stomach released a low, rumbly growl. "The food here looks SO good!"

"It *is*—ow!" Natasha winced, dragging the headband of her sparkly deely boppers through her purple tresses. On the tip of each antenna wobbled a round brown ball dotted with matching sequins, crowned with an undulating cap of white felt, two pointy fabric leaves, and three small red balls. "I love these, but they pinch my noggin."

Madeleine had figured out the sprigs of holly but had no idea what the round things were. She narrowed her eyes as she unbuttoned her coat. "What are those supposed to be?"

"Oh! Christmas puddings—*figgy puddings*, like in the carol?" said Natasha. "You'll see them everywhere here—on greeting cards, earrings, sweaters."

"They are *super* cute!" Madeleine smiled.

"Aw, cheers! Yeah, I'm obsessed with the real deal. Mum makes one every Christmas. Micah hates it, says it's disgusting, the wanker."

"What are they like?" asked Madeleine.

"Picture a dense, sticky cake made with dried fruit, eggs, spices, alcohol, sugar, *more* alcohol." Natasha giggled. "Basically, it's a sturdy, boozy sponge! We pour white brandy sauce on top, add a decorative twiglet of holly, then douse the whole bloody thing with more alcohol and set it alight!"

Madeleine's eyes widened. "On fire?"

"Yep." Sitting across from her, Julian slipped off his scarf, a subtle grin warming his cheeks. "My granddad got too close once, singed his eyebrows."

"He didn't!" Madeleine paled as Julian nodded.

"Thing is"—Natasha's tongue poked out as she anchored the boppers in her hair—"if nobody gets hurt and nothing gets broken, is it really Christmas?" Holiday headgear fixed, she flung her hooded black coat into the corner where their small banquette kissed a blue wall. "Last year, our cousins got into fisticuffs over what we call the little cheese-shaped thingies in Trivial Pursuit."

Cheese? No, they're pieces of pie.

Julian pulled his arms free from his car coat. "And to think I turned down this year's Cooper family Christmas invite…"

"It's never too late to reconsider, Jules. Then again, if you don't, more Chrimbo pudding for me! It's a win-win." Natasha beamed.

"I'll have to see one for real. I'm strangely fascinated." Madeleine wriggled out of her coat, leaving it pooled around her hips. "And getting hungrier by the second."

Natasha nodded. "Trust me, they're the dog's bollocks!"

And that's a good thing?

Julian hung his coat on the back of his chair. "To confuse matters even more, we call most desserts pudding, even if they're not technically a pudding. And then there's Yorkshire pudding, black pudding, and all the other savory puddings, which aren't actually desserts..."

"I can't keep up!" Madeleine laughed, but the British references and effortless repartee between Julian and his friends fanned the loneliness stirring in her gut. *They're kind and welcoming, but I can't help feeling like an outsider.* She absentmindedly toyed with her necklace. "Sorry, guys. I didn't mean to send us down a complicated pudding spiral."

Natasha waved her off. "Nah! Chatting about food is my favorite thing ever. That and romance novels."

"You're into love stories?" Madeleine's tone rose in approval.

"Hell yeah! Okay, I know I don't *look* it, but underneath this gothy goodness is a gal all about the swoons and happily ever afters."

"I'm with you on that score. I can't get enough of them."

"Aren't they the best?" Natasha dove into her army green messenger bag, studded with pins for London After Midnight, Alien Sex Fiend, and Bauhaus, and pulled out a historical romance with a kissing couple and a Scottish castle on the cover. "This is what I'm reading now, the new Cordelia Ross. It's ever so good."

"I think I've seen this one on Instagram. I'll have to check it out."

"You must!" Natasha stowed it in her bag. "Give me a princess finding her prince and I'm obsessed. That's why I couldn't wait to visit Buckingham Palace as a kid. Our Gran, bless her, brought me down on the train from Manchester when I was twelve. That was exciting. The Palace, not so much. It was a massive letdown. I expected romantic balconies, maybe a cheeky wave from Prince William from one of the windows. But what did I get? An eyeful of boxy Edwardian ugly!" Natasha's rant picked up speed and volume. "For fuck's sake, it's supposed to be a royal palace! If I wanted my photo snapped outside a wannabe train depot, I would've skipped down the road to Victoria Station with my Dolly Mixture."

Julian nodded. "You're *still* fond of fondant."

"Hey, Dolly Mix IS the freakin' best, especially the orange cylinders." Natasha licked her lips. "Yummy."

Madeleine's gaze climbed the twinkly strings of Christmas lights skirting the wall-mounted chalkboard beside their table. *HO! HO! HO! BURGERS & BRAINS aka QUIZ NIGHT! £50 voucher to tonight's winner PLUS £500 to the year's top team!* was scrawled across its surface in dusty white chalk. Loitering above it, a round blue plaque from English Heritage was affixed to the wall:

THE CASTLE
The Hatton Garden Heist
of Easter weekend, 2015
was planned here.

Madeleine's face pinched. *A jewel heist gets a historical plaque? Weird...*

Natasha's exasperated sigh reeled her back in. "So yeah. Sad to say, my sweets were the highlight of my Buckingham Palace visit. Seriously, the builders could've upped the fancy factor, that's all I'm sayin'."

"Its size is impressive." Madeleine added. "But when you compare it to the palaces in France and Germany..."

"Exactly!" Natasha nodded. "It's like the ugly stepsister or something."

"Tourists complain about it all the time," said Julian. "They say it's dull, architecturally uninspired, clunky..."

"Clunky." Natasha snickered.

"...but I like it. And the drive down The Mall can't be beat."

"That was my favorite part." Madeleine smiled. "All the huge trees lining the boulevard with the Victoria Memorial and the Palace at the end."

"You'll have to come back in the summer," said Natasha. "They fly massive Union Jack flags along The Mall and open the Palace for tours. Micah took me last year for my birthday. We saw ballrooms, grand staircases, thrones. It's proper swish inside and more than makes up for the crap exterior..."

As Natasha rambled on, Madeleine noticed the black concert tee lurking underneath Julian's unbuttoned black dress shirt. Written in a simple white font, the band's name was partially hidden until he reached past the blank piece of paper reserved for their quiz answers and retrieved a small tray with salt and pepper shakers and a bottle of malt vinegar from the end of the table. *The Divine Comedy? There's a tour shirt you don't see every day.* Madeleine was familiar with the indie group's hits thanks to her love of Britpop. *Julian has eclectic taste: these guys and Kylie Minogue. I like that he's not a music snob. I deal with enough of those at work.*

She trespassed a little lower as he rolled up his long sleeves and his toned forearms made their welcome debut. Madeleine fought back a smile. *Fit, handsome, a music geek like me—* A flutter frolicked through her chest. *And lives here, thousands and thousands of miles away from Boston. Figures. I crush on this amazing guy who I'll never see again!* Her gaze catapulted to Julian's face. Luckily, the cuff on his right sleeve begged his attention and he didn't clock her enamored stare.

"You agree, right?" Micah's sister urged with an elbow bump. "About the cathedral? It's beautiful inside *and* out."

Shit, which one? Madeleine took a stab. "St. Paul's?"

Natasha's bouncing Christmas pudding boppers signaled she'd guessed correctly.

"I didn't go inside. I spent too much time at the Tower."

"St. Paul's closed at four," Julian added, his shirt sleeves perfectly rolled and just shy of his elbows.

"The exterior, though, took my breath away," said Madeleine. "The size of that dome—it *owns* the sky. So big. I've never seen anything like it."

Julian smiled back. "You know what else you should see? Windsor Castle—"

"YES! Let's all go!" Natasha bellowed. "It's a bit of a drive, but we can sing carols and eat mince pies and get all festive before we arrive. Madeleine, you'll love it. Now THAT is what a royal residence should look like!"

Madeleine offered a kind grin and smoothed her black, smocked-neck blouse adorned with pink and purple lovebirds over the top of her dark jeans. "Um, I'm not sure how long I'll be here. I might be flying to Paris tomorrow night."

Natasha pouted. "But you just got here..."

Pressing his lips together, Julian picked up the blank sheet of paper awaiting their quiz answers and looked under the stack of menus. "Do you see a pen or pencil?" Leaning back, he checked the floor but found nothing.

"Use mine." Madeleine reached into her purse, pulling out a fat blue and white ballpoint pen crowned with four retractable 'plungers'—blue, red, black, and green—each delivering a different color of ink.

His easy smile returned. "Blimey! I haven't seen one of these in ages! They were the peak of excitement at school, only the cool kids had them. Cheers!" With his left hand, he clicked the black ink and wrote their team name on the paper.

Madeleine tilted her head, reading his neat penmanship upside down. *Beauty...School...* She broke into a puzzled grin. "Beauty School Dropouts? Like from *Grease*?"

"Blame Micah." Natasha reclined into the turquoise pillows populating their banquette. "I wanted to name us after these legends." She clutched two handfuls of the second-hand concert t-shirt she wore over her dress and angled the design in Madeleine's direction. A jagged lightning bolt struck the dome of the U.S. Capitol building.

"Bad Brains? I'm impressed!"

"Yep!" Natasha beamed. "It's the perfect team name, too: musical yet self-depreciating. I also liked the double entendre." Her thick false lashes fluttered. "Jules campaigned for Hold Me Closer Tony Danza."

Madeleine burst into a laugh. "W-what? From *Friends*?"

"You have to admit it's catchy, clever, *and* on point!" Julian smiled.

"The Elton John bit—'Tiny Dancer'—is brill, but the rest of it..." Natasha scrunched her nose. "Jules, remind me again—who the fuck is Tony Danza?"

"He played a cabbie on an American sitcom called *Taxi*." Julian's eyes flitted to Madeleine.

She nodded. "Danny DeVito was in it, too." Across the table, Julian's face lit up. "So was Jeff Conaway," she continued, "the actor who played Kenickie in *Grease*."

"Ah, bless!" Natasha laid her hand over her heart. "I've always wanted to be Rizzo. LOVE HER."

Madeleine gave Julian a wry grin. "Music and taxis, huh?"

"That's me in a nutshell, but I got outvoted. Tash here loves *Grease*, so Micah's Beauty School Dropouts won."

Madeleine's baffled "O-kay..." prompted an explanation.

"Meeks was training to be a hairdresser. Ages ago." Julian tapped the pen on the paper and stole a look over his shoulder. "But a year in, he got wanderlust and ended up in Thailand, doing his bit to help wildlife."

"Bollocks! He went raving!" squealed Natasha, her heavily kohled eyes tracking her brother as he approached from the bar. "It's not like he was saving elephants or dolphins or anything like that."

"Someone say dolphins?" Micah's brows perked. "Ah, love 'em." He slid a tray crowded with drinks and bar snacks on their table, bulldozing beer mats, menus, and Natasha's phone. "I ordered burgers, fish and chips, and crispy wings. Should be here shortly, but in the meantime"—he scattered colorful packets of crisps on the table—"get these down ya, peeps."

"Thanks!" said Madeleine. "I'm so hungry."

"Yay! Christmas crisps!" Natasha clapped like he'd dropped a stack of £50 notes. She rummaged through the festive flavors. "Turkey and stuffing, glazed ham, Brussels sprout. Oooh, pigs in blankets!"

Brussels sprout chips? Madeleine studied the bright packaging and looked up, catching Julian's eye. She smiled politely and glanced away. *I'll pass, thanks.*

Natasha turned over a packet of cheese and cranberry and a rogue bag of non-Christmassy salt and vinegar. "Show Madeleine your dolphin tattoo," she teased, relinquishing the crisps as she stole her G&T from the tray. "Go on, Meeks! Do it!"

He plonked down on the vacant chair beside Julian. "Give over! Like I'm gonna pull my keks down here." Micah plowed a hand through his hair. "I'm a respectable business owner."

"Like that's ever stopped you!" His sister leaned into Madeleine, confiding. "Our kid here strips when he's off his tits. Scarred me for life."

"You've seen nowt!" Micah shot his sister a peeved glare. "And whipping off my top while dancing hardly constitutes *stripping*." His face softened as he handed Madeleine a rum and Coke.

Sibling arguments. Madeleine felt nostalgic for home. Growing up in the Joy household with Shantelle and her two younger brothers, Antoine and Gabriel, familial disagreements and teasing were a daily occurrence, but they rarely happened now with everyone scattered around the globe.

"Thanks, Micah." She glanced across the pub where more strings of fairy lights glowed and curved, reflecting in the fogged-up windows like muted smiles.

"Jules told us about Paris," said Micah. "Bloody volcano, the fucker. Any word on flights?"

"I'm hoping for an update sometime tomorrow." Taking a sip, Madeleine studied his '90s Take That t-shirt, the group's five smiley faces indistinguishable in the faded cotton.

"What *is* tomorrow? The 22nd?" Micah squinted, placing a tall glass of sparkling water in front of his best friend, who responded with a quiet "Cheers, mate."

"Nope," said Natasha. "Tuesday the 21st. Nice try, but don't even think about celebrating your birthday early."

Micah rubbed his eyes with the heels of his hands. "My head's spinnin', days are blurring together, it's been so busy..." He melted into a wide, molar-flashing yawn.

Natasha clinked Micah's pint with her napkin-wrapped fork. "C'mon, 'respectable business owner'—time to get sozzled!"

Julian grasped his fizzy water and raised it high. "Now we have drinks, let's officially welcome our new, albeit temporary, quiz team member"—he smiled at Madeleine—"and wish her a safe trip to Paris *tout suite*! To Madeleine!"

"To Madeleine!" The Cooper siblings chimed in, clinking glasses with Julian.

She grinned. "Thanks for making a stray feel at home. I'm glad you don't mind an American interloper."

"Mind? I'm *thrilled*!" Natasha rested her drink on the table and threw her arms around Madeleine, hugging her tight.

No British reserve here. Madeleine relaxed into the embrace and squeezed back.

"Tash!" Micah winced over his pint. "Don't maul our guest—please?"

"Sorry." She loosened her grip and withdrew, her hands claiming the packet of Brussels sprout crisps. Tearing it open, she fished out a chip with a strange green hue.

Madeleine kept her cringe at bay as the snack neared Natasha's lips. *She's gonna eat that?*

"I'm not usually this touchy-feely, but I could tell straight away you were nice. Plus, you actually *talk* to me." Natasha bit the crisp in half and munched happily.

Madeleine smiled curiously. "Why wouldn't I?"

"Goth stigma."

Micah nodded, backing up his sister.

"There are loads of misconceptions out there," said Natasha.

"That's awful. I'm so sorry." Madeleine lifted her drink, her eyes bypassing the salt and vinegar snacks. "People can be really ignorant sometimes."

"Yeah. They wrongly assume we're fixated solely on death and graveyards. That couldn't be further from the truth," said Natasha. "Goths believe in balance. We celebrate life's dark *and* light moments—you can't talk about one and ignore the other. Life consists of both!"

"So true," said Madeleine. "I think goths are great."

"See? Like I said, you're sound as a pound." Natasha's friendly stare narrowed as Madeleine sipped her rum and Coke. "And I know it sounds bonkers, but I feel like I *know* you, strangely! Actually, you remind me of someone…"

Shoot. Not here, not now. Madeleine savored another sweet mouthful, hesitant to respond. *Don't tell me, Natasha's a fan* of Lost for Breath…

With their raven hair, bright smiles, and curvy figures, the Joy sisters were sometimes mistaken for twins, but while Madeleine had green eyes like their mother and favored contact lenses, Shantelle framed her brown eyes with glasses. Shantelle was taller and louder, loved sports and showing off, while Madeleine was well-read and more musically inclined, adored animals, and generally avoided parties. Often those differences were enough to throw people off the sibling trail and keep vampire-loving *Lost for Breath*-obsessives safely beyond Madeleine's orbit.

"You say that about everyone, Tash," said Julian, depositing the sole bag of salt and vinegar crisps in front of Madeleine. "You might prefer this flavor over the others…" He winked and picked up the blue and white pen.

He's such a lovely guy. "Thanks." Madeleine smiled demurely over the lip of her glass and took an ice cube into her mouth.

Micah squinted across the table. "No, I was gonna say the same thing. Madeleine, you *do* look familiar…"

Crunching the ice, she set down her glass. "Oh, I must have one of those faces." She reached up, tugging her musical note charm to the front of its chain. *Tash and Micah seem lovely, but I don't know them and I can't have a repeat of last week.* Her fingers flirted with the graceful curves of her Tiffany pendant.

"Then again"—Natasha pondered as she chomped another greenish crisp—"maybe I feel like I know you because you love music like I do. I mean—hello!—you work at Sensoria! That's hella cool, no matter what Jules says."

Micah sputtered on his pint.

What? Madeleine's raised brows met Julian's sheepish flinch. *My crush dissed me? But he's been so nice...*

"Our Jules is SUCH an old fart!" Natasha laughed. "Don't get him started on ebooks or the evils of Uber..."

So, it's not me. It's my job? Madeleine squeezed the silver quaver. *Well, if he's got something to say, he can say it to my face.* She let out a breezy half-laugh. "Julian, care to elaborate?"

SIX

MADELEINE

"Uh…" Clicking the pen, Julian's uneasy gaze slid across the banquette to Natasha and back again as Micah wiped beer from his lips with the back of his hand. "I didn't say it was uncool. I *said* I could never work for Sensoria—"

Natasha opened her mouth, but Micah jumped in. "Understatement of the century!" He yanked his chair closer.

"Oww!" Dropping her crisp packet, Natasha shot daggers at her brother and reached under the table, rubbing her shin.

"You okay?" Madeleine ducked down, searching past the purple curtain of Natasha's hair.

Julian glanced between the siblings.

"I'm fine…" Natasha pouted as Madeleine pulled back.

Micah carried on, ignoring his sister's scowl. "The sad fact is, Jules is the WORST at making playlists."

"I am." Julian's wince gave way to a self-effacing grin. "*The* worst."

That's what bugs him? The fact he can't do it? The tension in Madeleine's jaw eased. Guys were so weird. Why did they think they had to be great at everything? She shook her head slightly. "I'm sure you're not that bad."

"That's kind of you, but no. He's crap." Micah laughed. "I've heard his misguided attempts. Trust me, it's better for everyone if he sticks to what he enjoys most: listening to albums all the way through from start to finish."

"I like to get the full picture, find hidden gems," said Julian. "I like to absorb the overall message the artist is trying to convey. It's like a journey. If I make a playlist of just the hits, it creates a disconnect—at least for me."

"Old habits." Micah chuckled. "Once a music journo, always a music journo…"

Madeleine's glance shifted between Micah and Julian. "There's no right or wrong way to enjoy music…and what we get out of it, well, that's personal, too."

"But that's not to say I believe all songs or albums should have a message or theme. I don't. Music doesn't have to save the world to be good," said Julian. "Sometimes all I want is a catchy melody or a riff that sucks me in. No preaching, no lessons to be learned, just pure escapism and a dance around my kitchen!"

"If you could call it that…" Natasha snickered, fully recovered from her under-the-table injury.

"You having a go at my dancing?" He recoiled in mock horror.

"No! I'm talking about the tight squeeze you lovingly refer to as your kitchen. It's like an alleyway without the cool graffiti—"

"Or dumpsters," added Micah.

His sister sighed. "Totally useless for parties."

"Okay, okay—*kitchenette!*" Julian laughed. "But like I was saying, loving albums doesn't make me anti-playlist. The right songs, the perfect mix—I'm *so* there. Just don't ask me to make one. Best to leave it to the experts like you, Madeleine."

"Hear, hear!" Micah raised his glass. "I couldn't have said it better."

"It's hardly rocket science. I've just had a lot of practice, that's all." Madeleine picked at the edge of the salt and vinegar crisp packet. "I listen to *a lot* of music. Mostly albums, as it happens, but I skip the songs I don't like. I mean, why sit through all of Radiohead's *Pablo Honey* just to hear 'Creep'?"

"Oh good god, YES!" said Julian. "That album, definitely not their finest work."

"Pffft!" Micah sneered. "Give me The Prodigy over Radiohead any day."

"Ahhh, this feels like old times! Us getting lost down a musical rabbit hole." Natasha clasped Madeleine's forearm. "I've waited yonks for a female teammate who actually gives a toss about bands, and here you are!" She lobbed a smirk across the table. "Way to make up for Cherry-gate there, Jules! My lord, can you imagine how insufferable Caroline would've been tonight?"

Caroline from his call earlier? Madeleine waited for Julian's answer, but he didn't confirm or deny. He was otherwise engaged, running the tip of the pen back and forth, back and forth on the sheet of paper, creating a heavy red underline beneath Beauty School Dropouts. *Is that why he invited me? Caroline was busy?* She popped open the bag of crisps.

"I know 'Push It' when I hear it. I *lived* for Salt-N-Pepa when I was fifteen." Natasha leaned into Madeleine. "But that wasn't good enough for prissy pants Caroline and her '*I'm friends with the head of PR at BBC Radio 2*' bollocks. As if that makes her the master of musical knowledge!" As she shook her head, Natasha's Christmas puddings jostled violently above her cotton candy hair. "So like always, she ignored me and scribbled Neneh Cherry 'Buffalo Stance' on our sheet. And just like that"—she snapped her fingers—"POOF! Three hundred quid and a spot in the pub quiz finals GONE with a stroke of her pencil!" Her silvery braces glinted mid-snarl.

"Tash!" Micah stole a sideways glance at Julian. "Why don't ya yell a little louder? Manchester can't hear you."

Natasha stuck out her pierced tongue. "I'm just sayin'! As far as fiancées go, Jules really—"

"Natasha *Jade!*" Micah warned, eyes glaring.

Julian's engaged? Madeleine's stomach flipped as she crunched on a salty crisp, the sour zing of its vinegar puckering her face. *Well, can't say I'm surprised. He's wonderful. Not sure about this Caroline, though.*

"Let it go, Tash." Julian exhaled heavily, trading the pen for his water glass. "That quiz was a year ago."

"Well, feels like yesterday. I don't mind tellin' ya, I was *so* chuffed when you two broke up." Natasha snatched the bag of pigs in a blanket crisps. "Good riddance to bad rubbish. Now you can date someone nice. Like Madeleine here!"

She bit back the urge to grin while Julian took a long sip. *Awkward! He probably doesn't want to hurt my feelings.*

Julian lowered his glass tentatively and glanced up, meeting Madeleine's eyes. His lips pressed together with the faintest of smiles. "*Sorry,*" he mouthed.

Madeleine sat up, keen to change the subject. "So, I've been meaning to ask: what's the story behind your concert t-shirts?"

"They're our quiz team uniform," said Natasha.

"A lot of the questions are music-related," added Micah. "The shirts intimidate the competition, especially Tequila Mockingbird." He threw a dismissive sneer over his shoulder toward a table of plaid shirt-wearing twentysomethings. "Trendy chancers..."

Madeleine followed his side-eye. "Is that blond guy wearing...a monocle?!"

"Don't forget Panic at the Tesco." Natasha munched through a handful of crisps. "They're bloody good, too. Always score highly on anything food-related."

"So do the shirts work?" asked Madeleine.

"Well, I'll be honest with you and say no. No, they do not," Julian answered, straight-faced.

"Oh, ye of little faith! Of course they do!" said Natasha, brushing crumbs off her boob. "As a team, we ooze musical knowledge."

"Tash, love"—Julian cringed—"no offense, but I don't want to be oozing anything..."

Natasha scoffed. "What I'm saying is, music is our lifeblood. It's who we are!" She twisted toward Madeleine. "Meeks was in a few bands growing up. Our Sadie was a music journo. That's how Micah met Jules, through her. Their bromance has outlasted girlfriends, dodgy haircuts, and Micah's ridic fondness for Rickrolling."

"Eleven years strong!" said Micah, proudly raising his pint.

"Hands down, your longest, most stable relationship!" Julian tilted his glass toward his best friend as the pub's music faded.

Oh good. Madeleine grinned. *No more Christmas music.*

SSQQUEEEEEEEE! The quizmaster's microphone rebelled, its shrill feedback piercing eardrums throughout the pub. Madeleine's shoulders jumped to her ears. Julian and Micah flinched.

"Fuckin' hell!" Natasha cringed, her outburst accompanied by a pub-wide free-for-all of fruity expletives.

"Sorry, folks! Sorry!" The quizmaster turned away from the speaker and swept his dreads off his shoulder. "Good evening and welcome to our final competition of the year." Buying time, he straightened the hem of his *You Had Me at HO HO HO* Christmas sweater as the chorus of curses died down. "Just a friendly reminder, no phones, 'kay? If you're caught googling, your team will be disqualified and you'll be treating everyone here to a glass of our most expensive plonk."

"Wahey!" A sorority of fuzzy-antler-toting postal employees sputtered and high-fived one another, jostling their glass-strewn table. Their neighbors, a battery of steel-toe-boot-wearing construction workers grumbled and resumed shoveling their forks into large plates piled high with sausages, beans, and mash.

"Now for our stupendous prizes…" The quizmaster downed a mouthful of Guinness and stifled a burp before continuing. "Tonight's winners will receive a bottle of wine and a £50 bar voucher to be used at their leisure. We'll also be crowning the year's top team. They'll be taking home a sweet 500 quid to be shared between them. Who couldn't use that right now, amirite?"

"You know it!" Julian clapped as Micah whistled and whooped along with everyone else.

"We gotta win!" said Natasha. "I need the cash for Christmas shopping."

Micah toyed with his beaded bracelets. "I thought you'd finished?"

"For me, yeah. I found the coolest gold skull candle holder in Camden, but I still have to buy for everyone else."

Madeleine tucked her phone in her bag. *I hope I don't screw this up for them.*

The quizmaster waited until the noise died down. "As per December tradition, we'll open proceedings with general knowledge then move to Christmas-themed trivia. Some questions will be food-related, others pop culture-centric. We'll even play 'Name That Christmas Carol'…"

Shit. I didn't even think. Madeleine scrunched the napkin on her lap. *What have I signed up for?*

Barely pausing for breath, the quizmaster dove in. "Best of luck to all, and here we go. Question one: where was the first escalator located in London?"

"Ah, simples!" Micah leaned into their team huddle, whispering, "Earl's Court Tube station."

"On the Underground, yeah, but he said *in London*." Julian spoke behind his hand. "It was Harrod's in 1878."

"Nice one, mate." Micah smacked him on the back. "Go with yours."

Julian wrote down their answer as the quizmaster lifted his mic again.

"Question two: in October 1814, several beer vats burst in a London brewery, sending more than a *million* litres of beer rushing through the streets. The boozy tidal wave swept away houses and eight people died."

"What?!" Madeleine gaped, unsure whether to cringe or laugh.

"But what a way to go!" shouted one of the intoxicated mail carriers, her jingle-belled antlers tinkling with approval.

The quizmaster snickered. "Name the brewery where the London Beer Flood of 1814 occurred. And for a bonus point, name the street where that brewery was located."

"Somewhere in Spitalfields?" Natasha scratched the hair held hostage under her headband.

"It's the Horse Shoe Brewery," said Julian.

Micah winced over the rim of his pint. "So much for horseshoes bringing good luck!"

"I *think* it was the corner of Tottenham Court Road and Great Russell Street, near where the Dominion Theatre is now."

"How do you know this stuff?" Madeleine marveled.

"Jules reads A LOT!" Natasha laughed as he added the answers to their sheet. "When in doubt, we go with whatever he comes up with."

"So rather conveniently, it'll be me who catches it in the neck when we lose." Julian shifted out of the way so the server could set Natasha's stacked burger (sans pickles) and Madeleine's cod and triple-cooked chips on the table.

More food as well as questions followed about British football and rugby, Christine Keeler and the Profumo scandal, *EastEnders* and *Coronation Street* (which Micah aced). Audio snippets of Bauhaus and The Cure blasted through the pub's speakers and a giddy Natasha squeed with glee before assuredly whispering the answers through her indigo-colored lips. But it was the weekly round of 'Guess the Celeb from the Internet's Most Rubbish Fan Art' that collapsed the Beauty School Dropouts into breath-snatching laughter and brought tears to Madeleine's eyes.

"Oh my lord! Are you all right?" Clutching her stomach, Natasha gasped through her giggles.

Awkward. Madeleine reined in her laughter and swiped away the tears rolling down her reddening cheeks. "I'm okay, really!" She sniffed, the corners of her mouth bending into a sheepish grin. "I cry when I laugh hard. Hasn't happened for a long time…" Gently blotting her lashes with her napkin, she looked up from her half-eaten fish and chips, praying her waterproof mascara hadn't melted into smudgy panda eyes. "I know, I'm a freak."

"Nice try, Madeleine." A reassuring smile radiated across Julian's face as he fiddled with the curled edge of the fan art. "But the only freak here"—he held up the bizarre sketch of a discombobulated head and a goblet of wine—"is this bloke. Er, woman? Horse?!"

Micah choked back a chuckle. "How fucking tragic. Imagine seeing yourself like this? Buck teeth, googly eyes, flaring nostrils…and what's with the stringy hair? Mate, seriously, get some product."

Madeleine balled up her napkin, leaving it in her lap. "Is it Angelina Jolie…or Bono?"

"Oh, *please* let it be Bono," said Julian with a laugh.

"He's such a self-righteous twat," grumbled Micah. "He deserves this monstrosity."

"You are SO off base! It's Harry Styles, clearly." Natasha crossed her arms in triumph.

"Good point," said Madeleine. "There's a lot of scary Harry fan art out there."

The team agreed, and Julian added *Harry Styles* to their answer sheet as the quizmaster veered into Christmas-themed trivia, the questions now flying faster than Julian's taxi.

"The name of one of Santa's reindeer is also the name of another holiday's mascot. Name the reindeer."

"It's Cupid," whispered Madeleine.

"In the film *Elf*, Buddy wants to eat a whole roll of what?"

Natasha spoke behind her hand, eyeing Panic at the Tesco. "Tollhouse cookie dough."

"The much-loved Christmas classic 'Fairytale of New York' by the Pogues was written as a bet. Name the singer/songwriter who challenged Pogues lead singer Shane MacGowan to write a Christmas song."

"Easy! My man, Elvis Costello," said Julian.

As more questions were posed, the Beauty School Dropouts remained unfazed. Julian calmly wrote their answers in festive red ink, writing around Micah's unhelpful doodles of snowmen zombies and bug-eyed polar bears. For Madeleine, the holiday theme hadn't been as distressing as she'd anticipated, and thanks to the warmth of Julian and his friends, her first social outing in months felt like a huge win. She let out a relieved breath and picked up her drink.

"Final question!" said the quizmaster. "Name the U.S. state where Colin 'I'm Prince William without the weird family' Frissell meets four attractive anglophiles in *Love Actually*."

Oh... A lump grew in Madeleine's throat. "It's Wisconsin," she whispered and glanced away, retreating into the banquette with her rum and Coke.

"Nice!" A smile bloomed on Julian's face as he wrote down

their final answer. "Home sweet home for the win, eh?!"

Something like that. Madeleine nodded behind her glass and took a lengthy sip.

"We've won this, I swear!" boasted Natasha, nibbling on a curly fry as two members of staff brandished red pens and flicked through the answer sheets at the bar. Calculations complete, a woman scribbled something on a piece of paper and slapped it in the quizmaster's palm.

"Alrighty then!" He grinned above his microphone. "Before I announce the results, let me say that *no one* got the bad fan art question correct. I'm gobsmacked. Truly. I thought it was pretty damn obvious—c'mon guys, it's Mark Keegan."

Natasha's jaw dropped. "What?! Where's his kilt?"

"The actor from *Lairds and Liars*?!" Madeleine joined her teammates, all shaking their heads, flabbergasted. "The teeth, hair, eyes—all wrong!"

"Now, the news you've been waiting for," said the quizmaster. "We've got ourselves a draw, not once but twice!"

A loud groan caught fire, accelerating through the pub.

"Two teams earned the same number of points tonight. They're also now tied for our year-end crown. Congrats Tequila Mockingbird and Beauty School Dropouts!"

"Nooo!" Micah laughed playfully, pretending to bang his head on the table.

"Dammit!" Tequila Mockingbird's captain scowled. "We share the £500 with *them*? A washed-up journo, a daft goth, and some eco-raver..." A frustrated twitch popped the monocle from his eye as his friends, an influencer brandishing a handlebar moustache and a skinny noodle of a guy in rust-colored suspenders, gestured rudely at Madeleine's table and shared a sneery chuckle.

What a bunch of dickheads. She shot them a dirty look.

"It's a FIX!" The pissed posties and salty construction workers heckled the quizmaster. "Moustache twat used his phone—twice!"

"Trust-fund hipsters, all of them." Micah flopped back in his chair, resigned. "Haven't done a hard day's work in their lives."

Julian abandoned his half-eaten burger on his plate and raised his voice over the pub's collective grumbling. "Two-hundred and fifty quid split between us is better than nothin—"

"FIX!" hollered the mail carriers.

"All right, all right, keep your hair on!" The quizmaster chastised the room. "You honestly think I'd leave you hanging with a draw?" He pulled a folded piece of notepaper from his back pocket. "I've got the £500 tie-breaking question right here…"

"Bring it!" Natasha's holler was lost in a rising sea of whistles and claps.

"As this is a tie-breaker, remember—*only team captains may answer*," instructed the quizmaster. "First to call out the correct one wins the lot."

Madeleine glanced at the skinny hipster pensively caressing his bushy beard. She gave Julian a nervous grin. "Good luck."

"'Under Pressure'…" Micah sang under his breath as he doodled foxes on a beer mat.

Julian nudged his plate aside. "I apologize now in case I blow this."

"Here we go!" The pub fell silent as the quizmaster unfolded the tie-breaker. "In 1984, Band Aid's 'Do They Know It's Christmas' earned the coveted Christmas number one spot on the UK chart. Name the song and artist at number tw—"

"*Wham! 'Last Christmas'!*"

"*Frankie 'The Power of Love'!*"

Their answers collided in the air, their fallout sparking incendiary pop music discussions all around the pub.

"George Michael! Aww, I miss him!" one of the postal workers wailed into her pint.

Natasha sniffed. "That Frankie Goes to Hollywood tune is lush. Makes me blub every time."

Could be either one. Madeleine chewed her bottom lip.

Fanning himself with the shred of paper, the quizmaster sighed. "You know, I'm *really* disappointed, guys! Neither of you picked Paul McCartney and the Frog Chorus. What's up with that?"

"What's up? It's shite!" hollered Micah.

Julian laughed. "It is!" added Natasha with a straight face.

The quizmaster chortled, contemplating the answer in his hand. "Well, Macca's loss is someone's gain. In 1984, the #2 song on the UK Christmas chart was..." He paused as the crowd held its breath. "'Last Christmas', which means—"

"YESSSSS!" Natasha yanked Madeleine into a squeezy hug.

Julian won it?! Her eyes lit up.

"Beauty School Dropouts"—the quizmaster raised the dregs of his pint with reverence—"congrats! YOU are tonight's winning team AND our top team of the year!"

"For fuck's sake!" Like a petulant toddler, Tequila Mockingbird's captain chucked a beer mat across his table as the pub erupted into spirited whoops and applause.

The quizmaster spoke louder into his microphone, fighting the celebratory din. "The four of you are headed to the North London pub quiz challenge in February! Make us all proud, yeah!"

Micah slapped Julian on the back. "Well done, mate! I knew you'd do it."

"Bollocks, it was a team effort," he replied with a huge grin, meeting Madeleine's gape as she untangled herself from Natasha. "*We* did it."

"Congratulations, guys." Madeleine smiled. "So amazing!"

Julian reached across the table, covering her hand with his. "Did you have fun?"

The warmth of his caress blazed through her. "Yes! So much!" Her voice fizzed. "I've had the *best* time!"

"Good! We couldn't have won without you!" Julian gave her hand a squeeze and let go as the quizmaster dropped off their prizes: a bottle of wine, a £50 bar voucher, and an envelope stuffed with five hundred pounds in crisp twenty-pound notes.

"Congrats, Beauts! I couldn't be more thrilled. Our pub's rep is in great hands with you lot."

He high-fived Micah and swerved the sulky scowls of Tequila Mockingbird, returning to the bar where "Maybe This Christmas" by Tracey Thorn pulsed through the speakers and a well-earned pint overflowing with frothy Guinness awaited him.

Madeleine smirked at Julian, a twinkle in her eye. "Not hard-core trivia masters, huh?"

He scratched his arm, mid-shrug. "You weren't sure about coming. I didn't want to scare you off."

"Jules is our not-so-secret weapon," said Micah, pocketing the bar voucher as his sister took a selfie with a fistful of fanned-out pound notes. "He's like a walking, talking Google search engine. Remembers *everything*."

"Not everything." Julian pushed up his glasses.

"Modest much!" said Natasha, pausing mid-social media post.

This can't be the last time I see him. Madeleine leaned over her empty plate. "Julian, you might be busy already, but if you're not, could I book you tomorrow morning? It's probably my last day here, and I'd love to see Kensington Palace, Westminster Abbey, and Big Ben before I fly out. Maybe go for afternoon tea if I can swing it time-wise."

A joyful sparkle lit up his eyes. "Absolutely! Yeah, my pleasure. Can I get your number so we can coordinate?"

"Sure." Madeleine held out her hand. "Gimme your phone?"

Micah glanced over the lip of his pint, sharing a sly smirk with his sister.

"I'll make sure you see everything before you go." Julian leaned in as Madeleine typed in her contact details. "I know a brilliant place for tea near Kensington Palace, too."

"Perfect!" Madeleine looked up, smiling.

"Aw, lucky!" Natasha purred. "Jules, is that tea place the one I think it is?"

"Might be…"

SEVEN

"The future hasn't happened yet and the past is gone...
the only moment we have is right here and now."
Annie Lennox

MADELEINE

Four days until Christmas

Madeleine pressed her fingers to her lips, a slow grin flirting with her cheeks. *Is this what a religious experience feels like?*

Churches had never featured on her list of must-see places, but this one was different. Westminster Abbey was not only where Elizabeth Alexandra Mary Windsor became Queen Elizabeth II and Prince William married Catherine, but it was also the final resting place of monarchs, notable figures from science and history—and writers. If Madeleine had left for Paris without visiting Poets' Corner, her bookworm brain would've tortured her with unrelenting regret. Many of her literary heroes—Jane Austen, Charles Dickens, and the Brontë sisters—were either buried or honored in the south transept, and the opportunity to pay her respects and say thank you was one she grasped with both hands and her entire heart.

Toying with the headphones looped around her neck, she backed away from the life-sized marble statue of William Shakespeare and got stuck behind a doddering group of tourists, their ears glued to the Abbey's portable audio guides.

I should get going. Julian's been a saint, waiting patiently for me, and I still have my promise to keep.

Breaking free, searching for an exit, she rounded an unfamiliar corner and came to a dead end where several small steps led to a room labelled 'The Lady Chapel'. Her brows peaked. *What's this?*

She followed a cluster of tall, talkative Swedes who halted suddenly atop the stairs, searching for something in their London guidebook. Blocked by their human wall, Madeleine let out an impatient breath, her eyes flitting left to the chapel's open gates and their bronze carvings of roses, crowns, and thorn bushes, all beautifully ornate and indisputably royal. She fell under their Tudor spell. *Gorgeous. I so would've missed this if I'd rushed in.*

As the confused tourists moved aside, she entered the hallowed sanctuary where an unexpected calm embraced her. Morning sun poured through the stained glass windows, bathing the chapel's light stone, colorful heraldic banners, and oak choir stalls in a welcoming glow. Surprisingly, the shrine stood relatively quiet despite the multitude of visitors who, like Madeleine, had previously battled rogue elbows in the nave and transepts, straining for a glimpse of the Coronation Chair and the graves of naturalist Charles Darwin, actor Sir Laurence Olivier, and scientist Stephen Hawking.

She looked up toward the heavens where the intricately carved pendants and curved ribs of the chapel's vaulted ceiling unfurled like a symphony of aristocratic fans. *So beautiful and otherworldly...like lace woven by angels.*

Built between 1503 and 1516, the medieval addition to the Abbey was often called "the wonder of the world", and Madeleine wasn't about to argue. Mouth agape, she stepped farther into the chapel, careful not to bump her fellow visitors, each one joyfully reveling in the breathtaking sight above them.

Ensuring her flash was off, she snapped a barrage of images, capturing the ceiling followed by the vibrant stained glass windows, knowing full well her photos wouldn't do either justice. She wandered through the chapel and nipped around a corner, discovering the elaborate tombs of Henry VII, Mary, Queen of Scots, and Elizabeth I, who was buried on top of her half-sister, Mary. It would seem that even dead monarchs suffer from overbearing siblings.

Stealing another peek of the ethereal ceiling, a breath lodged in Madeleine's chest. *It's time.* Her phone, however, had other ideas, vibrating with a text accompanied by a cartoon image of a white hippo-like creature with a rounded snout and a long tail. It wore a red and white striped apron and carried a sturdy black handbag with a golden clasp.

Shantelle: Look! Here's the Moomin I'm voicing! Cute, huh?

She smiled at the Moomin, still clueless about what they were or where they came from, but if they made her sister happy…

Madeleine: Very cute! She loves fancy bags as much as you do.

She hit Send and paused, wondering if she should tell Shantelle that Cabbie Julian was Writer Julian. She wanted to. She wanted to tell someone. *It sucks having exciting news and not being able to tell the one person who would do cartwheels for me.*

Madeleine edged closer to the wooden stalls, keeping clear of tourist traffic. She had mentioned Julian and his writing to Shantelle before so…she typed a follow-up text.

Madeleine: Remember that UK music writer I had a fangirl thing for 10 years ago? It's Julian! My cabbie! Can you believe it? I'm seriously crushing hard.

The texting dots slid back and forth, back and forth, then blossomed into a burst of messages.

Shantelle: Soz, babe. Doesn't ring a bell.

Was worth a shot. Madeleine sighed dejectedly.

Shantelle: He's yummy tho. Snogged him yet? I hope you squeezed his crumpets.

She fought back a giggle as the dots danced again while Shantelle composed another message. *If this were Boston, if I had an*

THE CERTAINTY OF CHANCE

inkling he liked me back, I'd definitely ask him out, but here? Forget it. She glanced up, making sure she wasn't stood in anyone's way. *And honestly, I don't need another guy who doesn't understand grief. It's a total deal-breaker.* Her phone vibrated again.

Shantelle: So how was afternoon tea?

The seven-hour difference between Britain and Thailand created a few communication problems, usually involving Shantelle's comprehension of what her older sister might be up to. Madeleine ignored the prying crumpet query, keeping her response PG.

Madeleine: No afternoon tea yet. Still morning here. I'm in Westminster Abbey.

A flurry of message bubbles bounced up the screen.

Shantelle: Never been. Too crypt-y.

Shantelle: Like St. Martin's-in-the-Fields in Trafalgar Sq.

Shantelle: Did you know people sit beside moldy tombs in the basement and drink coffee? Ewwww!

Shantelle: You gone all religious on me now?

Like the rest of the Joy family, Madeleine considered herself spiritual but never gave much thought to God or prayers, and then Kellie died and a light went out. She couldn't believe in God, not now, not when he allowed horrible things to happen to good people—*her* people. But despite her lack of faith, she still felt awkward texting her sister under the stony gaze of the shrine's revered saint sculptures—all ninety-five of them. With a renewed sense of purpose, Madeleine left the tranquil Lady Chapel and rejoined the crowds milling past the Sacrarium as her phone impatiently pressed for answers again.

Shantelle: Having fun?

Sandwiched between a tour group of chatty seniors and several bored teens, she texted back.

Madeleine: The pub quiz was great. Was Xmas themed, which worried me, but I got through it relatively unscathed and WE WON! Julian gave me part of their prize—a bottle of wine. He's great, so kind and hospitable. I really like his friends, too. But every time I laugh or enjoy myself, I still get those guilty twinges like I'm forgetting Kel.

During a therapy session months earlier, her counselor Yoshiko had said, "Guilt is normal, feeling angry is normal—they're part of grief—and so are conflicting emotions. You'll feel sad and happy at the same time, guaranteed." But despite the expert advice, Madeleine struggled with her new normal, a new reality she'd never signed up for.

The yawning teens blocking her path budged slightly and she scooted through, bypassing the crowds on the altar's steps, yearning for a glimpse of the Cosmati pavement, a colorful mosaic of serpentine swirls and abstract patterns. Trod upon by history's kings and queens, its rare marble, onyx, and opaque glass dating back to 1268 was worth a proper look, but another message demanded her attention.

Shantelle: But laughing is good. The old Mads we know and luv will be back in no time.

Madeleine huffed. *'Cause the year of firsts is almost over, right? I should be 'done' with grieving?* She shook her head as she typed, her grief bubbling up. *I can't just pick up where I left off last December before Kel's death tore me apart. Grief doesn't work that way.*

Madeleine: The old Maddie is gone, Shan. Life will never be the same. I'll never be the same. Losing Kellie changed everything—it changed me.

Her phone screen blurred through a watery veil of tears. *Shan means well, but she's so insensitive sometimes.* Madeleine bowed her head. She was tired of platitudes and having her grief dismissed, and combined with her unexpected London layover, it all felt too raw, too much. What she needed was a session with her counselor. *If I can catch her before she heads to her family's cabin...* She dashed off a message.

Madeleine: Hi Yoshiko. Would you be able to fit me in sometime late this afternoon or even tomorrow?

She hit Send and kept walking, desperate for an escape from the crowds and Shantelle and the church's 'put your trust in God' ideology. As she followed a weary-eyed teacher and his never-ending gaggle of schoolchildren through the quire, her phone vibrated again.

Shantelle: I'm sorry. I get it. But I feel so HELPLESS. I wish I could do something to fix this.

Madeleine sniffed and glanced at her phone. *You can't, Shan. You can't bring Kellie back.* She hung back beside the wooden stalls and ravaged her purse for a tissue.

Shantelle: Maybe you should go out on a huge bender. Get totally sloshed. Forget everything for a while. Defo more fun than churches.

She wiped her eyes. *Forget Kellie? Never.* Her finger jabbed the phone's keyboard. *Shan says she gets it, but she doesn't...*

Madeleine: I'm not here for fun. I'm here to light a candle for Kel. Her mom texted, asked me this morning.

Her sister responded immediately.

Shantelle: I thought she was Jewish?

I don't have time for twenty questions. Thumbs flying, she sent her reply.

Madeleine: Her dad is. Her mom's not. Sorry Shan, phone's dying. Gotta go. x

She shuffled along the nave where, just shy of the poppy-trimmed grave of the Unknown Warrior, stood two large pillars on opposite sides of the space. Both were surrounded by a small pocket of people, their forlorn faces warmed by candlelight.

Madeleine slipped her phone into her coat pocket and joined the shortest queue. In front of her, a woman with a long silvery braid and a floor-dusting coat helped a young boy, his tiny hands clasping a votive candle. "Pierre, permettez-moi, s'il vous plaît," she whispered in her delicate French, guiding the candle's wick toward one of the flickering flames.

"Mais grand-mère...!" The little boy pouted, but within seconds of his protest, their votive burned bright and his face shone in wonder. His grandmother added their lit candle to the large display.

Her weary eyes met Madeleine's. No words were spoken, no grand gestures made, but they exchanged sad smiles, the two women...sisters in grief. A swell of gratitude warmed Madeleine's heart. If a stranger could acknowledge her grief, why couldn't the people closest to her?

"Bénissez-vous, ma chère." Nodding, the woman turned away and embraced her grandson. The pair then bowed their heads and recited something lyrical in French.

Madeleine fussed with the skirt of her black dress, its whimsical squirrel print peeking out from her open coat. She dropped several pound coins in the donation receptacle and selected a candle. Holding it steady, she lowered its wick to a lit votive, the orange flame catching. The heat warmed her fingers until she placed the candle in its metal home alongside the others.

She didn't really know any prayers. She didn't know hymns or any of the usual protocols required for such a solemn moment of remembrance. But she did know how much she loved and missed her best friend. Perhaps that was enough.

EIGHT

JULIAN

Sat on a low stone step across from South Kensington's famous 'thin house'—5 Thurloe Square, a Victorian dwelling notorious for being only six feet wide at its narrowest point—Julian crossed his legs at the ankle and updated Micah on Madeleine's adventures.

"Yeah, she had a mosey 'round Westminster Abbey, then went absolutely bonkers over Big Ben." *Which was so damn cute.* He switched his phone to his other ear. "She kept me there for a good fifteen minutes so she could hear him chime the hour."

"What about The Eye? Did she go up?" asked Micah, taking a well-deserved break from demanding Christmas shoppers.

"No, had to skip it. The line was too long. She wanted to visit Kensington Palace and pop into the V&A, so we couldn't risk missing our booking for afternoon tea at half twelve."

"Ooh, *our* booking?"

Julian stole a sip of coffee from his thermos and blinked furiously, hoping the tears would soothe the contact lens in his right eye, doing its best impression of a stabby lash. *Fucking things! Is it too much to ask? All I wanted was to look a little less nerdy today.* He closed his eyes, hoping that would help. "I can't let her go on her own, can I?"

"Uh, you could. People go solo all the time."

"But this is different." He blinked again, his gaze sweeping the red brick of the skinny house's most slender side.

"'Cause you fancy her."

"That's got nothing to do with it."

"Knew it!" Micah let out a smug huff. "You *do* fancy her!"

"What bloke in their right mind wouldn't? She's lovely and

smart, so gorgeous. Lives and breathes music. If that's not a turn-on..." Julian raised his voice, fighting the rattling rumble of an Underground train pulling into South Kensington Station. Hidden from view by the brick wall behind him and another across the street running perpendicular to the thin house, the aboveground Tube tracks sliced through the back gardens of Thurloe Square's terraced houses on its south side. "And before you ask, no, I didn't invite myself along to tea. After the Abbey, she asked me, said she'd like the company."

"Oh? Well, that's promising."

"Maybe. I've got no expectations. At least it proves she doesn't despise me, right? Speaking of which, thanks for the save last night. When Tash brought up Sensoria..."

"Hey, anything for you, mate," said Micah. "Tash doesn't engage brain before mouth sometimes."

"So, how is ol' Tash?" Julian dabbed the inner corner of his right eye, the stingy burn dissipating with each blink. "Did you apologize for kicking her under the table?"

Micah snorted. "My boot barely touched her! There's no bruise, no mark..." He paused, downing a gulp of his energy drink. "But, yeah, I felt bad. I apologized. Cost me twenty-two quid! Half a dozen fancy donuts don't come cheap."

Julian laughed. "Especially in Coal Drops Yard. Go Tash!"

"Anyway! What are you gonna do after your fancy tea?" asked Micah.

Julian set down his coffee on the stone step. "Nothing."

"Noth—you're NOT going to ask Madeleine out for dinner or drinks? You did last night—"

"I didn't. She was alone, and I was being kind. The pub quiz wasn't a date, Meeks."

"But you *wish* it were. Can't fool me. I know you better than you know yourself."

Why do I bother? Julian swept his hair off his forehead. "Fine, yeah. I would definitely ask her out, IF she weren't a customer, IF she were sticking around—but she is, and she's not, so all that kinda puts a spanner in the works, don't you think?"

Micah tsked. "Well, that's all rather convenient."

"What is?"

"You...blaming Paris. Only you would use geography to cock-block yourself! Love knows no borders, mate."

"Micah..."

"Where did old Jules go? The one who drove seven hours in a single day to bleedin' Edinburgh to surprise Caroline? Now, *he* was a romantic."

"*He* has been through a lot and wants an easy, uncomplicated life."

"Yeah, but not alone, right?" Micah blurted. "Besides, you're in luck. Madeleine dumped her boyfriend a few months back."

A breath bottled in Julian's chest. "How'd you find that out?"

"How else? My sister, the nosey goth. I swear she should work for MI5."

"Tash asked her?"

"No, but when we got home, she kept rabbiting on about Madeleine reminding her of someone. She scrolled for a bit on social media and hit the jackpot. Jules, Madeleine's sister is Shantelle Joy."

Julian fussed with a button on his coat. "And I should be impressed *why*?"

"Are you messin'? You seriously don't know who she is? She has over six million followers on Twitter, eight mil on Insta!"

"Okay. So she's like an influencer?"

"No! She's an actress and a bloody popular one, too, especially with the under-30s," said Micah.

"Ah, well, there you go. I'm too old to know who Shantelle Joy is."

Micah scoffed. "Don't be daft. Shantelle stars in that vampire film Tash goes on about. Not *Twilight*, the other one. Had that annoying French twat in it."

"Vampires, eh?" Julian half-laughed. "I rest my case!"

"Jules! You must've seen the adverts on the double-deckers. Or the trailer? It played on the big screens in Piccadilly Circus. Remember? The gorgeous brunette snogging the half-naked guy? Lots of rose petals, black lace…?"

"Sorry, mate. Can't say it rings a bell. I'm glad Tash is thrilled, though." A skulk of students on a break from an outing to the Natural History Museum planted themselves and their takeout lunches on the stone step to Julian's left. Their loud banter about football prised him free from his perch. "Sorry, just a sec…" He scooped up his thermos and sauntered down the street to where his cab was charging. "So what's Shantelle got to do with Madeleine's ex?"

"Tash found an old post of Shantelle's. She mentioned Maddie, her badass sister, kicking her loser ex to the curb, so there you have it, Jules!" Micah's voice brimmed with satisfaction. "The coast is clear. Madeleine's single! Spike that volleyball!"

"She's flying to Paris."

"Not if the airports remain closed—"

"Micah, would you give it a rest? Nothing's changed from yesterday, all right?" Julian paused beside a red and white triangular yield sign shouting GIVE WAY in black letters. He bent his neck, holding his phone against his ear with his shoulder as he tightened the cap on his coffee. "Plus, she's a paying customer."

"Yeah, one you're taking for afternoon tea."

"For fuck's sake, I'm not *taking* her." He tucked his thermos under his arm and retrieved his phone, lowering his voice. "She's paying. Now would you stop pushing this date stuff? God. Whatever happened to your *If it's meant for you, it won't pass you* shit?"

"But that's the *thing*, mate! What if she IS meant for you—"

"Micah!" Julian walked a few steps farther and unlocked his cab.

"Fine, I'll stop. Just don't come crying to me when the girl of your dreams disappears across the English Channel and meets some Gallic hunk…" Micah cleared his throat. "So, how much have you pocketed, then? Driving her about?"

"Six hundred pounds. I'm really chuffed." Julian unplugged the charging cable and stored it in his trunk. "Add that to my share of last night's winnings and what I'll earn the rest of this week with the tour agency and I'll be well on my way to paying off Winnie's surgery." He eased into the driver's seat. "The timing couldn't be better. I can't have Caroline painting me as an unfit pet parent in court."

"It's such a joke," said Micah. "Caroline is the unfit one, leaving him alone all day. I bet Wins misses you big time, coming home for breaks and his midday walks—" A ping from a text punctuated Micah's sentence.

"I should check that. I'm waiting for Madeleine to…" Julian lowered his phone.

Natasha: You ordered Micah's cake, right?

Yes, Tash. He smiled and returned to the call. "Nope, false alarm."

"Where are you taking her tomorrow?"

Julian sighed heavily. "I'm not. I'm driving a couple around tomorrow and Thursday morning. The agency arranged it."

"But you'll be done by tomorrow evening, right?"

"I'll be there, don't worry." Julian's soft gaze flitted up the road where Madeleine strolled along the sidewalk, pondering the mid-19th-century terraced houses with their white stucco façades and Doric columned porches overlooking Thurloe Square's gated garden. *There she is!* Wearing her headphones, her coat was unbuttoned, exposing a hint of a black dress. Fondness swelled in Julian's chest. *Micah's right, though. There's something about her that's special.* Madeleine's curiosity, her determination to make the most of being stranded in London, even that sweet but slightly sad smile she wore when she thought no one was watching…he couldn't get enough. "Meeks, I have to go. Madeleine is on her way."

"Say hi for me. Text later if you wanna meet for a quick pint. I'm meant to be helping Tash dye her hair, so any excuse to get out of that…"

"Will do. Cheers, mate." He ended the call and quickly texted Natasha back.

Julian: Yes. Cake is a GO! Picking up tomorrow.

He slipped his phone into his coat pocket and extricated himself from the car. "Madeleine, hey!" He waved.

Spotting him, she slipped off her headphones. "Found you!" She walked quickly, the gray-striped V&A tote on her shoulder bumping against her hip.

Julian shut the cab's door and strolled toward her. "You should've texted. I would've picked you up."

"Oh, no need." Madeleine tugged on the straps of the fabric bag, which was bulging with souvenirs. "It's such a beautiful day, perfect for walking." Her eyes swept the tall trees and overgrown shrubs peeking above the stone walls of the communal garden across the road. A gray squirrel scurried across the padlocked gate, which kept whatever else flourished inside secret, reserved for Thurloe Square residents only. "Ah, he's so cute and chubby." She tilted her head. "Makes me homesick."

"You see a lot of squirrels back in Boston?"

"Oh, yeah, but on weekends I volunteer for a wildlife rehab center. I help with the injured squirrels. I love them."

She must if the cute print on her dress is anything to go by. "Aw, that's wonderful. How long have you been doing that?"

"Almost a year now." She watched the furry friend climb up a tree. "I wish I had some almonds on me. I usually carry a small bag in my purse."

"For you or the squirrels?"

"For them!" Glancing away, a warm smile lifted her lips. "No wonder they're happy here. This neighborhood is gorgeous! I love the architecture and all the white stucco and gray brick..." Her quizzical gaze skipped back to 5 Thurloe Square. "But"—she began to sing—"one of these things is not like the others..."

Julian chuckled. "*Sesame Street*? Brought to you by the letters M and J."

"You know it? I didn't think it aired over here."

"It did for a while growing up. Team Big Bird or Oscar the Grouch?"

"Cookie Monster!" Madeleine beamed. "Always!"

"Excellent choice. I knew I liked you for a reason." He grinned back. "You're right about that building, too. It's definitely not like the others."

Madeleine cocked her head. "What's the deal?"

"Come with me."

He escorted Madeleine down the street to where he'd sat fifteen minutes earlier. The hungry students were long gone, replaced by a dust-speckled construction worker from the roadworks around the corner, scrolling through his phone.

"Oh, wait a minute..." She stopped and blinked at the sliver of brick, her mouth agape. "Is that for *real*? People actually live there?"

"Yep. A flat came up for sale recently. I had a look online."

"Was it obscenely small?"

Define small—it's larger than my flat. He nodded. "Only 670 square feet split over two floors. But it came with a not-so-wee South Ken price tag—an eye-watering one million US."

"Location really is everything, huh? So when do you move in?"

He met Madeleine's joke with a laugh. "Ah! Well, I'm still mulling over marble choices, arguing with the painters. You know how it is..."

She twisted her lips. "Is it five, six feet wide at most?"

"This end is six feet, but the far side where it touches 6 Thurloe Square is thirty-four feet wide."

"So it's a triangle—sorta."

Julian nodded. "Fun, eh? Such a great optical illusion."

"Goes to show you, things aren't always what they seem. Definitely fooled me." She raised her phone and took several photos. "So, I'm guessing it was built after the others?"

"Yeah, in the 1880s. The rest of the square was constructed forty years earlier. Originally, five houses identical to all the others stood here, but they were demolished when the Underground added the aboveground tracks connecting South Kensington and Sloane Square. A few years later, some enterprising bloke took the leftover land and built this skinny triangle. It housed artists' studios at first, but over the years they've been turned into flats."

"That back onto exposed subway tracks?" she asked.

"I know, right? Imagine the noise…"

Eyeballing the Victorian curiosity, Madeleine scrunched her nose. "For one million, I hope it comes with diamond-encrusted noise-canceling headphones and a subscription to Sensoria."

"At least!"

"When you move in, what's on your house-warming playlist?" she asked playfully.

"Old favorites, mostly. Elvis Costello, Blur, Janet Jackson—"

"Kylie Minogue, Australia's greatest pop export…" She smiled.

Julian scrubbed a hand over his chin. "Yep, Kylie too. What can I say? She's pure, pop-tastic joy and one of the nicest people around."

Madeleine clutched his arm. "You've met her? In your cab?"

Oh, I'm liking this. His gaze danced over her hand. "No, back-stage at an award show. She's tiny, really sweet and smiley. I was smitten, must admit…" *Kinda like I am now.*

"I would've been too." She withdrew her clench. "I adore Kylie! I saw her in concert once. Everyone was dancing and singing at the top of their lungs. It felt like a massive party no one wanted to leave. It's a shame she never really broke in America."

"How'd you discover her? Through work?"

Madeleine picked at her phone's case. "No. My best friend, she's Australian."

"Ah, personal recs—they're always the best. Do you listen to any other Aussie groups?" he asked.

"Yeah, quite a few. I went through a huge Australian phase: INXS, Tame Impala, The Church, Hunters and Collectors…"

Julian lit up. "Hunters and Collectors, eh? Now there's a name I haven't heard mentioned in a long time. 'Throw Your Arms Around Me' is such an epic tune—part booty call, part tender lament."

Madeleine nodded. "It's beautiful. Gets to me every time I play it."

"The yearning, the vulnerability..."

"Yeah and its message that everything is so...fleeting." She sighed.

"Seize every moment or..."

"Yeah." Madeleine slipped into a pout.

His eyes fell to her lips. *Is she thinking what I'm thinking?* A breath held in his chest. *Madeleine, I really like you...*

Her gaze lingered, settling on his mouth, the tease of her green eyes raising the tiny hairs on the back of Julian's neck.

If you kiss me first, I'll definitely kiss you back.

But Madeleine swallowed thickly and sucked in her bottom lip, dashing Julian's hopes. "Well, I, uh, guess we should..." Her hand flew upward, fidgeting with her hair.

Damn. I've made her feel uncomfortable. Julian disguised his inner cringe with a faint smile as he fumbled in his coat pocket for his keys. "Of course. Sorry. Get me talking about bands and I lose all track of time."

They crossed the road in awkward silence. Julian wished for a do-over while Madeleine's eyes remained glued to a trio of prancing Pomeranians yanking their portly owner along the sidewalk.

Break the stalemate. Say something but remain professional! She's a customer...but dammit, I wish she weren't. Staring blankly ahead, Julian chose a reliable conversation restarter. "We've definitely lucked out with the weather. So much sun..."

"I know, right?" Madeleine answered quickly. "So lucky." She waved casually toward his taxi. "And still no ash. Shouldn't it be falling by now?"

"You'd think, but last time we didn't see much on the ground either."

"That's weird." She squinted at the sun loitering behind a patchy cloud. "It's clogging airspace, canceling flights, but it's bright and cold and normal down here."

"Any word from your airline?" Julian asked.

"No, but I rang them again when I left the V&A and finally spoke to someone. Tonight's a no-go flight-wise, but she sounded hopeful for tomorrow morning."

She probably can't get out of here fast enough. He opened the passenger door of his cab, inviting her in. "Well, that's good news."

"Now I just need my sister to confirm she's flying tomorrow and we're all set." Madeleine leaned in, flinging her stuffed V&A tote onto the seat.

The famous sister. Madeleine hadn't mentioned Shantelle by name, so Julian didn't press. It had to be both thrilling and strange having a celebrity for a sister. "How'd you enjoy the Victoria and Albert Museum?"

"I feel like I barely dipped my toe in. It's huge!" A pleased warmth resonated in her voice. "But I found what I came for."

"And did Queen Victoria's coronet live up to your expectations?"

"Surpassed them! I didn't expect so much sparkle from something so dainty. All those sapphires and diamonds. I kept comparing it with the tiaras I saw this morning at Kensington Palace—ah, listen to me!" She climbed into the cab. "Just give me all jewels, all the time, and I'm a happy girl."

All Jules, all the time... A slow smile teased his cheeks. "Well, you got stranded in the right place, then."

"I guess I did."

He gently closed the passenger door and ran around to the driver's side, hopping in.

Madeleine's face contorted. "Ooh. Did you hear that?" She clutched her abdomen. "I think an alien's about to burst out."

Julian glanced in the rear view mirror. "Need feeding?"

"Oh god yes." Her grin rose in relief. "I'm so hungry I could eat Big Ben."

Julian turned the key in the cab's ignition. "Next stop, finger sandwich heaven!"

NINE

MADELEINE

Cozy amidst the crackling fire and booklined shelves of the stylish Kensington Hotel's Town House restaurant, local 'ladies who lunch' and well-behaved tourists wiled away the afternoon by indulging in fizzy champagne, exotic teas, and an eye-popping array of treats, both savory and sweet. The relaxed dress code, comfy chairs, and warm welcome along with their afternoon tea made the hotel's two Victorian drawing rooms popular destinations for famished guests seeking a decadent sojourn with a sprinkle of whimsy.

Finishing the first course of bite-size savories, Madeleine dug her spoon into her miniature steak and London ale pie. Despite the hectic morning rushing between tourist sights, the sense that a weight had been lifted lightened her mood. She could at least leave London knowing she'd fulfilled her promise to Kellie's mother.

However, a new conundrum tumbled in her mind: what to make of Julian's weighty gaze in Thurloe Square. Madeleine had felt every steamy second of it rippling through her. But was she reading more into it? Until that moment, her crush had seemed entirely one-sided, a flirty diversion from grief and loneliness. Sure, Julian had been charming and amiable, but wasn't that part of his job description? A way to earn tips? One intense look didn't mean he was hot for her.

She watched him intently across the table, eager for clues of something more than a business arrangement between them as he indulged in easy conversation and devoured his appetizer-sized Stilton and broccoli quiche. But she found nothing, all traces of romantic interest long gone…if they'd even existed in the first place. *This is what happens when you try to work on your novel before bed.*

Stop being ridiculous, stop making stuff up. He's not interested in you that way.

Scooping the last morsel of her meat pie from its miniature copper pot, she pushed aside her embarrassment and exclaimed, "Okay, *this* is delicious. I'm not usually a pie fan, but this one is tender and really flavorful. Love the puff pastry. Might be my favorite." The final spoonful of steak and gravy halted her enthusiastic ramble.

"You sure now?" Julian set down his cup of Earl Grey, a tease of a smile brimming. "Because ten minutes ago, you were all about the mini crab cake."

See? He thinks I'm a babbling fool who can't make her mind up. Mid-chew, Madeleine's eyes pored over her blue and white china plate, empty except for the copper pot and a dusting of flaky crumbs left behind from her mini quiche. "That was spectacular, too. I feel like a parent choosing their favorite child. I loved all three."

"But wait! There's *more...*!" With a wave of his hand, Julian gestured like an infomercial salesman.

Her gaze drifted, meeting two smiling servers on the approach, one carrying a three-tiered circular contraption shaped like the London Eye. "Oh. My. God." She squealed under her breath as their plates were cleared and the Ferris wheel-inspired metal stand boasting exquisite finger sandwiches and delightful sweets landed on their linen-draped table. "I didn't expect anything like this!"

Julian's eyes sparkled with playfulness. "I bet you thought you were coming for tea, not an edible tour through London."

Madeleine leaned over her plate, eager for a closer look. On the second of the stand's three tiers, eight mini desserts shaped like famous London icons—The Shard, a red telephone box, The Gherkin, and Big Ben—captured her glee and teased her taste buds. "This is too cute to eat!"

The server nodded with appreciation. "If you'd like, I can take a picture of you with it."

"Please!"

Madeleine handed the obliging server her phone, and he snapped several photos before delivering a quick introduction to the delicious fancies on display. Her head was buzzing with possibilities as he stepped away.

"My friends won't believe this! I'll have to post some pictures to Facebook and Instagram"—her eyes darted across the table—"if that's okay? I won't post any shots of you without your approval, but if you want, I could tag you?"

"Uh, sorry. You can't." Julian snapped his linen napkin, unfurling it over the lap of his black trousers. "I'm not on social media."

"At all?" she asked.

"Nope. It's not my thing."

Shoot. No snooping for me, then.

"But post away, share your pics," said Julian. "I don't mind."

"Okay. Thanks." She lowered her phone and ogled the top tier of the metal Ferris wheel. "What to try first?" A laugh escaped her lips. "It's sandwich heaven, a dream come true." Her eyes leapt from the egg and cress bridge roll to the smoked salmon on brown, layered with lovage pesto and soft cream cheese. "It's a given I'll love the cucumber sandwich, so I'll try something new first." Her stomach grumbled, dissatisfied with her dawdling. "How did you hear about this place?"

"A customer, actually. I picked him up here and he raved all the way to Pimlico. It sounded like something Tash would enjoy, so I told her sister Sadie and they celebrated her last birthday here." Julian smiled, letting the room's soft classical music fill his pause. "Go ahead, ladies first."

"Hmm, I guess"—her hand hovered over the row of sandwiches—"this one…" Madeleine claimed a dainty coronation chicken, its filling a British favorite created for the 1953 coronation of Queen Elizabeth II. The brown bread was soft and crustless, exactly how she had imagined tea sandwiches would be. *So elegant and fancy. Kellie would've adored this.* A ribbon of melancholy wound around her giddy heart.

"So"—Julian removed the linen bundle from the bottom tier

and unwrapped its soft folds, exposing an assortment of warm scones, both fruit and plain—"what are you most excited to see in Paris?"

Madeleine welcomed the diversion. "Everything! All the greatest hits: the Eiffel Tower, the Louvre, Musée d'Orsay, Luxembourg Gardens, Notre Dame Cathedral, the Champs-Élysées…" She bit into the sandwich and chewed ever so slowly, the tender chicken, fiery zing of curry powder, and sweet respite of sultanas and chutney rousing the corners of her mouth into a blissful grin. "Mmmm, *this* is divine."

"Not your average sarnie, eh?"

"I know I keep repeating myself, but this is SO good!" She watched Julian smooth a dollop of clotted cream on his scone. "Have you been to Paris?"

"A few times for the magazine." He added a splodge of strawberry jam and took a large bite.

"Oh, that's right! I remember! You wrote about Prince playing there. Didn't he do like, four encores or something that night?"

Julian nodded, mid-chew.

"Your review was so lyrical and poignant, it really stuck with me." She relegated the last chunk of her coronation chicken sandwich to her plate.

"Aw, thanks. Yeah, I'd seen him a few times before, but this gig blew all the others out of the water." Julian smiled. "I never saw Michael Jackson live, but Prince's take on 'Don't Stop 'Til You Get Enough' that night was probably the next best thing."

"I never had the chance to see either of them. I still can't believe they're both gone." She lifted her cup of English Breakfast tea.

"Gone way too soon." He licked jam off his thumb. "So young. So unfair."

"So true." Madeleine cleared her throat. "How are the scones?"

"Warm and fluffy, really lovely. The clotted cream and strawberry jam make a nice change. I'm more a marmalade bloke."

She lowered her cup after a soothing, body-warming sip and pinched one of the two milk chocolate replicas of The Shard. "I've never tried it."

"You should try mine."

Her lashes flitted up, leaving the small, triangular dessert. "Yours?"

"I make orange marmalade," said Julian.

She leaned in. "Get out!"

"I do! Mum taught me ages ago."

Oh, Julian. Madeleine audibly sighed. *Please stop being adorable. My crush can't take it.*

"If I'd known you'd never had it, I would've brought some. I make a big batch every year, put it in mason jars, and give 'em away as Christmas gifts. Beats fighting the crowds in Selfridges for presents."

"Plus, it prevents scurvy."

"Exactly!" Julian laughed. "Bonus!"

She cracked open one side of The Shard's chocolate shell. "Seriously, though, that's such a thoughtful gift."

"Provided I don't poison anyone. Hasn't happened yet. Micah's even selling a few jars in his shop." He set down his half-eaten scone and plucked one of the white chocolate Gherkin skyscrapers from the middle tier. "What's inside the Shard?"

"Well, it looks like tourists have been replaced by carrot cake and creamy white icing. See?" Madeleine spun her plate around, showing the tiny baked good. "So what's with all the weird names for London's skyscrapers? The Shard, the Gherkin, the Cheesegrater?"

"The Walkie-Talkie, the Scalpel, the Trellis?" Julian toppled the Gherkin and plunged his fork straight through, exposing a gooey, dark chocolate filling. "Why go by a boring street address when you can show off with a naff nickname?"

"So, it's a marketing thing?"

"Pretty much. In some ways, though, I reckon the architects are taking the piss. A cutesy name doesn't make up for an ugly building, and the problem with London is, they keep popping up."

"You don't like change, then?" asked Madeleine.

"I'm not a big fan, no." He looked up from his plate. "You?"

"I don't mind it, usually. Change keeps things interesting—except when it's a shock and you're not ready for it." She poked the broken Shard. "Like when your magazine folded."

Julian nodded, lifting a forkful of chocolate. "Like you getting stranded in London."

"Yeah…" Madeleine bit her lip. *Like my best friend dying.*

Tasting his dessert, Julian's brows peaked with pleasure. "Mmm…"

Madeleine blinked and painted on a smile. "Is that ganache inside?"

He nodded, savoring the flavor. "It's slightly bitter but nice. Balances the sweetness of the white chocolate outer layer. Have you seen the real thing?"

"The Gherkin? No, just in photos." Her fork lingered above her mini carrot cake. "I spotted the Shard from the Tower of London but haven't seen the rest. Which one is your favorite?"

"Probably the Gherkin. My least favorite is twenty Fenchurch Street—the Walkie-Talkie. You can't miss it. Just look for the ugly, top-heavy skyscraper leaning over the financial district. When it was being built, it got called the *Fry*scraper because it burnt up several parked cars."

"Holy shit! How?" she asked.

"All that curved glass reflects the sun's rays down into the street. Some bloke parked his Jag and returned an hour later to find the side panels and wing mirror all melted. Shops were hit, too. Carpets caught fire, the paint on their façades blistered, it was a right ol' mess. Of course, Londoners being Londoners, they rigged up their own street-level science experiments, frying eggs and toasting bagels on the tarmac."

"Taking street eats to a whole new level!" Madeleine giggled and cut through half of the small cake. "They fixed it, right?"

"Eventually. They installed these aluminum fin things to the façade to prevent further damage. Only in London! I bet something like this would never happen in Paris. Which arrondissement are you and your sister staying in?"

"The third, Le Marais?" Madeleine licked the icing on her fork. "My sister has a thing for the old-world charm and cobblestone streets around there. She booked us into a boutique hotel, which used to be Paris' oldest boulangerie. Apparently, it's where Victor Hugo bought his freshly baked baguettes."

"I bet it's gorgeous." Julian ate the last piece of the Gherkin's white chocolate shell.

She nodded. "They even kept the old boulangerie sign—" The buzz of a text stopped her short. "Sorry." She abandoned her fork and dessert, eyes darting to the lit screen just shy of her teacup and saucer.

Julian chose one of the smoked salmon sandwiches sans crust.

Jet Britannia: Travel update: Flight JB092 from LHR—CDG is delayed another 48 hours due to the continued threat of volcanic ash in European airspace.

What?! No! A rush of adrenaline spiked through her veins. *But the girl said...* Madeleine continued reading, the words stoking her worst-case scenario.

Jet Britannia: All British airports remain closed. Our next update will be Thursday, December 23. In the event the airports reopen that day, please be prepared to travel.

No, no, no. Her face fell as her free hand settled in her lap. *Not Thursday.*

Mid-chew, Julian pinched one of the two red telephone boxes made from rhubarb mousse. "Something wrong?"

"It's the airline. No flights will be leaving London for at least another 48 hours, maybe more."

Julian's eyes narrowed as he parked the phone box on his plate. "I'm so sorry—" Another buzz cut him off.

Shantelle: Did you hear? Still no flights into Paris.

"It's my sister. Looks like both of us are going nowhere fast." Madeleine glanced down again as Shantelle's follow-up texts landed.

Shantelle: At least J's keeping you company. I feel better knowing you're not alone.

Shantelle: Sending a surprise to your hotel. Something to cheer you up! Love and hugs. x

Madeleine typed Ok. Love and hugs, then hit Send, discarding her phone near her teacup. "Christmas in Paris is looking more and more unlikely."

"Are you sure you don't want to take the Eurostar?" asked Julian. "You could go and settle in before your sister arrives."

"But if the airports remain closed and she can't fly, I'll be alone. At least here in London—" Madeleine stopped short. *I have you. Sorta. Maybe?*

Julian offered a smile. "You've got someone to get you out and about. I'm more than happy to drive you around this afternoon, if you'd like to see more of the sights..."

Eyeing the green cabbie badge dangling from the lanyard looped around his neck, she slowly pressed back in her chair. *Right.* Disappointment kicked in her belly. *Well, that seals it. He's here because I'm paying him. I'm a customer, a guaranteed fare, nothing more. We are not friends, let alone anything else.*

"I'd suggest tomorrow as well, but I'm already booked with customers and won't be free again until Thursday afternoon..."

Adjusting the linen napkin on the lap of her dress, she raised a weak smile. "It's great you're so busy, especially before Christmas."

"It is, but I, uh"—he ran his hand over his mouth—"sorry about this. I'm on a tour company's roster and occasionally they send customers my way—"

"Julian, you don't have to explain or apologize. You've been more than generous with your time. Thanks to you, I've fit in so much already." She disguised her hurt by looking away and liberating a Big Ben made from lemon curd tart from the London Eye cake stand. "I can't wait to try the Tube and climb on a double-decker bus, get the whole London experience. It'll be great, I'll be fine."

"I don't doubt it, but call me selfish…I'm gonna miss driving you around." He toyed with his fork. "I've had more fun the past two days than I've had in a really long time…"

Nice of him to say.

A hard swallow bobbed his throat. "Would you be interested in hanging out tonight?"

She glanced up from her plate. *And what? I pay for the privilege?*

"But as friends? I can turn off the meter and we'll do whatever you like, wherever you want. That is, if you don't have other plans and your boyfriend won't mind…"

A flush of happiness roused her smile. "Nope! No boyfriend, no plans…"

"No worries." He grinned. "Great!"

Madeleine bit her bottom lip. "Julian, I—that's really sweet of you."

"Not as sweet as these." He nodded toward the remaining edible landmarks on the cake stand. "But seriously, name the place and we'll go: Camden, Soho, Winter Wonderland—"

"What's that?"

"Winter Wonderland? It's this massive holiday-themed fun fair held annually in Hyde Park. They have amusement park rides, carnival games, North Pole-themed bars, every sort of food you can imagine. It draws people from all over." He carved his fork through the rhubarb mousse of his red phone box.

Translation: super crowded, overpriced, and as cheesy as a Chicago-style deep dish pizza. "So it's more *Nightmare Before Christmas* than *It's a Wonderful Life?*"

He smirked. "You said it, not me!"

"If you don't mind, I think I'll pass."

"Thank Christ for that! I hate the place." Julian laughed. "So what do you fancy?" He tasted a forkful of mousse and nodded his approval.

You. She bit her tongue, halting what she really wanted to say. "I'd love to go for a nice meal and a chat, but I need to find some gifts for my sister first. My plan was to shop for her in Paris, but if I wait, I'll be cutting it too close."

"You'll have no problem finding something here. London has everything Paris does, pretty much. The sky's the limit. I'll take you wherever you want. I love a good shop, me."

Madeleine narrowed her eyes. "No, you don't. Every guy I know hates it."

"I'm not every guy…" He shrugged and broke into a playful grin as his fork returned for more mousse.

No. You're really not. She pressed her lips together, fighting the urge to smile. "Well, as long as you don't mind…"

"Never. I find it relaxing, strolling through the shops. It's good for me to see what's out there, too. Helps with the day job. Passengers are always asking for recs." He raised the fork to his mouth once more.

"And what do you usually suggest?"

Julian swallowed. "I'm so glad you asked, lovely Madeleine!" He relinquished his fork and pretended to roll up the sleeves of his shirt. "Tourists typically stay in central London. If they want department stores and high street shops, we go to Oxford Street and Regent Street. For something more upmarket, we head to Bond Street, the King's Road, and Harrods and Harvey Nichols in Knightsbridge."

Madeleine wrinkled her nose. "I can't afford posh."

"Me neither. That's where Camden and Soho, even Spitalfields come in for affordable or quirky. Seven Dials and Covent Garden are worth checking out, too. Lots of unique stuff there. And then there's always Piccadilly if you're thinking gourmet foodie gifts from Fortnum & Mason. They have something for all price points, it's always a winner. So, where we go depends on what you're after, really."

"I usually get Shan something practical because she's anything but." Madeleine explained. "She travels a lot for work and never has time to clean her place. Last Christmas I went with one of those round robot vacuums you can program."

"Gets the job done."

"Yeah, a little too well. It gobbled up one of her $500 bras."

Julian's eyes bulged. "*Five hu*—bet she was pissed!"

"Still is! So this year her gift has to be something innocuous, unique, and easy to pack. Bonus points if it isn't mass-produced or trendy, and doesn't break the bank. I know that's asking a lot...even for Santa." She giggled.

"Well, there *is* a place even Santa relies on when he gets stuck, but it might not be ideal if..." He scratched his temple. "Put it this way, it's like Christmas and the North Pole exploded all over the South Bank. Are you up for that kind of festive overload?"

Sounds like Christmas carol hell, but I'm running out of time and options. Madeleine inhaled deeply, her heart still bruised with grief but determined to find something special for her only sister. *I could play it safe, order a gift online, and send it to our Paris hotel—hoping we both make it there in time.* She poked her lemony Big Ben with her fork. *Or I hold my nose, dive into London's Christmas deep end, and maybe climb out with something spectacular...*

Madeleine glanced up.

...with Julian.

TEN

JULIAN

The setting sun disappearing behind Big Ben and the Houses of Parliament bathed the London skyline in sherbet pinks and fizzy oranges as laughter and the sweet scent of Belgian waffles sailed past on the brisk riverside breeze. With only four shopping days before Christmas, the Southbank Centre's Winter Market teemed with people, snapping up festive nutcrackers, handknit scarves, and gourmet delicacies such as plump gingerbread, artisan cheeses, and melt-in-your-mouth macarons available in a jaw-dropping rainbow of colors.

Strolling along the Queen's Walk, the wide promenade hugging the Thames, Julian and Madeleine sipped hot chocolate and zigzagged around phone-obsessed teens and distracted eaters munching crispy churros drizzled with Nutella. The scrumptious aroma of fried pastry sprinkled with cinnamon enticed Madeleine into a long, hard stare.

Someone's besotted. Julian licked his lips as she watched the treats pass by.

"Oh, London, why do you tease me so?" Her gaze snapped back.

"Churros are moreish, that's for sure." Julian's hair flirted with the wind. "Want some? My treat."

"I *so* would, but my stomach is screaming nooo!"

"Who'd have thought finger sandwiches and wee sweets would be so filling, eh?"

"I'm stuffed. I really shouldn't be drinking this hot chocolate…" Madeleine tossed what remained of hers in a recycling bin as another bone-chilling gust whipped through the trees, jostling their branches and the sparkly blue lights wound around them. She shivered into her scarf and gathered the hair frolicking across her forehead. "I could use a hat, though."

Julian gestured to a chalet peddling wool and fleece accessories, their top sellers featuring panda heads, lion faces, and English football team logos. "Looks like you're spoilt for choice"—he raised his voice over Elton John's 'Step Into Christmas' booming from the stall's tinny speakers—"if you dare!"

Madeleine's eyes lit up. "Challenge accepted! Wait here." She made a beeline for the chalet.

They're all novelty hats. She's not gonna find... Julian raised his hand in amusement. "I was joking! You don't have to...ah, she's going in." Chuckling, he dropped his arm, resigned.

She shot a look over her shoulder. "No peeking! Text Micah or something."

"That's me told." Julian hung back, but his gaze lingered as Madeleine engaged the owner in a lively conversation. *How is this woman single? She's damned near perfect.*

Eager for a sale, the stall owner brought out hats with cat's ears and fox faces with long furry flaps that would sweep her shoulders, but Madeleine donned a beanie boasting the Chelsea Football Club logo. *Ugh, the Blues?! Really?* Julian scoffed in jest and messaged his best friend.

Julian: No pints tonight. Going out with Madeleine.

A response bounced up his screen within seconds.

Micah: Maaate! I won't wait up. Lol

"So, how's this one?"

Julian looked up. Madeleine's windblown locks were tamed beneath a cozy brown and white knitted hat topped by two jagged green leaves and an impressive red pom pom.

She makes silly look absolutely adorable. Julian raised a quizzical brow. "You do realize you have a Christmas pudding on your head?"

"It was the lesser of ALL the evils." Madeleine tugged it down to her eyes. "Okay, who am I kidding?" She smiled, the smoky aroma of grilled bratwurst escaping from a neighboring stall. "It looked warm and fun and I had to have it."

Yes to all of the above. Julian's teasing smirk grew into a wide grin. "So cute. And the hat's not bad either."

A blush brightened her cheeks, but Julian wasn't sure if the culprit was his compliment or the cold.

"Thanks." A nervous giggle infiltrated her response as she gazed into his eyes for the briefest of moments.

It's my compliment! Julian's pulse quickened, but before he could do anything about it, Madeleine looked away, the row of human-sized 'snow globes' on their right stealing her attention. The clear plastic igloos offered round tables, fuzzy blankets, and dining for up to six famished revelers.

"You guys sure take your Christmas markets seriously," she said. "Ours are kinda half-assed. They'll sell hot chocolate and holiday knickknacks, might have a Santa for the kids or a beer garden, but that's it."

"No plastic igloos?"

"Nope." Looking up ahead, she pointed at the London Eye and its blue sparkle beyond the Golden Jubilee Footbridges. "Or a gigantic Ferris wheel."

"Or pudding hats…"

"*Especially* the pudding hats." Madeleine pulled her tote closer as they passed a hut doing a swift trade in steaming mugs of Glühwein, a time-honored spiced wine from Germany. "You were right about London being magical this time of year. This place is a whole new level of pretty. I almost don't know where to look."

Julian stroked his chin as they strayed toward a cluster of timber chalets bedazzled with blinking lights and fat tinsel garlands. "Is it too full-on? 'Cause if it is, we can go elsewhere."

"No! I'm okay, really. I'm glad we came." Madeleine adjusted her hat. "I might not be ready to deck the halls, but it's fun to walk around and see all this with you."

With me. Julian smiled to himself. "Good, I'm glad. I'm enjoying myself, too."

"And I know I've been a bit 'bah humbug' about London and Christmas, but thanks for being so kind and understanding. Not everyone gets it."

"Hey, I've been there. Sometimes you're not feeling it, you know? And there's nothing wrong with that."

"Thanks," said Madeleine. "I think my friends and family are giving me a hard time this year 'cause I usually love the holidays. I'm *that* person, the one who puts up their tree right after Thanksgiving and plays Christmas tunes non-stop till New Year's."

"And gets all their shopping done before December 1st?" Julian raised an accusatory brow over the rim of his hot chocolate.

Sheepish, she wrinkled her nose as he took a sip. "Usually, yeah. Don't hate me!"

He swallowed. "Hate? Never. Envy, more like. Do you bake, too? Send out cards?"

"Yep. Name the cookie and I probably make it. Few survive, though. I eat most of them."

"Well, you've gotta test 'em out, right?"

"Always. Every year for as long as I can remember, it's been Christmas dialed up to eleven in my family, especially for my dad," said Madeleine. "He's basically Clark Griswold."

Julian laughed. "From that *Christmas Vacation* movie?"

"Oh yes! He never blows things up or gets hurt, but he always has the biggest tree, hundreds of lights, the most sparkly garlands. People drive in from miles away just to see Dad's decorations on our house and front lawn. The local news usually stops by, too, filming all his moving Santas, glittery candy canes, and inflated snowmen."

"You must miss all that, being here on your own." His eyes drifted to the South Bank's famous golden carousel and its wooden horses forever mid-gallop. Parents lifted their children onto their brightly painted backs and snapped photos for posterity.

"Wow, that's gorgeous," said Madeleine, admiring the ride. "Christmas at home can be a bit of a circus, but yeah, I miss it—strangely. How about you? Where did your love for the holidays come from?"

"Hmm, not my family. They're not the most festive. We'd have presents and a nice Christmas lunch—Mum made sure of it—but by Boxing Day, the tree would be out on the curb. Maybe that's why I embrace it more now as an adult. I'm trying to make up for lost time, trying to recapture all the wonder and magic I missed out on as a kid."

They walked a little farther, perusing various booths, and Julian downed the last of his hot chocolate. He tossed the empty cup in a recycling bin while Madeleine wandered toward the sweetness of Dolly Parton's "Hard Candy Christmas" coming from a sparkly chalet festooned with multi-colored lights, astrological signs, and ceramic windchimes tinkling in the breeze.

"Julian!" She pointed at the shack and its unique jewelry. "This might be it! Shan *loves* zodiac stuff."

Joining the throng of stagnant shoppers eyeballing the display, Madeleine was swarmed by a rowdy bachelorette party live-streaming their mulled-wine-soaked antics on TikTok and ended up behind several vertically blessed German tourists. Ignoring the horoscope-themed treasures on offer, they were more enthralled with snapping selfies using polar bear filters.

She glanced back with a grimace and Julian inched closer, away from a couple wolfing down a hearty helping of gooey mac and cheese. He gestured ahead. "I think the bloke is waving at you."

"Hello, love?" The salesperson hollered over Dolly, keen for Madeleine's attention. "Can I help?"

"Hi!" Edging up on her toes, she yelled between the distended backpacks of the photo-obsessed Germans. "Do you have any birth month pendants that *aren't* zodiac signs?"

"Which month?" he bellowed.

"May."

"Just a moment..." He pivoted toward his shelves and rummaged through a pyramid of white boxes.

Madeleine looked over her shoulder, smiling. "I feel lucky!"

Julian's eyes popped. "Oh, watch your—"

She spun around as one of the backpacks swung with blind intent, its swollen cargo on a collision course with her face.

"Shit!" Madeleine blurted. She barreled backward, losing her balance as her souvenir-loaded tote scuttled down her arm and her boots stomped—hard—on Julian's shoes.

The pain, sharp and tingling, rippled through his right foot, but Julian gritted his teeth and blocked it out, his only concern Madeleine's safety. With adrenaline pumping, he caught her shoulders and drew her in, halting her fall. "You all right, Maddie?"

Her welcome weight leaning into him, the vanilla scent of her chestnut waves—Julian was a goner. Then, he realized his fingers were accidentally grazing the curve of her breast.

Fuck.

"Oh god!" Flustered, Madeleine scrambled free, her boots searching for the pavement. "I'm so sorry!" She tugged her tote back up her arm and faced him, her cheeks reddening. "Did I hurt you?! I trampled you like a baby elephant."

A half-laugh escaped Julian's throat. "No! I'm fine." The awkwardness coiling inside him lessened as he realized Madeleine hadn't felt the brush against her boob or, if she had, she figured it was an accident. "I'll live to tell the tale."

She readjusted the strap of her tote even though it hadn't budged from her shoulder. "You called me *Maddie.*"

"Oh, sorry. I should've asked first—"

"No! It's okay. I like it, sounds nice with your accent." A smile lingered, reaching her eyes. "Thanks for being here, catching me." Her stare slipped to his mouth.

"Always," he replied, as Madeleine's heated gaze conspired with his own simmering attraction. *We're friendly, flirty. We're no longer cabbie and customer, so...* His heart pounded, urging, asking, *Does she want me to kiss her?* He inhaled deeply. "Maddie—"

"Miss?" The seller foisted a small white box enthusiastically in her direction, stealing her smile and the moment.

Bugger. Cheers, mate.

Madeleine eased forward, her eager eyes zeroing in on her prize. "Oh, it's perfect!" She cradled the present in her hands. "Julian, see? Isn't it pretty? The flower inside is for Shantelle's birth month." She lifted the discreet sterling silver chain from the box and held its circular charm against her palm. "It's lily of the valley—for May." Artfully arranged, the gauzy white petals and delicate stems were captured in clear resin, the two tiny flowers in full bloom.

The seller cleared his throat. "There's a small card in the lid, tells you what it symbolizes."

Madeleine returned the jewelry to its box and removed the card.

Julian leaned over her shoulder, reading it aloud. "*Lily of the valley represents sweetness, humility, and purity.* Sound like her?"

"Not really." Madeleine smirked, catching the eye of the hovering salesperson. "How much?"

"Thirty-eight pounds, please love."

She returned the info card to the lid and tilted the box, admiring the charm's fragile flowers from different angles. "It's unique and pretty and it won't destroy her lingerie…"

Julian snorted as the seller's face contorted into a puzzled stare.

"I'll take it." She handed the box over the counter.

"Wonderful. I'll wrap it for you." The vendor removed the price sticker from the bottom and reached for a spool of thick green ribbon.

"Nice one," said Julian. "Definitely ticks all your criteria."

"I'll buy her some fudge to go along with it. Maybe a Moomin—whatever they are, if I can find one." Madeleine pulled her wallet from her purse. "Shan's wild for them all of a sudden."

Julian rocked back on his heels. "Need a Moomin? I'm your man. I know where it's all Moomins, all the time."

ELEVEN

MADELEINE

"This feels like I've entered a secret society." Madeleine half-laughed and squeezed past Julian as wide-eyed Snufkins, Hattifatteners, and Snorks stared back silently from racks and bins stuffed with toys, calendars, and homewares in Covent Garden's Moomin Shop. "I know squat about these hippo guys."

The wooden floor of the small, second floor boutique creaked beneath Julian's size tens as he leaned over a display of notebooks and bagged himself a mug. "Didn't you watch the cartoons growing up?"

"No. I wasn't aware of them until Shantelle got all Moomin-mad." Humming along to the final chorus of Joni Mitchell's "River" serenading from the shop speakers, she ventured farther down the customer-clogged aisle and pored over a rail of t-shirts and kiddie-sized pajamas, then flipped open a copy of *The Moomins and the Great Flood*. Vibrant artwork of an idyllic valley and a house topped with a jaunty flag gave way to a preface from the author, Tove Jansson. Beautifully written, one word jumped out: *Moomintroll*. Madeleine blinked, seeking clarity. "They're *trolls*?! But they're cute and roly-poly…"

Looking past ruddy-cheeked customers scavenging the shelves, she searched for Julian…and there he was, deep in conversation with four little kids and their mother. The newfound party of six were immersed in a four-storey playhouse—the house from the book in Madeleine's hands—complete with furniture, multiple staircases, and Moomins—lots of Moomins.

Toy fan, marmalade master, pub quiz king, Madeleine mused. *Julian is fun and interesting and irresistibly attractive. My god, the way he looked at me at the market. I thought for sure a kiss was coming. Or maybe it was just wishful thinking.*

Julian glanced over his shoulder, combing the crowd until his eyes locked on Madeleine's. His lips quirked into a boyish smile as he gestured enthusiastically. "This is AWESOME! Get your sister this!"

"Or you?!" Madeleine laughed, leaving the story book behind. *Love it. No pretense with this guy.* Holding her tote close, protecting the maple fudge she'd purchased on the South Bank for Shantelle, she threaded her way past elbows and shopping bags and reunited with Julian. His former playmates had moved on, enamored by a glowing Snorkmaiden nightlight. "Is that mug for you?" she asked, the pensive melody of Christina Perri's "Something About December" warming the store.

"For our Secret Santa—Tash, Micah, and me."

"You changed your mind about Christmas?"

Julian shook his head. "I don't really fancy the trip up to Manchester this year. Don't get me wrong, their family is hospitable and his dad's roasted potatoes are actually to die for, but when the Cooper cousins crack open the Baileys post-lunch, it becomes a fist-flying free-for-all."

"Natasha wasn't exaggerating?"

"Nope, and nothing is sacred. The Queen's speech, Quality Street, *The Sound of Music*—they've all sparked fights."

Madeleine scoffed. "Quality Street? The colorful chocolates in the tin?"

"Yep. Micah's got a cousin who is a tad territorial over the green triangles. Few years back, a relative scoffed the lot and the guy went ballistic, left him with a black eye."

"Those must be *some* chocolates!"

"Trust me, when the shot glasses come out, that's our cue—me and Micah's—to head to the pub. This year he'll have to go solo, though. I have too much on after Boxing Day, so I'll have a quiet Christmas down here."

"Will you see your family?"

"Uh, no. My dad walked out on us when I was six. Haven't seen him since." Julian scratched his temple. "My brother and I aren't on speaking terms just now and my mum is dead, so…"

"Oh, Julian." Madeleine squeezed his forearm. "I'm so sorry."

"Thanks. It was a few years ago." He shrugged.

Recent or long ago, it doesn't matter. It still hurts. She rubbed his arm. "The holidays are hard anyway, but when you're missing loved ones…"

"It sucks royally." Julian sighed, then flashed a wistful grin. "But that's life, unfortunately." He glanced around the shop. "So, this Moomin for your sister…"

Is this the 'stiff upper lip' Brits are famous for? He doesn't have to change the subject, not with me. Madeleine's heart dipped as she let go of his arm. "Julian, if you…you know, want to talk about your mom…"

"Aw, that's kind of you, but I'm okay. Thanks." He shifted toward the bins piled high with stuffed toys.

But are you? She followed closely behind. *I know what it's like, the loneliness, feeling like no one wants you to mention them.*

"Is there a particular Moomin she likes?"

I wish he'd open up. "Um, it's the one carrying a handbag."

"Like this?" Julian rescued a pudgy plush toy wearing nothing but a smile and a red and white striped apron from a bin of soft scowling creatures. "I think she was put in the wrong spot." He flipped the swing tag attached near her handbag and read the info. "Madeleine, meet Moominmamma."

"Moominwho-ha?" She laughed. "I'll take her. Thanks!"

They shimmied through the crowd of eager shoppers, many loaded up with teapots, books, and puzzles, and claimed a place in the queue snaking its way to the cashier. A low-fi version of "Blue Christmas" captured Julian's attention.

"Ooh, this is pretty. Actually, all the songs they've been playing are brilliant."

Brooke White, Christina Perri, Joni Mitchell…hold on. Madeleine gawped. "This…this is my holiday playlist."

"You made this?"

"Yeah, before I left Boston. If the next song is Ingrid Michaelson's version of 'Have Yourself a Merry Little Christmas', it's definitely mine."

"Great taste, Madeleine. It's really good!"

She flashed a grin as they stepped closer to the sales desk. "Thanks…"

"No, it is! My god, there must be, what, thousands of holiday songs out there? And you sifted through all that noise and found tunes that play nicely together. That's no small feat. So, what's your secret?" he asked.

"None, really. Just a lot of trial and error. I always start with an idea. Could be a mood, an occasion, or a story I want to tell through the songs."

"What's the story with this one? It feels a little…melancholy."

Inspired by heartbreak and loss. I can't talk to him about Kellie, not after he just brushed off his own grief. They edged forward in line, the question demanding an answer. "I, um"—despair pulled taut around Madeleine's heart, so she busied herself flattening a wrinkle in the Moomin's apron, hoping Julian would be none the wiser—"well, like we talked about, not everyone feels joyous in December. It can be lonely when the world is all about presents and parties—" She fell silent, unable to speak through the knots tightening her throat.

"That's why this playlist is so beautiful and poignant…"

Madeleine dipped her chin. She didn't dare look at him, fearful he'd see tears glistening in her eyes.

"…you know how it feels." Julian's glanced down at the mug in his hands.

She nodded. "I always hope someone will listen and feel solace and maybe…less alone, if that makes sense. If it can help one person…"

"If? I'd wager a guess you have, several times over," said Julian. "Think about it—how many times have you heard a song and thought, *They see me, they* get *me*? Lots, right?"

"Yeah."

"Well, I reckon a playlist telling a story through *several* songs would be even more powerful. Each one is like a space for listeners to feel their way through all sorts of emotions and situations. That's an incredible gift to give the world, Madeleine. They're amazing. And I think…you are too."

Propelled by his generous and unexpected compliment, her heart hurled into her ribs, thwarting all hopes of a coherent reply. "Uh, wow! I, um, don't know what to say to that. Thanks, I guess?" She pinched a Moomin magnet and handed it along with Shantelle's soft toy to the salesperson who promptly scanned their price codes into their payment system. "Listening to music is such a personal thing. I might adore a song for different reasons than you do, but we all love, we all hurt, we all feel lonely sometimes—our emotions are universal. That's my 'in' with listeners, so to speak. Everyone's going through something, right?"

"Definitely." He smiled as Madeleine pulled her bank card from her wallet. "So how *do* you find the right tracks? You must listen to a shitload of music."

She nodded. "Guilty! It's a miracle my headphones aren't fused to my ears by now. I'll listen to anything and everything: golden oldies and chart hits, unknown indies and big-label releases. Once I find songs that suit my narrative, I listen to them over and over, playing with their order, staying mindful of tempo and how the songs best flow together."

The salesperson leaned against her cash drawer. "That'll be £15.99, please."

"Thanks, I'll pay by card." Madeleine inserted it into the payment terminal and punched in her code. "There's always the chance someone will shuffle instead of listening in order, so it's best not to be too precious about that." Removing her card, she slipped it back in her wallet. "In that sense, I completely understand how an artist might feel when someone doesn't listen to their album from start to finish. Like you said in the pub, it's a journey. A story is being told, but not everyone necessarily wants to hear every chapter."

"So true," said Julian.

She picked up her Moomin-stuffed shopping bag. "Thank you!" Stepping out of line, her eyes followed Julian's mug as the salesperson scanned the tag stuck to the bottom and "Have Yourself a Merry Little Christmas", the Ingrid Michaelson rendition, eased through the speakers. "Yep, this playlist is definitely mine."

"What's your favorite thing about making them?" Julian tapped the payment terminal with his bank card.

"Other than listening to music all day? I love giving unknown artists a platform to be heard by a large audience. You know what it's like, being a music fan—we're always hungry for new tunes, new artists, but the business is so overly saturated, it can be impossible to find fresh favorites to enjoy. That's where we come in. Playlists can shine a spotlight on artists listeners might otherwise miss."

"There is that, yeah." He collected his small paper bag and smiled farewell to the salesperson. "Cheers. Happy Christmas!" His grin swerved to Madeleine. "You wanna look around some more?"

"No, I'm good, but I need to find a card store for wrapping paper and gift bags."

"There's a place in the piazza."

"Great!" Madeleine led the way through the obstacle course of shoppers and started descending the tight stairwell, admiring the Moomin murals painted on the wall. She also mulled over Julian's comments about playlists, his love of albums, and his apparent dislike for modern technology like social media and Uber. *Natasha called him 'an old fart'!* Giggling to herself, she reached the ground level of the Market Building and met the crisp air and unmistakeable aroma of roasting chestnuts. She paused for Julian to join her outside the Moomin's aqua-colored storefront. "Can I ask you something?"

"Sure." He nodded, fastening his coat's buttons.

"You're a devoted vinyl guy, aren't ya?"

Julian laughed. "Yeah! Is it that obvious?"

Her gaze swept up, across the massive silver baubles and

boughs of mistletoe hanging from the Market Building's arched ceiling. *I can't get enough of this, so pretty.* She scooted her Moomin bag up her forearm. "Maybe not to everyone, but…"

"You're a music geek—like me. You know the signs."

"Well, you have to admit, Julian, they are kinda flashing!" Madeleine smirked as they walked past the railings overlooking the building's lower ground floor where tourists nibbled on cupcakes and crêpes while fiddlers performed a jolly rendition of "Joy to the World". "There's your music journalist past, your passion for albums and listening to tracks *in order*"—she paused and snapped photos of the giant mistletoe looming overhead—"and your confessed playlist-making ineptitude."

"Sad but true." Julian lingered by her side. "It doesn't come naturally to me, unfortunately."

She lowered her phone. "But what Natasha blurted last night, it's not really about playlists, is it? It's about streaming." Her brows peaked. "You hate it, don't you? Be honest—you *loathe* where I work and what I do for a living."

Julian exhaled a heavy breath. "Madeleine, it's not about you, it's—look, I have my reasons."

She stepped aside, away from the flow of harried tourists and swinging shopping bags, and Julian followed. She threw a glance over the railing where a small Christmas tree crowded the tables, its scraggly branches dwarfed by a rash of red baubles. "Okay, vinyl guy. Let's hear 'em."

Julian leaned on the railing. "I've spent a LOT of time with musicians." His eyes strayed to the fiddlers below and back to Madeleine. "I've seen how hard they graft and how often greedy industry types, who couldn't hum a tune if their lives depended on it, snatched a sizable slice of a small financial pie. Making a living as a musician has always been tough, but it's gotten much worse with streaming. These services don't pay the artists anywhere close to what they deserve, unless they're someone like Taylor Swift or Beyoncé."

Madeleine nodded sympathetically. "I've seen it firsthand. Did you know the rights holder needs to rack up 250 streams of a *single* song to earn a dollar from Sensoria? And that amount gets split between several parties: the record label, producers, songwriters, the artist…"

"That's what I mean." Julian sneered. "Their business model is the modern-day equivalent of highway robbery."

"Yeah, it bothers me, too. I've complained a bunch of times, but no one cares because I have zero pull or influence. It's frustrating as fuck. My boss even had the nerve to say, 'Don't like it? Leave. I have a file stuffed with resumes from people dying to work here.'"

"Ooh, he's a charmer."

"He's an ass." Madeleine jutted out a hip. "But I need the paycheck and the creative outlet, so I swallow my anger and fill my playlists with lesser-known artists alongside the major names. My hope is that listeners will buy their albums, merch, and concert tickets, and more money will end up where it belongs—in the artists' pockets." Frowning, she played with the paper handle of the Moomin bag. "Julian, do you see me as part of the problem?"

"No! Never! Maddie, you're doing what you can to help, and you're not responsible for how they conduct business. It's just—big corporations like Sensoria act like they're God's gift to music. *That's* what pisses me off. But it is what it is. Times change and digital downloads and streaming are what people do now. Doesn't mean I have to like it, or that I can't miss the good old days of vinyl and CDs."

"You're *old school*." Her lips teased into a smile. "It's all good. I totally get it."

"You sure? You don't think I'm an old fart, stuck in my ways?"

"No, not at all…" She laughed. "Kids these days, huh?"

"Urgh! They're the *worst!*" Julian grinned.

Leaving the Market Building behind, they stepped onto the cobblestones of Covent Garden's east piazza where a gigantic silver reindeer dappled with white lights captivated every cell phone in sight. Ready to take flight, the reindeer's antlers were tilted back with glee while her front hooves pranced majestically above a green sleigh filled with presents and a minty candy cane or two.

Madeleine's jaw dropped. "Wow! That's amazing!"

"Isn't she gorgeous?" Julian nodded, taking in the sculpture's merriment.

Madeleine stopped and angled her phone, capturing the deer from antler to hoof. "I know loving horses is a rite of passage for many young girls, but I always preferred reindeer."

"That's a new one. How come?"

"No, you'll laugh." She lowered her phone.

"Try me."

"The Rankin/Bass Christmas specials!"

Julian tilted his head. "What are those?"

She playfully smacked his arm. "You know! The stop-motion dolls? *Rudolph the Red-Nosed Reindeer*, *The Little Drummer Boy*, *Santa Claus is Coming to Town*…?"

Julian shrugged as they walked toward a colorful stationery store tucked a few feet away in the corner of the piazza. "I know the Christmas carols, but…"

"*Really?!* You don't know *The Year Without a Santa Claus* or the Snow Miser…or Burgermeister Meisterburger?"

"What's that? Some kind of German fast food joint?" His brow rose along with his question. "Sorry, I don't think they aired on British telly."

"Aw, you missed out! They are THE best. I still watch them every year."

"The animated special we watched annually was called *The Snowman*. Heard of it?"

Madeleine shook her head.

Julian began to sing in a high pitch. "*We're walking in the air…*"

Her face crumpled with laughter. "What is *that*?!"

"The theme tune. It was a big hit!"

"Now I know why you wrote about music instead of perform-ing it."

"OUCH!" Julian snickered. "So, c'mon then, what's up with this Rankin/Bass person and his—her flying deer?"

"You were right the first time. It's two guys, Rankin *and* Bass. They produced a whole bunch of holiday specials, and their reindeer were cute and magical and could hop into the air and fly effortlessly all over the world!" She skipped a step or two ahead, whimsically mimicking Santa's most loyal helpers.

Julian swung his small Moomin bag in rhythm with each stride. "Hmm, I can see your point. Flying reindeer definitely trumps horses. Though, to be fair, horses have the advantage of being real..."

"Oh, shush. One year, our parents took us to a reindeer farm before Christmas."

"In Wisconsin?"

"Uh-huh. Their antler game was top notch," said Madeleine. "Never mind crowns—imagine carrying one of those racks on your head! Just amazing. That's where I found out only female reindeer have antlers at Christmas, so all of Santa's kickass flyers were actually women!"

"Slay, girl, slay!"

Madeleine laughed as she pulled open the door to the stationery shop. "Hey, if you want to get the job done, hire a woman."

"Can't argue with that!" Julian agreed.

Two steps into the celebratory world of all things colorful and happy, and Madeleine couldn't stop grinning. The glittery journals, fun desk accessories, wreaths made of Christmas tree baubles—everything was sparkly, more adorable, more fun than anything she'd encountered back in the States. And then she saw...

"Christmas pudding earmuffs?!" Their smiley round faces were in Madeleine's hands before Julian could speak.

"Uh-oh. We've created a monster."

"But look!" She beamed, separating the two pillowy puddings tethered together by a red felt headband. "They're so cute. Even the Grinchiest of faces will light up when they see these."

"You'd actually put those sweet treats on your ears and walk down the street?"

"Julian, I'm wearing a knitted pudding on my head…"

"That's true." He smirked. "And may I say, you look beautiful in it."

"Aw, thanks." She tucked away his compliment for safekeeping, ready to share a bit more about herself. "So, I have this *thing*…"

Julian lifted the lid on a gift box covered with animated Christmas crackers, their eyes crinkled and mouths wide with silent laughter. "A thing?"

"Yeah. It's not just these earmuffs. I have a thing for food with faces. Not *literal* food, obviously, but stuff like this, cute things." She gazed lovingly at the brown Christmas 'puddings' with their euphoric smiles and kind eyes peeking out from a sprig of holly and a smattering of white felt mimicking the traditional brandy sauce dripping down. "I know that might sound weird but"—she shrugged into a shy smile—"hey, that's me."

"Not weird. Fun. I had an inkling you might be into Kawaii stuff."

An inquisitive pinch of her brow tempered her grin.

"Your phone case with the ice cream cones?" He returned the lid to the box. "Kinda gave it away."

"I didn't know what Kawaii meant until my best friend, Kellie, filled me in. She'd been to Japan so…" Madeleine brushed her thumb over the soft brown felt face of one of the puddings. *Keep it at that. He's old school. If he doesn't like social media, he won't understand an online friendship.*

"Lucky duck. I'd love to go there," said Julian. "Great food, great culture…"

"Yeah, me too. Kellie said it was incredible. She brought back a big, plush popcorn with happy eyes and a grinning grilled cheese for me. Oh, and an onion."

"An onion?"

"Yeah, it has googly eyes and a surprised expression. It's…kind of an inside-joke thing between me and Kellie. It cracked me up when it arrived. I was laughing so hard I could barely breathe. My boyfriend—my *ex-boyfriend*—didn't find it as funny."

"No?"

"He said owning toys as an adult was a sign of immaturity."

Julian curled his lip. "What a dick. If it makes you happy…"

"Right? I hate it when people put down the things others enjoy."

"There's nothing deep or clever about raining on other people's parades. You're better off rid, there…" Julian picked up a small tray. "Hey, *look!*" The white plastic was decorated with cartoon holly, candy canes, tree baubles, and chocolate yule logs all with large, childlike eyes and easy smiles.

Madeleine lit up. "Ooh, I *love* that."

"Then you must have it—a little Christmas gift from me."

"Aw, Julian, thank you." She grinned wider, admiring the tray's snowflakes, reindeer, and Christmas trees, all happy, all adorable. "But I'll only accept it on one condition: you let me buy you something, too."

"Fair play." He flipped over the tray, spying its price sticker. "But only if it's under ten quid."

"Okay, hold that thought." Her eyes searched the store. "How 'bout…" She skipped down the aisle, her sweeping gaze stalling on a table of bento boxes, festive candy bowls, and journals. "Ah! A notebook? You could get all your ideas out of your head and jot 'em down on the go." She claimed a Nicola Metcalfe journal with colorful London icons on the cover including red phone boxes, teapots, and several small black cabs. It's price: £9. "This one is *so* you!" She held it aloft.

"Niiice! Loving the pink elastic ribbon."

Is he being sarcastic? Her finger skated down the elastic keeping the journal closed. "Do you?"

Julian nodded empathically. "Yes! Really, I do! My favorite dress shirt is pink."

"Then, this baby is yours. Merry Christmas, Julian!"

He glanced at her festive tray in his hands. "Merry Christmas, Madeleine!" With a smile, he leaned in conspiratorially. "And for what it's worth, I'll never make fun of your googly onion or your earmuffs, provided you don't take the piss about my fuzzy corgi slippers."

The image of Julian relaxing at home, listening to old vinyls with his feet tucked cozily inside plush corgi slippers warmed her heart. "God, how adorable are you?"

The words flew untethered, without filter, and Madeleine's stomach dropped, followed by her gaze. *That wasn't supposed to be said aloud.* She fussed with the red pom-pom holly on the earmuffs, desperate to escape her effusive slip of the tongue. *C'mon, Julian, say something...*

A grin tugged the corners of his mouth. "Well, err...thanks? I do try. Whereas I reckon you don't have to. You just wake up each day and be yourself—lovely and kind..."

Madeleine swore her heart stopped. *Yes, Virginia! There IS a Santa Claus. Julian Halliwell is definitely into me!* She couldn't hide in her earmuffs forever. Glancing up, she met his soft stare, losing herself in his blue eyes, undemanding and respectful, but with a cheeky glint that teased her in all the right places. Julian felt safe somehow, a risk definitely worth taking—and with giant mistletoe hanging just steps away outside in Covent Garden...

Maybe it wouldn't be such a terrible idea if I made a move? Kissed him, just the once—

"Can I put those behind the counter for you?"

Sorry, what? Madeleine blinked, reluctantly pulling herself away from Julian's warm smile. Jutting out a hand, a blonde shop assistant wearing a snowflake-patterned sweater glared at the earmuffs and journal in her grip. "I'll take those," she snapped through pursed lips.

Madeleine's focus pinged down to the cuddly felt faces. "Uh, okay. Sure..." Her eyes strayed, skimming back across the journal table. "Oh, one sec..." She reached over, rescuing a red and green skull-shaped candy dish. "This would be perfect for Natasha."

Then, it dawned on her.

I won't see Tash again before I go.

I won't see Julian.

Her heart spiraled in free fall. *This is it.*

The shop assistant whisked away Julian's journal, the Christmas tray, candy dish, and earmuffs, their stitched-on grins joyfully ignorant of the epiphany piercing Madeleine's merriment.

"That's really kind, Maddie," said Julian, toying with a unicorn-topped marker pen. "Tash will love that a lot more than my marmalade, and she loves oranges A LOT."

Moomin bag crinkling under her arm, Madeleine flashed a smile as they slipped past two teenage girls foraging through a box of cat-shaped highlighters. "I just realized, though—I won't see her before I go."

"Oh! Right." Julian nodded, her statement dimming his happy demeanor. "I can make sure she gets it, no problem."

"That would be great. Thanks." She joined the line for the sales desk. "I swear my jet lag is making me stupid. I'm mixing up days, don't know if I'm coming or going, if it's dinner or breakfast." She half-laughed, dampening any disappointment lurking in her voice.

Julian checked his watch. "Well, it's just gone six, so it's definitely dinner. What do you reckon? Want to go for a pub-style Christmas dinner? Turkey, pigs in blankets, roast potatoes—the works?"

She smiled sweetly. "I'd love to!"

"Great!" He beamed back. "You can even try a boozy Chrimbo pudding. I hear the Marquess of Anglesey pub around the corner serves up a good 'un. Comes with brandy butter ice cream."

"I like the sound of that." A loud buzz erupted from her pocket. "Ah, my sister's daily update. Today was supposed to be a floating market, massages, and sunbathing on her inflatable avocado."

Julian scratched his temple. "Tough life."

"Well, she works hard so—I'll just make sure she's okay." Madeleine tugged the device free from her coat and tapped the screen.

Yoshiko: Good news. My last appointment for the year just canceled. I'll FaceTime you on the hour.

The counselor's words collapsed her breezy bliss. *Nooo! I was hoping for tomorrow, not now!* Her smile loosened. *But Yoshiko is away till mid-January. I don't know if I can get through Kellie's anniversary without speaking to her.*

"All good with your sister?"

"Uh, it's not her..." Madeleine faltered, eyes squeezing into a squint. "But I, um—it's urgent. I have to video-call them back somewhere quiet." Her nose wrinkled. "Sorry, Julian. I'll have to pass on dinner. Could you help me get to my hotel?"

"Yes, of course." He nodded, but dismay seemed to linger in his eyes. "I'll get you there as fast as I can."

TWELVE

MADELEINE

Evidence of Madeleine's race to her ringing laptop lay scattered across her hotel room's plush gray carpet. Her tipped-over tote, shopping bags from Covent Garden, and a large unopened box from Shantelle wound their way to the king-sized bed where she turned on the TV (for company) and updated her grief counselor on the meddlesome volcanic ash, unexpected airport closures, and Julian's kindness.

Julian. Madeleine winced, recalling their goodbye. *I'd barely said thank you when the concierge rushed that family into his cab.* Late for a train departing Waterloo Station, they didn't dawdle, ordering Julian to take the quickest route through the capital and over the Thames. *I waved, but he didn't look back.* With a sharp sigh, Madeleine kicked off her ankle boots and tugged her pudding hat from her head, releasing a fright of static-charged flyaways. *Argh, look at me.* She tsked at the tiny image of herself on her laptop. *Would I look back for this?* She smoothed down her tresses and continued talking, sharing her unexpected London sojourn.

Yoshiko listened without interruption, taking everything in from her messy office in Boston's Back Bay as she occasionally jotted on her notepad. Barely forty with caring brown eyes, poppy red lips, and a defiant bolt of electric blue blazing through her dark shoulder-length bob, she had been Madeleine's lifeline for the past eleven months, bearing witness to her broken heart while providing a safe space for her to express her fears, thoughts, and feelings.

"I used to love surprises, the bigger the better," said Madeleine, wrestling free from her coat. She flung it beside her on the bed and shifted into a cross-legged position. "But the airport closing felt like a punch to the gut."

Lowering her pen, Yoshiko looked up through her large wire-framed eyeglasses as Madeleine whipped off her scarf. "I'm sorry you've had to go through this. Being stranded would be tough at any time, but with Kellie's anniversary coming up and it being Christmas week, it's a lot to deal with."

Her thoughtful words and soothing tone worked their magic, easing the tension knotting Madeleine's shoulders. It was a relief, feeling understood. "Yeah, but then I think, what's wrong with me? I'm in London. I *love* London. Coming here has always been on my bucket list, but—" Her face pinched.

"Not like this." Yoshiko's brows pulled together as she leaned in. "A year ago you were supposed to be there with Kellie."

"Yeah." Madeleine blew out her lips and swallowed, fighting the emotions thickening her throat. "To Kellie, London was *it*. Her happy place. I'd laugh and tell her, 'You can't say that. You haven't even been there in person.' But Kellie would shake her head and say, 'Maddie, I haven't met you in person, but that doesn't take away from how much I love you. My heart knows where it belongs.'"

Yoshiko smiled. "That's lovely."

The prickle of impending tears teased Madeleine's nose. "That was Kellie through and through. She always said exactly how she felt. She never held back. I loved that about her. I miss it. I miss *her*." Madeleine sniffed, her fingers plucking at her black tights. "London at Christmas was Kellie's lifelong dream and I'm here and she's not and this whole thing feels like some cruel joke. When I arrived, I seriously thought about staying in my room until the airport re-opened. Why give the universe the satisfaction of watching me struggle here without her?"

"What changed your mind?"

Madeleine swiped away a tear breaching her lashes. "I was watching people come and go on the Eurostar. My room overlooks the platform at St. Pancras."

"That sounds interesting."

"Yeah. It made me think, what if I never get back here again? It's possible, right? Things happen, plans change...people die." A staggered breath flew from her lips. "So despite all this hurting like hell and me feeling sorry for myself, what got me dressed and out the door was Kellie. She would've killed for a chance like this." Madeleine shook her head. "I can't take it for granted. I have to try to make London count—for her and me."

Yoshiko grinned softly. "That's a brave decision."

Madeleine's chin dropped. She fussed with the hem of her dress, rumpled across her thighs. *I don't feel very brave.*

"I'm proud of you, getting out, seeing the sights. How do you feel now that you've been out?"

"Conflicted," said Madeleine. "On one hand, I'm enjoying myself. I can't deny it, I am. London is incredible, better than I'd hoped, but it's making me miss Kellie more than ever." She toyed with her necklace, the last gift bestowed by her best friend. "Kellie was always the first person I'd call with good news or something to share and I hate that that's been taken from me. I hate that I'm making memories she'll never be part of, making friends she'll never know—and they'll never know *her*, the most caring, most important person in my life. And every time I laugh or catch myself having fun without her, it stings. It's almost like I'm betraying her."

"It's in our nature to feel all sorts of emotions, even when we're grieving," said Yoshiko. "Sometimes they creep in and set off alarm bells: I shouldn't feel happy when I'm so sad. But you're not betraying Kellie when these moments of light enter your life. You're being human."

"Then being human is scary and awful." Madeleine pouted. "It just seems the more happy moments I have, the more I worry I'll forget how much she meant to me." Her jaw flexed as a swell of longing ached in her chest. "Saying 'meant' or 'was'..." She paused into a cringe, her voice a whisper. "Past tense. I'm relegating Kellie to history without even realizing it, and it feels ridiculous because even though she's not here, I still love her—now, today. Present tense."

"And that won't change," said Yoshiko. "Love lives on, it never dies. Love lasts forever."

Rubbing her eyes, Madeleine slumped backward into a wall of pillows stacked high against the headboard. "I know this sounds weird, but I almost miss the days and weeks right after she died." *Uh, morbid much?* Madeleine sighed and tried again, her fingers smoothing several squirrels on her dress. "Okay, that's not exactly what I mean. It's not that I *miss* them, it's—" She closed her eyes. "Sorry, it's hard to explain."

Yoshiko leaned in, offering an encouraging smile. "It's okay, take your time." She picked up a red and green striped paper cup, its top edge overwhelmed by a swirly dollop of whipped cream and a generous dusting of dark chocolate curls.

Madeleine raked her hair off her forehead as her counselor took a careful sip. "It's just...all the sobbing and staring off into space back then, wondering how I'd survive the next hour—everything felt so raw and present. All-consuming. There wasn't room for anything else. My entire existence was Kellie and how much my body ached with her absence. It was like that gut-wrenching intensity made me feel closer to her somehow.

"But now, almost a year later, when I find myself actually looking forward to something, I feel sick...like I've turned my back on the pain, turned my back on *her*, and then it feels like I'm losing her all over again."

Yoshiko placed her peppermint mocha on her desk. "Those feelings are common and completely normal."

"Are they?"

Her counselor nodded. "It's natural to miss that immediacy, that closeness that comes from the most desperate, visceral moments of grieving, but Kellie's importance to you, your memories of her won't be lost. They live in the conversations you two shared and the stories you tell your friends about her. It's in the music she loved and the movies you watched together online. You're honoring her, remembering her whenever you enjoy them, too. And it's not just movies and music and conversation—Kellie's memory will always be part of you."

That's nice in theory. Madeleine sniffed. "I hope that'll be true, but..." The threat of tears tickled her throat again as her eyes drifted over the television and the bottle of wine from the pub quiz. "Right now, that feels like a consolation prize. I don't want second best. I want Kellie here, alive with me, even though *I know* that's impossible. Sometimes it feels like I'm torturing myself, desperately wanting what I can't have." She rubbed her nose. "I'm gonna feel like this forever, aren't I?"

"As months and years pass, your grief will feel...different," said Yoshiko. "Grief shifts and changes, but it never goes away, not completely. Like love, grief lasts forever. You will find new ways to cope with it, to live with it, but it won't magically disappear. Grief will always be in your heart, just like love."

Madeleine swiped away a tear. "Want to tell Shantelle that? She tries, but she doesn't really understand. Shan thinks I'll be back to my old self once Kellie's one-year anniversary passes, and if, for some reason, I'm still sad after our Parisian holiday, I'm stuck or grieving wrong, somehow."

"There is no right or wrong way to grieve," said Yoshiko. "We all handle loss differently. Unfortunately that doesn't stop others from projecting their norms onto us, like your sister expecting you to put away your grief after Kellie's anniversary. I know it can be hurtful and frustrating at times, but this type of encouragement often comes from a place of love."

"Doesn't always feel like it."

"I know. Shantelle probably feels helpless. It's hard to watch someone you care about suffer. I bet she'd do just about anything to alleviate your discomfort."

"And her own. She sighs every time I bring up Kellie. It's like she's tired of hearing about it, so she shuts off and only tunes in again when I change the subject or bring up happy things." Madeleine shrugged. "But I guess it could be worse. At least she doesn't avoid me. I've had friends lock eyes with me in a store then look away, pretending they didn't see me."

123

"Sometimes they don't know what to say," said Yoshiko.

Madeleine's mouth curved into a frown. "I don't know what's worse: saying nothing or using platitudes: *She's in a better place, Time will heal, Try not to cry.* I've heard them all, and not just from Shantelle."

Yoshiko scribbled something on her notepad. "How do those platitudes make you feel?"

"Like I'm receiving a patronizing pat on the head, telling me 'There, there, little girl, stop being a mopey drama queen.' Shut up and cheer up, basically."

"You feel silenced?"

"Yeah, I do. When they ask, 'How are you?', they're not interested in an honest answer, not really. They don't want to hear about me eating my feelings or crying in the shower for an hour."

"What gives you that impression?"

"Well at first, they wince. Then they fidget. They'll drop a platitude or two, make excuses, and then shuffle off. Or if they do stick around, they turn judgmental. Like last week at work, I was crying in the bathroom, and the woman in the next stall asked if I was okay. When I mentioned Kellie's name, she snorted and said, 'What? *Still?*'"

"Oh, Madeleine, that's awful."

"Then she mumbled something about the five stages of grief and I was like, not another one!"

"Someone mentioned them to you before?" asked Yoshiko.

"My boss—twice. Back in February and then again two months ago. Oh, and he dropped a lovely cherry on top, too, telling me to be strong. I *hate* when people tell me what to do or how to feel." Madeleine huffed. "I swear, other than you, no one understands, and I'm sick of it."

"I don't blame you." Yoshiko sipped her coffee. "Do you know where the five stages of grief originated?"

"I know there's a book. My boss said I should read it." She fussed with her dress. "I didn't."

"The author was a Swiss-born psychiatrist who worked alongside terminally ill patients," Yoshiko explained. "She collected their anecdotes and created a five-stage model for grieving based upon the emotions the dying exhibited: denial, anger, bargaining, depression, and acceptance."

"The emotions of the *dying*?" Madeleine squinted. "But I thought the stages were related to grievers, people like me?"

Yoshiko shook her head. "No. They were never based on or intended for individuals struggling with the loss of a loved one."

"So what changed? Everyone thinks they're about grievers."

"Over the years, her findings were misunderstood and misappropriated. People saw the word grief and made a flawed leap, assuming the stages were applicable to the bereaved, too. But in actuality, they have zero relevance to how the *living* experience or process grief. Sure, they might feel some of the same emotions as the dying, but the circumstances and outcomes are obviously not the same."

"Oh, okay," said Madeleine. "So that's why I've always had a problem with that five-stage crap."

Yoshiko nodded. "And as you'll know from experience, emotions following loss are fluid and unpredictable. One day you'll feel exhausted and depressed, then the next, anger or acceptance might take hold, followed by more depression or bouts of denial, but that's grief for you. It's messy. It doesn't follow a pattern or a projected timeline, and it definitely can't be organized into a handy 'how-to' instruction manual, not when emotions constantly change and surge."

"And kick your legs out from under you when you least expect it. So true," Madeleine mused, her lips twisting in thought. "I can see why the stages would be popular with non-grievers, though. Anything that rushes us through our grief or tries to fix it has got to be attractive. I love my sister, but I wish she'd stop trying."

"To fix it?"

Madeleine nodded.

Yoshiko picked up her pen and resumed taking notes. "Where do you think that comes from?"

"I think Shantelle has watched too many movies where the heroine's grief gets fixed by a vacation or some sexy stud. And then once the heroine"—Madeleine made quotation marks with her fingers—"'is better', there will be some redeeming, teachable moment that makes her life rosy again." She scoffed. "But being in the trenches, I know firsthand that idea is total bullshit. The only thing I've learned is grief sucks."

A buzz erupted from beneath her hat. Madeleine lunged forward, unearthing her phone. "Shantelle's ears must be burning." She read the message.

Julian: Hope everything is okay. I had fun today. Sorry for the awkward goodbye.

Me too. Madeleine's mouth quirked at the corners as she hastily sent the face blowing a kiss and smiley hug emojis, the sting of unfulfilled expectations and abrupt endings dragging her down.

"So, our time is almost up," said Yoshiko kindly. "I'm glad we had the chance to talk tonight. Madeleine, you're coping really well."

She discarded her phone on the bed. "Earlier you said I was brave, getting out, seeing things, meeting people…"

"I did. And you truly are."

"I don't feel brave. At all. I feel…*responsible*." She shrugged. "Maybe Kellie would still be alive if…if I hadn't pushed her to come here."

"I know this is something you've struggled with, but Madeleine, what happened to Kellie is *not* your fault."

"Isn't it, though? If she didn't get on the plane…"

Yoshiko's expression softened.

"I wish I could turn back the clock, made different decisions, listened. Maybe it would've changed the outcome? Kellie wanted to wait a year because work was so busy, but I knew Kel. She'd make excuses and drag her feet if I didn't push. So I did. I pushed 'cause I wanted to meet her so badly. I didn't want to wait another year—"

Her breath hitched. "If I hadn't been so selfish…"

"Kellie didn't want to wait either," said Yoshiko. "She wouldn't have traveled if she felt otherwise. Please don't blame yourself. Kellie was a grown woman. The choices she made were hers. What happened was no one's fault."

"But then, it all feels so random, and I hate that. It actually scares me."

"I know." Yoshiko set down her pen. "Our brains are wired to solve mysteries and random things, to figure out why tragic situations occur in the hopes they won't happen again. If we can just find a cause or someone to blame—even if it's ourselves—we'll find the *why* and be able to make sense of it. But sometimes there is no why, and the kindest thing we can do is let ourselves off the hook for events that are beyond our control. As much as it hurts to accept, sometimes horrible things just happen and there is no reason or blame."

Madeleine sighed. "That's really difficult to accept."

Yoshiko nodded. "It is. But will you think about it? Try to let go of the guilt?"

"Yeah. I'll try." Madeleine fidgeted and stretched out her legs, upsetting her pudding hat and phone, which slid beneath her coat.

Yoshiko smiled. "Will you do anything special in Kellie's memory while you're in London?"

"I lit a candle this morning at Westminster Abbey, but that was for her mom. I'd like to do something to commemorate the one-year anniversary, but I'm running out of time and ideas. I'd have to do it tomorrow or Thursday morning, whatever *it* is."

"What about the fan fiction you told me about, the stories you wrote with Kellie? Wasn't it Christmas or London-themed?"

"Some was, yeah. Wow, you remember that? Either you have a good memory or good notes—or both." Madeleine tucked her hair behind her ear. "We wrote a lot about *Love Actually* and *The Holiday*." She smirked. "That fic wasn't our best work. It was far-fetched, but we had a laugh writing it. We imagined all sorts of drama after the closing credits."

"Maybe you could visit the places from the films?" asked Yoshiko.

A flood of longing swelled in Madeleine's chest. "Kellie always wanted to see them."

"Do *you* want to see them?"

"I do, but—I dunno. It'll be bittersweet, you know? I'll probably bawl."

"You might, and that's perfectly okay."

Madeleine stared over the laptop at the TV. "At least it'll be less embarrassing on my own."

Yoshiko lifted her peppermint mocha. "How come?"

Two women on the television squealed as they set a Christmas pudding ablaze. Madeleine rescued the remote from the duvet, muting them. "The cabbie I told you about, Julian? He's booked tomorrow, so I'll be flying solo, which is fine. I'm sure I can find the movie sights online easy enough tonight, figure out directions…"

"It might be cathartic, though," said Yoshiko. "If it's something she always wanted to do, it could be a way to honor her."

Madeleine lifted her chin. Perhaps Yoshiko was onto something. Maybe this idea was one way to feel closer to Kellie? Paying tribute to her in the city she adored from afar but never got to visit? There was only one way to find out.

128

Thirteen

MADELEINE

Three days until Christmas

Dashing across All Saints Road in Notting Hill, Madeleine hugged her tote against her coat and dodged a passing black cab, its driver blonde and female and obviously not Julian. She paused on the curb, her eyes darting from driver to driver, searching as a shiny trio of taxis paraded past.

This is stupid. She pouted. *As if I'm going to magically bump into him here. Maybe I should send him a quick...* Pulling out her phone, she hovered over her texts, but guilt yanked her fingers away. *No! Today is all about Kellie—not me, not Julian or some holiday flirtation with no possible future. Honestly, if I was going to fix our crappy goodbye, I should've done it last night.*

Instead of texting Julian, Madeleine had spent the previous evening scouring blogs and entertainment websites for the UK filming locations from *Love Actually* and *The Holiday*. The former was shot mostly in London, unlike the latter which would require a train journey or a car, so she chose Hugh Grant's city flick over Jude Law's countryside romp.

Come on, girl, enough about the cute cabbie. Keep your head in the game and let's do this.

Straightening her shoulders, she breezed around a street corner, arriving on the sturdy cobblestones of St. Luke's Mews, a narrow road of terraced houses facing one another.

Charming and colorful with potted plants gracing doorsteps and whimsical Juliet balconies overhead, the structures on St. Luke's Mews were built in the late 1800s and served as horse stables, carriage houses, and servants' quarters for the wealthy residents on neighboring Lancaster Road and Westbourne Park Road. However, by the early 20th century when the clip-clop of horse hooves faded from the capital, the quaint buildings were reborn as residences for Londoners seeking a quiet, quirky respite.

London was home to many photogenic mews, but only one was made famous by a fictional art gallery owner named Mark proclaiming his unrequited love with cue cards on a St. Luke's Mews doorstep.

I spy pink! Madeleine adjusted her headphones and skipped ahead, bubbling with anticipation.

Four doors down on her right stood Juliet's house from *Love Actually*. Actors Andrew Lincoln and Keira Knightley were nowhere to be seen, but the spot was unmistakeable: windows trimmed in white paint with sparkly lights strewn haphazardly behind glass, cobbles underfoot, and the old stable doors hinting at an equine past. *Just one more thing to complete the scene.* Madeleine took a deep breath and hit play on her phone, and "Silent Night", the version sung by soprano Helen Snow in the film, filled her headphones.

I made it, Kellie. I'm here in front of your dream house.

Sorrow dampened her eyes as she gazed upon the home her best friend adored, once declaring during an online binge-watch 'To me, you are perfect.' The house was the same and yet different...the brick more rose pink than the blush in the film, and an interloper, a pistachio-hued bicycle, stood guard on its kickstand alongside three potted trees, adding an Instagram-worthy *je ne sais quoi* for passing film fanatics. The day's muted sunlight defied the nighttime somberness of the movie's best-known (and often imitated) scene, but it didn't matter, not to Madeleine.

"I don't need cue cards to tell you how much you'll always mean to me, Kel," her trembling lips whispered as she pored over the pink house and its neighbors, doused in sapphire and indigo blue paint. Standing silent and still, she sniffed away tears, committing the delightful mews to memory. *You always wanted to live here. I should be taking a photo of you, smiling in your happy place...*

Madeleine raised her phone and took a snap from a respectable distance, mindful that the house was someone's private home.

"TATYANA, THIS IT?"

The booming male voice rattled Madeleine's reverie. Draped in a black coat and a cashmere scarf tossed jauntily over his left shoulder, a slim twentysomething, all dark brooding stubble and growing impatience, rounded the corner dragging a large Louis Vuitton suitcase, its wheels click-click-clacking furiously over the uneven stones. He parked it with a disdainful thud beside the bushy tree shielding the house next door and whipped out a vape pen from his coat pocket as a sulking blonde caught up, her movements laboured as if walking through treacle. The blue, tarp-like item spilling from her arms didn't help, nor did her ground-grazing dress and its river of aqua ruffles fighting her legs with every step.

Madeleine pulled off her headphones.

"I want the pink house *and* the navy one," the woman demanded in a strong Russian accent as a steel pole slipped from the blue cloud in her arms, scraping its dissatisfaction across the peaks and valleys of the old cobbles.

What on earth is she carrying? Is that...a tent? Madeleine's nose crinkled as she stepped back.

The woman huffed loudly. "Sergei, help me!" She dumped her unruly cargo onto the stones, and a piercing metal clank reverberated down St. Luke's Mews. Several gauzy white curtains twitched across the street. "I need to change into the emerald gown NOW!"

On second thought, Kel, maybe you wouldn't want to live here... Swerving the Insta-invasion, Madeleine dove into her phone and walked away, following the directions to her next movie location.

Checking off from her *Love Actually* locations list both the Grosvenor Chapel in Mayfair where Juliet and Peter got hitched (to an impromptu rendition of The Beatles' "All You Need is Love")

and Selfridges on Oxford Street (disappointingly, not *one* of the busy jewelry clerks resembled Mr. Bean), Madeleine decamped south of the Thames.

First up, she wandered along Barge House Street in the lovelorn footsteps of Andrew Lincoln's Mark, playing Dido's "Here With Me" through her headphones. She paused and took photos of the old warehouse which 'portrayed' his flat in the film, then turned left and entered the cozy courtyard of the Oxo Tower Wharf complex. Relaxing holiday shoppers sat around small tables and drank frothy coffees in the shadow of the tall Christmas tree as she swept past, channeling Mark in his mournful escape. While his heart was heavy with yearning for the just-married Juliet (to his best friend, no less), Madeleine's was consumed with thoughts of Kellie and how much she would've loved this whirlwind cinematic adventure around the capital.

This scene was Kel's favorite. She loved the music, loved Andrew Lincoln's angst. Ah, that sweet agony of unrequited love. We've all been there.

Passing through the Oxo Tower's glass doors, she tugged her scarf tighter against the riverside breeze and joined the Queen's Walk, the footpath overlooking the Thames. Mark's Dido-themed scene ended here with him ruefully storming off, brushing his fingers along the brick railing, but Madeleine rewrote the script. She stopped for a few photos of St. Paul's Cathedral rising across the river, then headed in the opposite direction toward Gabriel's Wharf, an outdoor marketplace of restaurants, art galleries, and independent shops selling jewelry, clothing, and fair trade products. It was also home to a special bench from *Love Actually* where lovestruck little Sam shared a secret with his stepdad, Daniel.

A few new skyscrapers reached for the clouds on the other side of the Thames, but the river and the semicircle designs in the iron railings were *just* like in the movie. Two of the three wooden benches were free, so she claimed the middle one and turned off her music. She pulled out a bottle of water from her tote and downed a large gulp, but the refreshing drink did little to quell the flutters taking flight in her belly.

It's time to open it. There's no putting it off any longer.

Setting the bottle aside, she gripped her phone tightly with both hands and opened email. She scrolled down to the 'starred' file, tapping its sole resident.

From: Kellie Nguyen
To: Madeleine Joy
Date: Wednesday, December 23, 2020 at 6:06 a.m.
Subject: IN LONDON? OPEN ME!

The message had lived in her email for a year, untouched and unopened. It wasn't the last correspondence she had received from her best friend. That was a cherished text, a bubbly ramble. This email was one she hadn't had the heart to open...until now.

She sucked in a long, slow breath and tentatively let it go.

Hey, Mad Joy! If you're reading this, you're in London and we're one step closer to big squishy hugs—eight years in the making! Since your flight gets in five hours before mine, I've come up with a few ideas to keep you out of trouble. Knowing how you're completely up for new adventures, new people, new things, you'll probably check all these boxes before I even arrive at our hotel! LOL. But please save a FEW to do with me, okay? Oh, except the last one. With that, you're on your own!

Madeleine's heart pined and ached as Kellie's accent, all endearing sass and Australian casual, drifted through her head. *I can picture you so clearly. You and your adorable, crooked grin.*

1. Indulge in your weird sandwich flex. You'll see a chain of shops called Pret a Manger. They sell sandwiches to-go in triangle boxes. It's your nirvana, ya big nerd!

133

A ghost of a smile parted Madeleine's lips. *You know me so well—* Her mind snagged on her own words. *Dammit!* She scrunched her eyes and swallowed, fighting the sadness thickening her throat. *You* knew *me so well.* 'Knew' felt too final, too permanent, an unscalable brick wall separating yesterday from today. There was no going back. Shaking her head slowly, Madeleine blinked back her tears and read on.

2. Find the bombed-out ruins of St. Dunstan in the East, between London Bridge and the Tower of London. Two walls and a tower are all that's left of this Medieval church destroyed during WWII. It's now a beautiful public garden with trees, overgrown ivy, and a small fountain. Sounds gorgeous, right? It's perfect if you crave some alone time.

If Kellie recommended St. Dunstan, it was a must-see. Madeleine glanced up, her watery eyes skipping across the Thames and to the right where the red and white-painted steel of Blackfriars Bridge stretched across the river. *Can I walk there?* After a morning riding vertigo-inducing escalators and stuffy Tube trains, a leisurely aboveground stroll through the capital was as tempting as the Cadbury Wispa chocolate bar lurking in her tote.

3. One word: cookies. Okay, two more: Fortnum & Mason. Head to Piccadilly, find F&M. You'll thank me later, Cookie Monster. The ground floor IS Christmas with special teas, cookies, and confectionary as far as the eye can see. I'm telling you now, we'll be there A LOT!

4. Fall head over heels for a hot Brit boy! I know, I know— you'll bristle at my suggestion because you're faithful to he-who-ain't-good-enough-for-you, but hey, if I meet a gorgeous Englishman on the plane, you are SO toast! (I jest... *maybe?!*). But honestly, what would be better than a snog

(love that word!) with a cute British bloke? I want that for you. And if you don't find him, I'll just have to make sure to find him FOR you!

Madeleine's heart panged as she laughed through tears. *Like Julian?* His adorable smile, his quiet confidence—even the way "Maddie" slipped playfully from his tongue. *Oh, you'd like him, Kel. He's the kind of guy who walks on the sunny side of the street.* She sighed. *But I've blown it, before it even began.* Bowing her head, she reluctantly parked the cute cabbie in the back of her mind.

So there you go, Mad Joy! Just enough ideas to keep you busy until I arrive. I am SO freaking excited about exploring London with you—for real, in the flesh! We'll hit the best locations from *Love Actually* and *The Holiday*. Maybe we should resurrect our crappy fan fic—lol! (btw, calling dibs now on Jude Law's seat in that pub!), see all the Christmas lights, and celebrate the holidays like it's our last (that's my not-so-secret code for pub crawls, Brit boy snogs, and a Christmassy cocktail—or twelve)! And if we're lucky, maybe it will even snow.

Take good care of my London until I get there. WE'RE GONNA BE TOGETHER, FINALLY! Eeeeeee! Best Christmas present ever! Cheerio, babe—for now! See you soon and brace yourself for some mega hugs. Warning: I will *never* let you go.

Love ya more than tacos,

Kellie xoxo

Madeleine dabbed tears from her eyes and blew out her cheeks, avoiding the mouth-breathing stare from a passing jogger. *Oh, Kellie. Your excitement, your determination to meet me—it's all here in your own words. You didn't want to wait a year. I didn't force you to come.* A flood of relief rippled through her chest. Twelve long months of agonizing guilt and regret soothed by Kellie's email. *Yoshiko's right. I need to forgive myself, need to let my guilt go.* She sniffed.

I have to try.

Madeleine studied St. Paul's across the river, its magnificent dome piercing the heavens where a cluster of clouds rolled off toward the east. *Carrying on without you is the hardest thing I've ever done. Every day I wonder where you are, if you're okay. God, I hope you're okay.* She wiped her cheeks. *If you are, please tell me? Give me a sign...*

FOURTEEN

JULIAN

Escaping the lunchtime traffic, Julian expertly tucked his black cab into the vacant space between two parallel-parked taxis in the center of Kensington Park Road, his grin coinciding with the unmistakeable aroma of sizzling bacon invading his open window. *Bacon makes almost everything better.*

The welcoming scent was courtesy of a rectangular green shed—a cabman's shelter—boldly planted in the middle of the busy street. Serving up affordable hot meals, non-alcoholic drinks, and a warm space to sit (although with little to no leg room), the small, wooden huts first appeared on London's roads in 1875 and catered exclusively to a clientele of licensed cab drivers with horse-drawn carriages. As cars replaced horses, many shelters were abandoned or bulldozed to make way for the growing city, leaving only a lucky thirteen still standing. The Kensington Park Road shelter was Julian's favorite, and he made a point of visiting the Grade II listed structure for breakfast or lunch at least twice a week, hoping his patronage would prevent another invaluable piece of London's past from disappearing forever.

Despite his mouth watering in anticipation of a bacon sandwich smothered in salty Daddies Sauce, Julian hit pause on his lunch expedition and tapped a saved number on his phone.

"Hey, Jules!"

"Happy Birthday, mate!" He turned off the cab's engine and flung off his seatbelt. "How's it been so far?"

"Quiet, strangely," said Micah. "We've been open since nine and have had a grand total of three customers, tops. Tash is here, eating a chocolate orange and scouring the *Radio Times*, circling all

137

the Christmas specials she wants to watch. Oh, she's waving. Says hi."

"Hey, Tash!"

"Natasha"—Micah's voice strayed from the phone—"Jules says hi back...sorry, what?"

The younger Cooper mumbled something in the background.

"You need to know this *now*?" Micah tsked, his tone heavy with annoyance. "My sister is mid-circle and wants to know what you'd pick: the *Gogglebox* special or *Britain's Got Talent at Christmas*?"

"There's only one answer: *Top of the Pops*."

"Jules says *Christmas University Challenge*," he hollered back with a snicker. "Maybe she'll learn something—*hey*!"

"What am I missing?" asked Julian.

"She chucked a French hen at me."

"A what?"

"I'm finishing a custom order for three needle felted French hens, two turtle doves, and a partridge," said Micah. "No pear tree, though. Shame that."

"I know a few people I'd like to stick pins in..." Julian winced, his stomach snarling beneath his burgundy sweater.

"Today's Insta-tourists getting on your wick?"

"And then some. I've been driving them around for nearly six and a half hours. We started early, around six, so they could get Tower Bridge and Piccadilly Circus before they got too busy."

"Yeah—busy with annoying people just like them," said Micah. "I tell ya, the number of times I've arrived at the store and had to shoo people away from the doors. And the thing is, I get it. Yeah, Coal Drops Yard looks great on the 'gram, but all these Insta-fools seem to forget we live and work around here. It's not their virtual playground."

Julian picked up a red rectangular box from the console and parked it in his lap. "Oh, you'll *love* this: they brought along a tent."

"Whaaat? Why?"

"For costume changes on the street."

Micah snorted with contempt. "Bloody hell! You think you've seen everything…"

"You should see their itinerary. Everything's planned out with military precision."

"Okay, then, for shits and giggles, let's play London Insta Bingo!" Micah snickered. "They asked to see the Sky Garden…"

"Yep."

"The bakery in Belgravia painted pink, oh what's it called—Peggy Porschen!"

"Yep." Julian tilted the fancy cardboard, and three small chocolate-covered balls rolled into his palm. He promptly tossed them in his mouth.

"And the carousel and skating rink outside the Natural History Museum."

"Three for three, Meeks. Well done." Julian crunched away in lieu of a proper breakfast.

"Ergh, Jules, stop munching in my ear!" Micah tsked.

He swallowed sharply, remembering his friend's eating-on-the-phone phobia. "Uh, sorry! I haven't had breakfast and I'm bloody starving." Glancing over his shoulder, he eyeballed a large wicker basket. "My customers bought a huge £1,000 Christmas hamper from Fortnum's, then went to town on it in the back of my cab, scoffing smoked salmon, aged cheddar, caviar…"

"And just like that, my pimped-up bowl of porridge with sliced banana and chocolate chips feels rather unsatisfying," mused Micah. "I guess they didn't toss you any scraps."

"Just this box of sweets. They taste like posh Maltesers. They're"—Julian turned the festive packaging around—"Reindeer Noses." *Madeleine would love these.* Rattling the box, he unearthed the sole red one. "Oh! Found Rudolph's."

"So, where are they now?"

"The Russians? On Lancaster Road."

"Posing in front of the candy-colored houses?" asked Micah.

"Probably. Notting Hill should keep them busy for a while. They'll text when they're ready to move on to Harrods. To be honest, I could do without all this running around today. Normally, it doesn't bug me, but—"

"You're wondering what Madeleine's up to."

Julian paused. "There is that."

"So I take it yesterday went...well?"

"More than well. It was pretty damn perfect. We talked for several hours over tea, then decided to hang out. We wandered around the South Bank, saw the market." Julian left the box of candy in the console.

"And?"

"*And* we shopped, went to Covent Garden—"

"Home of the massive mistletoe. AND?!?!" Micah pressed.

"I didn't snog her if that's what you're digging for."

"Julian Halliwell, I'm *disappointed* in you. Didn't you want to?"

"Of course I did."

"Did you try?" asked Micah.

"No! I'm not going to jump her! Jesus, Meeks!"

"I wasn't suggesting that! What do you take me for?"

"Well?!" Another cabbie walked past, nose deep in a thick bacon sandwich. Julian closed his window and lowered his voice. "Stop banging on it about it."

"Jules, sometimes you need a little shove..."

"Not with this I don't. I'm not gonna try something when she sees me as just a friend. Trust me, she's not interested in anything more."

"And you could tell *how*? You are SO out of practice." Micah tutted.

"Ouch. Firm but fair. I'll admit—it's been a while."

"It wouldn't be if you'd listened to me. But no, you'd rather spend weekends crate-digging in Peckham instead of swiping right on your phone. Seriously, what hot-blooded bloke would choose searching through musty old vinyl over a shag?"

"This one." Julian's gaze flitted upward. "Micah, for the millionth time, I'm not interested in hooking up, not now, not ever."

"But mate, as lovely as all your records are, Kylie and Beyoncé won't keep you warm at night."

"Maybe not, but at least I know where I stand and I'm always guaranteed a bloody good time. I seriously doubt I could say that after using some ridiculous app—"

"But Madeleine's not on an app!" Micah stepped on Julian's words. "She's real and here and you're gonna miss your chance if you don't do something quick."

You don't think I know that?

"I think she's great, and Tash can't stop talking about her. It's so rare for people to give my sister the time of day. They see goth and look the other way, but Madeleine's a diamond. She was kind and chatty, never rude. Have you talked to her today?"

"No. It's been go-go-go this morning, and to be honest, I refuse to come off as some weird stalker dude checking up on her, especially now that we're friends and not just, you know—cabbie and customer." A frown brewing, Julian raked a hand through his thick hair. "Look, there's something you should know. Madeleine left early last night before we had dinner. She got a text while we were shopping and her whole demeanor changed."

"Who was it from? Her sister?"

"No, it wasn't Shantelle."

"Hmm. Maybe work, then?" asked Micah. "Emergencies happen, right? Even on holiday."

"I guess, but whoever it was, she wanted to video-call in private. I dropped her at the hotel and that was that. I texted later, but she sent me two quick emojis and nothing else."

"Oh! Which ones?"

"A face blowing a kiss and a smiley hug. I have no idea how to interpret them." Julian grimaced. "Was she feeling warm and fuzzy about me, my text? Was it a kiss *goodbye*? Or was she happy about whatever was going on with her call? This is why I hate emojis. So ambiguous."

"Well, at least she seemed to be in a good mood, eh?"

Julian closed his eyes and rubbed his forehead, frustrated with

Micah, with everything. "Like that helps."

"Mate, don't hate me for saying this, but is there any chance her call was with a bloke? A boyfriend?"

"Why are you asking me that?!" Julian sat up. "*You* were the one who told me she was single."

"But did you ask *her*?"

"She said she didn't have a boyfriend."

"Fuuuck!" Micah blew out his lips. "Maybe she lied…"

"Maybe?" Julian huffed into a wince. "But you know, I'm done speculating. I did enough of that last night."

"What about googling her? There's gotta be personal info out there, somewhere."

"I already did. Christ, now I *really* feel like a stalker, admitting that."

Micah snorted. "You are the antithesis of a stalker. Most guys would've looked her up on day one, not day four. Did you find anything good?"

"Only a Sensoria press release announcing her promotion. She has social media accounts, but—"

"You don't. Let me see what's out there. Gimme a minute."

While Micah searched online, Julian finished the box of Fortnum's sweets and tried not to read anything into the random cursing coming down the phone from his best friend. After a minute or two, Micah returned to the call.

"No luck, mate. All her social media is set to private. Did you check out Shantelle's?"

"I saw some of her photos. You and Tash were right, they do look a lot alike. But it was getting late and I had to be up early for work, so I put on some playlists and nodded off."

"Not Madeleine's playlists?" asked Micah.

"Er, yeah, they were."

"Fuck me, Jules! You must have it bad if you created a Sensoria account."

"Guilty as charged," he muttered and removed his glasses, rubbing his eyes. "Anyway…"

"Well, there's only one thing for it: you have to ask her out," said Micah.

"Mate, she's well out of my league."

"Bollocks! Stop selling yourself short. That's all Caroline's doing, and you know what? She's full of shit. So, c'mon! You have to find out a) is Madeleine truly single, and b) if your feelings are reciprocated."

"Yeah, that's a great idea." Julian scoffed. "Set myself up for some massive rejection, just in time for Christmas…"

"Go on! Put on your big boy pants and ask her. She might say yes and you'll have a smashing time."

"And when would I do that? She might be gone tomorrow. That leaves—"

"Oh shit, fuck, bollocks!" Micah groaned. "Tonight. That leaves tonight. Dammit!"

A text pinged in Julian's ear. "Meeks, gimme a sec…" He lowered his phone.

Natasha: I hear what my bro is sayin'. Don't you dare mess up his 30th. Tonight has to be stellar. I owe him so much and so do YOU. I expect you and that bday cake, all right? NO EXCUSES!

Bollocks, yeah, his cake. Have to get to Spitalfields. Julian pressed his phone to his ear. "Sorry, was a text—not from Madeleine…" He glanced up, catching his influencer clients on the approach as his stomach let out a long, dissatisfied growl. "Mate, I gotta run. My customers are headed back. Look, don't worry. I'll see you tonight. Your thirtieth is gonna be one to remember."

FIFTEEN

MADELEINE

The peal of distant church bells drew a smile as Madeleine slowly swiveled, admiring the quiet majesty of the ruins of St. Dunstan in the East. *Who ordered the beautiful bells? I bet it was you, Kel. You always loved them.*

Twisting toward the impressive Gothic-style tower and its surviving steeple designed by Sir Christopher Wren, the architect responsible for St. Paul's Cathedral, she snapped one final photograph and lowered her phone with a satisfied sigh. *Kellie was right, as usual. This place is special.*

Madeleine perched upon a wooden bench in what once was the nave and gazed at St. Dunstan's northern wall, one of only two left standing after an incendiary WWII bomb tore through the roof and destroyed most everything in its path. Through the years, winding vines, climbing flowers, and soaring trees had overtaken what remained, lending new life and a poignant resiliency to the scarred shell. She studied the arched windows, their stained glass long gone, replaced by overgrown greenery.

Such a beautiful church.

The unthinkable left you broken, but you survived...

A wistful smile slowly met her eyes.

But the rumbles growing louder in her belly weren't deterred by the breathtaking scenery or Madeleine's moment of reflection. Easing back into the bench, she removed a triangle-shaped box from her tote, a sandwich from Pret a Manger, the popular shop Kellie recommended. "*Christmas Lunch*, huh?" She peered through the plastic window. "I'm not sure about this, but let's give you a whirl."

She tore open the cardboard hatch and liberated half of the

sandwich, sinking her teeth into the soft granary bread. Layers of succulent turkey breast and herby pork stuffing mingled happily on her tongue with the tangy kick of port and orange cranberry sauce and a surprise burst of zesty mayo. Her lips drew into a taut grin. This sandwich was nothing like the turkey and stuffing crisps at the pub, thank goodness! Devouring another mouthful, her smile grew along with her gratitude as she watched a squirrel scurry across the church floor. *Whoever created this should be knighted. Christmas dinner between bread! Kel, you are on fire! First St. Dunstan, now this. You're two for two!*

She paused momentarily, resting her new favorite sandwich in its red and gold box on her lap. Two items remained on Kellie's email list: a trip to Fortnum & Mason and finding the perfect British guy. Happiness drained from Madeleine's eyes.

Yeah yeah, I know, you're probably cursing me out right now for choosing my grief counselor over Julian last night, but you're not here, Kel, living this weird new life. Sometimes I need to speak with someone who understands—someone who can help me find my way. She sighed, rummaging in her bag. *And as for Julian, he's a lovely guy, but I'm not sure.* The last thing Madeleine needed was to have her bruised and battered heart shattered by a holiday fling.

Over the past year, comforts had been few and far between, but food always stepped in, giving her a temporary lift—even if it meant she'd regret it later. Madeleine freed a plastic-wrapped cookie from her tote. Topped with a 'melting' snowman made from a smiley-faced marshmallow and a hardened puddle of white icing, the gingerbread biscuit was called Melvin—"*Melvin the Melting Snowman*". His wide chocolate eyes and skewed grin looked up innocently.

"Why did they give you a name?" Madeleine mumbled through her frown as she popped open his plastic prison. "It makes it harder to eat you."

Luckily for Melvin, his demise was put on hold by a soaring chorus of "Disco 2000". Her gaze darted to the lit phone and her black squirrel screensaver vibrating on the bench beside her.

Julian Halliwell

Eyes widening, her pulse took off with a gallop, the fizz of nerves mixing with unbridled glee. *What do I do? Apologize? Pretend nothing's weird? Ugh, the way I left things...*

As Madeleine debated and Jarvis Cocker sang on, curious stares flew her way. An older couple glared over their takeout teas and a family playing impromptu hopscotch on the stones halted mid-skip. *You're being a nuisance. Just answer the damn thing!* She abandoned Melvin on her lap and grabbed her phone. "Julian, hi! How are you?"

"Hey! I'm great! Works going well, it's not too cold, can't complain. You?"

"I'm good, thanks." She answered a little too quickly. "I'm in St. Dunstan in the East."

"No way! I was there this morning with my clients. They're Insta-influencers. I'm driving them around so they can fill their 'gram with picture-perfect images of their OTT jet-setting lives." Julian raised his voice, competing with the shrill wail of an ambulance's siren in the background as it sped past. "They even brought a TENT for costume changes."

Hang on—was that them on St. Luke's Mews? Bizarre. She shook her head. "Where are you now?"

"Outside Harrods. They're inside somewhere, probably drooling over a £9,000 advent calendar or posing beside a solid crystal bathtub filled with caviar."

"That's a thing?"

"If it is, they'll bloody well find it. I've been biding my time, stretching my legs and checking out the holiday windows. As per usual, they're completely over the top, lots of green and gold, plenty of glitz, but the displays down the road at Harvey Nics are more my thing. They reminded me of you, actually."

"Why?" She giggled nervously, returning Melvin to her tote. "Wait, don't tell me—they featured felt reindeer?"

"Sadly, no. Rudolph and his gal pals were nowhere in sight, but they did have silver stars, disco balls, and a huge neon installation spelling out BAH HUMBUG!"

"It's my Scrooge mother ship calling me!" Madeleine's eyes followed several little white flecks floating in the air. *Is that ash? Or snow?* The fine sprinkles landed on her wool coat.

"So, what have you been up to?"

She cleared her throat. "Well, I stared at my work in progress over breakfast, then wandered around Notting Hill and the South Bank, sat for a bit at Gabriel's Wharf watching the Thames. That was nice."

"Sounds like you've been trapped in a Richard Curtis movie." He chuckled.

Was that disdain in his voice? Madeleine winced. "Uh, yeah, kinda? I found Shakespeare's Globe and Borough Market. Had the best brownie of my life there, then crossed London Bridge, saw the Monument to the Great Fire, and eventually ended up here."

"Did you go up?"

"The Monument? Yep. Climbed all 300 steps. Nearly killed me! Great views, though." Her smile grew as a few more delicate flakes swirled on the breeze. "Now, I'm replacing all the calories I burned with a Christmas sandwich from Pret."

"Now *that* shop is your true mother ship, right there. How'd you like it?" he asked.

"I loved it. So many sandwiches, so little time, but this one is a Christmas miracle."

"It's also a London rite of passage. Congrats, Maddie, you're one of us now!"

"Well, that's nice of you to say, but my Cockney rhyming slang needs serious work. I went to withdraw some money today and found this wacky ATM."

"You're kidding?! The cashpoints with Cockney?"

"As a language option! I can't believe they're a real thing." She brushed the snowflakes off her coat, but they left behind an unfestive dusty smear. *Ah, yuck! It's ash.* She pressed harder, rubbing away the ghostly white grit.

"Well, I hate to break it to you, but they're not, unfortunately. A few were installed before the 2012 Olympics, but most are long gone now. Did it ask for your Huckleberry Finn or something?"

"It did! Thank god the screen said 'PIN' beneath it, otherwise I'd still be standing there, scratching my head. So I entered my code and then it asked me if I wanted 'fast sausage and mash.'"

"Cash! Were the denominations in Cockney, too?" His voice was buoyant and light. "Lady Godiva for a fiver, speckled hen for a ten?"

"Yep! Dirty for thirty pounds. I totally cracked up! I was laughing and uh, crying—"

"As you do…" Julian added warmly.

"And the shop owner was giving me some serious stink-eye from behind his newspapers. I couldn't figure out the last denomination, though. It said *double top*?"

"That's a darts reference," said Julian. "Means double twenty, so forty pounds."

"Well, there you go. I learn something new every day." She paused. As much as she loved chatting about fun, frivolous things, dancing around what she really wanted to say wasn't lessening the regret gnawing her belly. "Julian, about last night…I'm sorry I didn't text you back."

"But you did."

"Yeah, with emojis, but I meant to send you more than that. When you texted, I was in the middle of my video call with my friend and—"

"Is your friend okay?"

Typical Julian: thoughtful, concerned. And me? I'm being evasive, twisting the truth. Madeleine winced. *And for what reason? So he won't reject me? At this point, it doesn't really matter. It's not like I'll be seeing him again.*

She sucked in a big breath and let it go. "Actually, she's not my friend. She's…my therapist. A cancellation came up last night and it was the only time we could connect before the holidays. That's why I bailed in Covent Garden. I'm sorry I ran out of there with only a vague explanation." Closing her eyes, she waited. Waited for the usual awkward pause, followed by a flustered excuse and the call wrapping up. Grief wasn't the only thing that made people bolt.

But the pause never came, and Julian's lovely accent returned without hesitation.

"Madeleine, there's no need to apologize. Seriously." His tone sounded strangely relieved. "Your health and well-being are way more important than a pub dinner and some drinks."

She opened her eyes, lost for words. No stigma, no judgment? From the stiff-upper-lip British guy?

"Really, I'm glad she could fit you in," he said.

"Yeah, me too." She proceeded cautiously, wondering if Julian's empathy was too good to be true. "I always feel better afterward."

"I hear you on that score." His reply was overtaken by the crackling rumble of a motorcycle speeding past in the background.

Did I hear that right? Madeleine jerked her head back. "You see a therapist?"

"I did for a while, after I lost my job and then when Mum died." He quieted for a beat. "That's not something I share with a lot of people."

"I don't blame you. Not everyone understands or is supportive."

"Exactly. I mean, Micah's been great. Actually, all the Coopers have been. It's just a shame the same can't be said for my brother," said Julian.

"Ah, that's awful. I'm so sorry."

"Yeah, well, nothing weeds out your address book like an emotionally charged, life-changing event."

I had no idea we had this in common.

"That's why I'm selective about who I tell...and trust."

Warm gratitude embraced her heart. "Well, thank you for trusting *me*."

"Right back at ya." A smile rose in his voice. "Listen, I know how exhausting therapy sessions can be. Lots of times I'd be shattered afterward, so please don't beat yourself up over the emoji texts. It was just nice to hear from you. I hope you don't mind, me calling like this…"

"No, not at all." She grinned. "I appreciate it." *So much.* "And you are so right about therapy being exhausting. I fell asleep with my laptop, woke up at four a.m. with a crick in my neck, the TV still on. Oh, and there was this documentary about a jewel heist? They showed a street sign for Hatton Garden. Wasn't that the place mentioned on the blue plaque above our table at the pub quiz?"

"Yep, the very same. The guys sat at that table, planned the heist right there."

"And they were seniors!" said Madeleine.

"Just goes to show you, peer pressure is alive and well, even in your sixties." He laughed. "Did you get in touch with any of your sister's friends?"

Shantelle's friends had completely slipped Madeleine's mind. "Oh! Yeah, they're kinda busy, you know, Christmas stuff…"

"Ah, that's a shame. I'm sorry you've been on your own."

"Oh, it's fine. It's good prep for Paris in case Shantelle bumps into one of her old work colleagues. They don't mean to be, but sometimes they're a bit self-absorbed."

"Well, I know London isn't Paris, but"—his voice was full of warmth—"it has got *one* thing the French capital doesn't: us. Tash, Micah, me—you're not alone here, Maddie. If you want company, you got it."

She pined for him, his friends. "Thanks, that's really kind. I'd love to see everyone again, somehow."

"Well, that's why I'm calling, actually. Look, it's Micah's thirtieth birthday and he's throwing a house party later on. It'll be pretty laid back, lots of food, dancing…" The screech of a truck's brakes made him temporarily pause.

I'll get to see him again! A breath caught in Madeleine's chest.

"…and birthday cake! I was wondering if you'd maybe like to go with me…as my date?"

As his whaaaat? Her jaw dropped.

The cheerful birdsong high in the trees, Melvin the Melted Snowman, and the young family playing hopscotch on St. Dunstan's stone floor all faded away, evaporated by those three little words.

He wants to go out with me! Madeleine's eyes sparkled as sprinkles of ash fell gently from the cloudy sky. *Kellie, you might get your wish. But...is this ridiculous? We both know it'll be over before it really begins. I'll be in Paris in no time...*

Her delay sparked his concern. "Err...Maddie, you still there? Hello?"

"I'm here, Julian. Sure! What time are you picking me up?"

Sixteen

"Falling in love again was gradual,
like the volume being turned up."
Corinne Bailey Rae

MADELEINE

"This street looks like something out of a movie." Hugging a tin of chocolate, caramel, and confetti gourmet popcorn for Micah, Madeleine's eyes swept the tight semicircle of Victorian terraced houses on Keystone Crescent. The cobbled street, hidden away in a quiet pocket of King's Cross, featured tiny two- and three-storey homes on both sides, each one with a curved façade, Flemish bond brickwork, and black iron railings. Multi-colored lights blinked hello from several of the sash windows while a handful of sparkly Christmas trees peeked outward, suggesting that warmth, goodwill, and laughter awaited within. "It's so charming and tucked away, like a secret," said Madeleine, enamored by a whimsical ice skate wreath on a passing door festooned with trimmed evergreen boughs and silver baubles.

"It's always been a favorite of mine," said Julian, both of his hands occupied by a large box containing Micah's birthday cake. A bulging Sister Ray Records fabric tote hung from his shoulder, stuffed with two bottles of white wine, a six-pack of long-necked beers, and several small holiday gifts including his coveted homemade marmalade and the candy dish Madeleine purchased for Natasha. "Micah was stuck on the waiting list for a rental here for ages but finally got the call last May." With a tilt of his head, he gestured over his shoulder toward Caledonian Road. "A plaque back there says it's the smallest crescent in Europe."

"I believe it. The curve of the buildings is so sharp! It feels really intimate. Everyone must know each other, right?"

"And each other's business. It's hard to keep things on the down low here, living on such a narrow street. Meeks usually invites most of his neighbors to his parties. Cuts down on gossip and noise complaints." Julian slowed in front of a house on the crescent's inner circle, its five narrow black steps leading to an arched entrance and a door painted Manchester City blue. A glittery silver wreath made from mini disco balls hung above the metal mail slot between the door's two frosted windows. "This is it."

Madeleine adjusted the purse hanging from her shoulder. *My first party in a year.* She sucked in a breath, her eyes tracing the flashing blue and purple Christmas lights trimming the sole window on the ground floor. Poppy vocals and rhythmic trumpets rattled the glass, but a gauzy white curtain kept most of the inside festivities under wraps. *I'm out of practice, going to parties...and on dates.* Her knuckles blanched as her grip tightened around Micah's gift. "I'm a bit nervous. New people alert!" she half-joked, cracking a smile.

"Maddie, they're gonna love you! They're a good lot—like Micah and Tash, friendly and fun, always game for a laugh. But don't worry, I won't leave your side till you feel comfortable."

She laced her arm through his, her hand giving his bicep a squeeze. "Thank you."

Contentment warmed Julian's face. "Have I told you how gorgeous you look?"

"Maybe once or twice." She blushed, glancing at the skirt of her *Frill-Seekers* original, a surprise from Shantelle and her designer friend, Leia Scott. When Madeleine pried open the large box in her hotel room and sifted past several layers of tissue paper, her jaw dropped. What had she done to deserve this symphony of elegant lace and sumptuous silk? Romantic and chic in the most flattering lilac hue Madeleine had ever set eyes upon, the one-of-a-kind, up-cycled garment was *the* perfect party dress, and if Julian's rapt attention and multiple compliments were anything to go by, he wholeheartedly agreed, too.

Micah's door flew open and out spilled Natasha rocking freshly dyed cherry red hair and a knee-length corseted dress of black velvet flock. She gestured wildly from the top step as the celebratory cheer of Meghan Trainor's "Holidays" escaped from behind her. "Jules, hurry! Before Meeks sees that box!" Her heavily kohled eyes veered to Madeleine's hand on Julian's arm, launching her dark lips into a cheek-squeezing grin.

After spiriting away their booze, coats, and Julian's marmalade—about which she raved, "It tastes like liquid sunshine on a summer's day!"—Natasha thanked Madeleine for the skull candy dish by squeezing her so tight she could only croak a raspy "You're welcome."

"It's so perfect!" squealed Natasha, easing back from her death clench. "It's festive *and* gothy, my absolute fave combo! How'd you guess?"

Madeleine's ribs winced as her lungs expanded with air again. "You mentioned a skull candle holder at the quiz…"

"This girl's a gem, Jules!" Natasha clutched the red and green dish against her lacey bosom as her feathery false lashes fluttered. "She listens AND she gives kickass gifts!"

Madeleine met Julian's eyes, his agreement lingering on his lips.

"Yeah, she's all right." He smiled and leaned in, playfully touching Madeleine's arm while keeping the huge cake box upright. She pressed back, giving his black tie and pink dress shirt, which skimmed over his toned chest, an approving once-over. *He looks so handsome.*

"How you been enjoyin' London, Maddie?" asked Natasha.

"I love it!" she blurted. "I'm completely smitten. I wish I had more time to see and do everything."

"Well, you'll just have to conveniently miss your flight." Natasha winked as she set her candy dish on Micah's coffee table.

Madeleine snuck a sidelong look at Julian, who flashed a hopeful grin.

"So, Jules, show me this cake!" Natasha bounced on the spot.

"Oh, let me help." Madeleine carefully lifted the sizable lid and folded it back.

Natasha's jaw dropped. "THIS IS EPIC!" She stuck her nose in, ogling the ten-inch, six-layer piñata cake. "And it's got—"

"Sure does!" Julian slowly closed the box without decimating the creamy white icing, completely hidden beneath a profusion of blue sprinkles. "So, where's the birthday boy?"

"Try the kitchen or out back in the garden," said Natasha. "He'll be easy to spot. He's wearing my gift." Her eyes drifted, following a willowy blonde in a boho dress. "Hope *she* doesn't find him."

"Who?" asked Julian, scoping the crowd. "Sadie's friend?"

"Micah won't stand a chance. She's a total doppelbanger."

Madeleine laughed. "Doppel-what?"

"A doppelbanger. It's someone you'd like to fuck because they look like a famous person you fancy," Natasha explained. "Meeks has a thing for Saoirse Ronan, and that woman is a dead ringer."

"She's also married," added Julian.

"Not anymore she's not. Sadie says she divorced hubby number two and is rebounding all over the shop." Natasha pursed her dark lips. "Last thing our brother needs is another flighty fling." She motioned toward the cake. "I'll put this upstairs for safekeeping, yeah?"

"Good idea." Julian eased the box into her arms with the utmost care, and Natasha cradled it like a priceless artifact from the V&A.

"Follow us," he said. "We'll clear a safe path." He weaved his fingers gently through Madeleine's and stroked her hand with his thumb.

Delightfully warm with the perfect amount of squeeze, Julian's touch felt protective and reassuring, intimate. *I could get used to this.* Madeleine smiled to herself.

The threesome slipped past the Christmas tree and through the front-room crush of neighbors, toasting the holiday season with mulled wine martinis and the latest (and juiciest) Keystone Crescent gossip. Reaching the congested stairs, they parted ways: Natasha and the cake bound for the bedrooms while Madeleine and Julian joined the flow of guests descending to the lower ground floor. They took the steps slowly, inching past happy revelers headed in the opposite direction, hands filled with bottles of beer and topped-up wine glasses. One by one, their smiles grew as they spotted Julian and shouted over the laid-back funkiness of "Fools Gold" blaring from below.

"Jules, man!"

"Finally taking a night off, eh, Juzza?!"

"Happy hols, Halliwell!"

Julian hugged and backslapped his way down the stairs, introducing Madeleine with vigor, but his eagerness to include her was a mixed blessing. While his ebullient introductions softened the somersaults in her stomach, the social onslaught left her mind swimming in names and faces upon their arrival to the house's lowest floor where Micah's party raged all around them.

A sizable kitchen with white cupboards and walls occupied the right side of the space while what looked to be a dining room on the left had its table pushed against the wall and its surface crowded with bottles, a frothy red punch, and trays of food. A whirling disco ball hung above the action, throwing a kaleidoscope of silver stars over the happy guests while a door at the far side of the room was propped open, leading to a tiny walled garden. Guests, undaunted by the bone-chilling December damp, hung out under crisscrossing strings of Christmas lights, drinking, smoking, and playing Jumbo Jenga.

Madeleine squeezed Julian's hand. He crouched slightly so she could be heard above the music. "His house is like the TARDIS!" The subtle scent of bodywash drew her smile. *Nothing worse than a guy doused in cologne. Julian smells fresh...clean. Wonderful.*

Julian nodded at her *Doctor Who* reference and leaned into her ear, his smile flirting with her hair. "It's definitely bigger on the inside." Scanning the swarm of people, his eyes popped. "Oh, found him."

Wriggling through the jam-packed kitchen, Julian led Madeleine toward a guy wearing a black top hat, chatting and gesturing wildly within a pocket of people. "That's Tash's gift," said Julian. "Micah used to go raving dressed as the Mad Hatter but lost his original top hat somewhere in a field in Hampshire." Madeleine chuckled as Julian leaned in again. "Now it's just a nostalgia thing. He hasn't been to a rave in a while."

Steering close to Micah, they waited for a break in his conversation to say hi.

"That's asinine!" A woman winced above her martini. "He broke up with her because she was into Take That? They're a national treasure!"

Micah nodded, the animal faces on his green Banana Splits t-shirt contorting as he raised his beer bottle. "But here's the thing: could *you* ever be with someone, like long-term romantically, who loved the bands you *hated*?" He did a double take and caught Julian's eye. "MATE! C'mere!" With a megawatt grin, he threw open his arms and enveloped both Madeleine and Julian in a hug. "Ahhhh, I'm SO glad you BOTH made it!" Micah rocked sideways back and forth, jostling the couple.

"Happy Birthday!" Madeleine shifted her purse back onto her shoulder as he released them.

Julian plonked a hand on top of Micah's hat. "Nice lid, mate."

"Dead cool, right? Tash played a blinder."

"So did Maddie here." Julian nodded at the large blue tin in her grasp.

Micah's eyes flew to the popcorn. "I was hoping that was for me! May I?"

"Of course!" Madeleine offered the gift with a big smile. "Julian suggested it."

Micah pored over the label. "Ooh, confetti flavor—and chocolate! Nice one!" He nudged his hat above his brows with the tip of his beer bottle. "Edible presents are the best. What it is, right, is you have an enjoyable nosh, and then, bish bosh, they're gone! No clutter, no—"

"OH MY GOD?!" A screech cut him off.

A tall twentysomething with frizzy backcombed hair barged her way into the conversation, knocking Micah's empty bottle out of his hand. Mouth agape, her stare bored into Madeleine.

Who's this? She glanced at Julian, who rescued the rogue bottle from the floor. He looked as puzzled as she did.

"It *is* you!" The woman fussed with her faded *Lairds and Liars* t-shirt, which hung shapelessly over her black leggings. Stretched out of shape and washed too many times, it was obviously much loved. "Shouldn't you be in Paris?"

Madeleine squinted. "I'm sorry? Have we met?"

"Oh, my bad." Micah hugged his popcorn tin and gestured toward the guest. "This is Daisy. She's visiting from Belgium. Her auntie lives across the road." He grinned. "And these two here are Julian and—"

"I know who SHE is!" Ignoring Julian, Daisy invaded Madeleine's space. "Ah, you and Bastien—you guys are couple goals!"

Madeleine pointed at her ear. "I'm sorry, the music is..." She leaned in. "Me and—?"

"BASTIEN!" Daisy practically vibrated on the spot.

Oh shit. Here we go...

Julian's brows tensed in bewilderment, his gaze shifting to Madeleine. "Who's Bastien?"

He doesn't think me and Bastien are... Madeleine's eyes widened. *Does he?* Bastien Soulier was a French actor famous for his mop of shoulder-length mahogany curls and smouldering charisma. He wasn't just a fan favorite; he was also Shantelle's *Lost for Breath* love interest, the other half of her MTV Movie Award-winning 'Best Kiss'.

Madeleine shook her head. "Daisy, you've got me mixed up with my sister, Shantelle. I'm not an actress, and I've only met Bastien once." She reluctantly glanced at Julian, who pressed his lips together and slowly nodded.

Daisy blinked, considering Madeleine's response, then broke into snorty laugh. "Bwahahaha! You almost had me!" Edging closer, she stretched out her arm and snapped a bunch of uninvited selfies with Madeleine. "But don't worry! I'm cool—I won't text my friends you're here."

Oh dear. A slash of a smile tugged Madeleine's cheeks as she patiently waited for the brazen photoshoot to finish.

"Uh, Daze…?" Micah winced.

"She's telling the truth," said Julian, twisting the empty beer bottle in his hands. "Her name's Madeleine, not Shantelle."

Lowering her phone, the super fan's gape flew to Micah. He nodded, backing up his friend.

"It's an easy mistake to make. Shantelle and I look a lot alike," said Madeleine. "Can't say I've kissed Bastien either. I'm sorry to disappoint."

Daisy looked deflated. "Yeah…"

Despite Madeleine's frustration of yet another fan overreaction, she couldn't let Daisy walk away disheartened. "Listen, if you look up Shantelle's PR team online, I'm sure they'll send you an autographed photo."

"Really? That'd be awesome." Diving into her phone with nary a thank you, Daisy lumbered off.

"You handled that well," said Micah.

"Lots of practice." Her gaze flitted to her date. "I'm sorry I didn't tell you earlier about Shantelle. If people don't know we're related, I keep it under wraps for as long as I can."

Julian scratched his jaw. "Yeah, about that…we, um, knew."

"You did?"

Micah smiled kindly. "Tash figured it out after the quiz, and I told Jules. Matey here didn't even know who Shantelle was!" He laughed and spied his older sister, Sadie, on the stairs. An older, prettier version of Micah with doe eyes and shoulder-length brunette hair, she was enthusiastically waving at her brother. Micah liberated his beer bottle from his best friend's hand. "Uh-oh, looks like I'm being told to mingle. Oh, and one more thing—an insider's tip: steer clear of the punch. Tash made it. Catch ya in a bit, all right? Have fun." Clutching his beloved popcorn, he inched sideways through the throng of well-wishers.

Madeleine tilted her head. "You knew *nothing* about Shantelle?"

"Sorry, nope—not until Micah filled me in. I've never seen her movies. I don't read gossip websites." He held her hand. "Madeleine, I like you *for you*, not because you've got a sister who's famous."

Her expression relaxed. "I'm so glad to hear that. People get weird about it sometimes. They ask uncomfortable questions or want to be friends with me so they can get closer to her. I can't tell you the number of times I've had strangers ask me to call her up so they can say hi."

"That must feel…weird?"

Madeleine exhaled heavily. "Yeah, it can be exhausting. That's why I don't mention Shantelle or her job unless I have to. But it's hard. We're close—she's a huge part of my life, but now I'm more guarded, you know? I only talk about her when I'm sure that people aren't using me to try to become besties with my movie star sibling…"

Julian raised a speculative brow. "And do I pass the test?"

She smiled. "With flying colors!"

Arms flailed, fists punched the air, and lyrics were shouted at full volume as the lower level of Micah's house morphed into a sweaty, claustrophobic dance club. With friends and family taking turns playing DJ, the set list was eclectic and fun, spanning different genres and tastes, guaranteeing non-stop dancing in the kitchen, dining room, and even outside in the wee garden.

Madeleine and Julian jumped around and laughed, breathlessly singing the lyrics of Elvis Costello's "Pump It Up" until the final strains dissolved into a classic acid house track featuring a mournful saxophone and a haunting sample of a loon, a water bird common to North America.

"I'm dying for another drink." Chasing breaths, Julian loosened his tie.

Madeleine nodded and fanned her cheeks, her pulse pounding from their half hour of non-stop dancing. *I'm so gonna feel this tomorrow, but I don't care!* She wiped perspiration from her brow, but her perma-grin held firm. "I can't remember the last time I danced so hard." Truth be told, she couldn't remember the last time she'd had so much fun, period. *Just think, none of this would be happening if that manic guy in the fugly plaid coat hadn't stolen my taxi.*

Zigzagging through the sweaty bodies, Madeleine chased breaths while admiring Julian's ass in his black trousers. The cabbie hadn't been kidding at the pub quiz. He did like "a dance". However, his definition of dancing left out the fact he was fond of a sexy hip swivel and an impromptu body roll. Who knew?

He looked back, leaning into Madeleine's ear. "Oh, this song brings back memories."

"Good ones?"

"Loud ones!" His gaze washed over a cluster of wine and liquor bottles crowding the kitchen counter. "My corgi, Winnie, barking his head off. He hates the bird sample."

"You own a corgi?! You didn't say!" Madeleine tugged open the fridge door as Julian rescued a chilled bottle of white wine sitting precariously on top of a pile of napkins. "Pembrokeshire or Cardigan?" She grabbed a beer for Julian and stepped aside, allowing two of Micah's friends to help themselves next.

"Pembrokeshire," said Julian, pulling out the cork.

She smiled. "Are you pouring me a glass of wine?"

"I am." He grinned, spotting his beer in her hand. "Winnie's with my ex temporarily. I'll have him back after Christmas." He tilted the bottle above the lip of a long-stemmed glass. "I can't wait! My flat is so quiet without him."

"I wish I could have a dog." She watched the wine sparkle as it rose in her glass. "Do you have photos?"

"Now that's a dangerous question. We could be here all night…"

"Sounds perfect! Show me." Madeleine left his beer on the counter and budged closer.

Julian set down the wine bottle. "Okay, but I did warn you."

He opened an album on his phone featuring over 3,000 images of big-eared Winnie, his soulful brown eyes and boopable black nose beyond adorable. Flipping through, Madeleine spotted pictures of Winnie outside Buckingham Palace's gates, playing with a stuffed Paddington Bear twice his size, and sitting beneath the starry lights strung across Coal Drops Yard.

"He's absolutely gorgeous. Oh, Julian. I wish I could meet him."

"I wish you could, too. He would *love* you." He tucked his phone away in his trouser pocket and handed her the glass of wine.

"Thanks!"

"So, remember the clients I told you about earlier?" Julian grabbed his beer and a bottle opener from the counter.

"The Instagram influencers?" Madeleine sipped her drink.

Julian nodded, popping off the cap and discarding it in the trash beneath the sink. "They had a huge domestic in the middle of Neal's Yard this afternoon." He enjoyed a long pull on his beer.

"How come?"

"From what I could make out, the fella uploaded a photo of his girlfriend without any filters or airbrushing. She was so pissed, they canceled tomorrow."

"Oh?"

"So, if you want to hang out until it's time for you to go…" A familiar guitar riff pushed aside the booming acid house.

Madeleine lit up. "I'd love to."

"Great." Julian grinned back.

"OI, GUYS!" A passing Natasha snatched Madeleine's free hand. "Dance with me NOW!"

"Where have you been?" asked Julian. "We were out there for

ages. We just stopped, actually."

"Well, start again! *C'mon*, Jules," Natasha pleaded, swinging Madeleine's hand as an infectious surge of techno took over the song. "It's Madonna! We always swarm the dance floor when 'Ray of Light' comes on! You know, I *will* beg...!"

Madeleine bobbed her head and shoulders, unable to stand still. "I *love* this song! I can't remember the last time I danced to it." She set her glass on the counter and bit her lip, urging Julian to acquiesce with a bounce of her brows.

"Go on then." Julian's abandoned his beer and joined the women as they veered around a clique discussing *The Great British Bake Off* holiday special. Beneath the glittering disco ball, Madeleine, Julian, and Natasha dove into the pounding beat, swaying their hips and throwing their arms in the air with reckless abandon.

"MEEKS!" Natasha tackled her brother mid-pogo. "Great choice!"

"This song!" Micah shouted, leaping into the fray. "It makes me seriously nostalgic!"

Madeleine danced beside Julian, closing her eyes, losing herself in the swirling synths and electronic drums. *God, I've missed dancing so much!* Tossing her hair, she breathlessly sang along as Madonna's voice built up to the first soaring chorus and the entire room hollered...

"ANNA FRIEL!"

What? Perplexed, Madeleine's eyes popped open. *That's not the lyric. What are they singing?*

"ANNA FRIEL!"

Anna who?

"ANNA FRIEL...ANNA FRIEEEEEAAAAAAAHHH!"

As the synths and guitars careened into the second verse, Madeleine clasped Julian's arm and leaned in. "Why is everyone shouting Anna-something?"

"Oh right, sorry! It's *Anna Friel*. She's a British actress." He swayed for a beat then bent down again, speaking into her ear. "When this song came out, people misheard the chorus and thought

Madonna was singing Anna's name."

Madeleine snort-laughed. "I love it when people get lyrics wrong. It's hilarious."

"Well, this gaff is totally ridiculous, but we just can't help ourselves," said Julian. "It's become a *thing* now."

Kel and I used to change song lyrics all the time. Love it. I feel so at home with Julian and his friends. Madeleine grinned back. "Now I have to listen out for it."

She didn't have to wait long. The song whirled into the chorus again and like clockwork, the dance floor erupted in full boozy breath.

"ANNA FRIEL!"

"HA HA!" Madeleine's jaw dropped. "Unbelievable!"

"ANNA FRIEL…!"

She couldn't stop laughing. "Oh my god, it really does!" Her fingers whisked away a few stray tears.

"ANNA FRIEEEEEAAAAAAAHHH!"

Julian nodded and rocked along to the beat. "Stupid, right?"

"No! FUN!" She squealed as Natasha bounced closer. "I won't be able to hear the proper lyrics ever again!"

"It's better this way, eh?!" Natasha yelled back. The music slowed and quieted into the third and final verse. Micah's sister lowered her voice accordingly. "It's our gift to you. Now you'll always remember us whenever this comes on."

"I really will," said Madeleine. "My god, Tash, I'm having the best time!"

"Good!" Natasha beamed at Julian as the song swelled back into a frenetic pace and the dancefloor went ballistic with gyrating bodies, waving arms, and Micah holding on to his top hat as he bounced like a tipsy Tigger.

"ANNA FRIEL…!"

Madeleine punched the air and giggled, her heart feeling full and giddy. *I forgot what this is like. Dancing like mad with good friends, feeling like I could conquer almost anything.* She sidled up to Julian and flung her arms around his neck as the song built up to its spiraling crescendo.

"Hey you!" He smiled, falling in sync with her rhythm. They swayed in a playful bump and grind then jumped up and down as one, simultaneously letting out a final, high-pitched "ANNA FRI-EEEAAAHHH!"

Laughing so hard more tears began to fall, Madeleine dabbed her eyes as Julian lifted her up and spun around, his grin infectious and joyful. High in his arms, she matched his enraptured gaze and surrendered to the moment, holding on, refusing to worry about what would happen tomorrow.

And for the first time in a very long while, Madeleine didn't feel alone.

Seventeen

MADELEINE

Warm puffs of breath floated up into the inky sky as Madeleine, delightfully fuzzy-minded, curled up beside Julian on Micah's creaky sun lounger, the final flickering embers of the party dying out around them. Inside, Sadie's blonde friend, all roaming hands and urgent lips, made out with a shirtless Micah against the stairs while a cluster of holdouts, in no hurry to head home, drunkenly swayed and lurched along to Blur's "The Universal" stuck on repeat.

"Good thing we like this song," Julian joked as he pulled a wool blanket over Madeleine then covered himself. "You warm enough?"

Not really. "Um, can we cuddle a bit...?"

"Absolutely!" He opened his arms as she shifted closer, the lawn furniture squeaking in duress. He wrapped Madeleine in a firm but cozy hug. "Is this okay?"

"Mmmhmm." She rested her head on his shoulder and inhaled. *Still smells good. Sweaty but sexy.* Madeleine sighed, her gaze blissful. "This is nice." She glanced skyward. "Too bad we can't see any stars. It's the same back home. The city's too bright."

"Even if we can't, it's good to know they're still there, watching over us—"

"OWWW!" someone wailed.

They sprang up onto their elbows and peered through the darkness. A subtle glow from the dining room lit the shadowy figure from behind. They let out a low whimper and hunched over, grasping their foot beneath the hem of their dress.

"You all right?" Julian tilted his head as another groan left their lips. "Is that you, Tash?"

"Yes! Stupid Jumbo-bloody-Jenga! Why don't people put stuff away?" Natasha let go of her foot and drunkenly kicked the frost-kissed grass, missing the wooden game piece by a mile. "Guess I should clean up."

Madeleine whisked off the blanket. "Oh, we'll help—"

"NO!" A cloud of warm air burst from Natasha's lips. "You can't! I like to tinker about—alone."

Julian nodded and leaned back into the lounger. "She does. It's her thing."

"Okay, but if you change your mind, just holler." Madeleine re-claimed the scratchy blanket and pulled it up to their chests.

"I won't, BUT I *was* gonna ask, do you want more cake before I box it up?"

Grin rising, Madeleine glanced at Julian, who answered for her. "Yeah, save us another piece? Ta, love!"

"I still can't get over Micah's face when all those pale blue M&Ms spilled out," said Madeleine.

"Gotta love a Manchester City-themed piñata cake." Shivering, Natasha hugged her middle. "And I know he'll deny it, but I swear Meeks teared up when everyone followed 'Happy Birthday' with 'Blue Moon'."

"And that's really the anthem for Micah's football team?" asked Madeleine. "It's so old."

"Yes and yes," said Julian.

She giggled. "I thought it was another *Grease* reference."

"Funny, eh?" Natasha yawned widely. "Nicely played, Jules. I know how much you hate it."

"It's not the song I hate, it's the team! But I love the guy to bits. I'll do anything for him."

"You swear by that?" asked Natasha. "How 'bout tossing a bucket of water on him and that…woman." She threw a half-lidded glare over her slouched shoulder. "Please god, don't let them be loud. Our walls are paper thin—eurgh!" She punctuated her disgust with a snort. "Sod it, I'm gonna get a head start. I'm goin' to bed.

Lock up when you leave, Jules?"

"Consider it done. Oh, and Tash?"

She turned around mid-molar-exposing yawn. "Yeah?"

"You did good, girl. Micah had a blast. We all did."

Madeleine nodded in agreement. "I can't remember the last time I had so much fun."

A tired smile curved Natasha's barely there lipstick. "Cheers, guys. Night-night." She weaved her way through the empty yard back to the house and disappeared behind the door.

"How long has Natasha been a goth?" asked Madeleine, cuddling into Julian again.

"Eight, maybe nine years? She started dressing in black when their gran died. She was only seventeen at the time."

"Poor thing. Were they close?"

"Extremely." Julian adjusted the blanket, making sure Madeleine was fully covered. "Tash stayed over most weekends, watched movies with her, practiced knitting. Next to Micah, her gran was her favorite person."

"Did you meet her?" asked Madeleine.

"A few times, yeah." Julian gathered her in again. "She was this sweet northern lady famous for her homemade Lancashire hotpot and her crush on John Travolta."

"Travolta?"

"My god, she *loved* him! She first saw *Grease* in the seventies and she was a goner. No one else got a look in. That's why Tash and Micah are so fond of that film: their gran watched the VHS all the bloody time while they were growing up." Julian smiled. "One of many things they did together. She was always there for Tash. She'd make chips with curry sauce, listen to Tash's adolescent angst, and offer pearls of wisdom, but only if asked."

"That's lovely, having someone in your corner at that age."

"Yeah, her death hit Natasha doubly hard. Her friends weren't the most sympathetic either, which didn't help. They were too busy going out, having a laugh—being teens. Tash would tag along, but if she cried or mentioned missing her gran, they'd ignore her. Eventually, they started excluding her."

"Just when she needed them the most." Madeleine sighed.

"After a few weeks, Tash decided if she was gonna be an out-sider, she might as well embrace it," said Julian. "Becoming a goth seemed like the obvious choice. She'd always been fascinated by the Victorian era, and the way they openly spoke about death and lost loved ones felt liberating to her."

"The Victorians certainly weren't afraid to talk about dying," said Madeleine.

"And they would never tell someone to stop grieving and get over it. So Tash started to wear black and gravitated toward people who encouraged her to talk about her loss."

"Fellow goths?"

"Yeah." Julian stroked her shoulder. "And me too, I guess."

Madeleine's eyes widened. "You…?"

"You're surprised?"

"No, I just think…it's a kind thing to do."

"I had some idea of what she was going through," said Julian. "My mum died three years before their gran. I was twenty-two, had recently graduated from uni, and was in the midst of my probation-ary period at *Words and Music*. Taking time off to grieve wasn't on the cards, and I couldn't really speak openly about it with my new colleagues either. They were *impossibly* cool and older, and I want-ed to belong. Weeping into my computer keyboard was not the way to go about it, so I hid my feelings and worked my arse off, pretend-ing nothing major had happened."

Madeleine hugged him tighter. "Aw, Julian, that's heartbreak-ing."

"It wasn't smart, that's for sure. Holding in all that sadness made me anxious and angry, and the way she died…well, I *really* needed to talk to someone about it."

"Wasn't your brother around?"

"Not as such, no. He had his own way of dealing with things, which was basically escaping. The morning after the funeral, he left for a three-week hiking holiday in Turkey."

Madeleine's mouth tensed into a frown. "What about Micah?"

"I hadn't met him yet, and my old mates from Whitechapel were typical East End lads on the piss, looking for a shag and a good time. Talking about my dead mum? Buzzkill."

I can so relate. Madeleine gave him another squeeze. "I wish I knew you back then. I would've listened, been there for you." She bit her lip, knowing how important it was to have your grief recognized. The urge to share her own story grew strong, but Madeleine held back, remembering how it felt when people nudged her loss out of the way by talking about theirs. *I want him to know I understand where he's coming from, but this moment is not about me.* The best way to be empathetic and supportive was to let Julian open up uninterrupted, to just listen. "Want to talk about it now?"

"That's a lovely offer, Maddie, but it's Christmas and we've got a nice buzz on. I don't want to bring you down."

"Hmm, have you met me? Ms. Bah Humbug?!" She smiled kindly. "Julian, you won't spoil anything. I'm here, talk to me."

"Okay." He blew out a breath. "Well, Mum...she fell at home."

Madeleine's heart sank. "Oh no."

Julian pressed his lips together. "She was up a rickety ladder, washing windows. If I told her once, I told her a thousand times, 'Mum, leave it. I'll do it.' Obviously, she didn't listen to me." He exhaled heavily. "Her neighbor called with the news. I was out spending a Saturday afternoon in Camden with friends and raced home, but when I got there the paramedics said I was too late. Mum was gone."

"I'm so sorry. Were you two...close?"

"Window-washing stubbornness aside, yeah, we were. We talked every day. I'd treat her to dinner every week, sometimes twice. I just loved talking to her, hearing her stories. When our dad left, she did everything she could to make sure me and Alistair didn't want for anything. She was a grafter, worked at a grocery store during the day then babysat other people's kids on the weekend for extra cash, so she'd be home with us, playing in our dingy yard out back of our terraced house. She had a hard life but was a great mum." Tears glistened in his blue eyes.

"What was her name?"

"Veronica."

"That's pretty."

"Yeah, she was." He smiled wistfully and kissed Madeleine softly on her forehead. "Thank you."

"For what?"

"Asking about her." He sniffed. "She's been gone eleven years now, and other than therapy, I can't remember the last time someone asked her name or called her Veronica. It's like people think they'll make me sad if they do, but what they don't realize is a part of me will *always* be sad because she's not here."

"You'll always miss her." Madeleine blinked, soothing the sting of tears.

"And mentioning her by name kinda feels like she hasn't been forgotten, you know?"

"It does." Madeleine nodded. *I had no idea he felt like this. We have more in common than I thought.*

"Ah, what am I like?" Julian wiped his eyes. "Now I've made us both teary."

"It was worth it, learning about your mum. She sounds wonderful."

"Thanks. So, tell me about yours," said Julian. "You mentioned your dad yesterday, but not your mom. Is she…"

"Oh no, she's still around. My mom is the best. She's sixty-three going on twenty-three and always on the go. If she's not at her theater camp for kids, she's in her garden or making snow booties for dogs."

Julian broke out into a huge smile. "Dog booties?"

"Yep! They even got voted best in Milwaukee! Hey, if Winnie ever needs a pair, I can hook you up."

"I'll keep that in mind."

"Mom would've come with us to Paris, but she had a ton of orders to fill before Christmas," said Madeleine. "In case you haven't noticed, my mom has a fondness for Gallic things, including children's names. Her ancestry is French, so it's her little tribute, I guess. Even her business has a French-inspired name. It's called Faux Paws."

"That's brilliant!"

"That's my mom." Madeleine laughed. "She used to be a bookkeeper for a friend's business, but she's much happier making dog booties. It keeps the money coming in since Dad retired from his brewery job."

"How did they meet?" asked Julian.

"At a house party in 1982. Mom still remembers the song that was playing in her best friend's rec room: 'Vacation' by the Go-Go's."

"A classic."

Madeleine nodded. "Mom was so into all that '80s stuff. Belinda Carlisle, Blondie, and Janet Jackson were her heroes, then she switched to Cyndi Lauper, copying her second-hand clothing and hair. Mom's was long and bright orange when she met Dad."

"Was it love at first sight?"

"Dad says so. Mom disagrees. She said it took longer for her." Madeleine giggled. "My dad was a *total* metalhead with a mullet and everything!"

"Oh no!"

"Oh yeah! He had Iron Maiden patches sewn onto his denim jacket, chain-smoked cigarettes, and played guitar—badly." She snorted. "You know, it reminds me of what Micah said when we arrived tonight."

"About falling for someone with different musical taste? Yeah, how did your parents get past that?" asked Julian. "Sounds like a pretty wide gulf."

"Mom bought him an expensive pair of headphones for his stereo and insisted on a no-music policy when driving somewhere in his crappy Trans-Am."

"Well, it must've worked. You're here!"

She smiled. "Dad offered to chop off his mullet, but Mom said no freakin' way! She saw beyond the headbanging, long hair, and awful guitar solos. But Dad wanted to prove how much he loved her. He got a haircut, ditched the cigarettes. To this day, Dad says he would've given up everything to be with Mom."

"Aw, that's nice." Julian brushed her hair away from her face.

And so is this. Madeleine melted beneath the soft caress of his fingers and gently closed her eyes.

"Maddie?" Julian paused for a beat. "Have you ever been in love?"

Her eyelashes flickered. "Have you?"

"Oh no you don't. I asked you first."

She glanced away. "I don't think so. I thought it was love at the time, but...you know, when you're young and it's your first relationship, feelings can escalate *very* quickly..."

"How old were you?"

"Twenty-three."

"No way! *You?*" Julian's voice rose. "You didn't have a boyfriend in high school?"

"Nope. I was a pretty driven kid. I desperately wanted to get accepted by Emerson College and put all my energy into good grades and extracurriculars to make that happen."

"So, no crushes, no prom, nothing like that?" asked Julian.

"Oh, I had crushes and boys asked me out. I just didn't go on dates. Nothing was going to distract me from my goal, and besides, my parents had their hands full with Shantelle. She was always juggling boyfriends and creating drama. Some things never change!" Madeleine giggled. "More power to her."

"Did you date in college?"

"Yep, but no one rocked my world until Theo."

"And I hate him already." Julian grinned mischievously.

"Well, you asked!"

"I did. Carry on."

"Theo was the older brother of a friend and we started dating after I graduated," said Madeleine.

"So, what was so special about this Theo, then?"

"In hindsight, not much!" Madeleine grimaced. "I know that

sounds terrible, but what was attractive to me at twenty-three—well, let's just say, I've grown up *a lot* in the past ten years!"

"Funny, isn't it? What mattered then—"

"Doesn't even come close now." She licked her lips. "I thought I loved him, though. Briefly. Until he moved back to California, ran into his ex, and had a fling. Then all bets were off."

"What a wanker. Sounds like you had a lucky escape."

"Like you and Caroline?" She winced. "Sorry, that sounded mean."

"Not mean, true," he replied matter-of-factly.

"How long were you together?"

"Five years. We lived together for four, were engaged for three."

"Wow. That's serious." Madeleine's curiosity ran wild. *Is it wrong that I want to know why they split?* "What happened—if you don't mind me asking?"

"Well…"

He paused with a taut smile, a familiar one Madeleine felt in her gut. How many times in her life had she flashed a similar grin when *she* had minded? *Shit. He doesn't want to go there. Back-track—now!*

She cleared her throat. "Actually, scratch that. You don't have to tell me. I tend to ask too many personal questions when I've had a few. Feel free to tell me to mind my own business. I would!"

His expression loosened. "Maddie, it's okay, really."

"Great. Now you feel like you *have* to tell me."

"I don't. Not at all." Julian leaned his forehead against hers. "I promise."

"You sure? I haven't made you feel weird?"

"No more than normal." Julian laughed and lifted his head as Madeleine playfully punched him. "I was the one who asked about love and relationships in the first place." He trailed his finger along her cheek. "You answered, now it's my turn."

"Well, when you put it like that…" She smirked. "Spill."

"So, things were pretty good for the first while. We moved in

174

together, got engaged two years in, and then problems started to arise. It was nothing major at first, just typical arguments about money and whose friends to hang with on weekends and 'Why is your brother Alistair such a prat?'" A ghost of a smile passed his lips. "Then I noticed whenever I mentioned The Knowledge or cramming for my next test, she'd never engage or ask questions. She'd actually change the subject, which made me think she had issues with me becoming a black cab driver."

"Did she say why?"

Julian shook his head. "Initially, I thought she was worried about my safety on the job—in case I got robbed or worse. Then, I wondered if she was concerned about how much I'd be earning, which is fair enough. It's a legit worry, right?"

"Definitely, especially if you're living together or engaged and pooling your resources," said Madeleine.

"But then one night, we were dressed up and having dinner in Mayfair—"

"Ooh, look at you, Halliwell—so fancy!" She teased, tracing her finger along his bottom lip.

"Trust me, it was *not* my idea. I would've been perfectly happy with a pint and a plate of nachos from our local, but Caroline wanted to go somewhere special and wear her new Chanel dress."

Madeleine gawped. "Chanel? Forget what I said about pooling resources! Caroline was raking it in!"

"She was, yeah. Still is. She owns a popular PR firm…"

Of course she does.

"…and her clients range from major banks to big names in entertainment," said Julian.

"Don't tell me—she's on the UK Top 40 under 40 list, right?" Madeleine joked.

"Sure is. She's been named to it twice so far."

Julian's into rich, powerful women. Madeleine's stomach sank. *Didn't see that coming.*

"Anyway, Caroline had been working really hard with a new client and we'd been arguing a lot, so I gave in, hoping a night out at her favorite restaurant would make her happy." He rubbed his nose. "So, we were chatting away, having a great time, and she asked how my day had been. I told her I'd aced another cabbie exam, and she didn't say a peep. No 'Well done' or 'Congratulations', nothing. She took a long, leisurely sip of her wine then picked at her monkfish for what felt like forever." He gazed down at the blanket. "I knew the signs. Caroline was about to blow."

"In the middle of the restaurant?"

Julian met her eyes. "Well, here's the thing. She never makes a scene in public—ever—but she doesn't stew until she gets home either. Instead, she places a hand on your forearm and leans in, then, with a charming smile and a calm voice, rips you a new one. Servers, fellow diners—no one is any the wiser." He nodded. "Gotta hand it to her, it's a true talent."

"Yeah, a creepy one." Madeleine scrunched her nose. "She's a shark dressed in Chanel."

He half-laughed.

"So, what did she say?"

"*Your hobby was cute in the beginning, Jules—but if you want to marry me, stop pissing about and get a job! A proper one!*"

"Your hobby?" Madeleine snorted. "It's not like you were lying in front of the TV all day in your bathrobe, covered in Dorito dust. You were training for a new career."

"One she hated, as it turned out."

"But how could she? You weren't even doing it yet."

He nodded. "I was a year away from getting my license. When I reminded her that all my hard work would result in a *great* job with flexible hours, she finally came clean. It wasn't my safety or potential earnings she was fretting about. It was her friends."

Madeleine tilted her head. "I'm sorry, I don't follow…"

"All their partners and spouses were bankers, consultants, luxury real estate agents…" Julian swallowed hard. "To Caroline, a black cab driver for a fiancé just didn't compare. I was a huge embarrassment."

Madeleine's lips curled in disgust. "What a pretentious snob! I bet half those banker dudes *hate* their jobs. Meanwhile, there you were, working your ass off toward a profession you felt passionate about, and best of all, you'd be you own boss, an entrepreneur. She should've been extremely proud."

A slow smile reached his eyes. "That's…really nice of you to say. Thanks."

"Don't be silly. How else would I feel?"

"Well, it's just, when you asked what happened with Caroline, I hesitated because"—he nudged his hair off his forehead—"I thought if I told you why she hated my job, you might—"

"Agree?" Madeleine shook her head. "Julian, I don't care what you do for a living—as long as it's legal. But I can't lie. I would worry about you getting robbed or assaulted, but I figure you're careful and smart, know how to read people and situations."

"You'd worry?" A warm grin parted his lips. "That's nice."

Madeleine fidgeted with the blanket. "So, *have* you been assaulted?"

"Nope. Not yet, touch wood. I haven't been robbed either, but I have had fare dodgers—passengers who do a runner and take off without paying, which sucks 'cause I need every penny."

"What's wrong with people?" She pouted. "So, the closer you got to earning your cab license, the more weird Caroline was about it. What did she mean exactly by 'a proper job'?"

"A position with her father's consultancy firm. She wouldn't let it lie, so I went along to the interview. He offered me a sweet deal: six figures, an expense account, and a glass office high above Canary Wharf. It would've been a great gig for someone who enjoys wearing ties every day, who lives for corporate retreats…"

"I take it you turned it down?" she asked.

"I did, and Caroline moved out the next day."

"Thank god!"

"But she returned two weeks later, begging to try again, saying how much she loved me. She cried, too." Julian scratched his temple. "That was a first."

Madeleine fought the urge to barf. "And did she apologize for all her unsupportive, elitist bullshit?"

Julian paused. "No."

"Julian!"

"Maddie, I loved her…"

God knows why.

"…and things were much better after our break. The arguments stopped, we started house-hunting and planning our wedding, got Winnie. She even took an interest in my job. Our life was finally coming together, just in time for Christmas."

"Last year?"

"Yeah. We were due to spend the 25th with her folks, so I wanted to surprise her with a special Christmas Eve just for the two of us. I booked a reservation at her favorite restaurant, clocked off work early, and picked up a pair of earrings from Tiffany." Julian glanced away. "Thing is, she had a Christmas surprise for me, too. I came home and found her in our shower fucking my brother, Alistair."

Madeleine's jaw dropped. "What the actual hell?!"

"I didn't know where to look. I thought I was gonna be sick." Slowly shaking his head, Julian released a fleeting huff. "My Caroline, cheating on me. And with my abrasive, arsehole of a brother! She *hated* him, or so she'd said." He scrubbed his hand over his mouth. "I guess he wasn't such a prat after all—at least to her."

"You must've been furious."

Julian nodded. "Yeah, and then Alistair came clean, said they'd been going at it like rabbits for the past six months."

Madeleine paled. "Unbelievable. Did Caroline show any remorse?"

"Not much. She didn't cry, made zero excuses. She just wrapped herself in a towel, smacked her engagement ring on the counter, and said she couldn't do it, couldn't marry me. Said she deserved better."

"And your brother was 'better'?" Madeleine seethed. "What a bitch! Natasha was right—good riddance to bad rubbish, and that goes for both of them." She shook her head. "I'm so sorry. I hope they made each other miserable."

"No such luck. They're still going strong. They live together in Chelsea."

"Oh, Julian." Madeleine caressed his cheek. "They deserve each other."

"Yeah, I see that now. In hindsight, I knew things with Caroline weren't right. There were lots of warning signs, which I chose to ignore—at my peril. I should've ended it on my own terms, but making that leap and turning everything upside down is bloody heart-wrenching. Just the idea of having *that* excruciating conversation. Of course, now I realize it's better to have a tough talk than a horrible marriage." He sighed. "Caroline and I weren't a good match, pure and simple. It's the last time I'll be with someone hell-bent on changing me, that's for sure."

"I'm sorry it happened, but I'm glad you're not with her anymore."

"Me too." He smiled. "So! What's your Theo up to? Ever think about him?"

"No!" Madeleine laughed, spotting small, random flecks of white cascading gently from above. "He's a footnote in my history, nothing more. Just like all the others who have come along since."

"Same."

She fixated on the swirling flakes of ash as they settled on their blanket. "The volcano is saying hello…"

"Just had to make an appearance, I suppose." Julian softly ran his fingers along several strands of Madeleine's hair, removing the ash. He flicked his thumb across the flecks and they dissolved under his touch, leaving a damp residue. "It's snow." He looked up with a bemused grin. "It's actually snowing."

"In London…" A quivery smile played on her lips as she gazed upward into the night sky.

"We should probably—" Julian fought back a yawn but covered his mouth anyway. He leisurely glanced at his watch. "Blimey, did you know it's quarter past two?"

Her eyes widened. "Is it? And I'm still out, go figure! I haven't done anything like this for at least three years. Last time I stayed out all night, I came down with mononucleosis a week later. The worst part—I didn't even kiss anyone!"

"Talk about a raw deal! At least a good snog might've made it worthwhile." His lips parted slightly in a dare.

Madeleine felt every second of Julian's rapt gaze, but unlike Thurloe Square and the South Bank market, this was different. Whatever had pulled the brakes before was no longer holding him back. *Should I?* Her heart pounded, climbing higher into her throat, urging her to make the first move, but her nerves won out. "*Snog.* Such a funny British word," she rambled. "The way it sounds…"

"Know what's even better? The way it feels." His eyes, playful with want, slipped to her mouth.

"Is that an invitation?"

Julian nodded slowly. She watched his lips curl at the corners into a 'You can have me if you want' smile.

For months, surviving each day was all Madeleine could deal with. The idea of dating again, falling for someone new was as undesirable as a future without Kellie. Her heart had been so consumed with death and loss she had forgotten how to live.

I want this…I want him, however briefly it lasts.

Madeleine leaned in and kissed Julian softly, tentatively, until the teasing warmth of his parting lips, tender and confident, coaxed her deeper. She slipped her tongue into his mouth and he let out a blissful moan as his hands rose, cupping her face.

She responded in kind, her fingers tugging, curling through his thick hair as a wave of pleasure swept through her, settling between her thighs. She pressed closer, tighter, the thrill of kissing him growing increasingly frantic, knowing full well their time was running out.

EIGHTEEN

MADELEINE

Pleasantly tipsy and clutching a plastic container concealing two partially eaten slices of birthday cake, Madeleine leaned against the flowery wallpaper decorating the second floor landing as Julian fought with the lock on his studio apartment.

"I'm sorry, Maddie." Determination tensed his forehead. "It doesn't usually jam this badly."

Madeleine offered an empathetic smile, hoping to ease some of his stress. "Know what this reminds me of? Things you *never* see in Hollywood rom-coms."

A smirk curved Julian's lips. He paused and raised a mischievous brow. "Like foreplay?"

Madeleine giggled. "Oh god, yes, yes, YES! And where's the lube? Where are the condoms? And why don't we see the woman taking forever to *you-know*?"

Julian shrugged.

"Every woman in the movies climaxes with like, three thrusts. THREE! Jules, you're a guy—tell me, how does *that* happen? Is there some sort of magical penis involved?"

He scrunched his nose. "Don't reckon so."

"Well, a God-given talent, then?" She felt a blush rising but was too giddy with excitement to stop. "'Cause if it is, I hate to break it to you, but that one skipped me."

"What? You're kidding, right?" Julian abandoned the lock and key and threw his hands up, playing along. "Well, that's it. Tonight is *over*."

"Aw, dammit." Madeleine fake-whined into a stomping slump. "And here I was hoping for one of those rushing to the airport grand

181

gesture scenes."

Julian snickered.

"I'll have to remember all this when I edit my romance novel."

"Your work in progress is a romance?"

"Yep, it's unapologetically swoony and très sexy."

"I'm all for that!" Julian wrenched the key again. "Maddie, before we go in, I should warn you…"

Uh-oh. She sobered slightly. *What's the problem? An STI? He hates condoms? Hm, something else?* Her chest constricted. *Oh man! He did look tragic when I mentioned the magical penis.*

He winced. "It's small."

Fuck. Madeleine gulped, a swell of disappointment and compassion swirling in her belly. *Poor guy, he wants to give me an out.*

"It's not at all like in the movies."

Her lips twitched into a smile. "Hey, that's okay! We'll work with it. I'm not a size queen."

Julian sighed. "Ah, good. I'm glad! It's just…sometimes people have expectations, you know? And this is Islington. I can't afford anything bigger."

Hold on. She squinted. "You're talking about your flat…?"

He blinked, leaving the key in the lock. "Yeah. What did you think—?" His eyes widened. "Oh, blimey!"

They both stifled a laugh, mindful of Julian's landlord sleeping downstairs.

"So how small is it?" she whispered.

"Four hundred square feet, give or take."

"Shoebox dwellers, unite!" Madeleine inched closer. "Mine's six hundred, give or take."

"You'll feel right at home, then." Julian leaned on the door again. "Sometimes if I jiggle the key—"

CLICK!

His shoulders fell, and a collective exhale filled the stairwell.

"And you didn't even curse once—or pull a muscle! I'm impressed." Madeleine beamed, pushing off the wall. The loose M&Ms in the cake container rattled their approval.

"Good thing I had my Weetabix this morning." Julian half-laughed. He eased the door open, and brightness and "Goodbye Yellow Brick Road" greeted their grins. "Force of habit. I always leave the lights and radio on for Winnie, even now he's not here." He gestured ahead. "After you."

"Thanks." Madeleine weaved around the door and brushed past a parka and scarf hanging from a hook on the wall. The subtle scent of citrus—oranges—drew her lips into a grin, the fresh fragrance a lingering souvenir from Julian's recent marmalade-making spree. There wasn't much space to maneuver. The cramped entrance was basically a launch pad into the rooms and nothing more. *He wasn't kidding—this is small.* As the door closed with a whoosh, she turned, finding Julian pocketing his keys and wearing a sweet smile.

"Hi."

"Hello." Hugging the cake container against her chest, Madeleine wasted no time resuming where they'd left off in Micah's garden. She met Julian's lips eagerly for a long kiss that unfortunately ended too soon.

"Hey, beautiful." He rested his forehead against hers and gently stroked her cheek. "I'm sorry I didn't kiss you in the car. Bloody figures we get picked up by a cabbie I actually know."

Madeleine's fingers frolicked in the soft waves of his hair. "What are the odds, huh?"

"Welcome to my flat, Ms. Joy."

"Thank you for inviting me." She ignored whatever lurked in his quiet apartment and wrapped her free arm around his shoulders, tugging him closer, the tip of her tongue flirting with his lips. Julian groaned happily and let her in.

The faint flavor of vanilla cake, enjoyed during their journey, sweetened his kiss and gave the moment a playful, celebratory feel. Breathless, she pressed against him, feeling his smile growing beneath her lips until he reluctantly broke away.

"So, I wasn't expecting company. Sorry, my place is a bit messy."

She glanced over her shoulder. "Mess? Where?"

"Wait till you have a wander. I've got records scattered all over, a few dishes I've yet to wash."

"Thank god, you're human!" She squeezed his arm. "Apartments that look barely lived in creep me out. I always wonder, *What are they hiding?*"

"Want a tour? It'll take all of ten seconds."

Madeleine giggled as he motioned to his left and a square-shaped room with two sash windows facing the dark street. "This is my living area and bedroom…and this"—he gestured in the opposite direction toward an ajar door where a sink caught her eye—"is my bath. The kitchen is behind you. See? Like I said, ten seconds, max. Blink and you'll miss it."

"Could be worse. You could have a Tube train speeding through your back yard."

He brushed his hair off his forehead. "There is that. Here, let me take your coat."

Madeleine pulled her purse from her shoulder and eased free of her wool coat, keeping her arms tucked close to her body so she didn't strike Julian in the process.

"Would you like a drink?" He hung her coat up beside his parka on the narrow wall. "Some tea, a Coke, some wine?"

"Wine, please." She slipped off her shoes as Julian backed up into the bathroom's doorjamb and shrugged off his outerwear.

He laughed. "My place is so pokey, taking jackets off in here is a bit of a song and dance."

Stowing his coat on the last hook, he pulled off his shoes then dug around in his coat's pocket, unearthing his tie. His pink shirt, crinkled from dancing and cavorting, was completely untucked and, much to Madeleine's joy, unbuttoned to mid-chest, teasing a glimpse of dark hair on his pecs. "Make yourself comfy. Feel free to change the radio station or put on a record, and I'll"—he liberated the cake box from her hands—"take care of this. Be right back."

As Julian stepped into the sliver he called a kitchen, Madeleine padded across the honey-hued hardwood in her stocking feet and dove into her purse, pulling out a small bottle of eyedrops. *My con-*

tacts are drier than the Sahara. Tipping her head back, she squeezed a few drops into her eyes and winced through the sting, blinking continually and dabbing her lashes until Julian's apartment came into a sharper, more comfortable focus.

Despite his claim, it was far from messy. Like most homes, a few personal items were scattered about—his eyeglasses and a box of disposable contact lenses, some unopened bills, the London journal she'd given him—but nothing suggested a hoarding fetish or questionable hygiene practices, and his style, as expected, was more mid-century than modernist. *This furniture would've been perfect on* Mad Men*!* Madeleine smiled, inching past a small basket filled with dog toys and a sturdy wooden chair, one of two tucked beneath a round bistro table just outside the kitchen where Julian, hidden from view, ran the taps and rustled in cupboards. But it wasn't his dining setup or the small Christmas tree by the window that piqued her interest.

Skipping over the dark gray sofa dividing the space into living and sleeping quarters, Madeleine's eyes made a beeline for Julian's queen-sized bed and its indigo blue duvet dominating the left side of the room. A mountain of pillows, poufy like white marshmallows, rested against an upholstered headboard, and a cozy chenille throw languished casually across the neatly made bed, sending her thoughts tumbling toward naughtiness. *I bet he looks so good wrapped in that and nothing else!* Her fingers fussed with the clasp on her purse.

BANG!

A closing cupboard snapped her back into PG territory. Madeleine hastily hung her purse on a chair and edged past the sofa, picking up a vinyl copy of Depeche Mode's *Violator* from a stack of albums on Julian's rectangular coffee table. Her attention leapt from DVD copies of *Poltergeist* and *The Birds* to the jam-packed but neat display of books, movies, CDs, and records artfully arranged across a series of floor-to-ceiling built-in shelves. In the middle of Julian's pop culture collection stood an old fireplace no longer in use. A lone red Christmas stocking hung from the mantle, its owner's name, WINNIE, embroidered in black thread across the white felt trim.

I wonder why Winnie is with his ex. Leaning in, Madeleine held the record album against her dress and glanced past the sparkly Christmas cards on the mantle where framed photos held pride of place: Winnie with his dad lounging on a blanket in a grassy park; Micah and Julian, sunburnt and grinning, holding beers aloft at the Glastonbury Festival; and a mod-looking woman with a swingy jet-black bob, white go-go boots, and a green minidress on a bustling 1960s street.

"I see you've met Mum," said Julian, his smile wide and his hands occupied with a tray toting two glasses, a corkscrew, and a chilled bottle of white wine.

"This photo is incredible. Is that Carnaby Street?"

"Yep, well spotted." Julian placed the tray on his coffee table. Two small bowls kept the wine company, one filled with Quality Street chocolates, the other with a savory mix of pretzels and crisps.

"Wow." She admired the photo again. "If I could live in another era, I'd pick the swinging sixties in a heartbeat. I love the fashion and the music, so much going on. I bet your mum had some amazing stories."

Julian sat on the sofa and picked up the bottle of wine. "She bumped into The Rolling Stones once."

Madeleine's jaw dropped. "Get out!?" She turned sharply. "Really?"

"Yep, and Tom Jones. Her most cherished possession was one of his albums, autographed." He pierced the cork with the screw and began twisting the handle.

"Like mother, like son." She stepped away from the mantle and studied Julian's Christmas tree, occupying the small space between the window and his shelves. Barely reaching her shoulder, the fir tree was decorated with a modest assortment of multi-colored lights, a few baubles (including a David Bowie 'Ziggy Stardust' ornament), and a tinsel garland that wound down through the sparse branches like a river of spun silver. A needle felted corgi, a little larger than the one in Julian's black cab, guarded the top of the tree, and a single present—soft, bone-shaped, and wrapped in green tissue paper—lay on the red tartan tree skirt below. A warm fuzziness brimmed in her chest. *So lovely. There's no doubt who owns Julian's heart.*

"Like our whole family, really," said Julian, turning the corkscrew. "My grandmother worked for a spell as the tea lady at Abbey Road."

"Oh my god! Did she—"

"Meet the Beatles? No. She worked there a good decade or so before they appeared. It was mostly classical orchestras and big bands recording there during Granny's time. And my granddad, well, he ran a second-hand record stall in Petticoat Lane Market every Sunday. He sold vinyl, 8-tracks, and eventually cassettes and CDs. Did a fair trade, too. Mum helped out when she was a teenager, earning pocket money."

"Did you work there?"

"Yep." Julian pulled up the levers, and the cork dislodged with a delightful *pop*. "I started when I was nine, worked right through my teens." He gestured to the album in Madeleine's grasp. "I definitely shifted a few of those."

She glanced at the red and black album cover. "I love these guys. I see them every time they play Boston." Stepping back toward the shelves, she perused the rows and rows of records. "This is amazing and so organized." She slipped the Depeche Mode album into its rightful, alphabetical place then skimmed her finger across the spines. "What *don't* you own?" Her eyes darted over the names. "Death Cab for Cutie, Destiny's Child, Dua Lipa, Duran Duran…"

"Let me know if you'd like to listen to something." He filled their glasses with wine.

"Oh my goodness!" Madeleine squealed. "You have Hunters and Collectors!"

"Is that a request for 'Throw Your Arms Around Me'?"

"Ooh, I love that track so much, but…"

"It makes you cry," said Julian, parking the bottle of wine on the table.

He remembered. Slipping past the fireplace, Madeleine grinned to herself and studied the second bank of shelves. "Too much choice!" Her fingers skirted across the The O'Jays, Paul Oakenfold, Oasis— Her nose crinkled. *What did he say? Oasis is 'nothing special'? He owns their entire discography!* She bit back a smile and searched for S, spotting The Sex Pistols and Donna Summer. "Your collection is so eclectic. I mean, you've got Sia shelved beside Simon and Garfunkel."

"My mum adored them," said Julian. "Music doesn't get much prettier than 'Scarborough Fair'."

"Hmm..." Madeleine narrowed her search. "Got any—yep! You do!" She pulled out Saint Etienne's *Tiger Bay.*

"I didn't see that coming. You into them?"

"Big time. They sound so London to me." Madeleine removed the inner sleeve and handed it to Julian. "This one's perfect for three in the morning. Folky and melodic, a bit synthy, but not too loud."

"Excellent choice." Julian stood up and rounded the table.

She pored over the back cover as he turned off the radio and placed the record on his turntable. "Julian, can we play track six? 'Marble Lions'? I must admit, it was stuck in my head when we drove past Trafalgar Square."

He gently lowered the needle onto the spinning vinyl, releasing a series of warm, staticky clicks and pops until the song's sparse guitar chords took flight.

Madeleine smiled, feeling no pain. "Ah, love it." Leaving the album cover leaning against the shelves, she sat on the sofa and picked up a glass of wine.

Julian promptly joined her and raised his glass with a grin and a "Cheers!"

"Cheers," she echoed, enjoying a sip. Her eyes swept over a colorful, illustrated poster, art deco in style, hanging on the wall above his bistro table. Glamorous Londoners dined and danced with *Brightest London and Home By Underground* written beneath them. "I love your tree and your place. It's cozy. You've made great use of the space."

"Thanks. Yeah, it's all right. I'll have lived here a year come January. I can't complain. My landlord is dog-friendly and lets me park my cab in his space. He gave me a bunch of his old records, too."

"They'll be well loved here. So, how did you accumulate all this vinyl? Did your grandfather pay you in records?"

"He did, actually, yeah," said Julian. "Most of my older stuff came from him. The rest I found crate-digging around London."

She glanced at the pile of records on the table. "Does your family still have the market stall?"

"No, we had to give it up when I started uni. Alistair had no interest, and it was too much for Mum to handle on her own. It's a shame, but we had a good run." He sipped his wine. "Did you have a job as a teen?"

"I babysat, but I hated it." Madeleine smoothed the skirt of her dress. "It was hardly surprising. I was never one of those little girls who cooed over babies or played with dolls. Oh, except for Barbie. She was cool because she had boobs, a job, and a sportscar...and her feet were squishy and fun to chew on."

Julian laughed. "You what?!"

"Hey, *a lot* of us chewed Barbie's feet. It was a comforting, relaxing thing."

"God, we sure did some weird things as kids, eh?" Playfulness infused his words. "I used to pour glue on my hands in art class. I'd wait for it to dry, then peel it off. My goal was to remove it in one big hand-shaped piece."

"And did you?"

"Still trying."

Madeleine laughed. "In some ways, I still feel like a kid. I have to keep reminding myself 'You're thirty-three'. It doesn't help that I'm still waiting for my maternal instincts to click in."

"Well, you must have some, right? You love dogs, care for squirrels..."

"Yeah, but animals are awesome. Human babies"—Madeleine

cringed—"aren't really my thing." She leaned forward and traded her glass for the stack of vinyl on the coffee table. "My mom says it'll be different when—*if*—I have my own kids, but I dunno." She shrugged, bringing the pile of records with her.

"You don't want children?"

Does he? Shit, me and my tired, tipsy brain, bringing up babies on a date. Madeleine scratched her shoulder. "Hmm, not sure. Probably not." She peered up from the records, gauging his reaction. "Would you, one day?"

He blinked a few times over his glass, contemplative. "I like kids. I think they're great, but I want to travel, go on adventures." He paused. "Actually, I say that, but I'm not the best flyer."

"So you'll take the train. Or go on driving adventures instead."

"Exactly! But even so, that type of pick-up-and-go lifestyle doesn't really jive with raising a family."

Phew. Got out of that one unscathed. She eased back into the softness of the sofa and thumbed lazily through the albums while Julian drank his wine. "Yeah. My mom doesn't quite understand. At least she doesn't moan at me about it. My brother Antoine and his wife gave her the first Joy grandchild, so the pressure's off."

"Just don't ask you to babysit, right?" Julian smiled cheekily.

"Oh, I would for him. It's not that I don't *like* kids. I just prefer them a little older, when they can talk and understand things and no longer wear poopy diapers. I've had more than my fair share dealing with the Nine Circles of Hell."

He blinked again like he was trying to comprehend what she meant...or maybe his contacts were bothering him, too. "In what way?"

Madeleine turned over a Primal Scream album. "Oh, it's just the crappy job I had as a teenager: cleaning washrooms at a gas station off the interstate."

Julian audibly gulped.

"Don't worry, I'll spare you the gory details. Luckily, after two months, the manager moved me to a cashier position. Now *that* was an even bigger eyeopener, dealing directly with the public and discovering how horrible humanity can be."

"I hear you on that score. If I had a fiver for every time some-one talked down to me at the market or in my cab, I wouldn't need to work a day in my life." Julian reached over, draping his arm around her shoulders.

Oh, I like this! Madeleine nudged closer and nuzzled into the warmth of his neck. She closed her eyes and inhaled...deeply. *Mmm, I could do this for days.*

"Comfy?" He grinned.

"Very." She glanced up at him as he gently stroked her arm.

"So, how were they rude to you?" he asked.

"Oh, you know...I was talked over, screamed at when gas pric-es went up, told I knew nothing about cars 'cause I was a girl."

"I'm so sorry." He pressed a soft kiss in her hair. "You know, every single one of those asshats who threw a wobbler should've been forced to work in customer service. See what it's like to be treated like rubbish for absolutely no fucking reason."

"If only." Madeleine flicked past a few more records, pausing on an album by Run-DMC. "It's such a deal-breaker for me, too. There's absolutely no way I could be friends with someone who is rude to cashiers or waiters."

"One hundred percent." Julian nodded. "Same with people who litter."

"Ew, me neither." Madeleine lifted her head. "And people who talk in the cinema."

"And adults who paint their faces."

Madeleine choked out a laugh. "What?"

"You know, when they attend sporting events and all that?" Jul-ian shifted forward and picked up the colorful bowl of chocolates, offering it to her.

Madeleine took a green foil-wrapped triangle. "What? Like a small flag or logo on a cheek?"

"No, I'm talking full-face coverage, paint from ear to ear, fore-head to chin."

Freeing the chocolate from the foil, she giggled.

"Have you noticed women rarely do it?" Julian nabbed a pink rectangle and left the bowl on the coffee table. "It's always blokes, and they're always obnoxious. I'm all for showing team spirit, but these guys inevitably get rat-arsed and stumble into someone— usually me—and I'm left with a hefty dry-cleaning bill." He tore away the foil and popped the chocolate in his mouth before curling his arm around Madeleine again.

She savored the smooth hazelnut noisette melting on her tongue almost as much as Julian's clench. She rolled the green wrapper into a tight ball between her fingers. "It's a good thing you don't attend NFL games. A lot of the guys there paint their chests, too." Leaving the foil beside her wine glass, she leafed through a few more records, stalling on a cover featuring a photo of five guys wearing tartan-trimmed clothing. "Oh my god!" She squealed, holding the Bay City Rollers' *Dedication* album aloft. "My mom owns this! She loved Leslie."

"My mum was into Woody. Questionable name…"

Madeleine snorted. "This album is your mum's?"

"Well, it's not mine." Julian smirked.

"Can we play it?"

"To…take the piss or—"

"Because it's fun." She leaned into him. "Jules, you can play cool all you want, but the fact you still own this album *proves* you're not a music snob, which for a music nerd like me is a huge deal-breaker."

"Really? Hm." Julian lifted his arm from her shoulder. "Well, they *did* have some great pop songs…"

One of which plays during the funeral in Love Actually. Madeleine kept that pop culture tidbit hidden behind her gleeful smile as Julian stood and put away the Saint Etienne album, replacing it with the Rollers.

"Got any requests?" Julian whisked a carbon fiber brush across the spinning vinyl's surface, removing dust from its grooves.

"Should we abide by your habit? Side one, track one?" Her eyes flitted down the back cover. "'Let's Pretend'?" She opened the gatefold sleeve, examining the large black and white photo of frenzied fans packed into a city square in the late '70s. "I always liked this picture. All those screaming, happy faces. Fandoms rule."

Julian lowered the needle. "Have you ever screamed over a pop band?"

"Of course! I was a screaming, crying, card-carrying member of the Backstreet Boys fan club." She paused for a moment as the vinyl's scratches and pops gave way to the song's tinkling piano. "I loved the Spice Girls, too—still do."

"You weren't the only one." Julian dropped down onto the sofa. "Who'd you like? Baby? Scary?" Madeleine reached forward, returning the Bay City Rollers album and all the others to the coffee table. "No, I bet it was Ginger, right? All the boys at school loved her."

"Nope. It was always Posh for me. I like brunettes…"

Like me? Madeleine shifted back into the sofa, cuddling into Julian's embrace again.

"Do you know there's a connection between the Spice Girls and your hotel?"

"I found out yesterday!" She smoothed down his shirt and toyed with its buttons. "Can I make a confession?"

"Absolutely."

"I've acted out the 'Wannabe' video on the hotel's staircase three times now. I think the concierge hates me."

"Nah, they're used to it." He weaved through her hair, twirling the soft strands along the nape of her neck. "I have a confession, too. I listened to a few of your playlists."

Madeleine's eyes fluttered in bliss. "How'd you know they were mine?" Her fingertips explored, riding the defined curves of his chest lurking beneath the material.

"It took a bit of sleuthing, but I found several, including the Christmas one, credited to Mad Joy."

"Nice one, Sherlock."

"I love that you called it *More Meh Than Merry*," said Julian.

She snickered. "When art imitates life."

"I think it's brilliant. Then, I clicked on your name and listened to *Pub Night, Park Life Hangout...*"

"And what else?" Slipping lower, her hand diverted beneath the hem of his shirt, meeting his warm skin and the tangle of hair heading down his abs.

Julian sucked in a sharp breath. "The *Sexy Bedtime* one..."

"And...was it?"

"Definitely, yeah." He blinked slowly, his gaze heavy and unwavering as his fingers tenderly caressed her cheek.

The way he's looking at me... Madeleine felt the heat of lust in his eyes but also fondness and respect. She felt safe, his desire without demand or expectation. *If I stop, go no further, Julian will be fine with it.*

His kindness, his fun-loving *joie de vivre*, his talent with the written word—it all drew her in, but it was his empathy for others—for her—that had her smitten. She'd been crushing on him since she arrived, but this...*this* was different. It was reciprocal, mutual.

But Madeleine knew...like all good things, it would end.

This time it would be with an airline text, then a transatlantic flight. Her life would tick along in Boston while Julian's carried on in London, and they'd probably never see each other again. Madeleine's heart ached at the thought, but fretting over the future was squandering her enjoyment of today.

We can't have forever, but we can have right now.

Her hand ventured beyond his belt, flirting with the band of his boxers. *Should I lift the elastic and slide in?* The temptation to travel further taunted her, and so did the hard bulge pressing through his trousers. *I want to...* Her lashes flitted up, catching Julian watching her, his breaths short and intense as he dragged his eyes down to her pout.

"Maddie..." He nudged closer. "I'd love it if you'd stay—"

"I was hoping you'd ask." She met his lips, losing herself in the delicious boldness of his mouth.

Nineteen

MADELEINE

Two days until Christmas

A fiery beam of morning sun snuck through a gap in Julian's floor-length curtains and crept across the hardwood, setting the sparkly hem of Madeleine's designer dress alight. Hung from a hanger hooked over the top of his closet door, the frock sprayed dancing purple speckles across a sampling of records on the floor, left askew following the major make-out session the night before. All other evidence—the wine bottle and long-stemmed glasses, torn condom wrappers, and Julian's rumpled dress shirt—had been cleared away, victims of Julian and Madeleine's adulting. His suit's trousers, their hem in need of mending, lay over the back of one of his dining chairs just a step away from the kitchen where the mouth-watering aroma of sizzling butter and potatoes escaped. If only Madeleine wasn't hungover.

Shrugging off all signs of his own boozy overindulgence, Julian peered around the doorjamb and flashed a smile as he nudged up his eyeglasses. "Ham, cheese, and rösti potato sandwiches coming up!" He ducked out of sight, removing something from his tiny under-the-counter bar fridge. "Are you warm enough, Maddie?" He leaned around the corner again. "Do you need a top-up? Some more paracetamol?"

Yeah. A truckload. The two I took aren't conquering this headache. She smiled kindly and peeked in her *Words and Music* mug, the milky tea barely touched. "No, I'm good, thanks." She settled back into the chair and took a sip. Its warmth coursed through her but did nothing to soothe her pounding head or the growing unease twisting in her chest.

195

"If you change your mind, just say the word." He glanced past her, admiring the brightness being held back by his curtains. "Looks like it's gonna be a beautiful day." He returned to the kitchen and began singing along to "Perfect" spinning at a low, hangover-friendly volume on his turntable. The first track from the Lightning Seeds album *Jollification* was one of Madeleine's Britpop favorites.

He's way too chipper. She pressed her fingertips against her temples. *And I'm a lightweight. I've lost my touch. I shouldn't feel this hungover after four glasses of wine.*

The cute cabbie, though, couldn't do enough for her: making tea, pan-frying his 'hangover-curing' potatoes, offering his comfy (and clean) West Ham football club bathrobe, which was so fleecy and large it felt like a wrap-around hug from a humungous teddy bear.

Julian's kindness wasn't surprising, but the over-the-top nature of his hospitality left her puzzled. Was he *that* grateful for sex? Was he lonely, hoping she'd stay for the day? Or maybe, he could sense something was wrong that morning, trying to overcompensate...

December 23 wore many guises: forty-eight hours before Christmas, the date (hopefully) of her next flight update, and most weighing of all, the one-year anniversary of Kellie's death.

I didn't plan this very well. Madeleine pushed her eyeglasses up her nose. She traded her tea for a buttery slice of toast, slathered in Julian's homemade marmalade, and gave it a sniff. Citrusy and fresh, its zesty appeal was obvious. However, her appetite was not. *Last night was incredible, but what was I thinking, staying over?* Her stomach lurched as her phone buzzed. *Obviously, I wasn't.* She groaned. Dropping her weary head in her hand, she squinted at the message, too bright for her scratchy eyes.

Shantelle: I know today is extra hard. Call if you want. Love and hugs. x

Madeleine noted the time in the corner of the screen: 9:50 a.m. *Last year 9:50 Boston time, I would've been finishing laundry, packing my suitcase...* She nibbled the slice of toast, trying Julian's gooey jam. It would've been rude not to. An explosion of orange, bitter yet sweet, tweaked the corners of her mouth. Natasha was right. Julian's recipe really did taste like liquid sunshine.

He hit pause on his singing. "Maddie, what would you like to do today?"

I don't know. Cry? Curl up in a ball and hide? Go for tacos? How DO I mark the day my best friend died? She lifted her head and swallowed, avoiding the question. "Julian, your marmalade is delicious."

"Ah, cheers!" He popped around the corner, a rubber spatula in his hand. "I'm taking today off, so whatever you fancy... sightseeing, a movie and a meal, more sex"—he smiled—"I'm game."

But are you? Madeleine lowered her toast and licked her thumb as Julian reunited with their frying breakfast. *I'd like to honor Kellie, but to jump from orgasms to baring my soul, telling him my heart hurts because my best friend died a year ago today...er, talk about changing the temperature of the room.* She picked up her tea and slowly stood, searching for something to say as she rested against the kitchen doorjamb.

"Oh, I meant to tell you." Julian picked up a wooden cutting board and placed it on top of the pan of sizzling spuds. "There's this cool fundraising concert tonight in Chelsea if you're up for it. It's held in a beautiful church and raises money for a stray dog and cat rescue in Battersea—" With one hand firmly holding the board and the other grasping the skillet's handle, he flipped the combo upside down.

Madeleine's eyes bulged. "Holy f—what are you doing?!"

"I always hold my breath when I do that! You have to flip 'em to cook the other side." Julian lifted the pan and stole a peek. The rösti was perfectly golden and crispy. With care, he slid the potatoes off the cutting board, uncooked side down, back into the skillet. "Too many times to count, I mess up and the whole thing splats on the floor. Not that Winnie ever complained!"

Look at him. Chatty, flipping potatoes. Not a care in the world.

Her chest felt tight with dread. *Sharing my reality will drag him down. Jules doesn't deserve that, me dropping an emotional bomb then boarding a plane to Paris, knowing I'll never see him again. Best to leave things between us light and happy, just pleasant memories for him.*

Madeleine swirled the tea around her cup, settling on a way out for both of them. "Julian, about work...is that a good idea, taking today off? Last night, you said something about needing every penny, and with all the holiday shoppers and tourists, you'd be guaranteed *lots* of them."

"Yeah, but I'd rather skip today's pre-Christmas chaos and relax with you." He did a double take. "Unless you've got other plans..."

"No! I don't, it's just—"

"Maddie, it's okay, really. You won't hurt my feelings if you'd rather part ways after breakfast." He picked up the spatula and poked the potatoes crisping in the pan. "Or before. I can always wrap this up for you to-go and give you a lift back to your hotel. I know today might be your last day here and you have things to do, sandwiches to nosh..."

This man. He's lovely. He cooks, he dances, he's incredibly skilled at oral sex. Madeleine's eyes lingered on her late-night handiwork, Julian's epically mussed-up hair, and crept down his black David Bowie hoodie, its tattered cotton caressing the muscles in his back as he tended to the slices of ham frying in a second skillet. *And he's mine. Today. If I want him, and I do, but...TODAY...* The weight of the anniversary pressed, and she wrinkled her nose. *Kellie would say, 'Stay, you fool.'*

The admission loosened her shoulders and her resistance. "You know, I've never had a guy cook for me before. And I *love* rösti potatoes. The whole fluffy inside, crispy outside thing they have goin' on...delicious."

His face lit up. "Does that mean...?"

"If you're making homemade sandwiches, just try to get rid of me."

Julian laughed. "Ah, brilliant!" He leaned against the counter. "I know I've only known you for about five minutes, but last night, hanging out, exploring London with you—it's been absolutely cracking. You're lovely and fun and easy to talk to, not to mention *hot...*"

A bemused smile parted her lips.

"...and for me, last night was truly unforgettable," said Julian.

"I'll never forget it either." Her heart took a tumble. *And I'll never forget you.*

A wide grin reached his eyes. Sliding sideways, he began buttering generous slices of challah bread atop the cutting board straddling his sink. "These sarnies are gonna be epic!"

That ass is epic. Madeleine sipped her tea and stared appreciatively, the cheeky mistletoe print of his flannel pajama bottoms reminding her of all the places she'd kissed him a few hours ago. He slid across the floor again, and her gaze dropped. Two plush dog butts peaked out from beneath his pajama bottoms. *Corgi slippers. Of course!*

"Have a think about what you'd like to do after. We could hang here or shop, take a drive in the countryside somewhere, get some fresh air. That might do both our heads some good."

A surge of adrenaline spiked through her veins. *I could see* The Holiday *locations, commemorate Kellie!* Madeleine lowered her mug. "I like the drive idea."

"Great! We could head down south toward Brighton or west out Windsor way. It's totally your call. I'm up for anything."

I hope so. Madeleine shifted against the doorjamb. "I'd have to stop in at my hotel first and shower, though."

Julian glanced back and raised a flirty brow. "You're more than welcome to shower here."

"Thanks. I would, but all my stuff is there: my toiletries, my clothes..."

"Wait, hold on—you sayin' you don't want to wear your beautiful dress sightseeing?" He winked and returned to his stove.

"Dammit! I *knew* I should've packed my changing-room tent."

Her sardonic grin was tempered by a sip of tea. "Come to think of it, I should bring my carry-on and backpack with us. Not for Insta clothing changes, but in case I get one of those 'airport is now open' texts."

"Yep, no worries. You can leave it all in the cab." He lifted the searing ham with the spatula, checking its progress.

Ask him. She bit her lip. "Julian, could we visit the filming locations for *The Holiday*? It's a Christmas movie, a romance. I watch it every year."

"Aha! You're one of *those* people!"

She winced. "You think rom-coms are cheesy?"

"Nope, not at all. All I meant was, you're one of those people who makes pilgrimages to places of pop culture importance." He smiled over his shoulder. "I'm not pointing fingers. I'm the same! I've made multiple trips to Liverpool and Manchester for music stuff. I even hunted down the London street where Bowie shot his album cover for *The Rise and Fall of Ziggy Stardust*."

"Oh, I love that!"

"See? We're on the same page. And honestly, I would never judge, okay? I've been asked to drive people to pretty much everything. Nothing surprises me anymore. So, who's in this *Holiday* film, then?"

"Cameron Diaz, Jude Law, Jack Black, and Kate Winslet," said Madeleine.

"Kate! She's smashing! *Eternal Sunshine of the Spotless Mind* is one of my all-time faves." He glanced away from the potatoes. "Have you seen it?"

"I've heard of it."

"Oh, do yourself a favor and check it out sometime! It follows this couple played by Kate and Jim Carrey who erase sad and negative memories from their minds. It sounds kinda bonkers, people scrubbing away painful events and carrying on like they never happened, but trust me, it's an amazing, heartfelt film. Charlie Kaufman's finest hour. I highly recommend it—five glorious stars from me."

I would never erase my memories—good or bad. They've made me who I am.

Julian gave the spuds a nudge. "Where was *The Holiday* filmed? Outside London somewhere?"

"Most of it was shot in LA, but some scenes took place in a village called Shere."

"In Surrey?" he asked.

Her brows peaked. "You know it?"

"Yeah, I've never been, though. It's supposed to be lovely."

"It looks pretty in the movie. There's an old church, a river, some shops, and a pub." Her lips teased into a smile. "You can actually sit at the exact table where Jude Law sat when he spies Cameron across the pub."

"Well, that's cool. Shere is southwest of here, maybe an hour's drive, depending on traffic."

She pushed off the doorjamb. "Wanna go?"

"Shere!" Julian grinned.

Madeleine laughed and clutched her sore head. "Now *that's* cheesy!

TWENTY

MADELEINE

The charming village looked like a Christmas card come to life. Gently falling snow dusted the bare trees, quaint cottages, and shop roofs, and a narrow river dotted with paddling ducks, the Tillingbourne, babbled past shoppers and day-trippers searching for a festive bargain. Tourists strolled the narrow lanes, snapping photos of the village's war memorial and the lych gate leading to the broach spire of St. James' Church while locals lingered over pints in the White Horse Tavern, a Grade II listed building dating back to 1425. With its cozy nooks and spangly Christmas decorations, the English pub made the perfect location for a Hollywood love story.

Wrapped in an oversized sweater and the warmth of the tavern's crackling fire, Madeleine felt thankful for Julian's greasy breakfast, the brief nap in his cab during the drive, and the abundance of fresh Surrey air, all of which conspired to alleviate her pounding head and queasy stomach. She admired the exposed timber beams crossing the ceiling and the Christmassy pine boughs snaking around several nearby posts as a best of The Beautiful South album sang comfortably overhead. *Look at this place. So charming, so festive. It's exactly how I hoped it would be. Kellie would be over the moon. She'd be knocking back pints and chatting up the bartender.* Picking up her fork, Madeleine sliced open the flaky crust of her hearty chicken and mushroom pie, her appetite ravenous after their trek around town.

Julian, sleeves of his white Henley pushed up to his elbows, flipped through the Shere photos on her phone. "Ah, this one is brilliant!" He turned the screen around, displaying the shot of Madeleine channeling Cameron Diaz's character, Amanda, racing across the old stone footbridge in the falling snow.

"To think she did that in heels. Even in boots, I almost did a header into the river." Madeleine chuckled over her fork.

"Next time, we'll bring a stunt double." Julian set down her phone near her Coke and picked up his burger, turning it upside down.

She pushed her glasses up her nose and cocked her head. "Why do you...?"

"Eat it bottom-side up? The top bun is thicker, so if I eat the whole thing upside down, the juices and toppings won't soak the thinner bottom layer of bread." He smiled wantonly at his lunch then back at Madeleine, whose eyes widened with amazement. "I know. People think it's *hella weird*, to quote Tash."

"It's actually really clever." She watched him take the first bite, closing his eyes in complete hamburger heaven. A quiet "mmm" escaped his closed-mouth smile as he chewed happily.

Thank god it's delicious, especially after I dragged him all the way down here. She scooped up a piece of chicken covered in warm, savory gravy and gazed across the table again. *Kind, easygoing Julian.* His willingness to visit Shere, not to mention his enthusiasm for all her fangirlish photo ops, made her heart warm with gratitude.

"Julian, thanks so much for bringing me here."

He nodded until he swallowed his mouthful. "I'm always up for a beautiful drive, especially when it ends with a wander around a pretty village and a meal as good as this one."

"But are you sure I can't give you something toward the gas? At least let me pay half—"

"Nope. No. Sorry."

"Well, I'm paying for lunch, then."

He licked ketchup off his thumb. "That I'll accept."

"Good!" Nibbling the chicken on her fork, Madeleine's eyes strayed past him, their sparkle dimming slightly.

Her wistful stare didn't go unnoticed. Julian stole a look over his shoulder. Three seventy-something men sat around a table by the window, their husky chortling and bald heads overlooked by a small, framed poster for *The Holiday* hung on the wall behind them. The movie memorabilia marked the spot where Jude's character, Graham, sat during a pivotal scene. "Shame we couldn't sit over there."

"It's fine." Madeleine raked through her pie and speared a plump mushroom. "Just being here is incredib—"

"They're leaving!"

Her gaze catapulted away from her fork. Sure enough, the gray-haired gang were stiffly shuffling off, leaving behind a cluster of empty pint glasses and their table.

"Quick!" Determination creased Julian's brow as he grabbed both their plates. "I'll take these. You bring our drinks!"

Seconds later, the coveted table was theirs, and Madeleine's heart felt fit to burst. *Kellie, is this your doing?* She patted the bench. *Can you see me here? I hope so.*

"Someone looks like the cat who got the cream." Julian shifted the dirty beer glasses to a neighboring table.

"Jude Law's bum sat *right here*." She bounced in her seat and handed Julian her phone. "Could you...?"

"It would be my pleasure." Leaning back, he carefully fit in the film poster alongside Madeleine's beaming grin. He captured several photos from slightly different angles. "You really love this movie, don't you?"

"I'm a romantic, what can I say? I *love* love."

Julian's eyes crinkled behind his glasses. "You know, it's so refreshing, being with someone who—" Her phone buzzed in his hand. "Oh, new text." He handed it across the table.

Shantelle: My manager spoke to my travel agent. Calling you.

Before she could finish reading, "Disco 2000" sang out. Madeleine hit Accept and pressed her phone to her ear. "Hey, Shan! Got news?"

"Not the kind you wanna hear."

Shooot! Her smile collapsed.

"My travel guy says the airports in the UK and Europe won't be opening today and probably won't tomorrow either."

Madeleine rubbed the back of her neck. "But where'd he get that from? I haven't heard a peep from Jet Britannia."

Julian glanced over his upside down burger, concern darkening his brow.

"Dude got an email from head office," replied Shantelle. "He says the formal announcement is coming soon."

Unease knotted in Madeleine's gut. "Great," she muttered.

"You okay?" Julian asked quietly, wiping his hands on a napkin.

Eyes wide, she shrugged slowly. "Not sure," she mouthed back.

"I know! This sucks! I even called my psychic for a second opinion." Shantelle's beloved psychic was about as accurate as Punxsutawney Phil on Groundhog Day.

This gets better and better. Madeleine's face pinched.

"Thing is, she didn't agree. She says European airports WILL open tomorrow."

Madeleine shook her head. "Shan, no offense to your psychic and travel agent, but let's wait for the airports and Jet Britannia to issue *their* updates, okay? They'll have all the facts. They're who we should trust."

A huff filled her ear, a clear sign a pout was brewing on the other end of the line. "I was really hoping we'd fly today 'cause, let's face it, tomorrow is way too late." Shantelle moaned. "We'd just have to turn around and fly home three days later."

"Yeah, but Christmas Day and the 26th in Paris are better than nothing, right?"

"Not if everything's closed. Look, Mads, as much as it pains me to say this, it's time to call off Paris and head home."

Head home? How? Madeleine's pulse accelerated with throbbing intent, resuscitating her fading headache. "And—and what?" She leaned an elbow on the table and winced, massaging her temple with her free hand. "*You* decide for both of us and *I* don't get a say?"

The pointed question hung unanswered somewhere in between London and Bangkok. Shantelle didn't do awkward pauses. Something was up.

The knot in Madeleine's stomach cinched tighter. "You didn't book a ticket home already—did you?"

"I'm…I'm on my way to the airport—"

"Shan!"

Julian relinquished his napkin to the table and scrubbed a hand over his mouth.

So typical. So Shantelle. Madeleine slouched back in her seat. *Acts first and then expects everyone else to acquiesce.*

Shantelle sputtered. "It's just, if I leave tonight, I'll get to Mom and Dad's on Christmas Eve."

"Great—for you," said Madeleine. "Sucks for me."

"Mads, don't hate me."

"Did I say I do?"

"No, but you're annoyed."

"A little, yeah. If the tables were turned, I would've at least *told* you before I booked anything." Madeleine flicked flakes of pie crust from her jeans.

"I'm sorry. I didn't mean to upset you…"

"It's fine. I don't blame you." Madeleine looked up. Julian was scrolling through his phone, granting her as much privacy as he could sat two plate-widths away. "I'm pissed at the situation, not you."

"Okay, phew!" Shantelle paused. "Hey, want to hear something that might cheer you up?"

Madeleine braced herself. Her sister's mood boosters were usually related to a lucky break associated with Jupiter traveling through her ninth house. They rarely offered any benefit—or cheer—to anyone but Shantelle.

"I bought you the most amazeballs present!" she squealed. "It's on its way to Milwaukee as we speak. It wouldn't fit in my case."

What the hell did she buy me? In the past, Shantelle's 'amazeballs' gifts included a coffee table shaped like a sunfish and a patent leather purse with a clock imbedded in its side. "Oh, thanks, Shan, but honestly, you didn't have to. You've been paying for everything here."

"Yeah, but you still need a present to open! Wanna know something else?" Shantelle inhaled a deep breath, ramping up for her big reveal. "Baby Nolan is coming for Christmas!"

Madeleine's head jerked back. "What?" Her eyes fluttered down to her half-eaten lunch. "Since when? I thought Antoine was headed to the in-laws."

"Not anymore! Erin had an argument with her parents, so they're spending the hols with Mom and Dad! Oh, Mads, I had the *cutest* astrological chart designed for Nolan, and Gabriel bought him a pull sled, so we can give him rides in the snow on Christmas morning—"

"Wait, Gabriel is coming, too?"

Julian glanced up from his phone and adjusted his eyeglasses.

"And he's bringing his new boyfriend—the brave soul!" Shantelle laughed. "I offered to order in a twenty-pound turkey fully cooked with all the starters and sides and desserts, but Mom said…"

Shantelle rambled on breathlessly about their mom's cheesy broccoli casserole and buttery mashed potatoes, but Madeleine zoned out after spinach soufflé. *Everyone will be there—but me.* She closed her eyes and shook her head.

"Mads? *Madeleine*, are you listening?"

Her eyes snapped open, landing on Julian, who was lost in his phone again. "Uh, yeah. Mom's homemade bûche de Noël and French almond macarons. It just isn't Christmas without them."

Shantelle tsked. "Just come home as soon as you can, okay?"

"If I had a TARDIS, I would."

"I know, that's why"—static crackled through Shantelle's response—"my part."

"You—sorry?" Madeleine covered her other ear. "I didn't hear that. You were breaking up."

"I bought you a one-way, first-class ticket home," repeated

Shantelle. "I'm emailing you the deets now, 'kay?"

"Oh! That's really generous. Thank you." She rubbed her brow. *But I still can't fly.*

"I couldn't book it without a departure date, so it's set for to-morrow night," explained Shantelle. "But if the airport is still closed, you can easily bump it to the 25th or another day without penalty."

Madeleine nodded. "Okay, great."

"There's just one thing," said Shantelle. "It's not direct. There's a three-hour layover in Miami."

"In the middle of winter? Could be worse."

"Right?" Shantelle agreed. "So, that means your total flight time will be sixteen hours."

Sixteen hours! Madeleine cringed. *Shit.*

"Look, I'm almost at the airport now. I'll text again during my layover in Tokyo, 'kay?" Shantelle paused for a beat. "Maddie, I'm sorry Paris didn't work out, today of all days…"

"It's fine, I'll be fine." She weaved her hand through her hair.

"Stay safe, okay? Make sure you've got hand sanitizer and get up, walk around during your flight. And don't drink too much cham-pagne or talk to strange men!"

"Two of my fave things!" Shantelle snickered. "Don't worry, I'll be good. Love and hugs, Mads."

She nodded. "Love and hugs. Bye." Ending the call, Madeleine slid her phone on the table and met Julian's inquisitive nod.

"I take it your sister booked a flight?"

"Yeah—home. She's packing up her inflatable avocado and passing on Paris." She fidgeted with her necklace, smoothing her fingers over the quaver charm.

Julian's brows rose then furrowed. "What does that mean for you?"

"When the airports open up, I'll fly back to Milwaukee. Shan bought me a one-way ticket."

A ghost of a smile flirted with his lips. "Right. Well, that's good…"

"Yeah. My entire family is headed there, including Nolan, my brother's little guy."

"The first grandchild?"

"Yep."

"How old?"

"Seven months."

Julian picked up his sparkling water. "First Christmas, then."

Madeleine nodded as her phone buzzed once, then a second time, its persistence pulling her back to the screen.

Jet Britannia: Travel update: Flight JB092 from LHR—CDG is delayed another 24 hours due to the continued threat of volcanic ash in European airspace.

Jet Britannia: All British airports remain closed. Our next update will be Friday, December 24. In the event the airports reopen that day, please be prepared to travel.

I need to cancel my ticket and these Paris alerts. Madeleine crinkled her nose as she exited the messages. "Well, Shantelle's travel agent was right about something. Looks like I'll be here for another twenty-four hours at least."

"Can't catch a break, eh?" He lowered his glass.

I don't want him feeling obligated. She sighed. "Listen, Julian, you don't have to hang out with me."

"Yeah, I know. But what if I want to?"

"You'll lose out on all those fares. I'd feel awful."

"They're not going anywhere. The same can't be said of you."

Madeleine fiddled with her fork, stuck in her pie. "If you're sure…"

"Never been more." He returned to his burger.

Julian had gone above and beyond that morning: the homemade breakfast, driving through London's holiday gridlock and the British countryside, and passing up a golden opportunity to earn a sizable sum. His selflessness was heartwarming, and Madeleine wanted to pay him back. Not with money or sex (although the latter would've been fun), but with an experience he'd love as much as she was loving visiting Shere. Christmas was the season of giving, after all.

Think of something good. She dug her fork through her pie as Julian glanced out the window, his face softening into an irresistible smile. "Maddie, the most adorable bulldog puppy is outside. He's on one of the pub's picnic tables. Can you see him?"

Madeleine shifted in front of *The Holiday* poster and toward the window, looking through its paned glass. The stocky pup with his bowed legs, squished nose, and wrinkled face leaned into his owner's hand as she gave him a vigorous scratch behind one of his folded ears. A flush of happiness radiated through Madeleine's body. "Aw! Cute doesn't even begin to describe him."

"Who needs human babies when sweet doggos walk amongst us." Julian's voice bubbled with boyish glee.

Right then, Madeleine knew what she could do.

It would mean immersing herself in an evening of Christmas cheer, but after dipping her toe in slowly at the pub quiz, South Bank Market, and Covent Garden, she felt ready to take the plunge.

I can do this. I know I can do this...

With a smile, she turned back to their table. "Julian, that fundraising concert you mentioned, the one helping the dog and cat shelter? Still wanna go?"

TWENTY-ONE

MADELEINE

"*Eighty* Christmas trees?" she asked.

"And about 68,000 lights," said Julian.

"How is that even possible?" Madeleine stepped out of the path of two seniors overwhelmed with holiday shopping and raised her phone, filling her screen with the dazzling display outside the Churchill Arms pub in Kensington. The exterior of the boozer's ground floor and its two upper storeys were completely obscured by bushy Christmas trees of various sizes, illuminated with clear lights. The joyous glow set against the dark London night elicited excited exclamations and enraptured grins from people buzzing around the pub—including Madeleine.

"It's stunning." Her phone snapped away. "But I'd hate to pay their electricity bill. You say they do this every year?"

"Yep, since 1987. If you visit in the summer, it's covered in flowers."

She sighed, lowering her phone. "Just gorgeous."

"The inside is a bit more—well, you'll see for yourself," said Julian.

Once through the doors with drinks in hand, Julian led Madeleine through the loud, jovial crowd to a reserved table and a brown leather banquette with old-school diamond button tufting. Mahogany paneling rose from behind the back rest, meeting a bold display of black and white photographs of lords, dukes, and former British prime minister Winston Churchill. An intriguing array of curiosities and antiques—everything from musical instruments and chamber pots to lanterns and brass jugs—hung from the ceiling, creating instant conversation starters for shy couples out on a first date, but

Madeleine and Julian didn't have such trouble. So far, they hadn't run out of things to share or discuss.

They slipped behind the table, sharing the banquette and the view of the pub's bric-a-brac. Books, potted plants, and candleholders peppered every flat surface.

"I'm glad you suggested stopping at my hotel," said Madeleine, taking off her coat. "I didn't even think."

"Leaving your case in my cab in Shere is one thing, but London?" Julian shook his head. "Best to be safe. Can't have someone getting their mitts on your Christmas tray."

"I'd be heartbroken. I love it 'cause it's from you." She watched a grin bloom across Julian's face as he placed his phone on the table. "Any word from Micah or Natasha? They still planning to pop in?"

"I think so, but Meeks was feeling pretty rough after last night. He left his shop early, went home for a lie-down." Julian shifted free of his coat and left it behind him. "You sure you're not peckish? These guys do great Thai food."

"I feel like an overfed turkey: I'm stuffed." She grimaced. "But maybe we could grab a bite after the concert? Dim sum or tacos, something like that?"

"Absolutely."

"And maybe we could drive around and see some Christmas lights?"

Julian draped his arm along the back of the banquette. "You starting to feel the holiday spirit, there, Joy?"

Madeleine pulled the woolly Christmas pudding from her head. "I blame my hat. Its festive magic must be seeping into my brain." She rested it on top of her coat and retrieved her phone from one of its pockets.

Julian smiled and paused for a beat, his focus roaming the pub, landing on nothing in particular. "Ooh." His eyes zeroed in on hers. "Hear that?"

"Hear…?" She glanced at her phone and nudged up her glasses.

"Christina Perri just followed Joni Mitchell. I think the pub's playing your *More Meh Than Merry* playlist."

Madeleine exchanged her phone for her soft drink. "I wouldn't be surprised. Last week, it topped Sensoria's chart for most streamed this month."

"Congratulations! So what does that feel like, hearing your work played in shops and pubs so far from home?" Julian tipped the lemon slice off the rim of his glass into his sparkling water.

"It's fun and a bit...surreal." She gulped a mouthful of Coke.

"I bet it never gets old."

Madeleine swirled the ice cubes around her glass. "Not usually, but this year—well, I'm considering a change."

"Of job? Because of your boss?"

"Yes and no. He's part of it. It's just, I'm not enjoying it like I used to. I feel...indifferent, which is odd seeing how much I love music and messing around with playlists."

"Really? How long have you felt like this?" Julian asked.

"About a year. Since my promotion. I was excited when I got it, but now all the office politics and longer hours are making me question whether it's still for me. I don't want my job to turn me into someone I don't recognize. You know that whole 'live to work versus work to live' thing?"

Julian nodded.

"I've been mulling that one over a lot lately," said Madeleine. "But before I spiral into a 'what-should-I-be-doing-with-my-life' panic, I thought I'd put in for a transfer and see if working for a different boss gives me back my mojo."

"You can move around like that?"

Madeleine nodded and left her soft drink on a beer mat. "That's the best thing about Sensoria—the flexibility. We can work from home, a coffee shop, almost anywhere. I could transfer to, say, the LA office but work remotely from Boston. I'd just report to a boss in California." Her phone buzzed and she bent forward, reading the screen.

Mom: Thinking of you, sweetie. Love you so much. x

She pushed it closer to her Coke and sat back again.

"It's worth a try, right?" said Julian. "Life's too damn short to be unhappy because of a job." He tossed back a swig of fizzy water and set it down on their table.

Life IS too short. Madeleine's eyes followed the bubbles pinging upward in his glass. Sitting still for a moment without Surrey's pretty scenery or London's delights distracting her through the cab window, the gravity of the day closed in. *I've worried about the first anniversary for months. How I'd feel, what I'd do. Now it's here, and while my grief doesn't feel any less, it has definitely changed...and old fears are being overtaken by new ones.*

A lump grew in her throat. *Kellie, I used to feel you around me sometimes, your energy or spirit...something. I thought I'd feel you more strongly today, but I don't and that breaks me! Have I lost you again?!*

Another buzz and Madeleine's squirrel wallpaper lit up with a pair of texts and the time: 5 p.m.

A year ago, I was leaving for the airport. Snow was falling and I was waiting to hear back from you... She collected the phone and gazed at the screen pensively, the watery sting in her eyes begging her to blink. *...You never answered my text. Now it sits in my phone forever unread.*

Julian leaned sideways. "You all right? You seem far away."

Madeleine bowed her head and faked a yawn. "Oh, I'm just a bit tired. I'm sure the caffeine will kick in any minute." Amidst a flurry of tear-stifling blinks behind her eyeglasses, she opened the texts.

Shantelle: In Tokyo, having sneaky McD's in the airport. Saved you the Kawaii toy from my Happy Meal.

Shantelle: Next leg to Chicago will take 12 hours. Got my *Drag Race* marathon ready. Love and hugs! x

"I'll just message Shan back." Typing quickly, she kept her reply brief.

Madeleine: Thx for the toy. Be safe, ok? Text me from Chicago. Love and so many hugs. x

"Mate!" Micah, clutching a full pint, swerved around an amateur football team supping celebratory beers. "Sorry we're late. My phone died and..."

"Hangover 1, birthday boy 0." Julian smirked as Madeleine looked up.

"Not this time. Blame our kid." Micah tilted his head toward Natasha, bringing up the rear, a pair of candy cane deely boppers sprouting like two red and white question marks above her scarlet locks. "I had to physically drag her out of the donut shop." He pulled out a chair and gingerly lowered himself, preventing his beer from breaching the rim of the glass.

"I had a complaint!" Natasha's braces flashed as she plopped down in a profusion of black lace and velvet on the chair across from Madeleine.

Micah closed his eyes. "You *have* a crush—"

"And you have three fugly love bites!"

With a hard blink, he tugged at the Man City scarf draped around his neck. "So Madeleine, how was Surrey?"

Before she could answer, Natasha jumped in. "Sure, change the subject." His sister scoffed, digging in her cloak's pocket. Her hand surfaced with a bag of Dolly Mixture sweets and a packet of Marks & Spencer Percy Pigs. "He's pissed because apparently, I stole his superpower."

Julian's amused glance boomeranged between the Cooper siblings. "You what?"

"We saw a poster for the new Marvel film on the Tube and got talking superpowers," said Micah. "I chose shapeshifting."

Madeleine nodded. "Good choice."

"Right? It'd be a trip to switch things up, turn into someone else when the feeling strikes, you know?"

Natasha tore open her Dolly Mixture and fished out an orange cylinder. "And I said, you can't pick that because that's me—now. I'm a shapeshifter. I'm a goth today, but who knows ten years from now. I could be a metalhead, a mod..." She popped the sweet in her mouth and laid the packet on the table alongside the bag of soft, pink gummies shaped like smiley pig faces. "Madeleine, help yourself."

"Okay, thanks." She eyed the packet of Percy Pigs. "These look...interesting." Her fingers slipped inside.

"Oi, Tash, what you're sayin' isn't shapeshifting." Micah brushed a hand through his hair. "It's joining a musical subculture." He looked across the table. "Jules, Madeleine, back me up."

"I plead the fifth." Madeleine hid behind a bite of chewy candy and glanced sidelong at Julian.

"Well, I guess you could shapeshift into various subcultures..."

"Yeah, yeah, take Tash's side." Micah playfully tossed a beer mat at his best friend.

"Julian, what superpower would you choose?" asked Madeleine, the sweetness of raspberry teasing her tastebuds.

"I'd pick time travel..."

"Ooh, I like that!" Natasha sat up.

"...so I could go back in time, be in the audience for the greatest concerts of all time." Julian lifted his glass.

Madeleine lit up. "Like Bowie's Ziggy Stardust tour!"

Julian nodded enthusiastically. "Nirvana at Reading Festival in '92, Prince at Coachella—"

"Deadmau5 at Lollapalooza in 2011," offered Micah, gulping his pint.

Natasha let out a snorty laugh. "You were there, dumbass!"

"Like I can remember it! I was totally off my tits!"

"What about you, Madeleine?" asked Natasha.

"I think I'd like to control time. I'd slow it down or freeze it, so I could have more time with the people I care about."

A smile played on Julian's lips as he set his fizzy water on the table.

"Ugh, you guys!" Natasha wailed. "Your picks are way too *GOOD*. I'll have to change mine now."

Micah threw his hands up in the air.

"I'm going to swap shapeshifting for the ability to fly, see the world."

"Nice one, Tash." Julian's phone pinged with a text. "You could go all over, see friends you haven't hung out with in years. That's what I would do, and best of all, no planes necessary." He bent forward and squinted through his eyeglasses at the screen then sat back.

"I'd fly off to visit online friends, too," said Madeleine, re-claiming her soft drink.

Julian's forehead slowly creased as his fingers roamed beneath his sleeve and fidgeted with his watch. "Yeah, but I don't have any of those." He curled toward the table again, snatching his phone.

Of those? Of course. Madeleine offered a weak smile and sipped her Coke.

"Oh, blimey!" Natasha giggled. "Here comes the sermon from Jules on the evils of social media, online dating, the modern world, blah blah blah…"

"Ugh." Julian bristled, lowering his phone. "Caroline just sent me a text meant for Alistair."

"Oh gawd, it's not nudes, is it?" asked Natasha. "The thought of your brother wanking over that!"

"Now there's an image I could've done without. Cheers, Tash." Julian scrolled up. "No, she tripped and injured her wrist. She's having X-rays at A&E."

Micah feigned sadness. "*Oh nooo!*" His brow flexed sarcas-tically. "Anyway…"

Julian typed out his message. "Wrong…Halliwell. Send."

Natasha smirked. "Thanks for the texting play-by-play, old man."

He left his phone on the table and stood up. "Ignore it if she an-swers. I have to check on the cab, make sure it's charging okay.

Back in a sec." He squeezed past Micah and disappeared around the corner.

Madeleine leaned in, helping herself to another Percy Pig. "So what's the deal with Caroline? She's got Winnie now?"

"Yeah, god, she's such a nasty piece of work." Micah lifted his friend's phone and began swiping the lit screen with purpose.

"What are you doing?" Natasha's face pinched.

"My phone's dead and you never lend me yours. I need to check the time of our train tomorrow..." Micah tapped and swiped again. "So yeah, Caroline—she wasn't *always* awful. In the beginning, she seemed quite sweet, didn't she Tash?"

Micah's sister nodded. "She volunteered in the evenings, delivering meals to old age pensioners. She met Jules there, helping with the charity."

"She changed, though, when her PR firm became successful." Micah grimaced. "Stopped volunteering, dumped friends, hacked away at Julian's self-esteem for shits and giggles."

Madeleine swallowed her candy. "That's terrible."

"Yeah. She became a real power-tripper," said Micah. "Honestly, it was a relief when they split."

"Thank fuck Jules didn't propose with his mum's ring!" said Natasha. "Knowing her, she would've kept it—just because."

Micah looked up from Julian's phone. "They were supposed to meet and divvy up all their stuff, but when Jules was working late, Caroline came round with Alistair. They cleared out everything including Winnie."

Madeleine backed away, her eyes bouncing between the siblings. "Oh god! He must've been devastated, coming home, finding him gone!"

"It was such a dick move," sneered Natasha, peering into the bag of Percy Pigs. "Jules loves that dog more than life itself. You know, he *still* leaves the lights and radio on for Winnie? Force of habit."

Madeleine nodded as Micah continued. "Unlike Caroline, who barely gives a fuck about him."

"How can she not love a corgi?" asked Madeleine.

"She did when they got him. Wins was a cute novelty," said Micah. "Great for bragging rights, great for social media posts, but she didn't actually *do* anything with him. It was Jules who took Winnie to puppy class and checkups. Jules played with him, walked him, picked up his poop. He's the one who sat for hours at the vet during Win's surgery—"

Madeleine gaped. "Winnie had surgery?"

"Four months ago." Micah explained. "For hip dysplasia."

"Aww, poor pup! Julian must've been so worried."

"Yep, and he's got the gray hairs to prove it," said Micah, tapping Julian's phone screen again. "Rehab was tough, too. Weeks of exercises, laser treatments, water therapy—all on Jules, until a week ago. Now that the hard graft is over, Caroline's cut him off again."

"You serious?" Natasha scowled, scratching below her candy cane deely boppers. "Jules can't see him?"

"Bloody typical, right?" said Micah. "Until she books some fancy hols and wants him to dog-sit."

All this must've been so stressful, not to mention obscenely expensive. Madeleine puffed out her cheeks. *And he took today off work for me.* Guilt bubbled in her belly. "Did Julian try to get him back?"

"We were all set, ready to go over there, weren't we, Tash?"

Braces gummed up with chewy candy, his sister bobbed her head in a deep, emphatic nod.

"But Jules—you know what he's like, Madeleine: he's never selfish, always thinks of others first," said Micah. "We were about to head off in his cab, but he killed the engine and said he couldn't do it in good conscience."

Madeleine shook her head. "Why?"

"Caroline's got this massive back garden and a six-figure paycheck. And what's Jules got?" Micah shrugged, returning Julian's phone to the table. "He said he couldn't compete with all that. He thought Winnie would want for nothing living under Caroline's roof."

"Except for love." Natasha glared. "Tons of toys and Winnie photos on Instagram don't make up for a lack of affection. It's total bollocks. It's all for show. All she cares about is her flippin' image. Seriously, Madeleine, check out her feed: CarolinePeelPR. Winnie is her favorite prop. It makes me so mad."

She made a mental note. *I know what I'm doing later.*

Micah agreed. "Winnie's a trophy, nothing more. He's a prize she won, something to hold over Jules, and that is so fucked up."

"Unbelievable." Madeleine frowned.

"But now Julian is fighting back. He tried speaking with Caroline about sharing custody but got nowhere fast, so he's taken her to court." Micah glanced over his shoulder. Spotting Julian on the approach tugging down the sleeves of his Henley, he lowered his voice. "Hopefully, the judge will see sense and Wins will come home." Micah picked up his pint. "Tash, ready to crack on?" He guzzled most of his beer in one go as Julian rounded the table.

"I guess." She sighed, squirreling away her Dolly Mixture bag in the pocket of her black cloak. "Madeleine, you can keep the Percy Pigs if you want?"

"I will! Thanks!"

"What time is your train tomorrow?" asked Julian, reclaiming his seat.

Micah slammed his pint on the table and a mini wave of beer swirled around the glass. "Half-twelve. Bloody dreading it. You know it's gonna be a total clown show. If I wanted to be jammed in, sniffing armpits for two hours, I would've joined our local rugby team."

"A rugby match is eighty minutes, not two full hours." Natasha sat back all smug, her response drawing a brotherly wince.

"How do you even know"—Micah stifled a burp—"that?"

"Trivial Pursuit, two Christmases ago? Before the *Doctor Who* special?"

Julian leaned into Madeleine. "Another punch-up. The cousins disagreed on who was scarier: Daleks or Weeping Angels."

"And The Silence won, go figure." Natasha rummaged in her

cloak and produced a packet of cola-flavored chewing gum. She clocked Madeleine's soft drink. "Go on, Maddie! Have some! Tastes like the real thing."

She waved her hand. "Oh, I'm okay, thanks. I don't really chew gum."

Natasha snickered. "What? Did Jules get to you?"

"I'm...sorry?" Her glance pinged between Natasha and Julian, who shrugged.

"I have this *thing* about gum chewing," he said. "I hate watching people chew it, hate hearing that elastic-y snap. It's not a phobia, just a strong dislike, that's all."

"Ya weirdo! Let's hope no one sticks their gum under your pew tonight, eh, Jules?" Micah laughed. "So, this concert, got your vocal cords all warmed up?"

"It's a singalong?" Madeleine's lips quirked. "Julian, maybe they'll have that Snowman song!"

He shot her some amused side-eye.

"*We're walking in the air...*" Natasha sang, stashing her chewing gum packet in her voluminous cloak.

"Don't they usually have a celeb doing a reading?" asked Micah.

Julian nodded. "Last year it was that Irish bloke, the one from that Scottish Highlander show—"

"*Lairds and Liars,*" Natasha interjected.

"I'm all about the dogs," said Madeleine. "Can't wait to see them."

"Did Jules tell ya that's where he first spotted Winnie?" said Micah, buttoning his coat. "Adopted him the next day."

Julian shrugged. "When you know, you know."

"Aw..." Madeleine squeezed his hand. "That's so lovely."

Micah's eyes fell to their entwined fingers. "And they lived happily ever after," he mumbled, then caught Madeleine's double take. "Jules and Wins, I mean. It's like that saying: '*Happiness is a warm puppy.*'"

Madeleine's heart dipped, picturing the Charles Schulz quote tattooed on her best friend's forearm, a tribute to her Pomeranian. *Kellie loved Roo just like Julian loves Winnie.*

"Well, have fun tonight." Micah tugged on his Manchester City scarf and rose to his feet. "Madeleine, it's been mint! Cheers for hanging out."

"Thanks for making me feel so welcome." She let go of Julian's hand and stood, leaning over the table to hug Micah first, then Natasha.

The younger Cooper pouted as she withdrew. "Damn volcano! Can't it have another hissy fit? Anything to keep you here."

Madeleine smiled. "I'll come back." Her eyes strayed to Julian. "I promise."

TWENTY-TWO

JULIAN

Pews were filling up fast in St. Luke's Church, the demand for prime seats exceeding supply. This was great news for the dog and cat adoption shelter. For Julian and Madeleine? Not so much.

This is my fault. We should've arrived earlier. Julian dragged his hand over his mouth and scoped out the sea of festive faces. "Whaddya reckon? Near the front on the far right side and potentially obstructed by a stone pillar or"—he motioned to a vacant space for two in the last row—"sat on the center aisle in the back?"

"I don't mind sitting back there," said Madeleine, her fingers twiddling with the red pom-pom on her hat. "We'll still see everything."

Julian nodded as they retraced their steps, passing pew after pew, their sides adorned with sprigs of holly, red ribbons, and sparkly baubles. "And we'll be closer to the mince pies when we leave."

"Well, there you go!" said Madeleine. "It's a win-win."

She's amazing. Easygoing, fun-loving—and here with me. I still can't believe it.

Madeleine made way for an elderly man with a walker and sidestepped a jaunty Schipperke, the thick black ruff around her neck adorned with a red velvet bow. "I *love* those dogs, little black foxes." She smiled as the owner paraded by.

"You see all sorts here," said Julian, letting Madeleine enter the pew first.

Once they'd eased out of their coats and settled in, Julian thumbed through his concert program while Madeleine risked whiplash, looking everywhere with the exuberance of a little kid surrounded by a mountain of presents on Christmas morning.

All around were Londoners of all ages: families with small children, talkative seniors sharing the latest gossip, and long-lost friends greeting one another with hugs and "Let's meet for drinks soon! Text me!"

Madeleine smiled. "I feel like I've left tourist-land and stepped into real London."

Julian left his open program upside down on his lap along with his phone. "Loads of the same faces come back every year. It's become a holiday tradition."

"A lovely one." Madeleine craned her neck, studying the nave's vaulted stone ceiling and the imposing wood and brass organ overlooking the entrance behind them. Her eyes widened, taking in the instrument's design, which included a likeness of the church's tower. "I thought this place was going to be just another neighborhood church. You've seen one, you've seen them all, right? But I'm so wrong. This one's huge with tons of character. Julian, there are even flying buttresses outside!"

"Surprised me, too, first time I saw it. Get this—only St. Paul's Cathedral and Westminster Abbey have a higher nave roof than this place!"

"Incredible." Madeleine's gaze skated along the outer aisles and up the church's grand arches where the upper galleries hosted even more guests.

"Did you know Charles Dickens got married here?"

"No!"

"I'll show you his marriage certificate on the way out," said Julian. "They have a copy on display."

"That's so cool." Madeleine stared ahead, her eyes climbing the massive stained glass window behind the altar. "History really is everywhere you turn here." She opened her program and began reading the welcome messages from the church and the animal shelter.

She hasn't said anything about staying over tonight. Julian adjusted his glasses. *At times, she's seemed lost in her thoughts today.*

Quiet and reflective. I hope she's not having second thoughts about last night. He winced behind his hand. *I'm falling for her. I know geography complicates things, but like Micah says, love knows no borders. You can't help who you fall in love with, more's the pity...*

Madeleine's focus swerved off the page to a chubby pug waddling up the center aisle. Her expression lit up like the sparkly Christmas tree stood proudly beside the eagle lectern. "Look at *him*! Look at his *bum*! So soft and squishy! Don't you just wanna reach out and grab it?"

Her joy was infectious, lifting Julian from his spiral of doubt. "Hey, didn't you say the same thing about mine last night?"

She mock-frowned. "Hate to break it to you, Julian, but yours is firm, round, and *deliciously* biteable."

He covered his mouth with his palm, playing along. "Ooh, matron, what will the vicar say?"

Madeleine hid behind her program. "Whoops, sorry! Forgot where I was."

Julian lowered his hand as she fanned her face with the booklet, his gaze tracing her mouth. "I can't stop thinking about last night..."

"You're not the only one." She blinked up at him then looked away like she was self-conscious. "So, are all the dogs here up for adoption?"

Well, we are in church. Julian cleared his throat. "Most of them. Some are adoptees who've come back with their owners to celebrate."

"That's just—" She laid her hand over her heart. "Have you brought Winnie back?"

"I want to. Just haven't had the chance."

"Maybe next Christmas?"

Maybe. He nodded.

"If I were you, I'd include this concert in your book of London short stories," said Madeleine. "Tell your own tale. It's so beautiful, how you and Winnie found each other."

"Might do." He picked up his phone, muting it, then stowed it in his coat's pocket. "How's your writing coming along?"

"Oh, you know, fits and starts. I dabble—when I have time. It's nothing serious."

"But could it be? Why don't you make it a priority?"

"What, like you have?" She smiled mischievously, toying with the fringe on her scarf, still wrapped around her neck.

"Okay, you got me there." He licked his lips. "No, it's just I was thinking if Sensoria is bringing you no joy, maybe writing could provide an escape? You've got the talent and the degree. Why not put it into action?"

"I have—in a way," said Madeleine. "I've written two novels."

Julian lifted his chin. "Two?! That's brilliant."

"But I didn't query agents or publish them."

"Why not?"

She shrugged.

"Oh, there's a story!"

"Yeah, well, maybe this one is better left shelved." Her eyes trailed a fluffy black cocker spaniel, then a snow white Japanese Spitz. "They're so cute! Julian, let's buy a big farm near Shere and adopt *all* the dogs."

She's avoiding. Julian pushed his eyeglasses up. "Yeah, I could go for that, but before we talk leashes and dog toys, wanna tell me what happened?"

"Julian…"

"Maddie, I've had my share of bumps in the road, too, you know. Some even made me reconsider writing as a career. You already know the big one that ended it for good."

Her fingers fought through her scarf and grasped her necklace. She silently stared ahead, dragging the musical note charm along its silver chain.

Julian's lips pursed. *She's giving me nothing.* "I know how cut-throat the writing world can be." His tone was gentle, supportive. "All I'm saying is, whatever happened must've been heartbreaking if your finished manuscripts ended up abandoned in a drawer."

Madeleine closed her eyes and exhaled heavily. "It wasn't just

one thing"—her lashes slowly opened as she let go of the charm—
"and it was cumulative. One thing after another: fear of failure, syn-
opsis-writing hell…having an author I admire turn on me."

"What?! Who?"

"You won't know her." She watched a beagle and a Scottish
terrier meander up the aisle with employees from the animal shelter.

"Try me."

"Estella McKenna."

No clue. Julian shook his head.

"See, I knew you wouldn't—"

"Tell me anyway. And like they say, it's good to vent. A trouble shared is a trouble halved and all that bollocks." He draped his
arm around her shoulders. "So, come on—let's halve it."

Madeleine pouted. "It all started like, three years ago. I'd been
following Estella on social media as a fan and a book blogger."

"You reviewed books?"

"Yep, for five unglamorous years. One day, we had this amazing conversation about writing and novels. She shared her email
with me and we stayed in touch here and there. It was nice, having a
writer friend who took me seriously as an aspiring author.

"Fast-forward a few months and I'm working on a special project for Sensoria's board of directors. I'd been pulling all-nighters,
skipping meals, I missed a friend's birthday party…"

"One of *those* assignments," said Julian.

"Yeah, it was my life for two months, basically. I got most of it
done but was waiting on this guy in our New York office to send
me stats. I couldn't finish without them. I followed up several times,
left messages, and got no response." Madeleine let out a forceful
breath. "Then deadline day rolls around. I call, I email, and again,
tumbleweeds."

"You must've been pissed."

"And sick to my stomach. My boss was going to have a massive shit-fit, so three hours before our meeting, I call New York
again hoping someone can track down stats guy for me. Turns out,
he's in Uruguay and is unreachable."

"On holiday? The bugger!"

"Yeah, and he left the day after my *first* follow-up." Madeleine shook her head. "I couldn't believe it. He'd ghosted me! At this point, I was royally screwed, so I did what everyone does: I ranted online."

Julian flinched. "I'm almost afraid to ask…"

"Oh, it was nothing bad. I didn't swear, didn't name or shame. I just said it was mean and disrespectful to ghost friends or work colleagues."

"You're right," said Julian. "It is."

"Well, Estella saw it and assumed I was talking about her."

Julian's jaw dropped. "She what? Oh man, someone's self-obsessed. What did she say?"

"Nothing directly—to me. I spotted something online."

"You've *got* to be joking."

Madeleine weaved slightly. "She didn't name me, but she said any writer who publicly accuses another writer of ghosting when they haven't responded quickly to a message is a social-climbing user and shouldn't be trusted."

Julian bristled. "Blimey. That's pretty full-on."

"Yeah. Then I thought, *wait a minute*, she mentioned ghosting and messages—I'd sent her an email about ten days before—did she mean *me*? So I checked my follower list and yep, she'd unfollowed me."

His eyes widened.

"I don't have millions of followers like my sister, so a dip in numbers is easy to spot. Then, within the hour, two more dropped off—both authors, both friends of Estella."

"Bloody hell." Julian leaned back in the pew. "Regina George and her *Mean Girls* are alive and well!"

Madeleine sighed. "I can't say for sure, but they must've asked her who she was talking about. I doubt their unfollows were a freaky coincidence."

"Unbelievable." He shook his head. "Not only is she self-obsessed, she's also a bully."

"Which is ironic since she wrote a novella about a woman bullying another woman," said Madeleine.

"Did you get the chance to explain?"

"I sent her an email, told her about the project I'd spent months on, and said if she thought my rant was about her, it wasn't. I'd *never* drag her online. It's not my style."

Julian nodded as the organist began to warm up in the background. "What was her response?"

"Nothing. I never heard back. At first, I gave her the benefit of the doubt. I thought, maybe she was having a rough day when she saw my rant, assumed I was having a dig. I mean, let's face it—she's not the first person to think a social media post is about her. We've all done it, right?" Madeleine did a double take. "Well, *you* haven't."

"Yeah, but most wouldn't turn around and blast the person publicly or spread slanderous rumors based on ridiculous assumptions. Her behavior was completely uncalled for, not to mention juvenile and unprofessional."

Madeleine bowed her head and ran her finger along the edge of her program. "Yeah, well, obviously, Estella didn't see it that way. I was hoping for inclusion and friendship, to find like-minded people while pursuing what I love, but instead I got attacked for something I didn't even do. It soured me on the whole blogging and writing thing—and social media. I can see why you avoid it."

Julian scratched his chin and pressed closer. "But Maddie, all that says more about her than it does you. I reckon it's a lucky escape. Really, who needs friends like that?"

"That's what Kellie said." Madeleine nudged up her glasses. "It sucks, though. I thought Estella was different."

"Well, sometimes people aren't what they seem, right?"

She sighed. "Yeah, live and learn."

"Please don't let that silly cow ruin your passion for writing," Julian urged. "I know it can be hard. I've been there, dealing with egos and cliques and pettiness, but trust me, for every rotten egg, there are ten good ones. People like you—talented, decent folk who would never spread lies about another writer."

"I hope so."

"So, do us all a favor and write—please? The world needs a Madeleine Joy novel. Hell, I need one!"

"You say that now. Wait till you read it." She half-laughed. "Julian, thanks for listening. I feel better, talking about it."

"Good." Julian leaned in. "I'll always be around, you know, whenever you need me."

The organist segued into the opening strains of "Once in Royal David's City", the first carol of the evening. Latecomers searching for seats scattered, settling wherever there was free space.

"Does that apply to Carol Singing 101, too? I don't know this one." Madeleine grimaced.

"The lyrics are in the middle of the program." Julian flicked through the pages, showing her the words as all conversations and laughter dissolved into an impressive churchwide hush. "See? I got you."

Sharing a smile, Julian and Madeleine rose to their feet and began to sing.

TWENTY-THREE

MADELEINE

One ebullient welcome from the reverend, four carol singalongs, and two special readings later, the church broke out into applause as the evening's solo soprano finished her classical rendition of "Walking in the Air".

Madeleine bumped Julian with her arm, stifling a giggle. "All I could think about was you singing that in Covent Garden. Now I really need to watch that *Snowman* special."

"I have it at home somewhere," said Julian.

"Of course you do!"

The organ swelled again, leading into the next singalong carol. Madeleine stood up along with the rest of the church and leafed through the program, her mirthful grin vaulting past the jolly lyrics of "Good King Wenceslas" and the uplifting chorus of "O Come All Ye Faithful". With a final page flick, she landed on the next song.

Oh god. She froze, a breath bottling in her chest. *Oh god, no.*

Julian leaned in with a pleased smile. "I love this one," he murmured as the organist performed the opening notes, haunting in their simplicity and poignancy.

The entire church rose into song, leaving Madeleine behind. She swallowed hard, fighting the reluctance thickening her throat.

I-I can't do this.

The lyrics on the page began to blur and swim, her legs dissolving into jelly as the church's vaulted ceiling bowed and closed in.

I have to get out of here—right now.

Twisting sharply, she dropped the program on the pew and gathered her purse. Julian blinked away from the lyrics and bent toward her, his brows knotting with concern as Madeleine looped the bag's strap around her neck. "You all right?" he asked quietly.

Her ribs tightened like a vise, shortening her breaths into shallow, jagged gasps. "I-I'm not feeling well," she said, a quiver cutting through her voice. Scooping up her coat, she hid behind her hair, fearful of the secrets her tear-filled eyes might reveal. "I need some air."

"Oh, I'll come with—"

"No." Her heart rebelled, hammering in her chest, the need to flee creeping, scratching, growing by the second. "No, please, you stay."

"You sure?"

"Yep."

Julian dipped closer. "But you're coming back, right?"

She nodded tentatively and pressed her quivering lips into a false smile. "Of course." Fussing with her bundled coat, her eyes remained downcast, avoiding his unflinching gaze.

"Okay…" Julian's expression pinched as he leaned back, giving her space.

Edging past him, Madeleine rounded the end of the pew and rushed for the exit, the heavenly harmony of festive voices filling her ears and breaking her heart.

Fighting nausea and the pouring rain, Madeleine gasped for air and bolted across the church's driveaway, her boots sloshing through a river of puddles. She wrestled with her coat, punching her arms through the sleeves as her purse, flung haphazardly around her neck, bounced and pummeled her hip.

"Maddie! Wait!" Julian hurtled down the church's steps and stooped, rescuing Madeleine's pudding hat from the drenched pavement. "You dropped this!"

Shit! Glasses slipping down her nose, she stole a raindrop-speckled glance over her shoulder. *Forget it, keep going.* She swerved right through the church gates onto Sydney Street, barely missing a bickering couple schlepping a bristly Christmas tree. *Find a cab, any cab.* Her teary eyes searched the road, begging for a four-wheeled escape.

"Madeleine?" Julian caught up. "Maddie, please…stop."

She scuttled to a halt, her hair and coat soaked from the chilly deluge. "Julian, please," she muttered, chasing anxious breaths. "Leave me alone."

He yanked a compact umbrella from his coat pocket, and with the press of a button, a map of London's Underground bloomed above their heads. "Maddie, c'mon, get in my cab before you catch your death—"

"No! I can't…" She cried, yanking her purse hanging awkwardly inside her coat. "I can't do this!"

A flinch of panic rolled across his face. "Do what…?"

She gestured wildly back toward the church. "The—the Christmas carols and this place and, and *you.* This"—she rambled through hot tears, falling thick and fast—"this is a mistake. All of it. I should have never—I'm sorry. I've got nothing more to say."

I can't tell him about Kellie. He wouldn't understand. Madeleine spun away, but Julian rushed after her, hoisting his umbrella over her head again.

She shivered and kept her feverish pace, passing a docking station for bicycles for hire. *Why won't he listen?*

"You'll be hard-pressed to find a taxi in this weather." Julian hurried alongside her.

She threw her arms up. "I'll get the Tube!"

"Maddie, the closest Underground station is a soggy eight-minute walk away."

She opened her mouth as a red double-decker bus juddered by, but he spoke before she could argue.

"Look, I'll drive you straight to your hotel." He shook water from her Christmas pudding hat and held it out, a peace offering. "No questions, no prying. I'll just drive, okay?"

What were the alternatives? Getting lost on the bus? Drowning on the way to the Tube? Madeleine slowed to a stop, bringing Julian with her. Wiping her cheeks, she reclaimed her hat. "Thanks, but I mean it. I don't want to talk, okay?" She curled her arms around her waist and walked ahead, oblivious to the pained expression on Julian's face.

TWENTY-FOUR

"We are supposed to enjoy the good stuff now,
while we can, with the people we love.
Life has a funny way of teaching us
that lesson over and over again."
Sheena Easton

JULIAN

Minutes later, tires sloshing through puddles on Fulham Road, Julian glanced up in his rear view mirror. Madeleine was leaning against the door, staring outside as the rain raced down the fogging windows, transforming London and its Christmas finery into a distorted abstract painting.

She's crying less, he thought.

Returning his gaze to the road, he peered past his hyperactive wiper blades. The upcoming traffic light blinked from green to amber and Julian eased slowly on the brake, stealing another peak at the back seat. Head bowed, Madeleine was rifling through her purse on a quest for…something. She dropped a half-eaten bag of Percy Pigs in her lap, then her phone, and kept searching, finally pulling out a packet of tissues as the cab lurched to a full stop.

"Shoot," Madeleine murmured, scrambling for her sliding phone and snatching it before it tumbled to the floor. Eyes locking on the screen, she fell forward, bursting into a flood of breath-stealing sobs.

Julian's pulse began to race. He abandoned the restricted view in his mirror and threw a look over his shoulder. "Madeleine, you all right?"

The red light turned green and the car on his bumper blared its horn.

"Bugger," Julian cursed under his breath and reclaimed the wheel, pressing down on the gas. *I can't leave her alone like this.* He drove a few yards and flicked the left turn signal, diverting onto Pelham Crescent, a narrow, one-way street of Georgian houses facing a gated communal garden, their collective curve like a Grade II listed smile.

Quick but careful, he maneuvered his cab between two parallel-parked cars along the curb and killed the engine. He flung off his seatbelt, grabbed an unopened bottle of water, and abandoned the front seat, the slam of his door lifting Madeleine's quivering chin.

Julian climbed in beside her and gently closed the passenger door, the cab quiet except for her guttural sobs and the rain pummeling the glass roof.

"Madeleine, love…"

Slowly rocking back and forth, she stole a sidelong glance past her long hair. Her nose was red and swollen, and her cheeks were glossy with tears. "Why'd you pull over?" she shivered, her hands gripping a fistful of disintegrating tissues and her phone.

"I know I promised I wouldn't ask questions—and I won't—but I had to stop and make sure you were okay."

"*Okay?* What does that even *mean* anymore?" Shaking her head, she dabbed her nose, each wipe of the damp tissues drawing a wince. "Is it okay to, to hurt this much? To wish I could have m-my old life back?" she stammered.

Is this about work or…god, not that ex Micah mentioned? Julian softly squeezed her arm. "Madeleine, *whatever* has happened, I'm here. You're not alone."

Something in his words seemed to pry apart her steely reluctance. She dropped the crumpled tissues and phone on her lap and closed the distance between them, throwing her arms around his shoulders, drawing him in without pause.

The fresh scent of rain mingling with her shampoo was a heady tease, but Julian refused to be distracted. He left the water bottle in his lap and gently rubbed her back, offering comfort and support while fighting the urge to ask a flurry of questions.

Madeleine's fingers curled, clutching fistfuls of his coat. "All day I've been circling back, replaying what I was doing a year ago"—a sob stuck in her throat—"when Kellie died."

What?! Julian's heart fell. *Oh GOD! Her best friend...*

"I miss her SO much." She shuddered against his shoulder and dissolved into another cascade of tears.

...and today's the anniversary? Julian closed his eyes and gathered her tighter, cradling the back of her head. "Oh, Maddie. I had no idea. Here I've been asking if you're okay and obviously you're not. How could you be..."

"I'm sorry. I should've told you." She chased breaths between sobs. "I *wanted* to."

"You don't owe me anything, least of all an apology." He blinked, his focus blurring through the rear window as the driving rain pelted the glass. "This is so horrible. I wish there was something I could do or say..."

"I wish there was, too," she whispered.

"But I *can* sit with you and listen." He smoothed her wet hair. "Maddie, if you want to talk about Kellie or share stories, I'm here. I'd love to know more about her and your friendship."

Fingers loosening, Madeleine retreated from their embrace, her eyes puffy and overflowing with tears behind her glasses. She scavenged through the clump of damp, balled-up tissues on her lap. A few fell to the floor.

"Here, let me." Julian removed a fresh tissue from the plastic-wrapped packet on the seat and placed it in her hand.

"Thank you." Madeleine wiped her snotty nose as tears tumbled through her lashes.

Bearing witness to her pain, Julian ached with sorrow and concern. His thoughts rewound, revisiting their day together: her unease before breakfast, the wistful glances in Shere, her sad smile hidden behind a sip of Coke at the Churchill Arms.

She's been carrying this all day. She must've felt so alone.

He picked up the plastic bottle from his lap and tilted it slowly.

The water trickled from the bottom then glugged, rushing toward the cap. *If Maddie needs to cry and stay silent, so be it. But if she chooses to open up, maybe I can ease her pain a little by listening.* Whatever path she chose, it wouldn't be easy to watch, but Julian knew it would be a thousand times harder for Madeleine.

She helped herself to more tissues. "I feel like I need to talk about it, if that's okay?"

"Of course." Julian nodded gently. He cracked open the bottle then tightened the cap back up. "If you want some…" He laid the water between their thighs on the back seat.

"Thanks." She sucked in a stuttering breath. "A year ago tonight, I-I was at Logan Airport in Boston, waiting to fly here, to meet up with Kellie." Her words slipped out with a stuffy-nosed nasal twang.

Julian inched closer, softly laying a hand on her arm. "London for Christmas."

Madeleine nodded. "Kellie was on a layover in Italy—" A teary hiccup interrupted her. "She had a friend there, a guy she knew from university. I hadn't heard from her for a few hours but thought nothing of it. They were sightseeing, zooming all over Rome on his Vespa. She didn't have much time there, so they were cramming in everything before she left."

Fingers whisking away tears, her glasses bobbed. "My flight was delayed, so I wasted time in the store near my gate. Bought a magazine, some gum, and then my phone went off. I thought it was Kel, wishing me a safe trip, but it was her mom. She sounded weird, croaky like she'd been chain-smoking cigarettes or crying—maybe both." Madeleine swallowed thickly. "And that's when she told me: Kellie died that afternoon."

Julian's hand slipped down Madeleine's arm to her hand. He grasped it tight. "Christ, I'm so sorry."

A strangled sob escaped her throat. "I always thought if I got news like that, I'd immediately burst into tears. But I didn't. I couldn't." Madeleine rubbed her running nose. "My mind was stuck on '*Kellie died*' and everything else…stopped. The noise, the people, my breath—gone, sucked away into a vacuum of nothingness. I started shaking uncontrollably. Then my knees gave out."

"You collapsed..."

Her nod propelled fresh tears down her cheeks and chin. Drop by drop, they leapt from her jaw onto her coat, soaking into the wool. "People rushed over. Someone held my hand. I was crying so hard I thought I'd suffocate. In a way, I wanted to. My Kellie was gone, forever."

She glanced down and fiddled with the wadded tissues in her lap, the rainy tip-tapping on the roof slowing along with her jagged breaths. "I don't remember much else except for the Christmas song playing in the store. I recognized it straight away—'In the Bleak Midwinter'."

Oh! Julian's head jerked back. *So that's why...*

"Now it's forever tainted. All it takes is the opening notes and I'm back on that airport floor, on my knees, sobbing my heart out, reliving the worst day of my life."

Julian's heart ached. "Oh god. No wonder you couldn't get out of the church fast enough."

Madeleine let go of his hand and dragged hers through her hair. "Yeah, sorry about that."

"Don't be. I would've done the same."

"Usually, I'm pretty good at avoiding it. When I'm out in public, my headphones have been a saving grace." She weaved her fingers through the fringe on her scarf. "That's one of the great things about working for Sensoria. No one bats an eye if I wear headphones 24-7 from September onwards."

"September?" Julian flinched. "Sorry. I promised I wouldn't ask questions."

"No, it's okay. Ask away. September is when a lot of U.S. stores dust off their Christmas decorations and switch to festive tunes."

"Wow, that early?"

"It's ridiculous," said Madeleine. "Kids are just back in school, Halloween hasn't even happened, and there's my local pharmacy breaking out the red and green M&Ms and blasting 'Jingle Bells'."

"And there you are dodging grief landmines of the musical variety."

"Basically, yeah." She traded her scarf for the bottle of water and took a dainty sip.

Shit. Julian's face paled. "Everywhere we've been here—the pubs, the market—you must've been on high alert the whole time."

"Yeah, but sometimes I let my guard down a little." She screwed the cap back on the bottle and left it on her lap. "If they're playing Christmas favorites like they were at the market, they probably won't segue from Band Aid or 'Fairytale of New York' to something somber or traditional like 'In the Bleak Midwinter.' In those situations, I can usually skip the headphones and survive unscathed." Wiping her nose, she glanced over. "I'm sorry I didn't tell you before. I'm just so used to people being weird about death and grieving…"

"Please, Maddie, there's really no need to apologize." He held her hand again, his thumb softly stroking back and forth. "And I *completely* understand your hesitance to open up about it, especially if you've been let down by people who should have shown more empathy."

"Thanks. It's been a huge learning experience. If your loss isn't an immediate blood relative, *forget* it. People's patience wears thin pretty quickly. Most don't want to listen to a griever."

"Well, I'm a good listener. So are Tash and Micah, actually."

"If only I'd known you guys a year ago." She smiled softly. "Better late than never."

Julian paused, squeezing her hand. "Did you…ever find out what happened?"

"Yeah." She fussed with the fringe on her scarf again. "A week before Kellie died, she complained about a charley horse in her calf. She blamed it on working out. Kel was *always* exercising, even on holiday. Early on the 23rd, she texted and said she was going for a run and would call me before my flight. That text was the last I heard from her."

Julian let out a quiet "Fuck" as Madeleine sniffed back tears.

"Apparently, she felt short of breath while running. Thought it was her asthma, triggered by pollution or the excitement of being in Italy. It wasn't uncommon for Kel to have an attack when she laughed or felt giddy. She'd use her rescue inhaler and be fine, but this time her wheezing wasn't asthma. It was a pulmonary embolism."

He winced and blinked several times. "The charley horse? It was a blood clot—from *flying*?"

"And it moved to her lungs." Madeleine's chin trembled as she bowed her head and wound the scarf's fringe round and round her fingers. "A hotel housekeeper found Kellie on the bathroom floor..." Her voice cracked.

Julian dragged his hand over his mouth and looked away. "My god, the poor girl."

"Yeah. It breaks my heart that she died alone." Madeleine pressed her lips together as tears brimmed in her eyes. "I think about that all the time..."

Me too. Julian glanced over and gently rubbed her back, memories of his mum flickering in his mind. He remained silent, knowing there was no fixing, no words that would make things better. There was no remedy for this incurable hurt.

"...and I never got the chance to say goodbye." She patted her nose with a tissue.

"She didn't want a funeral?"

"No, she did." Madeleine sniffed. "They had one, but I couldn't get there in time. All flights to Australia over Christmas were booked."

"Right." Julian nodded. "Her parents. They lived out there?"

"So did Kellie."

How? His head tilted. "I thought she lived in Boston?"

"Uh, no." Madeleine's throat bobbed with her swallow. "Kellie and I were online friends. We were meeting in London for the first time."

They'd never... He blinked. "Oh?"

241

She pulled away her gaze and busied herself, collecting all the used tissues. "Look, I know that seems like a foreign concept for you…"

"Well, yeah. I've never made friends online, but to me, a friendship is a friendship." Julian followed her hands scurrying across the seat and to the floor, grabbing all her teary evidence. "It doesn't matter if you met online or down the local pub. It's the *connection* that counts. If it's meaningful and supportive, nothing else matters, right?"

Pausing her manic tidying spree, Madeleine sat back and dropped the dirty tissues in her lap. "Right, but at the pub, you sounded a bit…dismissive." Her posture grew stiff, wary. "You know, when I said I'd use Natasha's superpower to meet online friends?"

His mouth fell open. "Oh god, did I?" He leaned in. "Maddie, I didn't mean to be. I'd just spotted that text from Caroline and—I'm sorry if I sounded…flippant. I'm so sorry, hurting you like that."

Her shoulders softened. "You didn't hurt me. I was surprised, that's all. It's my fault. I assumed and shouldn't have." She licked her lips. "I get defensive sometimes if I think people are…what's the word? *Belittling* what Kel and I had."

"What you had—*clearly*—was an amazing, loving friendship," said Julian. "I'm so sorry it ended way too soon."

"Me too. I carry it with me, her loss, every day. Some are better than others. Today was always going to be a rough one…"

A kind smile curved Julian's lips. "Thank you for telling me about Kellie. Obviously, she loved you to the moon and back, flying all the way from Australia just to meet you." He gathered her hand in his.

"Yeah." Madeleine exhaled heavily. "But I wish I could turn back the clock and tell her—*beg her*—not to catch that flight…" She shrugged.

"I get that. That's the real reason I chose time travel at the pub—to go back and see Mum. I'd probably get in shit for changing the course of history or something, but I would've washed those damn windows. If I had, maybe she'd still be here."

"Julian, you can't say that…"

"Yeah, I know. It wasn't my fault. And it wasn't *yours*, either."

She shifted, studied his fingers folded through hers. "I know, but it's easier to…"

"Cling on to the guilt? Replay what-ifs?" He nodded. "Madeleine, you have to stop torturing yourself. You know that, right?"

"I guess, yeah." She stilled. "I'm trying to work on that."

"That's good. If you're anything like me, you'll be working on it for a while. It does take time, and that's okay."

She reached up and twisted the hair falling on his forehead, twirling it around her fingers. "You, Julian Halliwell, have a beautiful heart. You're lovely and kind and I'm so thankful I met you."

He grinned. "Likewise."

She leaned in and cupped his chin, gifting him with a chaste kiss, short but sweet. Julian savored the delicate press of her soft lips, even after she'd pulled away.

Madeleine held his admiring gaze then glanced up through the glass roof. Julian followed, craning his neck. The rain had slowed to a barely there trickle, plunging the cab's passenger area into silence. They sat quietly, staring up at the dark sky until Madeleine cleared her throat.

"Can I ask you a favor?"

"Sure." Julian squeezed her hand and let go. "Anything, you name it."

"The Christmas lights…can we see some?"

It'll be her last chance. "Absolutely. Got any requests?"

"The angels on Regent Street. Kellie wanted to see them…" She looked away. "Maybe she'll be there, in a way. I sometimes think she's watching over me."

"I know she is." Julian swept a piece of hair away from her eyeglasses. "I'm so sorry you've been dealing with this awful anniversary alone, Maddie."

A soft smile teased her lips. "But I haven't. You've been here, all along, right by my side."

TWENTY-FIVE

MADELEINE

Julian clasped Madeleine's hand. "Come on, I know a shortcut."

Escaping the chaotic pre-holiday hell of grumpy shoppers and slow-walking tourists otherwise known as December 23rd on Oxford Street, Julian guided Madeleine east along Princes Street. The nearly deserted road of offices and small restaurants ran parallel to its busier northern neighbor and spilled out onto Regent Street, a majestic thoroughfare of Grade II listed architecture and lavish shops, home to London's famous flying angels, The Spirit of Christmas.

Julian swerved a puddle. "Just up here, we'll turn right at the corner."

Can't wait! Spying a glimpse of mesmerizing sparkle, a whoosh of excitement surged through Madeleine. "Oh WOW!" Her jaw dropped. "Is that *them*?!"

Before Julian could respond, she darted ahead, tugging him along in her wake as she ogled the soaring spirits and their heavenly shimmer, high above the parade of cars and packed double-decker buses. The three-dimensional sculptures, boasting lacey wingspans of fifty-five feet and over 300,000 twinkling lights, dazzled harried Londoners and gobsmacked tourists alike with their ethereal beauty. Madeleine fell under their spell immediately and couldn't whip out her phone quick enough.

"Absolutely breathtaking! Wait till my dad sees these! He's gonna be *so* jealous." As she happily snapped away, the fizzy lights dramatically ebbed and flowed from angel to angel into an enchanting wave of luminosity rippling down Regent Street. "They're choreographed, too?!" She laughed. "Oh man, Griswolds, eat your hearts out."

Delighted by Madeleine's reaction, Julian flashed a toothy grin and rocked back on his heels. "They fly all the way down to Piccadilly Circus, too."

"And that's how far?" she asked, pausing her photo blitz.

"About half a mile."

"Wow. This is just—I've never seen so much pretty! Hang on, I'm gonna take some video..." She hit record and Julian stood by quietly, sparing her mini movie from needless talk and commentary.

Once she had captured several takes, she lowered her phone and gave his arm a tight squeeze. "Thank you!"

"C'mon." Julian gestured with a head tilt. "Let's walk down and see all the rest. The architecture along here is impressive, too."

"I was gonna say..." With an appreciative grin, Madeleine admired the street's grand façades. Uniform in style (Beaux Arts), materials (Portland stone), and size (five storeys—max), Regent Street's buildings offered harmonious curb appeal and weren't shy of a few sculptural flourishes. Fluted pilasters, ornate cartouches, and iron-railed balconies showcased grandiose flair along with Egyptian obelisks, roaring lions, and chubby-cheeked cherubs.

"London constantly surprises me. I love it." Madeleine caught Julian's eye. "Oh *god*. You must get so tired of tourists like me, gushing about *everything*."

"Not at all. It reminds me of how lucky I am."

"It must be incredible, leaving for work in the morning and having all *this* on your doorstep." Madeleine's gaze coasted across the street where the windows of Hamleys, the world's oldest toy store, enchanted visitors with a winter wonderland of skating penguins and sledding owls. "History, royalty, amazing shopping..."

"Yeah, but I'd imagine Boston isn't short on historical sites and cool things to see, too, right?"

"Not where I live." Madeleine left behind the exhausted parents with their bulging shopping bags exiting Hamleys and looked up at Julian. "Here's what I see when I leave my building: a payday loan place, a cannabis store, and a twenty-four-hour donut franchise."

"Well, that's *convenient*, at least," Julian reasoned. "You can get fast cash, puff away your problems, and satisfy all your late-night cruller cravings."

"True, but I'm already a scrupulous saver, pot makes me para-noid, and I prefer cookies—the crunchier, the better. I'd rather have easy access to that Pret place. Or Fortnum & Mason! Isn't it like, cookie heaven or something?"

"Biscuits, tea, chocolate—yep, all of the above."

"How quintessentially British." Madeleine lifted her chin. "And I say that as a good thing."

"But wait! There's more." Julian gestured playfully.

Madeleine laughed.

"You can shop for housewares, buy jewelry, grab a sandwich to-go. It's only a short walk down Piccadilly, actually. Fancy going now?"

"Sandwiches, jewels, biscuits—like you have to ask!" Made-leine studied the dancing lights again, her jovial expression soften-ing toward pensive. "And Kellie suggested I visit, so…"

"Then visit we shall," said Julian, taking her hand and giving it a gentle squeeze.

They walked in silence for a while. Madeleine added to her sparkly angel collection with more video and photos as Julian snapped a few of his own, letting her call the shots on whether they'd move ahead or linger a little longer.

Two-thirds of the way down Regent Street, Madeleine paused and stole a peek down a pedestrianized laneway cut through one of the buildings. "Where's this go?"

"It's Heddon Street. It leads to a courtyard of cafés and restau-rants. It's a lovely little respite."

"Hidden gems. Kellie would've loved this. She would've loved *all* of it." She spun slowly back toward him. "Julian, thank you for being so sweet and understanding tonight—and this afternoon. The trip out to Shere was for Kellie, too. *The Holiday* was her favorite film. She always wanted to visit that pub."

"Ah. I'm glad I could help make that happen. You know, I real-ly think you did Kellie proud today," said Julian thoughtfully.

"I hope so. I've struggled for months, trying to think of a suitable way to honor her. Nothing back home made sense, in a way. But *all* this, and Shere—even the dog concert—Kel would've been so thrilled." She gave him a quivery smile. "It's been nice for me, too. I haven't really been out much this past year. I've been hiding inside for the most part, thinking, questioning everything—my career, my friends...even my *hair*."

"Oh no, not the hair! Grief-fueled makeovers!" Julian grimaced. "That's a slippery slope."

"I know, but it's so tempting to just lop it all off!"

"So, what were you thinking?" he asked. "A change of color, a severe fringe...?"

"A pixie cut."

"Hmm." Julian studied her carefully then spoke. "Yeah, you could pull that off. You'd look kinda mod and cute. But..."

She raised an eyebrow. "Nooo! The dreaded *but...*"

"I'd wait. Don't do what I did a few years back. I had a particularly grim week, got pissed on cheap cider, and barged into an all-night barbershop."

"All-night haircuts? That's a thing?"

"In Finsbury Park it is." Julian chuckled. "I got the most tragic buzz cut ever, and what's worse, I discovered I have an odd-shaped head!"

She bit back a laugh.

Julian scratched his temple. "I regretted that hasty decision *for months*. The only saving grace was that I looked as shit as I felt."

"The joy of grieving, huh?" Madeleine half-smiled. "Okay, I won't chop my hair—yet."

"Good. In fact, don't go changing anything. You're damn well perfect in my book." Julian stepped back and raised his fingers, pretending to snap her photo. "I want to remember you just like this."

Oh my god. A flutter soared in Madeleine's chest. "Julian, I'll *always* remember you..." Her nose began to tickle. She threw her arms around his shoulders and hugged him, hiding her gathering tears. Blinking quickly, she spotted a jowly Great Dane and its owner on the approach.

I can't bawl here. Quick, change the subject.

She pressed a kiss to his cheek and withdrew, avoiding eye contact. "Hey, when will you see Winnie?"

"Boxing Day. He's coming to stay for ten days."

Madeleine squeezed him again. "Oh, Julian, that's great!"

"Yeah!" He beamed. "Caroline texted this morning. They're heading off to Courchevel to go skiing. They can't take Winnie along, so…"

Or don't want to. The thought creased Madeleine's brow. "But what about her broken wrist?"

"Oh, ended up being just a sprain. Looks like we both lucked out." Julian lifted his chin. "Caroline wouldn't normally leave Winnie with me, but she had little choice. Everyone else is busy, and she couldn't find a boarding kennel with availability."

Madeleine's pulse took off like a shot. "Kennels?!" She gasped. "At Christmas? What the *hell*?"

"I know, I know." Julian nodded, his expression beyond fed up. "I've warned her repeatedly, don't you *ever* board Winnie! She never listens."

"Honestly, if I were you, Julian, I wouldn't give him back." Her jaw clenched. "She shouldn't own a houseplant, let alone a dog."

"Hopefully the courts agree. We have a custody hearing after Christmas. We'll see." Julian wrapped his arm around Madeleine's shoulders as they continued walking.

She leaned into the comfort of him, her gaze tracing the gentle curve of the street up ahead. "How's he healing after his surgery?"

Julian's eyes widened. "How do you…"

"Oh! Micah and Tash told me. Hope that's okay?"

"Uh, yeah, it's fine. Winnie's doing well, really good, actually."

A slow smile nudged her cheeks. "I bet he'll love the bone you got him for Christmas. I saw it under your tree."

"Yeah, he'll love that daft thing. Every year, Father Christmas gets him a new one, and every year, he destroys it by New Year's."

"Hey, you've gotta have traditions."

"I also bought him this brilliant interactive toy," said Julian. "You'll like this! It's a plush honey pot with three little soft bees inside."

"Are they smiley?" she asked, her eyes catching the flicker and flash of Piccadilly Circus, its energetic lightshow bouncing off the surrounding buildings.

"Yep, surprisingly so, considering they'll be chomped and shaken to bits by a mischievous corgi."

"Dogs have the cutest toys," said Madeleine. "If I was a pet parent, I'd be permanently broke."

Julian tilted his head, glancing down at her. "Admit it—you'd dress him up, too."

"No way! Dogs in clothes *always* look so embarrassed. I would never!"

Julian laughed.

Madeleine did a double take. "Oh shit—you dress up Winnie!"

"Only in his football kit…and his crown, you know, for Trooping the Colour."

"Of course." Her giggle slid into a burgeoning yawn. She fought hard, holding back a full-on molar flash behind her hand, but exhaustion won out. "Ahhh, I'm sorry, Julian." She blinked away the watery remnants and slowed to a stop. "I'm fading—fast."

"No worries. It's been a long, emotional day," said Julian, easing his arm free from Madeleine's shoulder. He shifted around, facing her. "Do you want to grab a tea or something to eat?"

"I would, but I fear I'd fall asleep in my tacos. Is it okay if we call it a night?"

"Sure." Julian paused. "Would you like company?"

I've been both hoping for and dreading this question all day. She looked away. "Uh, I *would*, but…"

"Oh, blimey!" Julian shook his head and adjusted his glasses. "I didn't mean sex. It's not that I—my god, I do! It's just, I don't think it's right, you know, *today*. If that makes sense?"

Who is this man and why aren't there more like him back home? Madeleine broke into a relieved smile. "It does. And like you said, it's not that I don't want to..." She caught his hand and threaded her fingers between his. "So, what were you thinking? I'd stay over and we'd...cuddle?"

"I'll have you know, I could spoon for England."

She nodded, refusing to take her eyes off him. "That sounds amazing and really, really lovely."

"Your turn." Wearing Julian's West Ham bathrobe, Madeleine stepped out of his bathroom and tucked her toothbrush case back in her makeup bag. Her eyes strayed to a fruitcake sitting on Julian's small dining table. "How cute was your landlord, dropping off your Christmas gift?"

"Yeah, that was a surprise." He reclined on his bed in a concert t-shirt and navy boxer briefs. "I always give my landlords a small present, but this is the first time one of 'em reciprocated."

"He seems really nice," said Madeleine.

"He's great, but then again, Mr. Hannon *is* seventy-one and re-members what it meant to be neighborly back in the day. Helping one another, checking in, celebrating the season." Julian scratched beneath his t-shirt. "Acts of kindness like that don't happen too of-ten these days."

"Especially in a big city." She lingered by the sofa, stuffing her makeup bag in her purse. "So, are you a fruitcake fan?"

"Not really, but it's the thought that counts, right?" Julian yawned. "He seemed really chuffed to meet you. He's always on me about finding a nice young lady. Maybe now he'll stop!"

"Hey, happy to help." Madeleine gestured toward the kitchen. "Is it okay if I grab some wat—?"

The ping of his phone cut her off. "Go for it. Make yourself at home," said Julian, pushing himself off the bed. "Mugs and glasses are in the second cupboard. Oh, and there are biscuits in the next one over. Feel free to help yourself." He tapped the lit screen and his expression dimmed.

"Is everything okay?"

"It's the, uh, tour agency I'm signed up to." Julian plowed a hand through his hair as a grin flickered then vanished again. "They're offering me a last-minute job tomorrow morning..."

Oh? Madeleine's heart panged, the desire for more time together surrendering to the not-so-small matter of Winnie's surgical bills. Obviously, Julian needed the work, needed the money. *And I monopolized all of his time today.* Thinking about his kind selflessness, gratitude swelled in her chest, but it was quickly washed away by a tsunami of guilt. *If I'd known about his vet bills this morning...*

Tucking her disappointment away behind an encouraging smile, she let her breeziest, most positive attitude fly. "That's great!" Her gaze swept over his faded Franz Ferdinand tee and boxer briefs. "What are you waiting for? Say yes, say you'll take it."

He rubbed the middle of his forehead. "It's for a few hours...in Greenwich."

"Perfect. It'll give you something to do while I pack my souvenirs from Shere." She laughed, closing the door to any suggestions of a post-breakfast lie-in from Mr. Halliwell. "I have to be prepared to fly at short notice—so those airline texts keep telling me."

Julian's shoulders softened like a weight had been lifted. "Okay, great. We could always do something after?"

"Sure." She nodded, tugging the cuffs of Julian's robe over her hands. "Why don't you meet me at Fortnum's?"

As the question left her lips, her brain answered: *If there's still time.*

Her silent fear rolled around her mind, echoing and teasing, fueling the quicksand in her chest, swallowing up her faint hope. *If there's not, I might never see him again.*

"Fortnum's then—it's a date!" Julian grinned. His fingers texted at a snail's pace as he strolled into his bathroom.

Madeleine admired Julian's firm butt in his underwear until the door swung shut, ending the impromptu floor show.

I know we were just joking around, but if I could, I really would freeze time. I'm not ready to go. I'm not ready to say goodbye. She pulled her phone from her purse as the taps ran behind the closed door. *I'm crushing on him so badly...*

She wandered into the narrow kitchen and helped herself to a glass, filling it with water. As she drank, she leaned against the counter, her eyes skating over the cork board affixed to the opposite wall. Peppered with takeout menus for local Italian and Indian restaurants, the crowded rectangle also displayed old ticket stubs from concerts and football matches, adorable puppy pictures of wiggly Winnie, and silly photos of Micah and Natasha as well as one of Julian's Bowie articles ripped from an issue of *Words and Music*.

Julian loved his passions and people without reservation, and Madeleine had never met a guy quite like him. No toxic ego, no haughty pretense. Julian was selfless but strong, not a pushover. Stiff upper lip? Not this guy. Despite Madeleine's earlier assumption in the Moomin shop, raw emotions—his, hers—didn't require restraint or scare him off. She'd witnessed it firsthand when they talked about his mum at Micah's party, when she told him about losing Kellie...

He sat with me the entire time I ugly-cried in his cab. I know it couldn't have been pretty or easy, watching me fall apart like that, but he never shushed or judged me—or asked in a roundabout way: "Yeah, but when are you gonna be fun again?"

He encouraged Madeleine to open up, to share her grief. She didn't have to pretend or hold back. She could be her true self, and for once, Madeleine didn't feel rushed or embarrassed or self-conscious.

Imagine that.

Julian was remarkable. A rare gem. But even if he'd never be hers, Madeleine would leave him with no doubts as to how much his kindness meant to her.

She picked up her phone and typed a message, quick and succinct. Hey! I need you to do something for me.

TWENTY-SIX

JULIAN

One day until Christmas

"*Platform 10 for the 12:30 service to Manchester Piccadilly. Calling at Stoke-on-Trent, Macclesfield, Stockport, and Manchester Piccadilly...*"

The automated female voice cut through the drone of conversations and drove Julian's pounding pulse up another notch. He glanced down at his phone, devoid of unread messages. *Bollocks!* His jaw tensed as his eyes scoured London Euston's main concourse where the spirit of the season was collectively replaced by howling babies and stressed-out frowns. *Why aren't they answering my texts?*

Swerving a station employee mopping up something goopy, Julian barely missed a head-bobbing pigeon and two waddling toddlers barreling toward a bargain-basement elf (aka, another employee) handing out free candy canes. He paused for a moment, adjusting his tote on his shoulder. *C'mon guys, still be here...* His eyes roved past a pack of roaming carolers singing "Here We Come A-Wassailing", dressed in 19th-century costumes complete with hoop skirts, petticoats, and bonnets for the ladies, and velvet frock coats, ascots, and top hats for the gents.

Then, he spotted the Coopers, loaded up with magazines and confectionary in front of the WH Smith. The stiffness in Julian's jaw and shoulders subsided.

"Oh, thank god," he muttered, running the gauntlet of dawdling tourists. "Meeks! Tash! Didn't you get my texts?" He nudged up his glasses.

Natasha unfurled her arms for a rib-torturing hug. "Oh yeah,

253

soz, Jules. We're saving our batteries, you know, 'cause the charging ports on the train don't always work."

"Their wi-fi is proper dodge, too," added Micah, welcoming his best friend with a slap on the shoulder and a cheeky grin. "Ten more minutes, mate, and you would've been shit out of luck."

"I know, I know. I'm sorry." Julian nodded, running a flustered hand through his hair. "The drive back from Greenwich was a bugger. Everyone and their brother are on the roads today." His gaze shot to the Eastern Bloc tote bag hanging from Micah's shoulder. "You brought it, right?"

Micah gingerly reached in and presented Julian with a box. Perfectly square and wrapped in a shimmery, wintery blue paper, it was crowned with a thick silver bow, its fabric woven with a cavalcade of whimsical stars. If Madeleine couldn't see stars in the wilds of London, Julian would give her the next best thing.

He remembered the constellations. A smile raced across Julian's face. "Ah, cheers! Looks gorgeous, Meeks. She's gonna love it."

Natasha cleared her throat. "Uh, hello! Muggins didn't wrap it. *I* did." She tossed her rouge locks, which were kept neatly in place by a headband bedazzled with purple and blue tree baubles. "I thought it deserved a bit of feminine flair."

"As if! You were nosey." Micah scoffed. "I told you it wasn't a ring, didn't I? For one thing, the box is dead large!"

"Well, I dunno! It could've been a wee box inside a bunch of bigger ones." Natasha plunged her hand into her overstuffed messenger bag and rooted around.

"You read too much romance," said Micah, checking the time on his phone.

His sister rolled her eyes, her bag bulging and stretching as she searched. "I don't read *enough* romance." She unearthed a beat-up trade paperback and a red and pink packet of candy. "Anyway, ring or not, it's still a great gift. Jules, could you give her these, too?"

He accepted the loot with a wry grin. "Christmas Percy Pigs—"

"I'll have you know there's a special limited-edition Rudolph hidden in the bag," Natasha interrupted.

"And you're giving her a pre-loved book?" asked Julian.

"She'll know what it is. We were talking about it at the pub quiz."

He raised his brows. "I don't think you'll get it back…"

"That's okay! It's my way of saying Happy Christmas and thank you for being so kind," said Natasha.

Micah winced sympathetically as Julian carefully placed the wrapped gift and Natasha's book and candy in his Sister Ray bag. "So, you ready…for Madeleine leaving? I'm sorry, mate. On Christmas Eve, too."

"Actually, I think she might be staying." He lifted both straps onto his shoulder.

Natasha's eyes brightened. "For good?"

"For Christmas," said Julian. "I texted her about thirty minutes ago—"

"And?!" Natasha clutched his forearm and bounced on the spot, jostling him in the process.

"Still no word from the airline or the airport. I've been listening to the radio, but all they've been talking about is the Christmas number one."

"Oh god, yeah," said Micah. "Singing meerkats tipped to beat Ed Sheeran? British record buyers strike again," he mused sarcastically.

"Aww! But this is amazin'!" Natasha squeezed Julian's arm. "You and Madeleine together for Christmas! You'll have to video-chat with us!"

Micah smirked. "Something tells me the last thing they're gonna want to do is *chat*, Tash—especially with us."

His sister ignored him. "Oh, Jules, whatcha making for Christmas lunch? Your famous ham with rösti potatoes? God, that's mega lush!"

"Nope, I'm going for something special. I pushed the boat out, just ordered one of those dinner-for-two Chrimbo meals from Tesco—"

"NO! Not those Christmases in a box?" Natasha squealed. "With Yorkshires and bacon-wrapped turkey and *everything*?!"

Julian laughed, amusement glinting in his eyes. "Everything. Even the Christmas crackers and wine."

"Romantic Jules is back in town," said Micah.

"They're delivering it before six tonight. Mr. Hannon will keep it in his fridge till we get home."

"Nice one, mate!" Micah nodded. "I'm really chuffed for you." His eyes strayed to his left and the corridor leading to the train platforms.

"I should let you go," said Julian. "Don't miss your train."

Micah slapped Julian on the back and pulled him into a brief hug. "And don't you miss Maddie! Happy Christmas, Jules."

"YES!" Natasha bounced, giving him a quick squeeze. "Happy, happy Christmas! And if you do have time to video—"

"Tash!" Micah shook his head and tugged her by the arm.

MADELEINE

Musical merry-go-round tins filled with dulce de leche cookies, cardboard tubes of buttery dark chocolate biscuits…what to choose? Madeleine parked her suitcase beside her boots and perused the colorful products stacked impeccably on Fortnum & Mason's wooden shelves.

Or maybe a special tea, some wine, or something from homewares? She glanced down at the small rectangular box of Fortnum's Table Top Trivia and the doggy Christmas cracker for Winnie in her shopping basket. *All great gifts, but none of them truly convey how I feel. This is hard.*

Impatient arms reached in front of her, snapping up fruit and nut flapjack cookies and cinnamon and orange shortbread fingers, their quick decisions a reminder she needed to light a fire under her butt and hurry up.

Her eyes boomeranged back to a pretty blue, green, and gold tin with rounded edges and artwork of lions and whales on its lid—the Explorers biscuit tin. *Julian said he loves adventure.* Picking it up, the label promised maple syrup and coconut, English honey and macadamia nuts…tastes from around the globe. *A culinary getaway, no flying required—it'll have to do.*

She placed it in her basket and re-adjusted her backpack, then uttered polite "Excuse mes" and "Sorrys" as she carefully navigated her suitcase around distracted shoppers and glittering Christmas trees and display tables piled high with fancy milk chocolate pigs, polar bears, and…

"Squirrels!" Madeleine happily helped herself to a cheeky chocolate cutie and then panicked, trying to figure out how she'd get him home without breaking his tail. *Oh, worry about that later.* She gave her head a shake. *Gotta buy these things before Julian gets here.*

After zigzagging through the high-spirited maze of Christmas shopping chaos, she joined the long line for the cash registers, winding around the front of the store. A vibration tickled her left hip, setting off an anxious drum solo in her chest. *Flight news or Shantelle?* Rifling through her purse, she held her breath and yanked out her phone, afraid to look. *Please don't be Julian canceling!* She peeked at the lit screen, displaying 1:10 p.m. and a text from Shantelle: Your wish is my command. All done.

Madeleine exhaled into a smile as a second text shook her phone.

Shantelle: Chicago still getting hammered with snow, but my flight is finally ready to take off! Can't wait! One hour till Mom, Dad, and Nolan. I'll text when I get there. Flight attendant is giving me evils. Love and hugs! x

The couple in front of Madeleine budged ahead, so she followed suit then dashed off a message.

Madeleine: THANK YOU, sister of the year! Now I have to get you another gift! LOL. Safe flight, k? Love and the biggest, most grateful hugs. x

A few minutes later and fifty British pounds lighter, Madeleine waited by the exquisite spiral staircase in the center of the store. She alternated between staring at her phone, peeking over the stainless steel railing at the shoppers below, and scouring the crowd for any signs of Julian. His last text had been twenty minutes earlier, and she was starting to worry.

"Hello…"

That familiar accent. Her heart fizzed with excitement.

She spun around, finding Julian with a hint of stubble and wearing a chunky black sweater and dark gray trousers. A robin's egg blue Fortnum's shopping bag dangled from his hand.

"Hey! I'm so glad to see you!" Her eyes nosedived. "What's in *there*?"

Julian folded over the bag's handles. "Never you mind!"

It's for me! She lurched forward and squeezed him in a hug. "How'd you come in without me spotting you?"

Julian matched her embrace, but his hands ended up snarled in her backpack. "I came in the side entrance on Duke Street."

"Sneaky!" Madeleine let go first. "You cabbies know all the secrets."

"We do."

She softly met his lips, smiling into their kiss before breaking away.

Julian kissed her on the nose, his grin refusing to fade. "So, what do you think?" He marveled at the store's sparkling chandeliers and multiple Christmas trees. "Did you see the ice cream parlour? The fresh food hall downstairs?"

"Yes!" Madeleine beamed back. "I want to *live* in here. I could survive quite nicely."

"You reckon?" he asked.

"I should hide in the washroom until closing time—oh, speaking of, have you *seen* them?" Her eyes widened with wonder. "Marble countertops, yummy-scented soap, single-use hand towels, but fancy cotton ones—in a department store?! Kellie wasn't kidding. This place is incredible. No wonder the Queen loves it."

"Yeah, but Maddie, if you're hiding out in here tonight, you'll miss Christmas Eve dinner—with me." Julian adjusted his glasses. "The airports are still closed, right? Have you heard *anything*?"

"Nothing." Her expression went blank. "Looks like I'm gonna be stuck here for Christmas Eve *and* Christmas Day."

His gleeful gaze fizzled. "And how do you feel about that?" He glanced down at his Fortnum's bag and fussed with whatever lurked inside.

"Honestly?" She bloomed into a happy-go-lucky smile. "I'm thrilled! It means more time with you!"

Julian laughed, and the lines on his forehead faded away. "Hey, you won't hear me complaining! So what's next then? Do you wanna shop some more, go back to your hotel, or...?"

"I'm tired of dragging my luggage everywhere." She looped her arm through his. "Can we go back to your place and relax?"

"Yeah, absolutely." Julian claimed her suitcase handle. "We'll just have to make a quick stop at Sainsbury's, pick up something nice for dinner." They started walking across the red carpet, inching past shelves of elegantly decorated boxes of tea. "Whatcha fancy? Is there something Madeleine Joy traditionally eats on Christmas Eve?"

"Stuffed crust pizza—and lots of it. My family orders in because we're addicted to cheese and no one wants to cook." She smiled. "But how 'bout I make *you* something? I promise, it won't be a crisp sandwich."

"Like that's ever a bad thing."

"Never!" Madeleine's eyes softened. "Seriously though, that egg and crisp sandwich from Coal Drops Yard was the best sandwich I've ever had."

"Really? That good, eh?"

She looked up at him. "Yeah, because it brought me back to

you."

A grin raced across Julian's face.

They wound their way around the display cases of chocolates (over 500 sweet varieties!) as well as caramels and fudge, glacé fruits and decadent marshmallows, discussing Julian's job in Greenwich that morning until they reached the store's Duke Street side entrance. He carried Madeleine's suitcase down the four steps and held open the wooden doors, allowing her to exit first.

"I parked around back," he said, setting her case on the sidewalk. He grasped the handle and they headed toward Jermyn Street, her luggage's wheels clattering along the stone.

A snarly gust of wind whipped their hair. "I miss my woolly hat." Madeleine pouted.

"Lost it?"

"Packed it. Didn't plan that well, did I?" She clutched her phone with one hand and swung her blue Fortnum's bag with the other. "Ooh, I'm super excited about grocery shopping with you. I love seeing all the neat British things we can't get at home."

"Not even British chocolate?" asked Julian.

"We get some, yeah, but it costs a small fortune. There's a shop in Back Bay I go—" Her phone buzzed in her palm.

Then buzzed again.

Shit. Can't be Shan. She's in the air. A flutter of unease swooped in her stomach, slowing her confident gait. *And Mom will be busy, baking up a storm.* She swerved the awaiting messages and chose Julian instead, meeting his gaze. The happiness drained from his eyes.

Madeleine licked her lips as they both scuffed to a stop. "I'll just…"

"Yeah." Julian's smile wavered, fighting a losing battle.

She held her breath and tapped the screen.

Shantelle: My flight has wi-fi! Sweet! Hey, you'll never guess who's on my plane!

A relieved laugh escaped Madeleine's mouth. "It's *Shan*. Texting mid-flight."

"Oh?!" Julian's voice bounced up an octave and his grin rebounded, easy and elated. "She's not home yet?"

"Snow delay in Chicago. She'll land in Milwaukee in about forty minutes." Madeleine brushed her windswept hair from her eyes and read the second message.

Shantelle: Remember Jeff from DQ who got fired for putting extra Reese's in my Blizzards?

Her focus flitted upward. "Shan's bumped into an old ex. In college, she was convinced she was gonna marry this guy...until she met someone with a MINI and dumped him!"

"Ah, young love!" said Julian. "So fickle and fleeting."

They forged ahead and turned the corner onto Jermyn Street, only to be interrupted again.

"Someone's bored..." Madeleine's gaze drifted back to her palm. She read Shantelle's latest text aloud: "*He's got FOUR kids, Bucks season tix, OWNS that DQ!*" She snickered. "The future my sister turned down is flashing before her very eyes." She bit her lip as Julian liberated his keys from his pocket.

"Is that good or bad?" He unlocked the front door and left his shopping bag beside his Sister Ray tote.

"Good. Confirms she made the right decision. Shan *hates* the Bucks." Madeleine giggled and slipped her backpack off her shoulder, resting it on the sidewalk for Julian.

"And the Bucks are, what? Baseball?" he asked as the wind howled.

"No, silly—basketball!" Her phone quivered again and she dove back in.

Jet Britannia: Travel update—

Oh dammit. Madeleine rolled her eyes. *Forgot to cancel these updates AND my Paris ticket.* Out of habit, she skimmed the info despite it no longer being relevant with Shantelle flying 35,000 feet over the U.S. Midwest.

Flight JB092 from LHR—CDG departs today at—

Whoa, what?! Her heart kicked against her ribs. *The airports are OPENING?*

She glanced up. Julian was half in, half out of his cab, placing her luggage in the rear passenger area.

"It's mad, innit?" he mused, his voice muffled behind glass and metal. "How one decision can change everything."

"Uh...yeah." She faked a smile. *Okay, this text means nothing, right? Just because the Paris flight is happening doesn't mean my—*

Another text landed.

Fuck... A sour taste rose in her throat.

Julian scooped up her backpack and dove into his cab again, carefully stowing her belongings. Madeleine's gaze dropped slowly. *An unknown number.* Her stomach twisted as she tapped the screen.

Easy Air: Travelers, European airspace is now open. Flight EA0418 from LHR—MKE will be departing on 12/24 at 17:30, terminal 2. Please arrive 3 hours early to allow for long lines and security delays.

My flight to Milwaukee. A frown weighed down the corners of her mouth.

Julian returned, eager for her shopping bags. "What's up?"

Madeleine gulped, turning her phone toward him. "Our time."

TWENTY-SEVEN

JULIAN

"You warm enough, Maddie?" Julian looked up in his rear view mirror as they drove along Piccadilly.

Prising her focus away from the Ritz Hotel, she managed a half-smile and a flat "Yes, thank you." She chewed on her cheek, then added, "How long will it take to get there?"

"Less than an hour."

His answer didn't seem to sit well. Madeleine nodded solemnly and slouched against the side of the cab, staring through the glass as London flew by one final time.

Don't make her feel worse. Be upbeat, be chipper. Julian fought the lump in his throat and painted on an enthusiastic grin. "It'll be nice to see your baby nephew again, eh?"

"Uh, yeah." Her eyes flitted from leafless tree to leafless tree as Green Park sailed past. "I see Nolan every couple of weeks, though. I go back to Milwaukee regularly, visit my parents, take Nolan to the park…"

"Sounds lovely," said Julian.

Madeleine let out a heavy sigh. "Shan's the one who never goes back, never sees him."

"Oh, right." Approaching the bumper of another cab, Julian slowed to a stop, and their conversation hit the brakes, too. For five days, they'd chatted and laughed with ease and vigor, but now? Everything felt labored. Words were chosen with economy and care as if they feared the unsaid lurking deep in their hearts. The widening gulf, both verbally and physically (thanks to the cab's partition), rendered Julian frustrated and heartbroken.

I want to tell her: 'Maddie, I've fallen in love with you', but I can't burden her with my feelings. Not when I'm not sure if she feels the same way. Julian pushed his glasses up his nose. *Sure, she likes me, but like isn't love.*

He blinked up at the mirror again, hoping to meet her gaze, but Madeleine remained glued to the park, her interest, her thoughts elsewhere.

It's just not meant to be. Julian scratched the stubble on his chin, returning his attention to the road. *What's for you won't pass you by. Yeah, Micah, cheers for that, mate.*

As the taxi accelerated forward, the silence from the back seat pressed heavily on his heart, the distance between them growing by the second. In less than an hour, Madeleine would be gone, but Julian wasn't willing to lose her just yet. He cleared his throat, determined to make the most of the little time they had left. "Madeleine, you didn't say—what does your family do for Christmas?"

She shifted away from the window and the grayness swallowing up the sun. "It's pretty much the same year to year," she replied with a faint smile. "We play games, eat pizza, and watch movies on Christmas Eve. Then, in the morning, we make a big pancake breakfast and open presents—although this year the presents might come first with Nolan there. After that, Dad, Shan, and Antoine watch whatever NFL game is on TV while Mom, Erin, Gabriel, and I cook."

"What do you make? Turkey?"

"No, we always have ham. I wish it were turkey."

Julian's heart sank, thinking of the bacon-wrapped turkey breast, roast potatoes, and Christmas crackers scheduled for delivery to his flat that afternoon.

Madeleine's brow tensed. "Julian, what will you do? Could you and Winnie go up to Manchester on Boxing Day?"

"Uh, no. I don't really fancy it."

"But…you'll be alone." Her worried gaze widened as the cab swept down the cement slope leading to the A4 tunnel, a two-lane, underground roadway passing under Hyde Park Corner. "I hate to think of you by yourself, lonely…I feel so bad. I feel *guilty.*"

The word felt like a screwdriver to Julian's gut.

No, Maddie, no.

The dissolving ash cloud, their hastily canceled plans, his lack of social engagement on December 25th—none of these things were her fault, and Julian wouldn't allow Madeleine to feel even a smidgen of guilt. He had to keep things light, hopeful. He had to convince her everything was all right, that he was all right. "Nah, don't be! With my record collection? I'm never lonely."

"But what will you eat?"

"What *won't* I eat. I'll have turkey, potatoes, pigs in blankets…and with it being just me, I'll have loads left over for sarnies!" He glanced up in the mirror briefly then returned his attention to the monotonous, gray tunnel. "I might even sneak in a few crisps for good measure."

She gnawed on her bottom lip, her eyes fixed on the needle felted corgi swinging from the rear view mirror.

"I'll watch the Queen's speech and all the specials on telly. Probably video-call Micah at some point, make sure he's made it through Christmas lunch without a black eye. Then, I'll pick up Winnie on Boxing Day. So, don't you worry. I'll be fine." He did a double take. "And so will you. Christmas at home, eh? Nothing quite like it."

Madeleine wrapped her arms around her middle. "I *hate* this…" she mumbled mournfully, but the intercom picked her up, loud and clear.

Following a stream of cars and black cabs, Julian turned a corner and chose the second of four 'island' forecourts where passengers were dropped off before disappearing into terminal two's departures. A Range Rover sped away from the curb and Julian deftly swooped in, claiming the vacated space as Madeleine dipped into her wallet. He shot a furtive glance in his mirror and switched off the fare meter, then the engine.

The disappearing hum lifted Madeleine's chin. She peered through the partition, eyes darting to the dark meter. "Julian, what are you d—"

"I'll cover it." He unclicked his seatbelt.

"No!" She stiffened, struggling to escape hers. "I want to! You can't stop—"

Flinging his door open, Julian jumped out before she could finish.

I caused this. He slammed his door and rounded the nose of his taxi, shivering into the wind. *I should've stuck with the arrangement: cabbie and customer, no mixing business with pleasure, then no one would be hurting.*

Julian tugged open the rear door. Inside, Madeleine was backing away from the partition. Several folded pound notes sat in its small pass-through tray.

"Don't even try to argue," she said, gathering her purse and Fortnum's shopping bag from the seat.

A bone-chilling gust surged, propelling discarded coffee cups into the air and biting into Julian's skin. He braced against the open door and released a pent-up breath. "Okay, I won't," he replied, goose bumps prickling the back of his neck and beneath his sweater. "Thanks." As Madeleine slung the strap of her purse across her body, he reached in and collected her carry-on and backpack.

She followed closely, ducking her head and hopping out of the cab. Julian placed her luggage gently on the ground and clutched the suitcase's telescopic handle, extending it fully. Madeleine was ready to roll.

"Thank you." She nodded, fussing with her hair as it tangled in the wind.

Julian's brows jumped. "Oh!" He pointed in the air as he darted toward the cab. "You need a receipt—"

"No! It's fine." Stepping away from the open door, a heaviness seemed to plague Madeleine's smile. "I'm not writing this one off."

An airport attendant strolled past, chatting with a police officer. Julian tugged at the collar of his sweater then toyed with his watch, unable to settle. "So…"

"So…" Another gale burst across the forecourts, and Madeleine anchored a wayward lock of hair behind her ear. "Who would've thought, huh? I've been wanting to leave since I got here, but now, I just want to—" Her chin began to quiver.

Oh, don't cry, Maddie. Julian stepped closer. The need to gather her in, to comfort her, ached through his chest and empty arms, but he hesitated, fearful he'd never let go.

Madeleine shook her head wearily, her stare in freefall, plunging to her boots. "I wish things were different." She sniffed.

"God, so do I." Julian bowed his head slightly, eager to meet her eyes. "I've never hated a volcano or an ash cloud more."

"But if the volcano hadn't erupted…" She looked up and tears chased down her cheeks. "We wouldn't have met. I would've been alone—"

Fuck it. Julian reached out, collecting her in his arms. She trembled and sank into him, her warm, ragged breaths feathering his neck.

"I'll always be here, Maddie. I'm just a text or phone call away." He kissed the top of her head and hugged her tighter.

"But that's just it." Madeleine clutched his sweater. "You'll be here, half a world away." Her voice cracked and then the dam broke, her trickling tears dissolving into a river of gulping sobs.

Her tortured release strangled Julian's breaths. *She's right.* Stroking her back, his hand moved upward beneath her long hair, its thick softness pooling around her shoulders. He caressed the back of her neck tenderly, fighting the burning in his throat, his own tears churning, tightening his chest.

"I would've been lost here without you." Her whisper wrapped around his heart, unleashing the sting of hot tears.

"Maddie—"

"All right, people!" hollered the passing attendant. "Keep it moving!"

Madeleine jolted in Julian's arms, but he held tight, refusing to let her go. *Not yet!* He closed his tear-filled eyes, desperate to preserve this moment, this memory.

"You know the deal, cabbie." The airport employee threw them both an unsympathetic sidelong glance. "No parking, no long good-byes."

Curbing her sobs, Madeleine pulled back, swiping a hand under her nose.

With a huff, Julian blinked and wiped his eyes with the edge of his hand. "Yep, cheers." *You heartless bastard.* His glassy glare bore through the man as he waddled toward the next car.

Madeleine gathered her hair, dancing in the wind, and blew out her tear-stained cheeks. "Who knew the Grinch wore a hi-res vest, huh?"

A small smile broke Julian's frown. "I've got something for you."

"So do I," she countered, lifting the blue Fortnum's bag. "It's just a little something for you and Winnie…"

His heart swelled. "You got Winnie a gift?! Ah, Maddie!"

She bit her bottom lip as he accepted her present. "I'm sorry they're not gift-wrapped."

"That's okay. Mine aren't either. Means we can enjoy them quicker, without all that paper getting in the way." Julian refrained from peeking inside the bag and spoiling the surprise. "Thank you. I'll just get—" He darted to his taxi and opened the front door, trading Madeleine's gift for his own Fortnum's bag. Slinging his fabric tote over his shoulder, he snapped the door shut and joined her again.

"There's some candy and a book from Natasha, and the Fortnum prezzie is from me. It's a little taste of Christmas." He handed Madeleine the iconic blue bag.

"From London with love…" Her grin faltered as she looped her fingers through the handle. "Thank you, Julian."

"But wait!"—his eyes glistened, sharing their in-joke—"there's more." Reaching inside his record shop tote, he lifted out the small box Natasha had wrapped in silvery blue paper.

Madeleine's watery eyes widened as he placed the exquisite

present in her hand. "Oh, Julian, it's so pretty!" Loud voices pulled her attention to the car ahead of Julian's. The airport attendant was chastising a family of five for taking one goodbye selfie too many. Her gaze skittered back, jittery. "I guess I should save it for Christmas."

"If you like." Julian nodded, shutting out the noise. Only Madeleine mattered. "Save it or open it on the plane."

Madeleine lovingly touched the thick silver bow, admiring the constellations in its fabric. "Maybe one of these days you'll visit that cousin in Philadelphia." She swallowed and met his eyes wistfully. "If you're ever in Boston…"

"If you're ever back in London…" His lips parted as fresh tears brimmed in her eyes.

"*Julian…*" She inhaled sharply.

He swooped in and held her again. "It's okay, Maddie—"

"It's vacant!" A tall giraffe of a woman and her equally lofty husband scuttled past. "Quick, jump in." The pair clambered through the open rear door of Julian's cab.

He flinched. "Oh, wait a—" He pulled back from Madeleine. "I'm sorry, but I'm not picking up passengers here—"

"Well, you are now!" snarled the attendant, patting the hood of Julian's car. "Please, for the love of Harry Kane, just take 'em?"

Madeleine let go of Julian and stepped away, carefully stowing the gorgeous gift box in the Fortnum's bag with her other present.

This is not how I wanted to say goodbye. He rubbed his forehead. "Fine! Gimme one minute, mate and I'll go—promise."

"Good, 'cause if I have to ask again, you'll be paying my copper friend an £80 fine." With a terse nod, the airport attendant strolled off into the wind toward a fresh batch of unsuspecting travelers.

Madeleine's brow furrowed as she set the shopping bag on top of her suitcase and shuffled back to his side. "So, I guess this is—"

Julian curled his arm around Madeleine's waist and pulled her in, capturing her mouth with a firm, confident kiss. She didn't hold back, slipping her tongue between his lips, taking their kiss deeper as she clutched fistfuls of his hair, keeping him close. Every minute, every *second* had to count.

Breaths shallow, fingers digging into her coat, Julian pressed tighter, desperate to commit Madeleine's heady scent, her sweet gasps, the warmth of her embrace to his memory. It would have to do. Memories were all they had left.

But Madeleine eased back first, her hands retreating, slipping from his messy hair. She cradled his face and kissed him softly once more. "I'll never forget you," she whispered, her eyes overflowing with tears as she released him.

A gust of brisk wind blew between them, the growing distance thickening Julian's throat. "Will you text me when you land?"

"It'll be late…"

"Just text me. The time doesn't matter. You do."

She nodded and lifted her backpack onto her right shoulder then clutched the blue bag containing Julian's gifts against her chest. "Please give Winnie a kiss from me, okay?"

"I will. So many." He nodded solemnly, refusing to say good-bye. "Merry Christmas, Maddie."

She flashed a tight smile. "Merry Christmas, Julian."

Gripping the handle of her carry-on, she turned and plodded toward the departure entrance. Julian stood quietly for a moment, watching her until a certain policeman cleared his throat. *And happy fuckin' Christmas to you, too, mate.* Dragging his feet, Julian pulled his keys from his trouser pocket and rounded the front of his cab.

"JULIAN!"

She changed her mind? He halted, turning toward her buoyant voice.

Arms aloft and fingers bent, Madeleine was snapping a pretend photo of him. She blew Julian a kiss and grinned.

Returning her smile, Julian whispered "I love you" into the wind as she collected her belongings and headed into the terminal, disappearing for good.

TWENTY-EIGHT

MADELEINE

"Here you go. Please let us know if we can get you anything else."

Madeleine glanced up as the lounge hostess set her steaming tea on the small table she shared with a sweet grandmother who was flying to Scotland to visit her grandkids. "Thank you," she said, picking up the china mug. "But I think I'm good."

With a nod, the black-haired Brit in her crisp blue and red uniform took her tray and accommodating grin and navigated through an obstacle course of carry-ons, strollers, and overwhelmed travelers.

Billed as spacious and quiet, the Easy Air departure lounge on Christmas Eve was anything but. Every club chair and sofa was occupied, and a rowdy group of gin-soaked Geordies competed with a clique of trust-fund brats moaning about the lounge's prosecco for the title of 'Travelers You'd Hate to Sit Beside on a Plane'.

Madeleine blew on her hot, milky tea and took a wary sip as the senior seated beside her slowly stood.

"Och, these wee chairs. Made me stiff!" The old woman's Scottish brogue was thick and endearing. "Well, love, Happy Christmas. I wish you a safe, comfy flight."

"Thanks. You, too. Happy Christmas," said Madeleine with a grin. "I hope your grandson loves his sweater."

The grandmother's thin lips bowed into a smile as her gnarled fingers curled around the handle of her suitcase. She tottered off, and once again, loneliness descended around Madeleine.

I miss Jules. Setting down her tea, a pang reverberated through her. *I wonder if he's still working or if he went home...*

Picking up her phone, Madeleine shifted in her seat. *If I'm gon-*

na pine for him, do it full-on.

She plowed inside her backpack. *What to listen to? Kylie? Madonna?* Her hand ventured past her laptop, one...two novels, her carefully wrapped chocolate squirrel, and her refillable water bottle. *Wait—how 'bout Hunters and Collectors? Yeah, I need "Throw Your Arms Around Me" and I need it now.* She dug further, but the buzz of her phone hit pause on her search.

Shantelle: In Milwaukee. OTW to Mom & Dad's.

Shantelle: JUST HEARD! Airports are open in London!

The three 'texting in progress' dots danced, then stopped, then started again, giving way to Sorry! Leia calling me. Have to speak now or I'll miss her. Will text back. x

The whiny trust-fund boozers were reaching new heights of headache-inducing annoyance, so Madeleine lunged into her backpack again. Her hand flirted with a magazine, a bag of salt and vinegar crisps, and landed on...canvas. *What?* She flinched and her fingertips scooted through crumbs. *That's it?! No, no, no...*

Breath bottling in her chest, her other hand dove in, pulling, yanking, clearing a path for her panicked gaze. Nose-deep, she came face to face with the stark reality. Her fingers weren't lying. All that sat at the bottom of her bag were cookie crumbs.

FUCK! Her shoulders slumped. *You've got to be kidding me. I FORGOT them?*

Madeleine closed her eyes and sagged back in the chair, her bum sliding, hanging off the seat. *Shit! Those headphones are my life.* She huffed. *Well, I hope the hotel's housekeeper enjoys them.*

"Uh, pardon me, but is this seat taken?" The male voice was British and oh so posh.

Eyes popping open, Madeleine blinked and pulled herself up, reuniting her butt with the chair. "No, it's all yours." Her attention swerved toward her new neighbor.

Tall and blond, the guy wore the hell out of his black designer suit, but over his arm hung a long, tailored coat in the most obnoxious red and purple plaid she'd ever seen.

"Thank you." He nodded politely.

Wait a minute?! No way! Madeleine's pulse took off on a sprint. *IT'S THAT GUY!* A flashback six days in the making pinched her gut. *The taxi thief! With the ugly coat!*

He sank down into the vacant seat beside her and pulled his carry-on close to his polished shoes. His garish coat, laid across his lap, erupted with the five iconic tones from *Close Encounters of the Third Kind.* "Er, sorry..." he mumbled, diving into a hidden pocket.

At least he's more polite this time. Sneaking a sidelong glance, Madeleine's gaze fell from his face to his coat and its vertical and horizontal crisscrossing bands of red, purple, yellow, and white. The inside label stared back. *That monstrosity is designer?!* She reeled in her shock and turned away.

Plaid Coat Guy pressed his phone against his ear. "Bruce, hey. How's New York?"

Madeleine picked up her own phone. *3:47 p.m. Where would Julian be now?*

Filling time, she tapped into her photos and scrolled through her London memories, starting with her gorgeous hotel room, the junior suite in the St. Pancras Renaissance. She adjusted her position on the firm chair, pining for the softness of the hotel's king-sized bed...and the privacy her headphones usually provided.

"Er, no, that's just it." The guy sighed mournfully and shook his head. "It didn't work out the way I'd hoped. My grand gesture—flopped horribly..."

Madeleine's finger swept down the screen, pulling up her Tower of London pictures, including the selfie with Julian, the pair of them together in front of the Queen's Guard. Spreading her fingers, the image grew on the screen. *Look at him.* She ached with longing. *So smiley and adorable. If I'd known six years ago that Julian Halliwell was a beautiful person inside and out, I would've gotten on the first flight over here.*

"Didn't have the chance, mate," said Plaid Coat Guy, his shoulders slumped as he confided into his phone. "I left it all too late. She met someone, a fellow teacher. He proposed two weeks ago, apparently. Even had her students in on it."

Ouch! Poor guy. Madeleine fought the urge to glance over.

"On the upside, you won't have to write that best man's speech." Plaid Coat Guy paused for a few seconds, slipping into a wince. "Yeah, I guess. But talk about *mortifying*, walking back into Harry Winston asking for a bloody refund..."

Madeleine stole a peek. The taxi thief looked tired and defeated, and she couldn't help but feel sorry for him. Then, his gaze slid left.

Shit.

Pressing her lips together, she returned to her phone, and with a flick, the photos from the Castle pub quiz rolled under her finger: making faces with Natasha; Julian and Micah, arms around each other, singing along to Take That's "Could It Be Magic"; sharing a laugh and a gooey, molten lava cake with Julian. *Tash sent me this one the next day.* A soft smile lingered on Madeleine's mouth. *I had no idea she'd taken it. Tash captioned it 'Couple goals'.* Her heart stuttered. *She wasn't wrong. Julian and I were so great together.*

Her blond neighbor cleared his throat. "Well, mostly I *feel* like a bloody idiot..." Closing his eyes, he pinched the bridge of his nose and let out another heavy sigh.

Madeleine scrolled to a photo of Julian, lips puckered, eating the lemony Big Ben from their afternoon tea...

"I know! I royally fucked up. I should *never* have taken the job offer." The guy covered his face with his hand. "I-I should've stayed with her in Oxford."

...then, a selfie appeared, Madeleine and Julian together amid the magical sparkle of the South Bank Christmas market. Hot chocolates aloft, they were cuddled up close, but Julian wasn't looking into the camera. He was gazing lovingly at her.

A lump lodged in Madeleine's throat. *Am I doing the right thing?*

"No, Bruce, none of this is on her!" exclaimed Plaid Coat Guy. "It was *me* who said we couldn't make it work long distance. A year's a long time, and New York isn't just a hop, skip, and a jump down the M40. For all she knew, I was never coming back..."

A mix of Madeleine's and Natasha's pictures from Micah's party glided under her thumb: sweaty and smiley, Madeleine was wearing the birthday boy's top hat as she and Julian lip-synced upstairs to Kylie's "Kids"...playing Jumbo Jenga in the frosty garden against Sadie and Natasha...jumping around wildly to Guns N' Roses (Julian was doing that full-body Axl Rose 'snake dance' thing)...and a moonlit selfie, mid-kiss on the sun lounger.

Reliving that moment, a flutter swooped in her belly: the warmth of Julian's embrace, his soft lips, persistent yet tender, and the little sounds of pleasure he made when she took their kiss deeper.

What would be better than a snog with a cute British bloke?

Kellie's words—her familiar Aussie voice—careened into Madeleine's mind.

I want that for you. And if you don't find him, I'll just have to make sure to find him FOR you.

Scrolling through her images from Shere, Madeleine's heart pounded through her ears.

And you found him, didn't you, Kel? Were you here all along, setting up these coincidences? Making sure we met and fell...

An ache rose in her throat. Madeleine lowered her phone. Her eyes clouded with tears, but for once, she could see clearly.

Oh god. I LOVE him. I'm in love with Julian.

"I'm telling you, mate, I swear to god"—Plaid Coat Guy's quiet voice cracked with emotion as Madeleine stole a sideways glance across the table—"I think I'll *always* regret leaving her."

A buzzing tickle in her palm yanked her away from his palpable angst.

Shantelle: Sorry, Mads! Had to speak with Leia 'cause you know, time zones. SO! What's the latest?

TWENTY-NINE

JULIAN

A garland of jaunty snowmen, hung across the frosted windows of the Kensington Park Road cab shelter, danced in the wind as Julian huddled behind his steering wheel, sipping hot coffee from his thermos. The radio rambled on about traffic havoc around Heathrow, but Julian didn't hear a word. He was too busy staring into the evening's encroaching darkness, convincing himself he'd done the right thing: letting Madeleine leave without fuss or fanfare…without making the case for a long-distance relationship.

It wouldn't have worked. His eyes followed a well-dressed couple across the street, holding hands as they sauntered down the steps of an elegant, terraced house. *Here's me, freaked out about flying with barely enough money to pay for my dog's surgery. And then, there's beautiful Maddie, using up all her holiday time just to see me, using up her savings to fly back and forth. How fair is that?*

He screwed the lid on his thermos, ignoring the comforting aroma of fried bacon, ketchup, and thick toasted bread calling out from a paper bag sat in his lap.

Plus, Maddie didn't suggest it either. At the end of the day, we're still on the same page. At least I can take comfort in that…

A text pinged his sleeping phone, cradled in the console to the left of his thigh.

Madeleine? Julian's heart leapt into his throat. Dropping the thermos in his lap, he snatched the device, his fervent gaze poring over… Tour driver needed Xmas Day noon to 14:00. Text yes if interested.

The tour agency. His racing pulse hit the brakes. *What am I doing?* He swallowed, refocusing. *So, am I interested?*

277

Julian looked up from the screen and nodded at a fellow cabbie trundling past, his hands (and mouth) busy with a takeaway sausage and egg roll. The cab shelters usually closed after the post-lunchtime rush, but with London buzzing with shoppers, tourists, and Christmas parties—and drivers in need of affordable sustenance on the fly—they were keeping their kettles whistling and griddles sizzling until six p.m.

I could definitely use the cash. Taking this job will boost my rating with the agency, too. As Julian placed his thermos in the console's cup holder, "Never Gonna Give You Up" by Rick Astley blasted in his palm.

"What the—?"

Smiling beneath 4:36 p.m. and a crooked Santa hat, Micah waved a half-eaten mince pie, his request for a FaceTime chat beckoning. Julian promptly hit Accept, trading the 1980s earworm for Nat King Cole's "Caroling, Caroling", a favorite of Micah's dearly departed grandmother.

"Hey, mate!" Micah shouted as the red and green lights on the Cooper family tree blinked in time with the nostalgic Christmas classic.

"So, get this," said Julian, switching off the cab's radio. "My ringtone miraculously changed to Rick Astley. Anything to do with you, Meeks?"

Micah snickered and lowered his pie. "You're just noticing that now? I changed it like, last night at The Churchill!" His head turned as his niece and nephew—Sadie's kids, nine-year-old twins—flew by in the background, arguing about who started 'it'.

Julian paused, waiting for their chaos to die down. "You're my first call in twenty-four hours. Everyone texts me these days."

"Wow, look at *you* and your texting! Maybe you're not such a dinosaur after all." Micah chuckled, tugging at the Man City scarf flung casually around his neck. "But never mind that." His cheeky grin gave way to a tempered brow and a piercing gaze. "I heard about the airports. Is Madeleine *going*?"

"No." Julian plowed a hand through his hair. "She's gone."

Micah's face contorted in empathy. "Oh shit! Oh mate! That's fucking rubbish!"

"MICAH *SPARROW*!"

He dropped his pie and his hand flew up, fumbling with his scarf, pulling the blue and white knitting over the cluster of purple hickeys on his neck.

Mrs. Cooper, a stickler for swearing, especially at Christmas, only used her children's full names when she was royally pissed. She lurched behind Micah, her 'Knock, Knock, It's Prosecco O'clock' apron hiding her ample curves.

"Who you cursing at?" Her heavily mascaraed eyes squinted beneath her bleach blonde bangs.

Julian waved. "It's just me, Pam."

Pamela Cooper's face lit up brighter than Blackpool's illuminations. "Ah, Julian love! We *miss* you, darling!"

"Yeah, we do," added Micah. "Drop everything, mate—come join us! Sadie baked an epic Battenberg, Mum made her award-winning Bakewell tarts—"

"I did!" She thrust out her chest. "Got top prize down the Legion."

Micah laughed. "And Tash—"

"Is eating *everything*!" Natasha invaded Micah's shot, holding up a plate with what looked like a massacred slice of Banoffee pie. "Jules! *Pul-lease* tell me you're on your way? I need someone with active brain cells on my Trivial Pursuit team."

Julian gave a ghost of a smile. "You know, I'd love nothing more, but I'm gonna hang out here. I'm picking up Winnie on Boxing Day. He's staying till January 3rd—"

"Oh, bring Wins up!" Natasha squealed. "I need some corgi lovin'!"

"Ah, Tash, another time, eh? I'm not feeling very Christmassy," said Julian. "I'm gonna hunker down with Winnie and take advantage of the quiet here, make a start on my London book."

Sadie poked her head in. "Jules, did I hear that right? You're writing?"

Natasha's heavily kohled eyes widened as she stuffed a forkful of bananas and toffee between her lips.

"Planning to, yeah."

Sadie smiled. "Our *Words and Music* star, on the rise again!"

Julian glanced away sheepishly. "I'm not sure about that."

"Well, the fact you're even trying—I'm happy to hear it. Happy Christmas, Jules!" Sadie tapped Natasha on the shoulder. "C'mon, Tish Tash. If we're gonna finish our Victoria sponge before *Strictly*, we better get a move on."

Natasha rolled her eyes. "I'm not *six*! Stop calling me that!" With a huff, she waved through the screen, "Jules, see you later!" as Mr. Cooper stormed into the room. Jacket slick with rain, he muttered about the iciness of the roads.

Micah glanced over his shoulder. "Gimme a minute, mate..." Standing, he carried his phone and his pie somewhere more private, leaving Nat King Cole, the flashing tree, and his grumpy father behind. From the long pause, jerky picture, and the *thump, thump, thump* of Micah's feet up some stairs, Julian guessed they were headed to his best friend's childhood bedroom.

"So"—a door squeaked closed and a burst of overhead lighting brightened Micah's face—"Madeleine just...left?"

Julian gave the smallest of nods, resigned. "It was messy. She cried...I started to lose it—"

"Aw, Jules. I'm so sorry." Micah plopped down on a twin-sized bed, overlooked by Man City and Prodigy posters.

"Yeah." He expelled a heavy breath. "But what did I expect, eh? It was always going to end this way, sooner or later."

"Right. Well, I feel awful, pushing you..." said Micah.

"Listen, mate, this is *not* your fault. I went into this willingly, okay? I knew what I was doing."

"But still..." Micah winced. An incoming call on Julian's phone bumped his best friend's face (but not his voice) from the screen. "Jules, if there's anything I can do—if you want, I could come back down early—"

"Oh bollocks." Julian's pained gaze flitted upward. "It's Caroline calling."

"Ergh." Even without seeing Micah's face, Julian knew his nose and eyes were scrunched like he'd huffed a stinky smell. "Do you wanna take her—"

"Christ no." Jabbing Decline, Julian banished his ex to voicemail and reunited with Micah's live stream, his expression full of loathing. "I'm not in the mood for Caroline's bullshit."

"Don't blame you." Micah rubbed his eye with the heel of his hand. "Ah, this really sucks, Jules. If only, eh? If only you'd never asked her out, if only we'd never walked past the sandwich shop... if only she'd hopped into someone else's cab." He exhaled loudly and dropped his hand, his watery eyes wearily focused on something across the room. "Could've spared you all this angst—and on Christmas Eve, too."

"But that's the thing, Meeks," said Julian, leaning against his door's armrest. "I don't regret any of it with Maddie. Not a second."

"No?" Micah chewed on his fingernail. "Not at all?"

"Well, obviously, I regret making Maddie cry. She was full-on sobbing."

"But you know, mate, that speaks *volumes*," said Micah. "She was into you, man—like, *big* time."

Julian tilted his head. "Maybe, who knows, but seeing her like that broke my heart. I couldn't take it." He stared down at the wrapped sandwich waiting in his lap. "That's the *only* thing I regret. Everything else, I wouldn't change a bleeding thing. I'd rather have five days of *spectacular* than five years of so-so."

"Oooh, burn!" Micah snorted. "Take *that*, Caroline!"

Julian offered a tired smile. "That's just it, though. Everything about her—it felt...*right*. Like we were meant to find each other. I've honestly never—"

TAP-TAP-TAP.

Julian flinched and shifted away from his door. On the other side of the glass, two thirtyish women, a blonde and a redhead weighed down with designer shopping bags, grinned expectantly. He lowered his window.

"Sorry for startling you," cooed the tawny-haired half of the stylish duo, her plummy accent in contrast to the smiling Christmas pudding earmuffs peeking out from her expensive blowout. "By chance, are you available?"

Julian's heart dipped. "Yeah, I'm free." He pressed his lips together. "Do you need help with your bags?"

Micah nibbled on his mince pie, waiting.

"We're good, but thanks!" The redhead nodded and pulled open the rear passenger door.

"You gotta go?" Micah licked pastry crumbs off his bottom lip.

"Yeah. Sorry, mate." Julian pulled on his seatbelt. "Unfortunately, the holidays don't stop for heartache."

THIRTY

JULIAN

One fare to Sloane Square, a round-trip—plus waiting time—between Mayfair and Harrods, and jaunts to Vauxhall, Bermondsey, and Hackney later, and Julian was spent: stiffness in his legs, tightness in his shoulders, and an unbearable ache in his heart.

Maybe some air will help. Leaving his black cab charging on Hemingford Road, a short stroll from his flat, Julian set out to stretch his tired legs before heading home.

He wandered over to Caledonian Road. The street was busier than usual, clogged with traffic, both vehicles and pedestrians. The rolling laughter of loved-up couples headed to dinner echoed between passing double-deckers, their windows fogged and seats crammed with exhausted Londoners and their hard-earned shopping. In their wake, packs of pink-cheeked teens wandered from pub to pub in search of sneaky pints and maybe a festive snog. Watching them on the prowl, Julian tried to push away all thoughts of his dismal love life: two back-to-back Christmas Eves, two back-to-back punches to the gut. Both were devastating but for completely different reasons.

The breakup with Caroline was, as Micah called it, "a swift kick to the bollocks"—the wake-up call Julian had long needed. As time went on and Caroline became more status-obsessed, his sense of unease about the relationship had grown, but he'd bitten his tongue and made excuses, to himself and friends. But, as Micah noted, there was a *reason* they'd never 'named the date', and when her betrayal with his brother exploded last Christmas Eve, some small part of him was relieved. The pretense that all was well came to a crashing end. As he picked himself up again, he held out the hope that he'd meet someone new—someone kind and supportive who wasn't so hung up on shallow, unimportant things...

And then, almost a year later, she magically appeared on the back seat of his cab. Lovely Maddie with her fondness for sandwiches, squirrels and reindeer, Kawaii smiley faces, and Brit bands few Americans knew about. She was the polar opposite of Caroline: empathetic, vulnerable, deeply caring...in a world that often didn't understand loss. Madeleine wasn't perfect (*She hates Oasis! Doesn't know* The Snowman?*!*), but she understood through experience that life is precious. She was *real*; there was zero artifice about her. She understood what mattered—family, friends, fun. And, as luck would have it, she liked him for who he was—cab, corgi, and all.

Losing Madeleine felt like losing his hope for happiness. His present, his future...his heart.

Oh man. This one is gonna hurt. Badly.

But what could Julian have done differently? He couldn't follow her. Couldn't beg her to stay. Well, he could've, but sometimes you have to see a situation for what it really is.

Maddie was on holiday, passing through, and then there was me, flitting from place to place in my cab. A fleeting connection if there ever was one. What we shared...shone brilliantly for a few days, but it was too bright a flame. It was never supposed to last forever...

Ah, fuck it! He wandered into a bustling corner shop and purchased two Lion Bars, a bag of Wispa Bites, and a red plastic tub of candy, inappropriately called Celebrations.

A broken heart and Christmas, both worthy reasons for a chocolate binge.

Just get through tonight and tomorrow, and then at least Winnie will be with me. Cuddles with the pup, while not the same as cuddles with Maddie, always make me feel better.

Dainty snowflakes twirled in the air, looking for a safe landing as Julian parked along the curb of terraced houses on Ripplevale Grove. He breathed a sigh, turned off his cab's engine, and glanced up at his empty flat, its windows aglow for Winnie. A swell of angelic voices sang out from the ground floor, the apartment owned and occupied by Julian's landlord, the fruitcake-loving (and hard of hearing) Mr. Hannon.

The annual BBC carol service from King's College in Cambridge. I'm so not feeling any of this...

Julian checked his watch: *8:25 p.m.* He stared ahead, talking stock of the evening. *Maddie will be flying over the Atlantic by now. Meanwhile, in another half hour, Old Man Hannon will be headed to The Drapers Arms for his traditional Christmas Eve tipple. That gives me a few minutes upstairs to decompress before I knock on his door and collect that Christmas dinner for two I ordered. Good thing I love leftovers.*

He unfastened his seatbelt and gathered his thermos, coat, and the Fortnum's bag containing his gifts from Madeleine. His phone, lodged in the console beside the balled-up wrapper from his bacon sandwich, pinged with a message. Julian's eyes darted, a flicker of hope quickening his pulse as he collected the trash and his phone.

Caroline: How the fuck do you know Shantelle Joy anyway?

What...? Oh, wait. Snooping through Tash's social media again, Caroline? Julian shook his head and stowed the phone with Caroline's text and earlier voicemail (which he'd ignored) in his coat's pocket. He cracked a tired smile. *You know what? Let her think we're together. Why not? Madeleine does look a LOT like her sister.*

Arms full, he exited his cab just as he realized he'd forgotten to text back the tour agency. The Christmas Day job offer was probably long gone, but Julian wasn't that bothered. The money would've been nice, but a December 25th spent in bed feeling sorry for himself seemed like the way to go.

He plunged his key in the front door's lock and let himself into the hallway, the full brunt of "Hark! The Herald Angels Sing" assaulting his ears with Mr. Hannon's tipsy-sounding dulcet tones in accompaniment.

At least Mr. Hannon is full of the joys of Christmas, bless him.

Trudging up the stairs, Julian's long shadow weaved along the flowery wallpaper and rounded the landing's banister. His mail—a few bills, a magazine, and a late Christmas card or two—laid on the mat outside his door, brought upstairs by Mr. Hannon. Tomorrow, the senior would be off to Brighton on the train to stay with his daughter for a few days, and the lovely old terrace house would be quiet and still, ideal for writing.

He bent over and scooped up his mail, dropping his crumpled sandwich bag in the process. Crouching again, he picked it up, and something else, too—a song, straying beyond his apartment door. Julian recognized the pretty melody instantly. It was "Gently", a sweet, sparkly charmer of a British Christmas song by Terry Emm, often overlooked and definitely underrated.

The radio's on. Old habits...

Shaking his head, Julian unlocked his flat and nudged the door open.

"WOOF!"

The sharp bark was followed by nails scampering across the hardwood. A jolt of anticipation rushed through him.

"Winnie?!"

Elbowing the door closed, Julian dumped his belongings as the corgi's boopable nose and wiggly bum veered around the living room doorjamb. He ecstatically fell to his knees. "Winnie Winks!" Laughing raucously, Julian bundled the squiggly dog into his arms as the canine's chorus of whimpers and happy cries rose around them.

"But how did you—?"

Winnie answered with excited, sloppy licks across Julian's chin.

"Merry Christmas!"

Wait, what?! Mid-dog hug, the breath stalled in Julian's chest. He blinked and slowly lifted his head, his eyes sweeping up black tights and an oversized striped sweater, its shoulders swathed with silky brown waves. Her pouty lips parted in a hopeful smile, and for a moment, all Julian could think about was their softness and her exquisite taste.

She didn't leave?! Julian's heart soared, higher than Big Ben, higher than the Shard. He gave Winnie a loving pat and rose to his feet, meeting her gaze glistening with happy tears.

Madeleine had never looked more beautiful.

She gently raised her hand in greeting and let out a small shuddering breath. "Hi."

Winnie weaved happily around Julian's legs then lolloped into the living room, grabbing his Paddington Bear.

Julian blinked. *Is this really happening?*

Longing swelled in his chest as he inched forward. "B-but I thought you'd gone—?"

Madeleine didn't let him finish. Throwing her arms around his shoulders, she pulled him close, meeting his mouth greedily with urgent, needy kisses.

Julian didn't need convincing. He scooped her up and breathed her in, his lips breaking away, pressing smiling kisses along her jaw and down her neck.

"I just can't believe you're *here!*"

As he kissed her again and again, a delighted laugh escaped his throat as Madeleine wrapped her legs around his waist and tilted her head back, gasping with pleasure, an irresistible sound Julian thought he'd never hear again.

"I couldn't get on the plane. I knew I'd regret it..." Sliding her hands up into his hair, she leaned in, her eyes tearfully determined. "I love you, Julian."

She loves me?

He paused mid-kiss against her neck, lightness and joy tingling through his chest. Easing back from the softness of her skin, he smiled tenderly. "Oh, Maddie! I love *you*, so damn much!" His mouth claimed hers and Madeleine didn't hesitate letting him in, their deepening kiss becoming faster, more desperate, making up for lost time as they pressed and tasted and reveled in their unexpected reunion.

Cupped in Julian's hands, the luscious curves of Madeleine's bottom teased the growing hardness in his trousers. *She can have no doubt how much I want her.*

Madeleine broke free first, her eyes heavy and full of want, brimming with impatience as her thighs tightened against him. "Care to join the Naughty List with me?" Her fingers twirled the downy hair at the nape of his neck.

The best Christmas present ever. Goose bumps pebbled Julian's skin. "Join it? I'm already on it." With a cheeky laugh, Julian bounced her in his arms and swept toward his bed.

"Well, YOU, Julian Halliwell, are no one-hit wonder!" Chasing breaths, Madeleine melted into a plump pillow and wiped perspiration off her brow. "*That* was even better than our first time, which is saying a lot 'cause"—she swallowed—"that was amazing, too."

"Ah...yeah it was." Chest rising and falling fast, Julian blinked blissfully up at the ceiling, lost in reverie...the softness of her thighs, her taste on his tongue. "I was nervous, though."

"The first time?" she asked. "Really?"

He nodded and ran a hand through his hair, sweeping it off his damp forehead.

"Aw, Julian, I thought it was just me." Madeleine shifted closer. "When is the first time *not* stressful?"

"Never. Not for this bloke, anyway." He half-laughed. "And with you, well..." He rolled onto his side and faced her, propping himself up on an elbow. "It's been a while, you know? I haven't dated or been with anyone since my ex, and breakups do all sorts of weird things to your confidence."

"That's true." She agreed.

"So the whole anxiety-riddled, getting your kit off in front of each other for the first time thing felt more intense, but then when we kissed and held each other…I just knew it would be okay."

Madeleine caressed his bottom lip with her thumb. "'Cause it will be."

I'll never tire of this. Julian kissed her finger and smiled. "Hey, that's another thing to add to our list—the Hollywood rom-com list."

"YES! The *awkwardness*." Madeleine snickered, lowering her hand. "You never see it. Everyone on screen is uber confident and uninhibited. Oh, and of course, they're all perfectly shaped. No fat thighs, stretch marks, or cellulite allowed."

"But *you're* perfectly shaped," said Julian.

Madeleine grinned. "I'm really not, but thank you!"

"Bollocks! You are! I *love* your body." Julian's finger traced circles along her hip. "I fancied you something rotten from the minute we met."

She scrunched her nose. "*Really?*"

"Yeah."

"So you like sullen girls who don't talk much and stare wistfully out your cab's window, avoiding eye contact?" She bit back a grin.

A flicker of a smile curved Julian's lips. "You had good reason—more than one, actually." He pressed a lingering kiss to her forehead. "I thought you were gorgeous, and obviously your interest in music had me intrigued. Only the *coolest* girls have a Pulp ringtone!"

"Yeah, yeah. I bet you say that to all your lady passengers…" She laughed.

"No, actually! I've never…you know, met *anyone* that way." He played with a wisp of her hair. "Customer/client romantic entanglements are frowned upon when you drive a black cab."

"Well, good. I'm glad to hear it!" Curling into him, she nuzzled into his neck.

"I'm sure some cabbies blur the line, but I never have. That's why I waited until we were obviously clicking before I asked if you wanted to hang out. You know, in case you felt the same way about me."

Madeleine lifted her head. "Oh, I did. I *do*! I really did read everything you wrote for *Words and Music*." She cuddled into him again. "I was a huge fan, crushed on you and your writing for years. And the whole time, I had no idea what you looked like."

"That was an editorial decision: no journo headshots, no schmoozy photos with the artists—they wanted the attention on the music, not our ugly mugs," said Julian. "Quite right, too."

"Didn't matter," said Madeleine, her fingers splayed and toying with the hair on his chest. "I was hooked on your personality, your wry sense of humor. I fell head over heels for your word choice and turn of phrase."

"*That* is geeky!"

"Hey, that's me. I'll own it!" She glanced up, searching his eyes. "It was like I'd found a kindred spirit, you know? I knew if we ever met, we'd get along famously. I've never crushed so hard on someone I didn't know in *my life*."

Julian's brow furrowed coyly. "Not even your beloved Backstreet Boys?"

"Shit." Madeleine gulped. "I guess I should apologize to Nick Carter, huh?"

"Immediately," Julian deadpanned.

"That's why I got all wild-eyed when you told me your last name. Not only was my writing crush talented, he was also friendly and helpful and oh so *handsome*..."

Julian winced playfully. "Oh, stop. My ego can't take it."

They both laughed.

"And then you mentioned going for therapy and I crushed even harder—if that's possible."

"Therapy, a turn-on?" Julian reached up and captured her hand, threading his fingers between hers. "Who knew?"

She laugh-snorted. "Joke all you want, but for me it is. Listen, I've dated guys who think therapy is for losers, and funnily enough, one of those guys—my ex—also believed grief can be conveniently wished away."

"That's awful." He kissed her hand and held it tight against his chest. "I'm sorry he made things tougher for you."

A soft smile graced her lips. "But you get it. You've *lived* it. You know we never get over losing a loved one. The loss becomes a part of you. It gets into your bones and stays with you forever."

Julian nodded pensively. "It does feel like an 'us and them' situation sometimes."

"It's a relief, though, knowing I can just sit with you and be myself," said Madeleine. "This, being with you...feels amazing."

He brought her hand to his lips again for a tender kiss. They gazed into each other's eyes for a moment, then Madeleine spoke.

"Okay, so confession time." She squeezed his hand as he lowered their clench. "I stifled a squeal when you asked me out. There were seniors and little kids around, so I held back. I didn't want to scare them."

"Civically minded, that's good!" Julian brushed his thumb across the back of her hand. "I nearly keeled over when you said yes, actually."

She giggled. "So *that* was what I heard!"

"Oh bollocks, you caught it?"

"Uh-huh." Madeleine bit her lip. "Weren't you outside Harrods or something?"

"Yeah, I was so wrapped up in our conversation, waiting for your answer, I tripped over a raised bit of pavement and barely avoided two women taking selfies with a box of cupcakes."

"Yikes, that wouldn't have looked so good on the 'gram!" She snickered. "Imagine if you went viral?"

Julian winced. "Kill me now!"

"So, asking me out..." Madeleine cocked her head. "You thought I'd say no?"

"I wasn't sure *what* you'd say. I knew we got along well, but...I don't know, there's always the risk, right? Misreading things. Being seen as just a friend?" He gently let go of her hand

and scratched his temple.

"Well, I'm happy you took that risk. I had a blast at Micah's party. That whole night—unforgettable."

"So was your dress," said Julian.

"Now it's all rolled up in my carry-on. I hope I didn't ruin it."

"You looked absolutely stunning. You took my breath away. You still do…" Julian leaned in, kissing her eagerly as she edged closer, pressing against him.

She grinned, leaving their kiss. "I never expected this, meeting a great guy, falling in love…"

He brushed a finger along her jaw. "What are the odds, eh?"

"It just goes to show you," said Madeleine. "You can be sad and hurting but still feel happiness. They can sit together, side by side, the bitter and the sweet."

"Yeah, it took me months and whole lotta therapy to figure that one out," said Julian.

Madeleine swept a lost eyelash off his cheek. "It's still new to me, but I'm slowly coming to terms with it…and not feeling guilty about it."

They shared a wistful smile.

"By the way, how did your family take it?" he asked. "You staying here and not coming home for Christmas?"

"That is such a *Julian* question."

His head tilted. "Why?"

"You always ask about other people," she said. "It's one of the things I like the most about you."

He flipped down the bed sheets. "Not my pumped-up pecs, eh?"

"Your body is sexy as hell. Toned in all the right places, but not too toned"—she scrunched her nose—"if that makes sense?" Her expression relaxed. "I'm not into all those super-hard-body dudes that show up on dating apps or at the gym."

"Thank god for that!" He chuckled. "So, about your mom and dad…?"

"Oh, they don't mind me staying. They'll miss me, but more

than anything, they want me to be happy. They're already used to Shan flying here, there, and everywhere, so me being in London isn't that big a shock."

"So Shantelle is okay with it, too?"

"Oh, she was *ecstatic*! Once I told her you were a Sagittarius, she rambled on for like, twenty minutes. Apparently, we're a match for the ages. She wants to meet you, of course."

"And I her. Good to know the stars are on our side." Julian slipped his fingers through Madeleine's again.

She grinned. "I'll have to find a post office in a few days, send on all their presents."

I guess Shan put her up in the hotel again? Julian cleared his throat. "So, are you back at the St. Pancras?"

Madeleine nodded and glanced away. "For the next week, yeah. After the holidays, I'll find a place to rent."

Rent? She could move in here with me, but is that...too soon? Julian's heart skipped. "You're gonna stay? For how long?"

"Six months."

His smile took off like a shot. "Maddie, that's great! Wow, you're transferring here with Sensoria?"

"No, I'm taking a leave of absence. I'll work on my writing, see more of London...hopefully, figure out if I want to return to Sensoria." She rubbed her nose. "Six months is as long as I can stay on a visitor's visa. I did a LOT of googling and emailing during the drive from the airport."

He squinted humorously and squeezed her hand. "Uber or black cab?"

"Cab, of course! Hey, I gotta support my boyfriend's industry."

A warm, fuzzy sensation bubbled in Julian's chest. "Boyfriend, eh? Like the sound of that."

"Yeah, so did your Mr. Hannon downstairs!" Madeleine giggled.

"Oh!" Julian gaped. "So *that's* why he let you in!"

"Yeah, I guess he approves. Although, I think he was also looking to offload Winnie."

293

"Wait—he was already here?" asked Julian.

"Yep. Got dropped off an hour or two before I arrived…"

Julian slowly nodded. "Okay, that makes sense. That must be why Caroline called me. I pushed it to voicemail. Should probably listen to it. They must've left for their fancy skiing trip two days early."

Madeleine sucked in a breath. "Actually…that's *not* what happened…"

His brows lifted. "Oh?"

"Caroline is still in London…" She gave him a tight smile. "Julian, Winnie's here because of Shantelle. I asked her for a little favor."

He blinked. "A favour? Like what?"

"I asked her to convince Caroline to let you have Winnie permanently."

She what? Julian swore his heart stopped. "You're *kidding* me?!"

"Nope. Last night, I told Shan what's been going on and gave her Caroline's social media details. She privately messaged her, out of the blue, saying she wanted to discuss something over the phone. I guess Caroline couldn't believe her luck 'cause she called Shan straight away." Madeleine rubbed her eye. "After some small talk, Shan let her have it with both barrels: if Caroline didn't stop using poor Winnie as some kind of pawn and hand him over to her *dear friend Julian* immediately, she'd make sure ALL her British acting buddies steered clear of Peel PR."

His pulse began to pound. "Bloody hell, no way!"

"Shantelle's a *tough* cookie," said Madeleine. "She's involved in all her contract negotiations, and she knows a LOT of people— BAFTA winners, Oscar winners. Plus, there's her eight million social media followers. One tweet from Shan and…"

Julian's jaw fell slack. "Caroline's perfectly cultivated PR bubble *pops!*"

Madeleine nodded. "Apparently, Shan wasn't on the phone long. Caroline didn't need much persuading."

"I bet she didn't!" Julian eased up on his elbow and collected his eyeglasses. "Where *is* Winnie?" He scratched his bedhead.

The cute dog lay sprawled out on top of Julian's corgi slippers, his belly rising and falling with satisfied snores.

Madeleine pushed herself up and hugged the covers around her bare breasts. "Ahhh, he's sleeping beside his Paddington, near your tree. It's been a long day for him."

"He's totally content, bless him," said Julian, a full-on grin rising. *Safe at home with me...for good.*

They retreated under the sheets and Julian rolled back to the middle of the bed and Madeleine. "I owe your sister a phone call and a massive thank you—I owe *you* one, too. My god, Maddie." His eyes began to sting. "This is the sweetest thing anyone has ever done for me."

"I just wanted you to be together again. For Christmas." She smiled sweetly.

Julian gazed at her and slightly shook his head, feeling happy, exhausted, in awe. "You know, I can *never* thank you enough for this. I love you so much, Madeleine."

"I love you, too."

"Please say that again."

She laughed. "I love *you*, Julian!"

"That's music to my ears." He tenderly cupped her face and leaned in, kissing her softly until they fell asleep tangled in each other's arms.

THIRTY-ONE

MADELEINE

Christmas Day

Cocooned in Julian's cozy bathrobe while Frank Sinatra's holiday favorites crooned from the stereo, Madeleine sipped her tea and scratched Winnie's soft belly. The corgi's back leg, healed from his September surgery, scratched the air as his eyes gently closed and his tongue lolled out the side of his mouth. The picture of unbridled happiness. By chance, Madeleine had found the sweet spot.

Her eyes, sore from falling asleep in her contacts, strayed across the room to the closed bathroom door. Behind it, the whoosh of surging water nearly drowned out Julian's singing, his spirited rendition of "We Need a Little Christmas" featuring a wrong word or three. Intentional or not, it made Madeleine grin.

So much can change in a year.

She adjusted her glasses and glanced back at Julian's twinkling tree with its cute corgi and glittery Ziggy Stardust.

Twelve months ago, I would've sworn I'd be spending this morning in Wisconsin, hiding under the overstuffed duvet on my childhood bed while Mom begged me to come downstairs for pancakes.

Reaching toward the coffee table, she traded her tea for the sealed box of Fortnum & Mason reindeer noses from Julian, the perfect gift if there ever was one.

But here I am in London—of all places—freshly showered with a tummy full of egg and soldiers cooked by this amazing British guy. What are the chances?

A familiar ache stirred in her chest.

But that's just the thing, isn't it, Kel? None of this happened by chance. I owe you so much…

She tipped the box, and a cavalcade of milk chocolate-covered treats rolled past the cellophane window. In their midst was a single red one.

Merry Christmas, my darling Kellie. I hope you know how much you are loved.

Wiping away a few tears, Madeleine set down the chocolates and clasped the sterling silver musical note hanging around her neck then pulled Winnie close for a tender hug.

Celebrating Christmas three thousand miles away from home was one thing, but being banned from Julian's pokey kitchen was quite another.

"You *sure* I can't help?" Madeleine loitered by the dining table, the spicy waft of sage and onion stuffing driving her to mouth-watering distraction. "I could stir the gravy or turn the potatoes?" She smoothed down the skirt of her blue cocktail dress, an A-line beauty awash in a merry snowflake print that she'd bought especially for Paris. "Really, Julian, you shouldn't be stuck doing all the work."

"Maddie love, I appreciate your kind offer, but no, you're my guest! The wait is almost over, though. I'm mere minutes away from my big reveal. Gordon Ramsey, eat your heart out!" Julian chuckled, the snap of a closing cupboard punctuating his glee. "Besides, this isn't really work. It's just heating things up!"

Heating things up or not, Madeleine wasn't good at being waited on. Thirty years of helping her mom peel vegetables for Thanksgiving and Christmas dinner was a hard habit to shake.

"Well, he can't stop me from pouring the wine," she murmured to his Christmas tree, having lost her four-legged furry companion. Fifteen minutes earlier, Winnie had skedaddled, intoxicated by the aroma of bacon-wrapped turkey filling the kitchen.

One popped cork later and their wine glasses were waiting with a dry chardonnay.

What to do next? Picking up a silver foil Christmas cracker from her side plate, Madeleine gave it an inquisitive shake and peered down one of its cylindrical ends. No luck. All its treasures remained tucked away, safe from prying eyes.

One mitt of a two-handed potholder emerged around the door-jamb, followed by Julian's earnest grin. "Okay! Sit and close your eyes, please."

Madeleine was too hungry to argue. She claimed a chair, scrunching her eyes tight, determined not to cheat and spoil Julian's surprise.

Winnie's dog tags jingled as he romped into the room, his excited panting a huge tell: Julian and their Christmas lunch were on the move.

Accompanied by the rustle of his dress shirt, a plate came in for a soft landing in front of her, then a waft of air tickled the peach fuzz on her arm. Julian must've ducked back into the kitchen for something, but a growing clickity china-on-china cacophony signalled his speedy return. A discreet clank on the table was followed by a scraping sound—*his chair?*—across the hardwood.

"Okay, *now* you can look!" Julian sounded extra breathy, like anticipation and apprehension were playing tug of war in his chest.

Her lashes prised open. She glanced down.

Where's my plate gone?

The china was barely visible under several slices of moist turkey and a colorful medley of roast carrots, broccoli florets, and Brussels sprouts. A mini mountain of crispy roast potatoes bordered a trio of bacon-wrapped pork sausages and a generous helping of peppery stuffing. A small popover-type roll—an individual-sized Yorkshire pudding—balanced triumphantly on top, waving the flag for beloved British cuisine.

"Merry Christmas to me!" Madeleine beamed. "Julian, this looks *amazing*! You've definitely got the wow factor going on here! Truly!"

Julian blew out his lips and picked up his napkin, flinging it open. "Fingers crossed it tastes as good as it looks." He draped the linen on the lap of his black trousers.

"Where should I even start?" she asked.

Julian leaned in. "How 'bout a toast?"

"Oh! Okay, sure!" Madeleine grasped the stem of her wine glass as Julian raised his. "What are we toasting to?"

"To absent loved ones?"

A warm flush coursed through her. "Julian, this is…" She gasped, a knot cinching in her throat.

He reached over and clasped her hand. "If it's too much…"

"No." Her nose itched as she blinked. "It's lovely."

Julian drew in a breath and licked his lips. "Dearly missed but forever in our hearts." Holding Madeleine's hand and her misty gaze, he lifted his glass higher. "To Kellie and Mum."

She lifted her chin and softly smiled. "To Kellie and Veronica."

"Look, Tash, it's a Christmas bloody miracle!" Micah gawped as his FaceTime feed jerked abruptly with the arrival of a pair of sparkly white snowflakes popping into frame. Jiggling atop wires, the festive flurries were followed by Natasha's red hair and dark eyebrows. Her ink-lined eyes widened.

"OH MY GOD?! You're *together*!" She bounced into the air, knocking her brother and slopping his beer.

Micah tsked and shook his wet hand. "All right, settle down!"

"Ah! Looook!" Natasha squealed. "Aren't they freakin' adorable in their paper crowns?!"

Madeleine laughed and lovingly glanced at Julian sat next to her, his green Christmas cracker hat clashing with her orange one. "I'm officially obsessed. I don't know how we do Christmas back home without crackers! A loud bang, paper crowns, silly jokes, and a small gift? What's not to love?"

Micah's lips twisted. "Wait? You don't have them in the States?"

"No. I've seen them in *Doctor Who* episodes, but never in real life," she said, shifting her plate out of the way. Madeleine had devoured her second helping of turkey and potatoes as quickly as her first. "But then, I saw the doggie version at Fortnum's and got one for Winnie." She glanced down. Smothering her feet, Winnie chewed on the plush bone Julian had given him. "Oh"—her eyes darted back to Julian's tablet—"but before you panic, Winnie's didn't bang when he opened it. It was totally pet-friendly."

"With a crown and a rope toy inside." Julian nodded.

"Which took a back seat to the cardboard tube," said Madeleine. "I think he liked that the best."

"Gotta love dogs." Julian laughed. "He did have a little barkfest, though. Maddie and I snapped through an entire box of crackers, just to see what was inside!"

"My kind of people!" Natasha beamed, nibbling on an After Eight mint.

Madeleine gathered her haul for show and tell. "We got a keychain, a magnifying glass, a plastic moustache, and a little airplane."

Julian joined in. "And a compass, a sewing kit, a mini ring toss—"

"Ooh, we got a ring toss," said Natasha, her snowflakes bobbing with glee.

"My favorite was the harmonica." Julian held it up with a lighthearted laugh. "We may start that band yet, Meeks!"

"Mate, I'm on it!" Micah pointed at the screen. "Hey, Jules, did your crackers have any decent *sayings* or jokes in them?" He winked over his beer.

Madeleine caught it. *Must be an inside joke.*

Julian glanced at her and shook his head. "Nah, you know how it is. They're always rubbish."

"My dad would love them. He's a sucker for a crappy pun," said Madeleine. "I'm gonna send them over to him. I'm sure my brothers won't thank me." She giggled.

A distorted mumble off-screen grabbed Micah and Natasha's

attention. "Oh? Right. Cheers." Micah waited until the person had left then shifted close to his tablet's camera and whispered through his grimace. "Pray for us. Our cousins have cracked open the Bailey's and Trivial Pursuit."

Natasha budged forward, rolling up the sleeves of her black velvet dress. "Bring it!"

"I'll keep my fingers crossed you don't end up in A&E," joked Julian.

"Oh, Micah! Before you go." Madeleine leaned in. "The gift Julian gave me, the needle felted squirrel? It's beautiful—I *adore* it."

"Aw, good! I'm glad," said Micah. "Yeah, Jules said you had a thing for them—"

A crash in the background cut him off.

"Dammit! Not the tree!" Natasha's braces flashed with her snarl. She jumped up, disappearing from view.

Micah rolled his eyes. "We gotta run." He saluted the screen. "Happy Chrimbo, lovebirds. See ya on the flip side."

"Happy Christmas!" Madeleine and Julian chimed in at the same time as Micah's image froze then vanished.

Julian laughed, pushing his chair back. Winnie shifted from Madeleine's feet and came out from underneath the table, wondering where his dad was going. "Well, looks like we got the Cooper family's seal of approval."

"Ah, they're lovely." She glanced away as Julian tossed his tablet on the sofa. "And so are you, Winnie!" Bending down, she gave the perky-eared pup a deserving hug and kiss.

"I think he's smitten," said Julian, sitting back down.

"And that makes *two* of us!" Madeleine sat up, her heart full of gratitude and contentment as Winnie slipped back under the table and wedged himself between their two chairs. Her eyes sparkled as she pored over her empty plate. "This dinner. *Turkey!* We never have it for Christmas. It was so damn good!"

"Are you missing home at all?" Julian picked up the wine and refilled Madeleine's glass then his.

"Thanks." She smiled as he returned the bottle to the table. "I thought I might, but no, not really. I'll still get to see everyone when we FaceTime later."

"Meeting the parents!" Julian's eyes widened.

"Ah, you've got nothing to worry about. They're gonna adore you and Winnie." She adjusted her orange crown. "Today's been wonderful. Although, it does feel strange eating a big dinner just after midday. I can see the appeal, though. Going to bed on a full stomach is *so* not comfortable."

"Or fun." Julian edged closer, lowering his voice conspiratorially. "Especially if we're not planning on sleeping..." His lips teased, parting wantonly with a flick of his tongue.

Madeleine melted into his gaze, remembering the grind of his hips, the desperate caress of his tongue, and how she cried out as one orgasm rippled into another and another. *The best sex of my life.* A yearning ache flirted low in her belly. "Oh, I think I'm going to enjoy London."

Julian leaned in and left a kiss in her hair. "I'm *so* happy you're here. We're going to have the best time inside *and* outside the flat." He bounced his brows comically, reaching across the table.

She watched Julian's forearm muscles flex as he picked up the gravy boat and returned it to its saucer. *Madeleine, get a grip: we cannot 'shag' our brains out ALL the time. And Julian paid a small fortune for this meal, so...behave!*

"You reckon you might be ready for dessert?" he asked, licking gravy off his thumb.

Madeleine lifted both arms in a satisfying overhead stretch. "Ooh, I shouldn't. Have you *seen* me today, eating everything in sight?"

"Enjoyed the reindeer noses and Celebrations, did we?" The smile in his voice held zero judgment.

She patted her stomach. "As my sister would say, '*Nice food baby.*'" Madeleine dropped her hands into her lap. "Poor Shan. The woman is always on a diet. If she gains like, two pounds, her agent has a meltdown."

"That must be tough." Julian stole a sip of wine. "Her willpower must be astonishing."

"Yep. That's why she's the movie star and I'm not!" Madeleine tugged at the bodice of her dress. "I could never go on vacation and eat nothing but salads and smoothies."

"Part of the fun of travel is all the eating," said Julian.

"Yeah. You know, I was meaning to ask—could we maybe check out some of the pretty cake shops I keep seeing on social media? I spotted one with a Love Heart wall."

Julian nodded as he patted his mouth with his napkin. "We can definitely do that, yeah. We can take our time now, too, go off the beaten path. There are some great places in Wandsworth, even Richmond."

"Oh, I can't wait!" Madeleine gazed up at the vintage Tube poster and smiled at the Londoners wearing their yellow party hats as they downed champagne. "I'd like to know every inch of London. Maybe we could bring Winnie with us?"

"Sure." Julian agreed.

"I'd like to explore all the parks."

"Well, we've got loads of those. Perfect for picnics—perfect for writing, actually." Julian enjoyed a quick sip of wine. "When you were in the shower, I started making notes for my London book."

"Julian, oh, that's great!"

He scratched his temple. "Yeah, enough time has passed, I think I'll make a proper start. No more excuses."

Madeleine shifted to the edge of her chair and looped her arms around his neck. "I'm so proud of you. The world needs more of your words, Julian." She planted a kiss on his cheek.

"And yours." He reciprocated with a sweet peck on the nose. "So, how about that dessert?!"

"Oh, go on then…" She smiled and rolled her eyes, giving up the food fight.

"Wait right here!" Julian scooted back in his chair.

"At least let me help clear…"

"Nope!" Julian stood, taking their plates with him into the

kitchen. Winnie got up and waggled after him.

A few minutes and several oven door slams later, Julian returned with Winnie at his heels and a dessert ablaze with flickering blue and orange flames. The boozy brandy scent, spongy cake texture, and jaunty sprig of holly could only mean one thing: a traditional Christmas pudding.

Madeleine cracked a huge grin. "Oh wow! It's the real deal!"

Julian nodded fervently as he placed the lit confection carefully on the table. "Look, Maddie, I make FIRE!" He laughed and dramatically waved his hands in front of him.

"It's awesome!" Her eyes darted up to his face, sweeping his forehead. "Yup, brows still there!"

Julian plunked down in his chair, his hand reaching, fingers folding through Madeleine's. "Once the flames fizzle out, I'll grab some bowls and the ice cream."

The gorgeous meal, the delightful crackers, and now the Christmas pudding—Julian did all this for me. A warm flutter swelled in Madeleine's chest as her fingers flexed, keeping him close. Hers.

I've fallen for this sweet man, so deeply it almost hurts. Who'd have thought my life could change so quickly?

Volcanic ash, a canceled flight, stranded alone and grieving in her deceased friend's 'happy place'—six days earlier, Madeleine's December had been hurtling toward disaster, but fate, it seemed, had other plans for her.

With a boyish grin, Julian gathered her in and gestured at the pudding's fleeting flames. "Well, is it everything you hoped it would be?"

A soft smile pinched her cheeks as she gazed up at him. "It's more, Julian…so much more."

Epilogue

JULIAN

Not quite one year later...

Julian opened the rear passenger door of his cab and peeked inside. "Okay, sleepyheads, we're home."

"Oh...what time is—?" Madeleine's raspy whisper morphed into an eye-scrunching, teeth-baring yawn.

"Just gone half four," said Julian, his smile growing as Winnie lifted his chin from Madeleine's lap. "You two were *totally* out for the count."

Tail sweeping the back seat, the corgi scrambled to the floor then leapt to the sidewalk, his leash dragging behind him. He nosed around, sniffing a crunchy brown leaf before parking his butt near their front door, the perfect vantage point to keep tabs on Mom and Dad.

"Winnie, you *stay*, okay?" Julian shuffled toward the front of the cab. "I'll get your case, babe. Take your time."

"Thank you." She blinked away the watery remnants of her yawn. "God, I really needed that nap. Didn't sleep much on the plane." She stretched and let out a long, satisfied sigh. "I'm so happy to be home! Thank god the volcano didn't erupt this year."

A breathy grunt escaped Julian's throat as he hefted her large suitcase free from the luggage area beside his seat. *Someone had a wee shopping spree!*

Looping her backpack over her shoulder, Madeleine ducked her head and hopped out of the cab, crouching for more corgi cuddles and licks. "Ah, you're just my favorite little munchkin, aren't ya, Winnie Woo?" She wound his leash around her wrist and kissed him between the ears. "Just you wait! I have the cutest koala bear

305

for you!"

"We didn't half miss you," said Julian, closing the taxi's front door. "That was the longest three weeks ever."

Madeleine giggled as Winnie landed a slobbery lick on her glasses. "Go on, admit it!" She looked up, smiling. "You *enjoyed* it! I bet you did all the things you never do when I'm home."

"Like what?"

"You know, like binge-watching scary movies or playing Oasis at full blast." She stood up, removing her glasses.

Julian shrugged. "Oh, I play Oasis when you're here. Yeah, I just do it when you're volunteering at the dogs home."

Cleaning her lenses with her scarf, a wry smile bent Madeleine's mouth. "Well, at least you got to sleep in without this early riser disturbing you."

"Not a chance." Julian's eyes danced. "I'm hardwired to wake up at half six now, thanks to my horny girlfriend who insists on a shag before breakfast."

Madeleine coyly fluttered her lashes. "So, you *did* miss me!" She put her glasses back on, giving them a little boost up her nose.

Julian wrapped his arms around her waist and pulled her close, locking her in. "That's why I've booked tomorrow off."

She curled her leash-free hand behind his neck. "Yeah?" Her fingers inched up into his hair.

"Yeah, so we can get reacquainted…over"—he kissed her forehead—"and over"—he shifted lower, kissing her nose—"and over again." Tilting his head, he hovered above her lips, his unwavering gaze heated and loving. "I could snog you silly right here."

"You might want to wait." She wrinkled her nose. "I'm kinda stinky from the flight."

"Then we can be dirty together…" He tenderly cupped her face and leaned in for a slow, deep kiss. The softness of her lips, the way her tongue flirted with his…for Julian, nothing else mattered: not the whistling postie strolling past, not the twitching curtains next door…

"WOOF!"

Except that. That mattered.

Madeleine broke their embrace with a laugh. "Grumble Bum wants in—now!" Smiling, she stooped down and scratched Winnie's chest. He slumped to the right, his back leg drumming the ground with pleasure. "You like that, Winnie? Aw, I missed you. I missed our little family."

Julian grinned and pulled out his keys. "Let's get you both inside."

Halfway up the stairs with the second floor landing in sight, Madeleine leaned against the flowery wallpaper and surrendered to another big yawn.

She's fading. Julian hoisted her suitcase onto the stair in front of him. "You sure about the pub quiz tonight?"

Madeleine looked over her shoulder. "I'm *very* sure. We have to defend our title." She took another step, then another. "Beauty School Dropouts forever!"

"But aren't you knackered though?"

"A bit, but my nap in the cab helped," she said, meeting a panting Winnie waiting on the landing. "And the three-day layover in Tokyo has definitely helped with the jetlag."

Julian hiked her case up the final stairs. *Blimey, I reckon she has most of Japan stashed in here.* He plonked it on the landing. "How much Kawaii stuff did you bring back?"

"Um..." Madeleine paused, pulling her backpack around her side. "Just a few things." Unzipping a small pocket, she fished out her keys. "I have souvenirs for Micah and Tash, too—oh, and Shantelle gave me gifts for you and Winnie, but don't get too excited. They're typical Shan!"

She unlocked their apartment door and pushed it open. The lights were already on, and The Weeknd's "In Your Eyes" sang softly from the radio as Winnie scampered ahead in search of his latest toy obsession. Madeleine stood back and took off her backpack and coat in the hall so Julian could go in first.

"When's she done filming there?" He guided her case through the small entryway and left it near the sofa.

"Next week." Madeleine followed, placing her backpack on the floor. "Then she's off to Honolulu for a bunch of flashback scenes with Benedict." She hung up her coat then yanked off her boots and paused for a moment, wiggling her toes. "Ah, that feels *so* good," she murmured, letting out a relieved sigh.

"I hope Cumberbatch is as friendly as people say he is." Julian stepped out of his shoes and closed the apartment door.

"You and your man crush." Madeleine grinned as she toddled past her case, headed for their bed. She flung herself on the duvet, bouncing once before sinking in. "Home sweet home."

Julian turned the corner, his eyes straying to his bedside table. *Oh fuck, fuck, fuck!* A tightness twisted in the pit of his stomach. *I didn't stash it away!*

"I missed you, little bed." Rolling onto her back, Madeleine stared blissfully at the ceiling, her splayed arms and legs resembling a star shape. "I'll never take you for granted ever again..." Her words faded off into a long, contented yawn.

Julian stared at the table, a mere pillow-length away from her upturned hand. *If I could just sit in between...*

He gingerly sat beside her, blocking her view. "You know, we don't have to go back out. You could have a long soak while I make us some dinner."

"I *am* hungry," she mumbled.

Julian played with the zipper on his Bowie hoodie, dragging it up then down. "A lovely pasta, a salad? Or just a crisp butty, yeah? Doesn't that sound good?" His pulse hammered beneath his moving hand.

"Mmm, sandwiches with crisps..." Madeleine balled up her hands and rubbed her eyes, her lips twisting, considering.

Winnie barked and galloped around the living room, dragging a chubby Moomin.

"Winnie!" She turned away, toward his bark. "Whatcha doing?"

Now! Julian's right hand flew stealthily across the bedside table, snatching his prize. He shoved his fist into his hoodie's pocket with Madeleine none the wiser and eased sideways onto the bed, propping himself up on an elbow. *Phew! Got away with it.*

She sprawled over the edge of the bed, playing tug with Winnie. "That all sounds so tempting, but after a shower and some tea, I think I'll be more than ready to kick some Tequila Mockingbird arse!" With a sharp yank, the corgi won his Moomin and scooted away. "Ah, I'm out of practice," Madeleine giggled and rolled across the bed, meeting Julian again. "I can't wait to see Micah and Tash tonight and tell them all about Australia."

An ache filled Julian's chest. "I'm proud of you, ya know," he said quietly, sweeping a strand of hair from her eyes.

"For what?"

"I know this trip wasn't easy."

Madeleine glanced down, her expression softening. "Yeah, but I'm glad I went. I should've gone years ago..."

"Hindsight, eh?" Julian pressed his lips together.

"Yeah, don't put off what you can do today..." Madeleine fiddled with the hem of her sweater, tugging it down over the top of her tights.

Julian collected her hand, giving it a squeeze as she let out a wistful breath.

"I know I keep saying it..."

"It's okay," he whispered. "You can say it again."

"Seeing her name carved into the headstone"—she shook her head—"felt so surreal." Madeleine's throat bobbed. "I know I talk to Kel all the time, but *being* there...it was like we were together, finally." She sniffed and dipped her chin.

Julian's heart panged. "Were you able to find her favorite flowers?"

"I did, yeah. Stargazer lilies." Her eyes widened as she glanced up. "Oh, I forgot to tell you. When I got back to Kellie's parents' place, I took Roo out for a walk."

"Aw, I bet you enjoyed that."

Madeleine nodded. "Roo's such a beautiful boy. We went to his favorite park, sat under a big tree, and he was looking all around—" Her reverie dimmed. "Like he was looking for Kellie..."

She trailed off and chewed her lip, slowly untwining her hand from Julian's and pausing briefly before pushing herself up.

"Anyway, it was a good trip. Bittersweet, but I'm so glad I went. And now I know where Kel got her awesome sense of humor from." She smoothed her hair and tucked a thick strand behind her ear. "My god, Julian, her parents and brothers had me in stitches. I think I freaked them out a bit, though, the first time I cried mid-laugh."

"Yeah," said Julian. "But I bet they found it as endearing as I do."

They shared a muted smile.

"Hey, I have to show you something." Madeleine stood and headed toward her backpack.

Julian sat up and checked his pocket again. *Safe as houses...*

She picked up her bag and turned, walking back to Julian as she browsed inside. A soft smile warmed her face, indicating she'd found what she sought: a plain, rectangular box. "Mrs. Nguyen gave me this." She sat on the bed, retiring her backpack to the floor.

Julian kissed Madeleine's temple and wrapped his arm around her as she lifted the lid.

A nest of white tissue paper appeared first, but as Madeleine peeled away the protective layer, a sparkly tree ornament peered back, a small angel with a silver halo and diaphanous wings.

"Oh, love, it's beautiful," said Julian.

"Isn't it gorgeous?" She nodded, gazing down with reverence. "It was Kellie's favorite. They wanted me to have it."

"We'll find a special spot for it on our tree."

Madeleine looked up. "Are we still getting one on Saturday?"

"Yep. And we can also swing by Maltby Street Market if you want, pick up some of those Love Bites you're addicted to?"

Madeleine folded the tissue paper over the tiny angel. "Ah, brownies with pretzel bits in them—*perfection*. I'll have to get a bunch of their Christmas treats, too."

"Maybe you should buy some for Leia. Butter her up a bit," said Julian. "Three weeks without you? I bet she's been counting the days till you're back."

She returned the lid to the box, cradling it in her hands. "I'm really looking forward to going back on Wednesday." Madeleine paused, her eyes crinkling. "Who *am* I? I don't remember ever feeling like that about Sensoria!"

"It feels good, doesn't it? Knowing you made the right decision?"

Madeleine nodded. "I'm so grateful to Leia. Sponsoring me, offering this amazing job. Just having the opportunity to write all day—and be paid for it! And I love her upcycling designs and what she stands for—and all the stories I get to tell on her website. It feels like I'm doing something good for a change instead of padding some overpaid music mogul's pocket."

Julian slung his arm around her shoulder and gathered her in, leaving a kiss on her forehead. "You, Mad Joy, are a rock star."

"God, I've missed you." She budged closer. "I missed Winnie, our lovely flat...our life." She kissed Julian tenderly and stroked his chest.

The warm press of her hand skating over the fabric, her mouth claiming, tasting him again—there was no better feeling in the world. Julian's heart skipped. *Our life...is beautiful.*

She eased away slowly and caressed his chin. "Sorry about the texts at all hours, FaceTime calls in the middle of the night."

"Don't be sorry. They were the highlight of my days—er, *nights*." He grinned. "Speaking of writing, did you..."

"Do any? I did." She wrapped both hands around the ornament box. "Every morning before breakfast."

"And how'd it go?" asked Julian.

She blew out her lips. "I am *so* done."

A flicker of concern creased his forehead. "Done, like—"

"THE END, done." She broke out into a smile.

Julian pulled back, gauging her reaction. "You finished? Babe! That's fantastic."

"Well, it only took me, what? Three and a half years? But it's finished and I'm gonna query agents, starting this week."

"Go Maddie!" He pulled her close again as Winnie plunked himself on top of her feet.

"Yep, I'm putting myself and my book out there, and we'll see where it lands—well, *if* it lands." She reached down and patted the corgi.

Julian nodded assuredly. "It will. It's brilliant. It's touching and romantic and so *you*. Heartfelt and gorgeous." He kissed her on the cheek. "Ah, this is the best news."

"Shame you're not an agent." She snickered. "Did you hear back from yours?"

"Uh, yeah, three days ago." His brow furrowed. "Two publishers passed, but two others started a bidding war—"

"*What?!*" Her jaw dropped. "You're telling me this *now*?"

"I wanted to tell you in person! I've been absolutely busting, actually, haven't told a soul. Well, except Winnie. He gave me a sloppy lick then chewed a hole in my favorite jeans. Keeping it real, our Winnie Bum."

"Julian, you know what this means, right?! Your book will be in Waterstones! We'll see it on the way to Fortnum's." Madeleine's eyes were wild with happiness. "We *have* to celebrate! It's another reason to go out tonight. You know Micah and Tash will want to buy you a pint."

"Sounds good!" Julian tugged on the zipper of his hoodie. "Hey, don't we have something on Saturday? Tickets for something, just me and you?"

"Theater," she said. "The Andrew Scott play at The National."

The South Bank. Perfect. Julian nodded, giving Winnie an ear scratch before the pup wandered off toward his toy basket. "We could have drinks first, see the play, go for a stroll after?"

Her face lit up. "Along the Thames…"

Julian finished her sentence. "…with the blue fairy lights in the trees."

"I love it there." Madeleine swooned.

I know you do.

"You twisted my arm, it's a date!" She leaned in for a quick kiss. "Right, so I better jump in the bath and wash the plane off me. I feel all grubby. Need to shampoo my hair, too."

"Okay, just don't fall asleep in there!"

"If I'm not out in thirty minutes, come join me." Madeleine winked and leapt off the bed.

"Ooh, take your time then." Julian laughed as she set the box with Kellie's angel on her dresser.

Winnie returned, carrying one of his squeaky, plush donuts, and dropped it at Julian's feet. "Who's the boss, eh? You are, Winks!"

He played tug of war with him for a minute or two while Madeleine opened her suitcase, rescued her toiletries bag, and scattered dirty clothes all over the floor. She disappeared behind the bathroom door where the roar of the taps eventually gave way to her voice softly singing a Christmas tune Julian didn't recognize. Something about a Snow Miser—a Mr. Icicle—who was "Too much", apparently.

Her voice filling the silence, her stuff strewn around the flat...Julian's heart was fit to burst. The past year with Madeleine and Winnie had been the best twelve months of his life, full of laughter, love, and the odd sandwich or two.

Julian gave Winnie a hug. "Happy your mum's back?"

Winnie answered with an extra wiggly butt and an impatient grumble.

"Yeah, me too. It's just not home without her, is it? We're so lucky. I hate to think, what if someone else had picked her up that day...?"

Julian dug in his hoodie pocket. Winnie pressed forward, his nose twitching eagerly back and forth, curious.

"No treats this time, mate. I've got something even better."

He pulled out a small velvet box and eased back the stiff lid. An elegant yet understated round diamond in a classic white gold setting sparkled under the apartment's lights.

"This little beauty used to be my mum's. So, what do you think, Winnie? Will Madeleine like it?" Julian grinned. "We'll find out Saturday night!"

ACKNOWLEDGEMENTS

Serendipity, fateful events, chance encounters—my life has been blessed with them. I love the magical whimsy, the haphazard coincidences, the *how the hell did this happen*-ness of these head-scratching moments, and they keep popping up in my life. The biggest one involved meeting my future husband. I met him during a two-day trip to New York to see a Northern Irish band called The Divine Comedy (yep, the one in this book). I flew down there from Toronto just to see the band. My husband flew from the UK with the same purpose. We met and the rest is history. I often wonder, 'What if I stayed home that weekend?' It goes without saying my life would've been completely different.

I wrote this book in the shadows of losing our Zoey. The first anniversary of her death had passed and it was surprising how some people's tolerance for my grieving changed. I could hear it in their voices, in their messages: "Shouldn't you be over this by now?" Luckily, not one person uttered "She's just a dog" to me. I think they knew they would've lost a testicle or a friend for life if they had. *The Certainty of Chance* gave me the opportunity to show the reality of grief, especially when it involves a relationship that others don't always understand. With all grief, you don't 'get over it' or 'move on'. You end up living with it, and there's no magic potion or vacation or new lover who can lift the weight and magically make things better. In a world where people avoid talking about grief and the griever is left to muddle along with few to confide in, we need to change. We need to speak about how grief really feels and not shame grievers for the pain they carry day in, day out. If you, my lovely reader, have lost someone dear and are struggling, I hope Madeleine and Julian's story helped you feel seen.

If you've read my other books, you'll know how much I love online friendships. *The Certainty of Chance* is another tribute to my friends who I met online. If you've been fortunate to make besties through social media, chat rooms, or email groups, you'll know how special, complex, and deep these relationships are.

Big love to my incredibly supportive family: Heather and Bill, Val and Tony, Jason, and Therasa. To my mum and dad and Zoey—I love and miss you *so* much every single day.

I write amazing fictional friends because my real life friends are so fantastic. Sheila, Maria & Curtis, Esther & Ian, Charlotte, Vicki, Lynsey, Cristina, Nicole, Kristin, and Sally & Bruce—love you.

Thanks to the team at Grey's Promotion (Tiffany and Josette) for getting the word out!

Much thanks and hugs to Melena (my Keeganites United Book Club queen), my beta and sensitivity readers (special shoutout to Jennifer and Jacqueline), as well as my amazing editor Caitlin (Editing by C. Marie), who puts up with my excessive love of commas.

And then there's Darren, my husband, the Brit boy at the New York concert. You are my world. This year has been rougher than most, but we're together and that's all that matters. I love you and Charlie Floof and our messy, cookie-crumb-sprinkled life.

Last but never ever least...to my Keeganites (the members of my Facebook group, Keeganites United) and my readers, as well as all the librarians, bloggers, reviewers, bookstagrammers, and booktokkers, THANK YOU! You are the unsung superheroes of the book community. Your adoration for stories like mine, which celebrate hopeful romantics with messy lives, make all this worthwhile. I love you more than tacos—and that's a lot! xoxo

*Btw, the Iceland volcano eruption
really did close European airspace in 2010!

GLOSSARY

Some people, places, and things mentioned in *The Certainty of Chance* might not be familiar to all readers. Here are a few helpful explanations.

Charing Cross: Charing Cross is the point in Westminster where all distances to and from London are measured. Charing Cross isn't London's most central point, but it's been used to measure mileages since 1291. A statue of King Charles I riding his horse and a small plaque embedded in the pavement memorialize the spot.

Disenfranchised grief: A term created by mental health counselor and gerontology professor, Dr. Kenneth J. Doka, in the mid-'80s. A griever can experience disenfranchised grief when their loss isn't socially accepted or openly acknowledged, and they're made to feel that it's inappropriate to mourn publicly. Unfortunately, this lack of empathy happens too often to individuals dealing with pet loss, the aftermath of miscarriage, the loss of a limb, or the death of anyone who isn't an immediate blood relative.

The dog's bollocks: British slang for the best.

Dolly Mixture: Small British sweets of various colors and shapes (cubes and cylinders) made from soft fondant and jelly.

Off his/her/your tits: British slang for extremely drunk.

Lady Chapel: A chapel dedicated to the Virgin Mary typically located at the easternmost end of a church. They're often elaborately decorated and beautiful. Many were destroyed during the Reformation, so few exist today.

Get on my/your wick: British slang for someone irritating you.

Grade II listed properties: In England, the government classifies old properties as 'listed' to protect their historical or architectural significance. There are three categories (Grade I, Grade II*, and Grade II), which rank their importance.

Moreish: British word to describe food so yummy you'll crave more and more.

Cockney rhyming slang: Originating as a secret code in London's East End in the mid-19th century, Cockney rhyming slang replaces a word or phrase with another word or phrase that rhymes (examples: stairs = apples and pears; curry = Ruby Murray; believe = Adam and Eve).

Bûche de Noël: A chocolate yule log cake from France dating back to the late 19th-century (although different variations exist elsewhere). Chocolate cake is filled with buttercream and rolled into a log shape then it's covered in yummy chocolate ganache. Mmm!

Harry Kane: English professional football player.

MENTAL HEALTH RESOURCES

**If you or someone you know suffers from
anxiety or depression, help is available.**

United States
Anxiety and Depression Association of America
www.adaa.org

Canada
The Canadian Mental Health Association (CMHA)
www.cmha.ca

United Kingdom
Mind
www.mind.org.uk

GRIEF RESOURCES

If you are grieving, here are some empathetic resources:

It's OK That You're Not OK by Megan Devine
(In addition to her book, Megan also has a wonderful website:
refugeingrief.com)

What's Your Grief website
whatsyourgrief.com

Speaking Grief website & documentary
speakinggrief.org

MEET MY OTHER BOOKS!

My novels are written as standalones.
However, they all take place in the same 'world',
and characters from one book often appear in another.

LONDON BELONGS TO ME
Contemporary coming-of-age story with a touch of romance.
Tropes: friends to lovers, found family,
actor/Irish hero, playwright/American heroine
(has open-door kissing scenes but all sex is off the page)

LONDON, CAN YOU WAIT?
Contemporary romance and the sequel to *London Belongs to Me*.
However, it can be read as a standalone.
Tropes: angsty, relationship in trouble,
actor/Irish hero, playwright/American heroine,
tragic past, soul mates, second chance, starting over
(open- and closed-door sex scenes)

UNTIL THE LAST STAR FADES
Blurs the line between contemporary romance and women's fiction.
Tropes: angsty, slow-burn, friends to lovers,
Scottish hero, American heroine, tragic past, found family, college
(open- and closed-door sex scenes)

SAY HELLO, KISS GOODBYE
Contemporary Romance
Tropes: fling to forever, opposites attract,
wealthy English/Scottish hero, divorced Canadian heroine
unrequited love, girl squad, tragic past
(open- and closed-door sex scenes; my steamiest book)

All titles available in paperback and ebook from all major retailers.
London Belongs to Me is also available as an audiobook.
Content warnings can be found on my website under 'Books'.

The Certainty of Chance

Enjoyed Madeleine and Julian's story?
Please consider leaving a review on the retailer's website.

Stay in touch!
Follow Jacquelyn:

Instagram: @JaxMiddleton_Author
Facebook: JacquelynMiddletonAuthor
Twitter: @JaxMiddleton
and join her private Facebook readers group
to hear book news first, participate in her book club,
and have the chance to enter exclusive giveaways.

Visit Jacquelyn's website
for book playlists, behind-the-scenes exclusives,
and to sign up to her newsletter.
www.JacquelynMiddleton.com